To Paula, with love in Him and many blessings.

The Door Where it Began

A Novel of Yeshua, Israel and the Early Church

And Yeshua cried out with a loud voice, and breathed His last.

Then the veil of the temple was torn in two from top to bottom. So when the centurion, who stood opposite Him, saw that He cried out like this and breathed His last, he said, "Truly this Man was the Son of God!" (Mark 15:37-39)

Raymond Robert Fischer

Olim Publications
P.O. Box 2111
Tiberias, Israel
E-mail: olim@012.net.il

The Door Where it Began

© 2005, Raymond Robert Fischer
Cover painting: Sonne Krohn
Cover and Layout: David Coddington

Copyright © 2005 by Raymond Robert Fischer
P.O. Box 2111, Tiberias, Israel

ISBN 965-90874-0-3

Unless otherwise noted, Scripture quotations are from
the New King James Version of the Holy Bible.
Copyright © 1979, 1980, 1982
Used by permission of Thomas Nelson, Inc.

Printed in Israel

The Door Where it Began

Dedication

It is with a deeply thankful and love filled heart that I dedicate this book to the greatly treasured memory of my parents, Lillian Gelson Fischer and Alfred Max Fischer, and to my maternal grandmother, Amelia Silverman Gelson.

Acknowledgments

I would like to express my great appreciation to Donna Jean Goade Fischer, my darling wife of more than 45 wonderful love-filled years, who diligently reviewed each succeeding draft of this work and who once again served as an indispensable sounding board as this work progressed. Her many excellent content related ideas and editorial suggestions were of tremendous value and are reflected throughout the entire book.

My great appreciation also to Bill Eldridge who dedicated many hours to meticulous editorial reviews of the first and final drafts. Bill has stood at my side every step of the way in the production of my four most recent books. His stamp of professional excellence can be found on all of these many pages.

My great and abiding thanks also to Reuven Schmalz, my dear friend of many years and co-author of *The Messianic Seal of the Jerusalem Church*. Reuven's review of the manuscript for historical accuracy has added significantly to the credibility of the significantly new ideas set forth in these pages.

Finally, my special thanks to Sonne Krohn who went through several versions to capture the vision I tried to describe to her in mere words. I am thrilled with the cover painting that is exactly as I had "seen" it on display in my mind. Her wonderful talent and dedication to this work is greatly appreciated.

RRF

The Door Where it Began

Cast of Characters
(In order of appearance)

Marcus Frank Sterling, nee "Mark Francis Sterling:" A young American Jew struggling to survive in the "Great Depression" of 1929. Father of Andrew Scott Sterling ("Drew").

Leila Cittrenbaum Sterling: Mark's wife and mother of Drew.

Daniel A. Brandon, nee "Daniel Abraham Berkowitz:" Director of Sales and Technical Services, National Carbon Company, Mark's boss and mentor.

Matthias: Appointed as "The thirteenth apostle" after the betrayal of Yeshua by Judas Iscariot.

Eliezar the High Priest: a son of Zadok, leader of the Essene Sect at Qumran, adoptive father of Matthias and Yochanan (John) the Baptizer

Yochanan (John) the Baptizer: Adoptive brother of Matthias

Andrew Scott Sterling (Drew): A messianic Jew, retired Chaplain Colonel, U.S. Air Force, dual citizen of the United States and Israel.

The Johnsons: The Sterlings' Southern Baptist neighbors in Portland, Oregon

Franz Friedrich Mueller: An extreme anti-Semite

Yeshuah ha Mashiach (Hebrew): Jesus Christ: King of the Universe, Son of God, Messiah, Redeemer, Great God among the Gods.

Amelia Grossman Cittrenbaum ("Grandma Amelia"): Drew Sterling's maternal grandmother

Ariston: A citizen of Hippos; father of Heliodora (Dory).

Theodora: Wife of Ariston; mother of Heliodora (Dory)

Euclid: Brother of Heliodora (Dory)

Heliodora (Dory): Citizen of Hippos; wife of Matthias

Yahweh: Anglicized expression of YHWH, (Hebrew "I will be") the name of God as designated by Himself in the Torah

Father John Lassiter: Roman Catholic priest, Rochester, New York

Mike Ryan: Drew's roommate and best friend at the University of Rochester

Kefa: (Hebrew) the Apostle Peter

Athanasios (Athan): A resident of Hippos who became demon possessed as the "chained man" of Kursi who was healed by Yeshua (Matt 8, Mark 5, and Luke 8). He later became a leader of the Gentile Christian movement at Hippos.

Sheldon Thurman: A U.S. Air Force Chaplain who led Drew to the Lord and later became his mentor and best friend.

Hank Tyler: A U.S. Air Force fighter pilot assigned to the F-101B test project at Eglin Air Force Base

Carla McKenzie Sterling: Drew's beloved wife

Dory Ann Sterling: The first of Drew and Carla's three daughters

Rebekah Ruth Sterling: Their second daughter

Rachel Florence Sterling: Their third daughter

Judah: A son of Miriam and Yosef, blood brother of Yeshua

Ya'akov: (later known as "James the Just") A son of Miriam and Yosef, blood brother of Yeshua who was to become the first Leader of the Body of Believers in Israel.

Glossary

Chuppa: (Hebrew) traditional Jewish Wedding canopy.

Elevated: New York City mass transit train system operated on elevated tracks.

Goy, Goyim: (pl. Hebrew) Literally, nation or nations (other than Israel). Meaning: non-Jew, Gentile.

Kinneret: (Hebrew) Sea of Galilee

Komerim: (Hebrew) deacons

Komerot: (Hebrew) deaconesses

Kotel: Western Wall of the Temple in Jerusalem

Kippah: (Hebrew) *Yarmulke* (Yiddish) Skullcap worn by Jewish men during prayer. Many wear the *kippah* at all times, both as a statement of being Jewish and as a statement of God's presence everywhere.

Olim hadashim: (Hebrew) new immigrants

Meerpesset: (Hebrew) balcony

Mikvah: (Hebrew) Biblically mandated Jewish purification by immersion in water. The precursor of Christian baptism.

Nazarene Essene: The Nazarenes were by far the larger of two predominant sub-sects of the Essenes who dwelled at Qumran and mostly throughout the Galilee before and during the time of Yeshua. The Nazarenes were expecting a Messiah who in every way, as they described him in their scrolls, was like Yeshua. Thus, when Yeshua appeared among them, they embraced Him in large numbers and they became, principally, the very first believers we read about in the Book of Acts and elsewhere.

Scarsdale: An exclusive suburb in Westchester County, just north of New York City.

Shofar: (Hebrew) Biblically mandated ram's horn sounded by Jews on specified and traditional occasions.

Shekinah: A visible shining manifestation of the divine presence as described in Jewish theology.

Tallit: (Hebrew) Prayer Shawl worn by Jewish men

Tenach: (Hebrew) The entire Old Testament

Torah: (Pentatuch) The first five books of the Old Testament

Tudat Zahoot: Israeli national identity card

Wannabee: (Want to be) Describes those who want to be something they are not or cannot become as restricted by physical limitations; e.g, a person born as a Gentile wants to become an ethnic Jew.

Way: (the Way) The early believers in Yeshua were also known by some as "the Way" as can be seen in several references in the Book of Acts, e.g.; 19:9, 23; 24:14, 22

Foreword

From the outset, I intended the *The Door Where it Began* to be a heartfelt, loving testimony of thanksgiving to *Yeshua ha Mashiach* (Jesus Christ) my Lord, my God, and the font of my salvation. Both my darling wife, Donna, and my dear friend and editor, Bill Eldridge commented upon reading the first draft that I had succeeded in doing so. Bill wrote:

> I really like this book. It is extremely well written! It flows like the Jordan River on a spring day. I found it to be not only exciting from the perspective of what is going to happen next, how are the lives intertwined, what is the relationship going to be, etc, but also it is clearly the most glorifying historical fiction book written that I have read.

> Let me explain: Drew, Carla, Sheldon, Matthias, and Dory are not really the central characters of this book. And whether I was a Christian or not I would come to the same conclusion: *Yeshua* is! There is no debate on the subject. I know that was your intent, but I don't know if you realize just how powerfully that has come across. The presence and impact of the Almighty God of Israel is evident in every chapter and on just about every page. There is not a single character, who does not in some fashion glorify God through actions or words. He truly is the focus.

If indeed Bill's glowing assessment of this work is by any means correct, then any attendant glory arising from all this, most assuredly, is not creditable to me. Whatever glory there may be is entirely His, the Lord God of Israel's. Throughout the entire almost two year process of bringing this novel forth, I had the clear sense I was being held closely in the hollow of His Holy Hand, and guided every step of the way.

Unlike any of my earlier work, I found my role in this current writing to be more that of a recorder than a creator as the intertwined millennia, life's challenges, and relationships of its characters played out before me in the theater of my mind.

By way of example, in March, 2004 I was completing a photographic based DVD teaching on the many Bible sites in the Galilee. I had, for no particular reason, saved nearby Capernaum for last in the process that had already yielded well in excess of 1,000 digital pictures.

Thus, one fine morning, as I was about to turn my car into the parking area at Capernaum, I heard a "still quiet voice" in my inner being tell me quite clearly: "No, my son, not here---continue on around to Tel Hadar on the other side of the Lake."

Given that we had already lived in Tiberias for nearly thirteen years and I had never before been to Tel Hadar, nor had the slightest understanding of its significance or even its location, I was quite taken aback by this clear direction which I immediately set out to follow.

During the previous thirteen years, I had driven around the Lake any number of times and had never seen even a hint that a place called Tel Hadar was anywhere to be found along the eastern shore. Even so, it came as no surprise to me that about a third of the way heading south along the shore-side highway, two remarkable simultaneous events occurred: I saw a clearly visible sign "Tel Hadar" with an arrow indicating I should turn right at the next primitive road. At the same moment, I once again heard the "still quiet voice" instruct me simply. "Turn right here."

A few moments later I found myself standing in front of a shore-side monument that had been identified and marked in 1969 by the famous Catholic archeologist, Bargil Pixner. It seems this was the site of Yeshua's second feeding of the multitude where he miraculously fed some 4,000, many of whom He also healed (Mark 8:1-10).   It wasn't until very late that night, as I prayerfully tried to find some relevance   in all this, that the Lord began to reveal His purpose. He did so by posing two questions, to which He almost immediately supplied what seemed to me to be His own responses.

"Who were these four thousand whom I fed and healed at Tel Hadar?" He asked. "And, from where did they come and then where did they go?"

Then I heard at once: "They were mostly Gentiles---non-Jews---pagans some of whom had followed me to this place all the way from Sidon." (a city now in modern day Lebanon). The answer continued: "The rest of these dear ones were mostly from communities located along the Eastern shore of the lake, and among these, most were from the nearby ancient mountain top city of Hippos."

Then, in a sudden revelation I understood that many of these miraculously fed, divinely healed, and most certainly newly "born again" non-Jewish believers in Yeshua, even as many as several hundred of them, immediately returned to Hippos, which up to that point had been a blatantly pagan community. Certainly, it was there on their home turf in Hippos, that these very first Gentile believers must have sought some way to communally worship their newly embraced Yeshua. It is thus my studied conclusion and contention that they did indeed establish the very first Gentile Christian Church on that site.

Let me say, trying not to get ahead of the amazing story that follows, there is a convincing body of both documented and anecdotal evidence: scriptural, historical and archeological that, I believe strongly supports this idea. There was a Gentile Christian Church, not only in Hippos, but scattered throughout the vast region of the Decapolis, at least some twenty years before the Apostle Paul took his first evangelical journey.

There is *enormous significance* in this! If this pre-Pauline Church hypothesis can be proven, then Church history, as it has been known for two millennia, has, perforce, been remarkably re-written. Consider this: the Gentile Christian Church would thus be shown to have its origin in the Decapolis of Israel, not in Rome! The first Gentile Christians would likely have been discipled by Torah-observant Jewish believers who dwelled in large numbers on the Western shore, extending all the way to nearby Kursi, just 3 kilometers north of Tel Hadar. There would have been, at least at the outset, a presumed sense of unity between the two groups of believers: the Jews to the West and the Gentiles to the East.

Taking this new understanding of early Church history as a point of departure, the book you hold in your hand traces the development of the two parts of the Body of Yeshua (a.k.a. the Church) though parallel stories of representative characters from the first century and from modern times. I am certain that the lives of all born again believers, irrespective of the barrier of time, are and forever will be inexorably and gloriously intertwined. One of my purposes in telling these two intertwined parallel stories is to add a new, refreshed meaning to the words of our Lord, Yeshua who told us:

> *I pray for them. I do not pray for the world but for those whom You have given Me, for they are Yours. And all Mine are Yours, and Yours are Mine, and I am glorified in them. Now I am no longer in the world, but these are in the world, and I come to You. Holy Father, keep through Your name those whom You have given Me, that they may be one as We are.* (John 17:9-12)

If I were asked to forthrightly state the central theme of this book in one word and then briefly state why I, by His hand, have brought it forth, I would have to say that the central theme is *Unity* and the purpose of this writing is to promote anew, *Unity in the Body of Yeshua* as I have become persuaded it likely existed in the very early years of this blessed Body's existence.

Finally, you will note that the format I have used for this work is quite unique. I have "officially" labeled this as a novel; i.e., a work of fiction. I have done so in the interest of good scholarship since a portion of the evidence I have used along the way is anecdotal---"a portion" but certainly not all. Given this mix of documented and undocumented evidence from a great variety of sources, I have made it a point to document the book, as if it were a scholarly work of non-fiction, with a number of endnotes for the reader's guidance. I have also used a number of photographs of selected subjects that will, I trust, add further credence to the ideas I have brought forth.

In the end, my prayer is that you will find this reading at the very least entertaining, as you might any good work of fiction, but even more, that it might be otherwise edifying and cause many to reevaluate what has up to now been regarded as "accepted" Church history.

Finally, I pray that you will indeed find Yeshua and His blessed gospel among these pages and having done so that you will be greatly blessed.

RRF

Tiberias, Israel,

September, 2005

Chapter One

Manhattan, November, 1930

Marcus Frank Sterling, who, since his early adulthood had presented himself to the world as "Mark Francis Sterling," shivered under the meager protection of his inadequate summer weight overcoat. Now, as the biting cold wind assaulted him head on, he hurriedly made his way toward the Union Carbide building at 247 Park Avenue.

It wasn't only the near freezing, early snow threatening conditions of this particular Monday morning that produced in Mark what he vainly hoped were no visible signs of his growing terror. Rather, it was far more the critically important employment interview, scheduled to begin in just 15 minutes that seriously compounded what had become his tremble producing, soul deep uncertainty concerning his future.

Indeed, the outcome of this forthcoming meeting represented much more than potential employment. Rather, it was a matter of basic survival; not just his own physical survival in the New York-centered deeply troubled economic depression wracked world in which he inescapably dwelled, but also, the very survival of his deeply loved and indescribably adored new bride, Leila, who now waited expectantly, and trustingly for him in their tiny, almost entirely unfurnished apartment on Allerton Avenue in the Bronx.

Mark's heart surged at the very thought of Leila, and the nine most wonderful months of his life since they had stood together before a somewhat reluctant young rabbi in the small, exclusively family attended ceremony in her mother's apartment.

Leila was everything to him: extraordinarily beautiful, deeply devoted, the very essence of sweetness with a lingering naivety that was something more deeply rooted than simply the unbridled innocence of her youth.

Mark's trembling surged in a sudden new wave as he once again acknowledged the great depth of his newly acquired responsibility for another person's well being. Leila was a mere child, only eighteen. She not only adored him, but she was totally dependent upon him in every way and for every thing.

Mark's mind raced as the elevator hurriedly transported him to the offices of the National Carbon Company that occupied the entire eighteenth floor. Suddenly, he found himself standing before the imposing closed heavy wooden door upon which the occupant who waited for him on the other side was duly identified by imposing hand carved raised wooden block letters as "Daniel A. Brandon, Director of Sales and Technical Services."

Daniel Brandon's seemingly instinctive ability to instantaneously screen, analyze then evaluate those whom he encountered had never failed him, and now he was immediately impressed with the strikingly handsome, dark complexioned, brown eyed, twenty-three year old job applicant with whom he exchanged a gripping introductory handshake.

"Have a seat, Mark," Dan invited warmly and encouragingly, as he pointed to the simple office chair that stood imposingly in front of his large mahogany executive desk. "You come to us highly recommended by our mutual friend, John Samartano. John told me all about your impressive technical and sales skills," Dan set the stage for the probing interrogation to follow." But, if you don't mind, I'd like to learn more about you personally; your ambition and life's goals."

***

An hour later, Dan had learned even more, than he had wanted to know about Mark Francis Sterling who had stood up well under the pressure of his deliberately intense probing that was now winding to a conclusion. "Mark," Dan announced warmly, smiling broadly for the first time since they had begun their exchange, "I think you will fit in quite well as a member of the team of technical representatives I am assembling to deal with the public regarding our revolutionary new product, *Prestone* antifreeze. How does a starting salary of $200 a month, a generous expense account and a company car strike you?"

Mark tried to contain his excitement but didn't quite succeed. "I'm very flattered, Dan," he exclaimed, "and I am more than pleased to begin this relationship with the company that I know will grow into an exciting and rewarding career."

"Okay, then," Dan stood and once again shook Mark's hand strongly. "As far as I am concerned, you're hired, but there is the formality of the official employment application that you'll need to complete for our personnel department. Mind you," Dan's tone suddenly took on a subtly warning tone that Mark immediately sensed: "This application is only a formality, but it is *very* important. Mark, I must be very honest with you---I want you on my team---okay," he hesitated for only a brief moment before he went on. "The application form requires that you state your religious preference---. You would be very well advised to exercise due caution on this matter---Mark, if you want this job---well, I'm sure you understand----."

"Say no more, Dan," Mark interrupted, "I understand perfectly, and I, ah, ah--- I can't thank you enough."

"You are more than welcome," Dan replied as he handed Mark the two-page formal application. "Please complete this, and drop it by our personnel office before you leave us today. I'm very anxious to get you on board so I'll push them to expedite your application. If all goes well can you begin next Monday?"

"I'll be here with bells on!" Mark relied, making no effort now to conceal his growing pleasure and excitement.

Some time later, Mark had been efficiently ushered into a small private cubicle by a most helpful personnel clerk who offered to provide any assistance he might require regarding any part of the application Mark had already labored over for nearly an hour. He had quickly responded forthrightly to all of the many self obvious questions that confronted him on this imposing and now suddenly threatening formality that stood between him and the financial security he so desperately sought for himself and his precious Leila. Only one question remained---just one more blank to be filled in--- and it was here that he had hesitated, now, unseemly, for almost a half-hour. The remaining blank space lay before his eyes accusingly---- "Please state your religious preference."

"Why do I care?" Mark tried unsuccessfully to diminish the gravity of the moment, as he, for the umpteenth time during the past half hour once again reviewed his own religious, or better described non-religious upbringing. After all, his own father had faced a very like situation many years ago when he had opened his now highly successful machine shop in an exclusively Christian Upper East Side neighborhood that serviced a mostly Christian clientele.

"Mark," his father had explained to his confused only son about the time most Christian boys are "confirmed" and nearly all Jewish boys are *Bar Mitzvah-ed*: "This is America and America is a *Christian* country---Jews need to fit in--- to be absorbed!"

"But why?" Mark had innocently responded, "Why can't Jews be Americans too?"

"Of course we can be Americans, my darling son! But, in order to survive, *first* we must be Jews. If a Jew can pass as a Gentile, he'll find it much easier to make a decent living in this troubled world---even to survive! Tell me, Mark," his father had continued, "do you think it was a painless matter for me to change our family name from Silverman to Sterling? Do you really believe it would be just as easy for you to live in the neighborhood, even in this free country where we live if your name was "Marcus Frank Silverman," like your mother insisted that the *Mohel* write on your certificate of circumcision?

Although he consciously struggled to be resolute in his decision, Mark's hand nevertheless perceptibly trembled as he entered the single word "Protestant" in the last remaining blank.

***

Dan Brandon was delighted that the personnel people had honored his request to expedite Mark's application. Here it was only Wednesday morning and the approved "New Hire" personnel package had been hand delivered to his office.

Dan smiled knowingly as he began to dial Mark's home number in order to share the good news of his new prodigy's imminent employment As he did so, his eyes were fixed in a contemplative stare at the single word response to what he instinctively had understood would be Mark's most difficult moment.

In a vain effort to somehow ameliorate his own sense of responsibility, he who had been *Bar Mitzvah-ed* as Daniel Abraham Berkowitz, whispered entirely for his own benefit: "Strange that we both decided to be 'Protestants'---. At least *he* didn't have to change his name.

Chapter Two

Qumran, Autumn A.D. 26

Even though Matthias looked to him with the same indescribable awe shared by his many thousands of sectarian brothers, there was something very special about his own, deeply personal relationship with their shared spiritual leader---a bigger than life, giant of a man who was known to his Essene brothers, and even to the world outside of their monastic community at Qumran on the Dead Sea, as Eliezar the High Priest, a son of Zadok.

How greatly Matthias treasured this dear man among men, and how thoroughly he loved him---after all, by the grace of God, Eliezar, whom Matthias knew intimately as Abba (father), had personally chosen him and only one other from among the many newly circumcised Jewish male infant foundlings who were left each year at Qumran to be raised and nurtured by the sect into manhood.

Matthias deeply loved and adored the other exclusively selected male child who was now, like himself, a vital young man in his late twenties. It was as if the two of them were genetic, real life twins---this is how their mutual Abba had treated both himself and this his very special, Godly brother---a wonderful, Spirit filled young man who had only recently become known by his quickly growing group of passionately loyal followers as "Yochanan (John) the Baptizer."

Matthias had a deep, soul nourishing love of Shabbat---the twenty-four hours of divinely ordained rest when *all* Jews, and most emphatically, *all* Essenes, because of their rigorously religious sectarian devotion, were called to focus every waking moment on drawing ever closer to Yahweh, the Lord God of Israel, King of the Universe.

But for Matthias, Shabbat was an even more wonderful and compelling holy gift than it was for most of his universally worshipful sectarian brothers. For Matthias, Shabbat was the one day of the week when he could joyfully spend several private hours, together with Yochanan, in the intimate presence of their beloved Abba.

On this particular Shabbat afternoon, as he was about to enter Abba's private chambers, Matthias was not unselfishly aware that he would have Abba all to himself. Yochanan, had earlier announced that he was planning to sleep under the stars at nearby Bethabara on the Jordan River so that he could resume his special work for the Lord as the rising sun confirmed the beginning of the first day of a new week. It was thus that Matthias praised God from the depths of his soul for the intimate private time that he would have with his beloved Abba as he entered Eliezar's unimposing, modestly appointed chambers.

"Greetings in the name of our Lord, Yahweh," Eliezar exclaimed as he joyfully embraced Matthias with a near crushing bear hug, the power of which was easily absorbed by his adoring, athletically built, strikingly handsome, olive complexioned adopted son who stood a half-head taller than himself. "You are looking well, my son!" he exclaimed. "What news do you have of your brother, Yochanan?"

Matthias, who had hungered for this moment, once again marveled at Abba's ability to discern his thoughts and immediately go to their heart. "Abba, I'm told that Yochanan has been performing a holy mikvah on an already very large band of followers, and proclaiming the soon coming of *Mashiach*," he replied.

"Indeed, my precious son," Abba smiled knowingly, his huge, dark brown, Holy Spirit filled eyes, providing instant confirmation that the words his lips were about to utter would flow from the very heart of God, "Your brother Yochanan is the one whom the great prophet Isaiah spoke of : 'The voice of one crying in the wilderness. Prepare the way of the LORD; make straight in the desert a highway for our God. Every valley shall be exalted and every mountain and hill brought low; the crooked places shall be made straight and the rough places smooth---.' Matthias," Eliezar proclaimed with unabashed fatherly pride, "Your brother has been called to a very special purpose---to proclaim to all who would only listen that God Himself was about to come into the world and dwell among men."[1]

"Abba," Matthias replied, instantly caught up in the overwhelming magnitude of what Abba had shared, "Surely this holy one that Yochanan speaks of must be the first coming of *Mashiach,* just as our fathers divinely anticipated and recorded long ago in our sect's sacred scrolls?"

"Indeed He is the *Mashiach,* my son," Abba replied, "but be careful not to confuse Him with the very different *Mashiach* who is anticipated by the Pharisees. They look for a man sent by God to come at the end of days as a prophet, priest and king, but by no means as God Himself, come in the flesh as a man to be sacrificed once and for all for the sins of men. I can tell you, my son," Eliezar sighed deeply, making no effort to conceal his profound, wrenching sadness, "I know with a certainty that this gross error that flows from the evil heart of Satan himself will indeed condemn legions of our brother Jews to eternal damnation, both now and throughout the coming ages."

"But, Abba," Matthias exclaimed incredulously, "How is it that the *soon to come Mashiach* will not make himself known to the world as someone far greater than just a prophet, priest and king? Why won't He proclaim Himself as the one whom our fathers precisely wrote about in our sacred scrolls that: He would be descended from the line of King David; he would come into the world as a perfect sacrifice to atone for the sins men, He would appear twice, both imminently and then again at the end of days--- and, most importantly, He would be a 'great God among the Gods'"?

"Remember, my son," Abba replied with continuing sadness, "It is also written in our scrolls that men will reject Him, even though they have heard the undeniable truth of who He is."[2]

"But why, Abba? Why will there be those who know clearly who He is and why He has come---how will any of these still be able to reject Him?"

Eliezar responded with a deliberate firmness to underscore the extreme importance of his reply. "My son, it is also written in our scrolls that to know *Mashiach*---to embrace Him, to follow Him---to have eternal life that can only be gained through Him--- even so, this knowing of Him cannot be willed by any man---it can only be given to each of us through our faith, and then only as an individual gift from God by His loving grace."[3]

"I have heard all of what you have taught, Abba--. But, it is still too awesome for me to fully understand."

Eliezar, smiled with rightful fatherly pride. "You speak with such wisdom for one so young, my son, and you have only erred in one important part of your understanding."

"In what way have I erred, Abba?" Matthias replied, suddenly taken aback.

"You could have had no way of knowing this, my son," Eliezar fell to his knees as he replied under the power of the awesome truth he was about to share. "The *Mashiach* is no longer *soon to come*---He is already in the world! He will soon be with your brother, Yochanan---you must go to them without delay!

Chapter Three

Portland, Oregon, August 1943

"Listen to me, Leila!" Mark nearly shouted, trying but failing miserably to keep his growing frustration under control. "For God's sake, Drew is already *nine* years old. Stop being so overprotective and give me just one reason why he shouldn't go by himself to the movies in the middle of the day?"

"Okay! Okay!" Leila relented, submitting, as usual, to the will of her husband. "It's just that Drew has had--- ah, ah," she hesitated, looking for the right words to express her own inner turmoil without evoking further provocation--- "It's just that he's had such a hard time adjusting since we returned from our visit to New York----."

"I suppose that you're still blaming me when it was *your* family who screwed up his mind with all their Jewish gobbledygook?" Mark retorted. "Leila, let's put this whole mess behind us and go on with our lives! Drew is a good boy---he's smart and he's sensitive! Believe me, he'll get over this thing if we just turn him loose and let him grow up!"

"Mark, darling," Leila moved close to her now fully agitated husband and took his hands comfortingly in her own. "All of this had to happen sooner or later and it is just as well that the truth is finally out in the open so we can all deal with it."

"I've only done my best to provide for my family," Mark continued, defensively. "You know, being Sales Manager for the Company's Northwest operations isn't such a bad thing?" Suddenly, his own inner turmoil came to the surface as he continued, "Honestly, Leila, I really believed our move to Oregon was a Godsend---that we could put all of this behind us and simply live like everyone else!"

"How could we possibly escape from whom and what we are?" Leila broke the intimacy of the moment as she moved away from him, still trying, but not succeeding to comfort her husband, and instead revealing her own growing frustration. "How could we simply put *all of this behind us* when we are Jews living in one of the most anti-Semitic places in the world?

For God's sake Mark!" she nearly screamed. "Your own Jewish son was already a nine year old anti-Semite from all the poison of this place when I tried to find some easy way to tell him: 'Oh, by the way, son, you're a Jew.'"

"Maybe we should have told him sooner?" She sighed deeply, again questioning the wisdom of the lie they had been living in order to protect Mark's rising career.

"I'm telling you Leila, it isn't *your* fault! Drew had to know before you introduced him to your observant family during Passover---. Just maybe it was a mistake taking him back to New York in the first place, much less, exposing him to all of this during the holidays? Listen to me!" he shouted. "It wasn't *your* fault! It was Amelia, your darling mother, your screwball sisters and your idiot uncle, Nathan!"

"How can you blame *them*?" She shouted back. "Why *wouldn't* they put a kippah on his head and a tallit around his shoulders? Mark, *my family is Jewish* and guess what, *so am I*! And, just in case you're beginning to believe your own facade, *so are you Mark*! *And so is Drew*! Jews do Jewish things during Jewish holidays!"

"That's just fine, I suppose." Mark almost whispered, as tears began to cloud his eyes. "But why did they have to do them all to my nine year old anti-Semitic son who had just been told he was a Jew?"

***

Andrew Scott Sterling, known to all within his rapidly expanding nine-year old world as "Drew," was greatly emboldened by his just granted independence as he made his way alone along the one mile route between the Sterling residence on Hazelfern Place and the Starburst Theater on Sandy Boulevard.

Even so, despite the joy of his newly found independence, Drew nevertheless found himself struggling to suppress his still very much lingering torment and confusion. As far as he knew, he pondered, as he walked along on this lovely summer day, he was the only Jew in all of Laurelhurst Elementary School's large student body. He understood that this terrible, deep family secret was not to be shared with anyone. After all, he knew well that his father's job depended upon the secret being kept---anyway, why share such a terrible thing with anyone---his nine year old reasoning questioned. Why tell anyone such a hateful truth about himself when no one seemed to care or even guess the terrible reality that lay just beneath the masque of the Sterling family's face upon the world around them?

All of them---his parents, whom he loved intensely, and he, as his mother had so lovingly yet clumsily explained during their recent fateful train journey to New York: Yes all of them had, seemingly, successfully "passed" themselves off as just another unremarkable family in the Gentile Christian world wherein they lived and prospered. Yes, Drew understood: He and his family were simply non-religious Jews---no one knew and no one cared and therefore, what did it matter?

Drew struggled to regain the anticipatory joy of the newly released war film, *Guadalcanal Diary* that lay just ahead as he hurried along his way. He fondly turned his thoughts toward the Johnson family, their lovely Christian neighbors with whom they had grown close during these five years of living in close proximity. It seemed good to him that they had been taking him to Church with them for the past several months.

Even now, after his father had continued to bless this attendance, although he had emphatically let it be known that the Sterlings were not, by any means, Baptists like the Johnsons. But, it was still okay for him to go to church with them, as long as he didn't take any of this too seriously---. Drew began to sing quietly: "Jesus loves me this I know, for the Bible tells me so. Little ones to Him belong. They are weak but He is strong---."

As he neared the large, grey-with-age, wooden bridge crossing over the double railroad tracks that lay about half way between the Sterling residence and the Starburst Theater, Drew was filled with a sudden inexplicable foreboding that snapped his attention back to the moment. There was something dreadful about this old grey wooden bridge, something totally beyond his own understanding. He struggled with himself, trying to regain his now shattered composure, at least sufficiently enough for him to ascend the twenty wooden stairs; transit what had to him become a fearful obstacle, and then descend the twenty steps that led to the graveled pathway on the other side.

Drew resumed his singing as he struggled to suppress the dread and unaccountable, chilling fear of his present situation---"Yes, Jesus loves me. Yes, Jesus loves me. Yes Jesus loves me. The Bible tells me so---."

The graveled pathway on the other side of the bridge wound its way through the massive grounds of the Eagle Lumber Company's well stocked yards. There were huge stacks of lumber of various dimensions and lengths scattered about seemingly everywhere along the both sides of the path. Drew's mind raced out of control with a sense of fear and foreboding the likes of which he had never previously known or imagined. He increased his pace----. "Yes, Jesus loves me. Yes, Jesus loves me. Yes Jesus loves me. The Bible tells me so---."

***

Franz Friedrich Mueller was a German born immigrant to America whose father, Heinrich, had been a highly decorated non-commissioned officer in the service of the Kaiser during what the Mueller family still spoke of as the "Great War."

While Heinrich had passed on to his eternal reward just after the beginning of the current "Great War," Franz, his son, still continued to regard several aspects of his intensely German heritage with a near reverence that dominated his very being. He deeply lamented the outcome of the first "Great War." And, like his heroic father before him, Franz directly attributed his beloved country's crushing humiliation to the detestable Jews of Europe who even now seemingly still controlled the banks and all commerce. It was they and they alone, Franz had long ago concluded, who were the true and enduring enemies of his beloved Germany.

It was this intense, all consuming hatred of everyone and everything Jewish that greatly helped Franz mentally replace and therefore occasionally escape the unfortunate physical realities of his birth. It seems that Franz had been born with a hair-lip, cleft palate and club foot, all of which had been only hurriedly and clumsily repaired by the only medial staff available just before the end of the "Great War," a newly drafted, just graduated, totally inexperienced German Army physician, one Doktor Lieutenant Benjamin Liebowitz, who also just happened to be a Jew.

The outcome of all these life's hardships in the living reality of Franz Mueller, as he struggled to survive as a minimum wage yard man in the employ of Eagle Lumber Company, was predictably dreadful. The intensity of the self induced hatefulness which dominated him was only equaled by the extreme physical unattractiveness with which he was forced to present himself to the world.

On this particular late morning in August, Franz' thoughts were suddenly diverted from his fanaticized visions of the coming glory of the Third Reich as he caught his first glimpse of Drew who now approached the large stack of "two by fours" behind which Franz had just now been lazily policing the grounds.

Franz *knew* at once that the approaching young lad was a Jew. After all, he looked Semitic---dark complexioned, black hair, and, his first evaluation confirmed as Drew came ever closer---his nose---his nose was hooked, surely an ugly Jewish beak!!

Franz leaped out from behind the stack of lumber like a man gone wild onto the graveled pathway just in front of Drew! He began to take the last of the few steps that physically separated him from his prey, his arms extended threateningly as giant claws, his deformed leg dragging behind him, thankfully slowing his advance. He screamed accusingly: "Jew boy!!

Dirty, filthy Jew boy!!"

In the stark terror of the moment, Drew struggled to regain his breath, as his reflexes took over and he leaped to the left, just barely escaping the approach of his gone wild pursuer's grasp, yet close enough to smell his foul tobacco breath and to literally feel the reality of his blind, intense hatred.

Drew's legs seemed to churn beneath him, his feet barely touching the ground as he ran, terrified, the remaining half-mile to the Starburst theater all the while hearing again and again the dreadful outburst: "Jew boy!! Dirty, filthy, Jew boy!!"

Drew sat in the back row of the near empty theater where he quietly wept during the entire showing of *Guadalcanal Diary*. He never told his parents or anyone else about his horrific experiences of that day.

Chapter Four

Bethabara on the Jordan River, November, A.D. 26

Matthias felt the intense heat of the noon day sun reflecting up through the soles his thick leather sandals and his usually impervious heavily calloused feet. Even as his parched mouth and throat made each successive breath more labored, the joy of his anticipation enabled him to suppress his growing discomfort as he hurriedly made his way through the barren, three-mile stretch of boiling Judean desert wilderness that separated Qumran from Bethabara on the Jordan River. This was the place where his beloved brother Yochanan was ministering.

Matthias whispered a brief prayer of thanksgiving as he saw, on the distant horizon, the first hint of the thick, bright green band of vegetation that sprang forth from the perpetually irrigated rich soil on both sides of the river.

He quickened his pace and now hurried toward the cool, lush attraction of this unseemly continuing oasis that snaked its way along the sixty miles from where the river exited the Sea of Galilee in the North and the Dead Sea, where it was to be eternally entrapped by its bitter, mineral saturated terminus in the South.

As he hurried along his way, Matthias continuously uttered praises to God, whose presence with him was intensely evident. He *knew* with clear assurance that there would be an immensely holy significance connected with the events he was about to witness. He found himself enraptured as he cried out joyfully: "Holy, holy, holy is the Lord God Almighty; the whole earth is full of your glory."

And so, intimately in communication with the God he so deeply loved, Matthias looked toward the north and took notice of what appeared to be the gathering, moisture laden black clouds of a quickly approaching early winter storm. He took this manifestation to be a sign in the heavens, and in response he increased his pace to a slow run as he delighted at the thought of the relative coolness and shelter of the river-centered oasis just ahead.

As he neared the thick band of vegetation that separated the perpetually sun baked desert from the lushly protected cooling waters of the river, Matthias trembled at the intense power of the gathering storm that had already coalesced into an immense cloud with flashing lightning, surrounded by brilliant light. The center of the fire looked like glowing metal---.[4]

Matthias cried out to his God, seeking protection, and, instantly a response came in the still quiet voice with which he had become so familiar, speaking to him from the depths where it dwelled, deep within his spirit: "Take heed my son," for the wondrous things you are about to witness I first revealed to my great prophets."

Then, just as this supernatural communication ended, Matthias at last reached the thick cool band of vegetation. He took a few more steps, and then fell prostrate onto the inviting, soft, cool, refreshing carpet.

***

Some time later, Matthias was awakened by the dripping remnant of the just passed torrential rain. It fell upon him soothingly in a persistent sprinkle from the carpet of leaf laden tree branches under which he lay. His spirit within him soared as he remembered the awesome message from the Lord that had thrown him into a swoon---an intimate encounter with his creator.

As he once again became increasingly aware of his immediate surroundings, Matthias discovered that he had fallen on his face just inside the beginning of the thick verdant band that lay between himself and the rushing river. He estimated from the sound of its rushing waters that the stream could be no more than one hundred meters or so from where he now stood. He struggled to find something recognizable in his new and very different surroundings that would show him how next to proceed.

Once again he received what he knew instinctively to be supernatural guidance, the still quiet voice he knew so well telling him that he was to proceed straight ahead, toward the river. He immediately responded, pushing aside the dense undergrowth as he moved toward the sound of the rushing water.

Matthias had only to take a few steps before he broke out of the dense green carpet and into the brilliant light of what was now late afternoon. What he beheld literally took his breath away, and it took him a few moments to recover so that his overtaxed sensibilities could begin to translate the meaning of all this to the beginning of his understanding.

Just another one hundred meters or so upstream Matthias saw a large clearing on the other side of the river. And there, he observed with unabashed joy, he beheld his greatly adored brother Yochanan, standing waste deep in a gently swirling pool of seemingly living water that took its jade green color as a reflection from the umbrella of trees that framed the scene.

Matthias suddenly *knew* in the depths of his being that what would happen here on this late autumn afternoon was indeed something most holy and unspeakably profound in its significance for all men who lived in the present age and also for all generations to come. He *knew* instinctively that these were the wondrous events ordained and conducted by the hand of God--- the events that had long been recorded in the sacred scrolls by past generations of his sectarian Essene brothers.

When Matthias had drawn very close to the pool where Yochanan stood and ministered, he fell to his knees. The presence of the Spirit of God was so powerful that Matthias could do no more than reverently observe what was taking place before his eyes.

"There must be more than one hundred men, and even some women," Matthias quietly observed, from their manner of dress and different dialects that he could now overhear, who had come to this place from all over the

Land---from Samaria, Judea, the Galilee and perhaps even beyond. Here they, he observed--- all seem to radiate with a holy light---themselves glowing externally from the inward fire that was being transferred into the depths of their beings by some supernatural process that Matthias himself was only just beginning to fathom.

One by one they fearfully yet reverently came forward, as if in a holy trance, to be ministered to by Yochanan, who proclaimed to each of them in turn as he supervised their purifying mikvah-like, squatting in-place, self immersion: "*I baptize with water,---but among you stands one you do not know. He is the one who comes after me, the thongs of whose sandals I am not worthy to untie.*"[5]

Suddenly, Matthias observed, a complete and utter silence fell upon the scene as if all discernable human perception had been abruptly replaced by an intense, brief interlude of heavenly, indescribable peace.

Matthias blinked his eyes several times, testing the reality of the moment. Then, almost at once, he again began to hear the sound of the river's rushing water ---but also, he heard an overriding, incredibly powerful, awesomely beautiful, heavenly chorus. A chorus rendered in perfect sixteen part harmony by an enormous choir of angels, repeatedly singing their glorious offertory of praise to God --- "To him who sits on the throne and to the Lamb be praise and honor and glory and power, for ever and ever!"[6]

Matthias, overcome by the utter awesomeness of the moment, once again fell prostrate, face down upon the cool earth, his entire being physically and spiritually refreshed in a way far exceeding anything he had ever previously experienced or even imagined, as if he were, somehow, being gently held in the loving protection of the very hand of God.

It was his beloved brother Yochanan who broke the utter silence of the moment as he cried out in a voice like that of the clarion announcement of a perfectly tuned and presented *shofar*--- "Behold! The Lamb of God who takes away the sin of the world! This is He of whom I said, 'After me comes a Man who is preferred before me, for He was before me.' I did not know Him; but that He should be revealed to Israel, therefore I came baptizing with water." [7]

And then Matthias saw with his own eyes of whom his brother spoke as he simultaneously heard the long familiar still silent voice whisper in the very depths of his being---- "This is my beloved son, the Messiah, who is one with me, in His first appearance; the one of whom your scribes wrote---the Holy One of Israel whom you have been expecting. Make no mistake; it is He of whom the great prophet spoke:

> *But, oh, how few will believe it! Who will listen? To whom will God reveal his saving power?   In God's eyes he is like a tender green shoot, sprouting from a root in dry and sterile ground. But in the eyes of men there will be no attractiveness at all, nothing in his appearance to make us want him. In fact, you will despise him and reject him-a man of sorrows, acquainted with bitterest grief. You will turn your backs on him and look the other way when he passes by. He will be despised, and you will not care. Yet it is your grief he will bear, your sorrows that will weigh him down. And you will think that his troubles are a punishment from God, for his own sins! But he will be wounded and bruised for your sins. He will be beaten that you might have peace; he will be lashed-and you will be healed! You-every one of you-have strayed away like sheep! You, who will leave God's paths to follow your own. Yet God will lay upon him the guilt and sins of every one of us!* [8]

Matthias, remained prostrate, face down upon the ground just a few feet away from where his brother had now fallen to his knees in the water, leaving only his shoulders and head above the surface. Ever so slowly, Matthias opened his eyes and raised his head just enough to take in the awesome, God directed scene that was unfolding before him.

It was then, for only a brief fraction of a moment that Matthias made eye contact with Him who approached. Matthias swooned as if he had been struck deaf by a strangely silent bolt of lightning that encompassed the entire collective power of the universe---yet he felt not even a hint of violence or force---rather Matthias found himself overwhelmed, even totally consumed by what he clearly understood to be an outpouring of intense love---all the love in the universe coalesced and focused upon himself in this fraction of a moment during which he understood the essence of *eyn sof*, eternity. This was the perfection of love revealing to Matthias precisely who it was who approached, as he heard the familiar still voice within him saying: "--- love one another, for love comes from God. Everyone who loves has been born of God and knows God. Whoever does not love does not know God, because God is love."[9]

In a flash of divinely orchestrated recognition, Matthias unmistakably understood that this very ordinary looking Semitic man who approached was at once both God and man, the one for whom his beloved father, Eliezar the High Priest had been waiting all of his many years--- the one of whom the scribes had written in their sectarian scrolls:

[---] and he will be great over the earth---[. . .] great will he be called and he will be designated by his name. He will be called the Son of God, and they will call him the Son of the Most High---His kingdom will be an eternal kingdom, and all his paths in truth and uprightness. The earth will be in truth and all will make peace. ---The sword will cease in the earth and all the cities will pay him homage. He is a great God among the gods.[10]

Although Matthias had never before encountered the one who approached, instinctively, almost inaudibly, he whispered his name for the first time---

"*Yeshua*"----Salvation.

Moments later, Yeshua stood before Yochanan who knelt in the water before him. He lovingly placed his hands upon Yochanan's shoulders and said, "Arise Yochanan, my beloved brother, I have come to be baptized by you."

Matthias, who was near enough to see and hear what was taking place in the nearby pool saw Yochanan tremble as he replied, "I need to be baptized by You, and You are coming to me?"

Yeshua answered and said to him: "Permit it to be so now, for thus it is fitting for us to fulfill all righteousness."[11]

Yochanan rose up from the water and stood before Yeshua. Gently, he placed his hands upon Yeshua's head and while exerting only a hint of pressure, Yeshua went down into the water until he was entirely immersed.

At this wondrous moment, Yochanan cried out to heaven: "I baptize you with water --- But you who are far mightier than I, whose sandals I am not worthy to carry---you will baptize with the Holy Spirit and with fire."[12]

Then, just as Yeshua began to come up out of the water, Matthias and all of the others who were there assembled witnessed the fulfillment of what had been spoken of long ago by the prophets: Daniel, Isaiah and Ezekiel. Above the expanse over their heads they saw what looked like a throne of sapphire, and high above on the throne was a figure like that of a man. They saw that from what appeared to be his waist up he looked like glowing metal, as if full of fire, and that from there down he looked like fire; and brilliant light surrounded him. Like the appearance of a rainbow in the clouds on a rainy day, so was the radiance around him.[13]

What followed in the next instant would be forevermore etched into the very fiber of Matthias' heart, soul and spirit. At that fraction of a moment he saw heaven opened and from there he saw the Spirit of God descending upon Yeshua like a dove and lighting on him. And he heard a voice from heaven say, "This is my Son, whom I love; with him I am well pleased." [14]

The unseen glorious choir of angels continued to sing their praises in wonderful sixteen part harmony as Yeshua embraced Yochanan and silently began to make his way from the clearing, moving north, toward the Sea of Galilee. All who were there assembled remained totally silent, as if frozen in place by the awesomeness of what they had just witnessed.

Finally, after some considerable time, when the angelic singing had ceased and some sense of normalcy had returned to the scene, it was Matthias who was the first of many to be baptized by Yochanan that very day and in the same manner as had been their newly revealed Master, Yeshua: King of the Universe, Son of God, Messiah, Redeemer, Great God among the Gods.

Chapter Five

The Bronx, July, 1946

Drew's navigational self confidence soared as he confirmed, from the address posted above the entrance to the red brick, ten story Bronx tenement in front of which he now stood, that he had successfully found his way to Grandma Amelia's apartment at 1087 Allerton Avenue. His mother had driven him to the station early that morning, and he had journeyed forth from there by New York Central commuter train, transferred to the correct "Elevated" and here he was, all the way from the Sterlings' posh new Scarsdale residence. The family had recently relocated from Portland following Mark's latest promotion, along what was already a well established meteoric pathway to the top management of National Carbon Company.

Drew smiled as he remembered his father's earlier strong protestations to this weekend visit pronounced over breakfast: "Leila, you must be crazy altogether!" Mark had bellowed his objection to his mother-in-law's suggestion. "Drew is only twelve---he has no business taking a train all the way to the Bronx by himself!" He paused for a moment, smiling at the presumed cleverness of what was to be the continuation of his outburst. "Did it ever occur to you that he just might get lost in the bowels of the Bronx--- and even worse *he might actually find his way* to your mother's apartment?"

"Why are you carrying on so about this?" Leila countered. "What could be so terrible about your son visiting his grandmother for the weekend---you know, it was *her* idea?"

"Of course it was *her* idea!" Mark got right to the real substance of his objection, now addressing his response as an earnest appeal directly to his son. "Drew, I don't have to tell you how important it is for us to continue living our lives, just like we did in Portland! We are now a part of a new community---we live in a high end Westchester County neighborhood---you could count the number of Jewish families that live here on one hand! Son," Mark sighed, looking for the right words to express his frustration: "Your grandmother is a practicing Jew. She simply cannot and will not accept the fact that we have different ideas about religion and how we choose to live---."

"Dad," Drew responded earnestly, "I understand---honestly I do! I like being the same as everyone else---you know, fitting in! I have absolutely no interest in being Jewish---in fact, *I hate being Jewish*! I *know* that your job depends upon us keeping this whole rotten Jewish thing quiet---."

"Watch your tongue young man!" Leila interjected. "Being Jewish isn't a 'rotten thing.' We Jews didn't choose to be Jewish. God chose us from among all His creation to be His chosen people---its just that, out of *necessity*, we must be quiet about this particular wonderful blessing."

Mark seized the moment. "Son, when you grandmother learned we were coming back to New York she launched a campaign regarding your---ahh---religious education, and she hasn't shut up since! She is absolutely insistent that you are going to be Bar Mitzvah-ed, just the way she insisted that you be ritually circumcised!" Mark's demeanor and tone lost any semblance of warmth, revealing his genuine dislike and continuing battle with his mother-in-law as he continued---"I caved in on the circumcision but you will be Bar Mitzvah-ed over my dead body--- unless of course, you personally, ahh---."

Drew interrupted, letting his father off the hook as he almost shouted "Mom and Dad, *please understand*! I DON'T WANT TO BE BAR MITZVAH-ED!"

Leila broke the silence following Drew's outburst. "Enough already! Hurry, or you'll both miss your trains!"

***

Drew paused for a moment before he pushed the fifth floor door bell labeled "Amelia Grossman Cittrenbaum" that would open the way for his visit with his beloved grandmother. He took a deep breath, as if to better take in and somehow prolong the soul thrilling uniqueness of his Bronx, New York surroundings.

He could not then begin to understand, much less explain, even to himself, why it was that his heart surged in seemingly visual consonance with the living essence and substance of New York spread out all around him, in a very like manner, even as it was so gloriously captured and musically expressed by George Gershwin, another New York Jew.

Instinctively and unconsciously Drew struggled to score, harmonize then orchestrate the divergent strains of this, his own, uniquely private sensory New York rhapsody that called out to him for recognition: The young mother sitting in a folding chair in the relative comfort of a shaded part of the sidewalk, who, to avoid an unnecessary trip to a stifling hot upstairs apartment was loudly encouraging her five year old son to urinate in the street— "It's okay, darling, Pish! Pish!"—The not unpleasant odor of floor covering sawdust strangely blended with that of freshly grilled all beef kosher hot dogs that scented the air like an olfactory trademark flowing from the open door of the nearby delicatessen—The almost palpable taste of three-cent chocolate egg sodas that were the thirst quenching specialty of the shop adjacent to the entrance to Grandma Amelia's tenement.

For Drew, this potpourri of sights, sounds and scents that were uniquely New York and more specifically Allerton Avenue, the Bronx, were crying out to him to recognize and accept the compelling, inescapable visceral essence of whom and what he was—a Jew, one of the chosen—chosen by whom and for what he then could not even begin to understand or imagine.

***

Grandma Amelia carefully surveyed the hand she had just dealt herself in their now traditional, seemingly never ending game of Hollywood Gin, and then clumsily exchanged the bottom card from the deck with one in her hand that was evidently not to her liking. Drew had always been drawn to this dear woman, his only surviving grandparent, for reasons he could not completely explain.

For starters, Drew unabashedly (by necessity, most often silently) sided with his grandmother in her continuing battle with his father. Even at his tender age, Drew was well aware that Amelia had appointed herself, as if by some divine commission, as Mark's ultimate advisor on any and all matters; such advise, most often preceded by the inciting, trigger phrase, "Mark, Darling, wouldn't it be better if you---??"

The specific circumstances didn't really matter—Amelia knew exactly how to taunt her son-in-law into a nearly immediate explosion and she played him to this purpose like the director of the New York Philharmonic calling for the perfectly timed crashing report of mighty cymbals.

Fondly, breaking into a broad grin, Drew recalled Grandma's final visit to Portland, just before they returned to New York. Mark, typically, had retreated from what was shaping up to be an inevitable argument with Amelia and had sought refuge by slipping out the back door to take out his aggressions by chopping wood for the family fireplace.

Drew, had joined his father at the wood pile, wanting to observe the encounter he correctly suspected that was soon to follow. He thus was not at all surprised when Amelia quietly slipped out the back door and, unobserved by Mark, stood closely behind him where she carefully evaluated his current activity as he repeatedly swung his ax with more than necessary tension relieving force to accomplish the physical task at hand. After a few moments, she placed her hands firmly upon her hips, noticeably stiffened her just over five foot, corpulent, square frame as if to physically challenge her over six foot impending, self chosen adversary as she exclaimed: "Mark, Darling, wouldn't it be better---?"

Without the slightest delay, Mark spun around in place, thrust the ax forward into her hands that she protectively raised in front of herself, and, in one of his finest moments, quietly responded. "If you have a better way, then, *you* do it!"

"Marcus," she used his unchanged name as another weapon. "You know that I love you."

Mark did not respond, but rather calmly retreated into the house.

***

"Nuuu! Drew, Darling," Grandma Amelia pulled her greatly adored grandson from his recollections, anxious to get on with the game the inevitable outcome of which she had, as usual, already assured: "Stop grinning already and play a card!"

At that moment, their eyes met and held fast in a soul level exchange that reflected the sweet, confident solidity of their relationship. After a few moments, Drew spoke from his heart, "You know," he almost whispered adoringly," I love you very much grandma."

Tears began to well up in Amelia's large blue eyes that were the central feature of what her son-in-law not affectionately but quite accurately described as her "bull dog" like face. She wiped them away with the sweep of a hand as she quietly replied, "So, Darling; put the cards down already. We need to talk."

Drew was not surprised by her intensity and obvious concern as he expectantly awaited her opening comment.

"Drew, Darling," she began, her heavy Yiddish accent seemingly even more pronounced than usual, as if to underscore the basis of her concern. "You know, in just a few months on your birthday you will be a man!"

"Grandma," Drew responded with some surprise, I will only be *thirteen*!"

"By me and by our people you will be a man, Drew, no longer a boy!

"I don't understand, Grandma, I'll just be starting high school--- I won't be able to drive for another four years---I can't even get a part-time job after school for at least another year! How do you figure that I am suddenly going to be a man?"

"Drew, Darling," she reached across the table and caressed his arm lovingly as she tenderly explained: "You are now a nice Jewish boy, one of God's chosen people, and nice Jewish boys become men when they reach thirteen." She paused for a moment as if to emphasize her forthcoming central message. "Drew," she continued resolutely, you *need* to be Bar

Mitzvah-ed!"

Drew paused for a few moments, collecting his thoughts before he finally replied, attempting at first to lightly dismiss her challenge and change the subject. "God is really wasting his time with me, Grandma---maybe he should have chosen someone else? I don't think of myself as being Jewish!"

"Drew, Darling," she replied tenaciously, "Your father can masquerade as 'Mark Sterling' instead of the 'Marcus Silverman' he was born and, he can give his son a *goyish* name like 'Andrew Scott' but it doesn't change *anything*! Drew, you are a Jew and you must learn to accept whom and what you are!"

He was overcome by the intensity of his adored grandmother's outburst. Suddenly, the self erected up to now impenetrable mental barrier that had insulated him from the unspeakable recollections of his still very young years was breached, bringing forth his own tears as the barrier broke and the flood of terrible memories returned: the revelation of his Jewish-ness delivered to him awkwardly by his mother as they traveled to New York to celebrate Passover with her family—his insensitive decoration with a kippah and tallit when he had been forced to take his unwanted place at the Seder table—the unspoken horror of his encounter with whom seemed to be the very devil himself at Eagle Lumber yard—. "Not in this lifetime, Grandma!" he replied resolutely. "Not in this lifetime!"

Chapter Six

Tabgha, on the Western shore of the Sea of Galilee, Spring A.D. 27

The huge orange ball of the sun now rising just above the Golan Heights on the eastern side of the Lake burned its way through the heavy morning mist. It manifested itself in a glorious display of infinite tiny diamond-like sparkling fires reflecting from the deep blue water into the eyes of the growing party of commonly clad men and women who made their way along the rocky shore reverently in trail behind Yeshua, their beloved Master.

Matthias was filled with unfathomable joy as he took in the wonder of this wonderful, heavenly moment from his unassigned but self assumed place in the entourage, just behind the twelve whom Yeshua had already chosen as his closest disciples.

Matthias' spirit leaped within him as he recalled the incredible events he had witnessed during the past several weeks since he'd faithfully been following the Master about the Galilee and then Syria. He thrilled as, in the theater of his mind he once again witnessed in kaleidoscopic recall the miraculous happenings to which he had so recently born witness: Yeshua's teaching in many synagogues, preaching the good news of the kingdom, and healing every disease and sickness among the people.

News about Yeshua spread all over the region as he healed the many people brought to him, all who were ill with various diseases, those suffering severe pain, the demon-possessed, those having seizures, and the paralyzed.

How deeply privileged he was, Matthias marveled, to be in this, his ordained place, near the front of the large crowds who came from Galilee, the Decapolis, Jerusalem, Judea and the region across the Jordan who followed his master, Yeshua.[15]

Now, as the rapidly growing assemblage progressed along the one mile or so that remained between their present position, just beyond Tabgha, to their destination, the looming slope of Mount Ermos, rising just to the north of the shore; Matthias took special notice of what to him was a surprising diversity in the crowd that gathered behind him.

While, Matthias reasoned, most of those who now enthusiastically followed, could easily be identified as Jews, mostly Galileans, by their dress and language, there was also a large contingent who had come from the Decapolis. The Decapolis, he understood, was a widespread group of ten Greek founded pagan populated communities that spread from its beginning at Hippos, just on the other side of the Lake, to Pella in distant Trans Jordan.

"Why was his precious *Jewish* Messiah, Yeshua of interest to these Goyim?" Matthias pondered. "Certainly, the scribes had recorded in his sect's sacred scrolls that the Messiah would come into the world to redeem *all* men---not just the Jews,[16] but Matthias was surprised to find that apparently some non-Jews were to be included among those who would apparently embrace Yeshua from the very beginning of his ministry."

In fact, even now, Matthias noticed, glancing back over his shoulder, what appeared to be a family of Gentiles from the Decapolis who were following along, immediately behind him.

While Matthias noted the middle aged husband and wife, and he who was apparently their teenage son, he was especially drawn to the striking, extravagant beauty of who he assumed must be their older daughter. She was tall, full bosomed and lithe and in his eyes she seemed to move with extraordinary grace as she made her way along the rock strewn mountain-side they had just begun to ascend. But even more it was her lovely, even angelic deeply tanned face, punctuated by the large deep blue eyes of her Greco-Roman heritage, all of this framed in long, flowing jet black hair that cascaded to just below her waist. Matthias nearly swooned as their eyes met for the first time.

Now, drawn by a motivation beyond simple hospitality, he slowed his pace, until he was walking alongside the head of this family of non-Jews from across the Lake, and he introduced himself warmly. "You are most welcome to the Galilee. I am called Matthias and I am a drawn follower of the Master."

"I am called Ariston," the head of the family responded with matching warmth." We have heard many wondrous and astounding things about your Master in our city, Hippos, and we have come to witness these things for ourselves."

"Then you have come at a perfect time, Ariston," Matthias replied. "I am told that on this very day the Master will speak many deeply important truths from the slope of this mountain we are now ascending."

"Behold, you speak with prophetic truth. Apparently, your Master is about to begin," Ariston observed as he looked ahead and saw Yeshua, facing the crowd, sit down upon a large boulder that seemed to be at the very center of what was an enormous natural amphitheater.

Yeshua waited silently as the multitude, now grown to many thousands, spread themselves out in a huge semi-circle immediately below where he had taken his place. They sat upon what was a gorgeous natural green carpet decorated with a sea of multi-colored spring wildflowers.

As they found their places, Ariston warmly invited Matthias, "We would be greatly honored if you would sit with us."

"The honor would be mine," Matthias replied, sensing that his hidden agenda was about to be accomplished.

"Let me introduce my family," Ariston offered: "My wife, Theodora---my son, Euclid, and, my daughter, Heliodora."

Matthias, who bowed reservedly as each name was mentioned, was quite startled when each member of the family, in turn, embraced him and kissed him on both cheeks, as evidently, he assumed, was their custom.

It was no accident that Matthias found himself sitting among the wildflowers close by the last member of the family to be introduced who whispered in his ear as she kissed his cheeks, "I am called Dory."

It was only the riveting voice of Yeshua that could have diverted Matthias' attention away from Dory, and it did so, even abruptly.

The Master began to speak in a firm voice that could be heard clearly by all of the many thousands who had assembled in that place, the natural acoustical system of which had been designed for this very purpose since before the beginning of time:

Blessed are the poor in spirit, for theirs is the kingdom of heaven. Blessed are those who mourn, for they will be comforted. Blessed are the meek, for they will inherit the earth. Blessed are those who hunger and thirst for righteousness, for they will be filled. Blessed are the merciful, for they will be shown mercy. Blessed are the pure in heart, for they will see God. Blessed are the peacemakers, for they will be called sons of God. Blessed are those who are persecuted because of righteousness, for theirs is the kingdom of heaven.

Blessed are you when people insult you, persecute you and falsely say all kinds of evil against you because of me. Rejoice and be glad, because great is your reward in heaven, for in the same way they persecuted the prophets who were before you.

You are the salt of the earth. But if the salt loses its saltiness, how can it be made salty again? It is no longer good for anything, except to be thrown out and trampled by men.

You are the light of the world. A city on a hill cannot be hidden. Neither do people light a lamp and put it under a bowl. Instead they put it on its stand, and it gives light to everyone in the house. In the same way, let your light shine before men, that they may see your good deeds and praise your Father in heaven.

Do not think that I have come to abolish the Torah or the Prophets; I have not come to abolish them but to fulfill them. I tell you the truth, until heaven and earth disappear, not the smallest letter, not the least stroke of a pen, will by any means disappear from the Torah until everything is accomplished. Anyone who breaks one of the least of these commandments and teaches others to do the same will be called least in the kingdom of heaven, but whoever practices and teaches these commands will be called great in the kingdom of heaven. For I tell you that unless your righteousness surpasses that of the Pharisees and the teachers of the Torah, you will certainly not enter the kingdom of heaven. [17]

As Yeshua paused for a moment, Matthias who was thrilled beyond measure by what he had already heard, whispered excitedly for Dory's hearing alone: "This is amazing!" he exclaimed, "It is truly amazing! The very form and substance of what the Master is saying has long been written in the sacred scrolls of our sect!"

Dory took his hands and held them warmly with her own. "I beg you to teach us about your Torah and about your sectarian scrolls," she requested expectantly."

"I shall!" he replied, as if responding to a divine calling. "I shall indeed!"

Chapter Seven

Rochester, New York, December, 1955

Drew greatly loved the delightfully unique sound and feel of new fallen snow crunching beneath his feet. He increased his pace to more quickly close the remaining block or so of his two-mile weekly trek from his University of Rochester River Campus dormitory to the embracing warmth of Father John Lassiter's study at Saint Agnes' Roman Catholic Church. In a way, Drew pondered, he was saddened that this would be his tenth and final session with Father John. He had grown to genuinely like and admire this dear man of God during their open and intense time together.

Having just celebrated his twenty-first birthday, Drew relished in the full flower of his young manhood. He breathed deeply, filled with a great sense of contentment and well being as the crisp, very cold, early winter air filled his lungs with its tingling, invigorating and somehow deeply satisfying goodness.

He paused for a moment as he reached the sheltered portico entrance of the church, brushed away a two inch layer of accumulated snow from a cement bench with a gloved hand and sat down.

Despite the bitter cold of his surroundings, he was immediately mesmerized by the rhythmic, nearly palpable, quickly frozen exhalations of his breathing. His thoughts quietly drifted back to his first meeting with Father John, some two weeks after the beginning of what was now the final semester of his senior year at the "U of R".

***

"You come highly recommended by your roommate," Father John had begun their first meeting, "Mike Ryan is a wonderful and faithful member of our congregation and he speaks very highly of you."

Drew found himself fully at ease as he took the proffered seat in front of the frock clad priest's simple wooden desk. "Mike has become my best friend over these past three and a half years," he replied warmly, "I've come to love him like a brother, a brother who has something very special in his life that I don't. "Father Lassiter," he added bluntly. "That's why I'm here."

"He has the Church," Father John had quickly replied, "and through the Church he has found his salvation."

Drew hesitated for a moment, looking for the right words before he turned to the heart of his need---"I suppose Mike has told you about my family being Jewish and all?"

"Yes, my son," Father John, replied, suddenly and naturally transformed at once into Drew's sincere teacher, mentor and concerned counselor. "He shared with me that you have grown up in a kind of spiritual limbo--- that you are seeking a greater understanding of God." He smiled knowingly, unconsciously sharing the beginnings of his own deep conviction. "You have come to the right place. The Church is what you have unknowingly been seeking."

***

Now, ten weeks later, Drew once again pondered all of this as he sat on the frozen cement bench in the portico of Saint Agnes' Catholic Church. God and the Church---that was the crux of his problem. During their several lengthy, probing and sometimes emotional discussions, Father John had always come back to the central focus of his teaching:

- The Jewish people and the Land of Israel have been replaced by the Roman Catholic Church in the plan and purposes of God. Thus, the Church is the rightful and historic continuation of Israel to the exclusion of the former.

• The Jews are now no longer a "chosen people" and are no different from any other ethnic group or nation.

• Apart from repentance and conversion into the Church, the Jewish people have no future, no hope, and no calling in the plan of God.

• The term "Israel," as found in the New Testament, refers to the Church.

• The promises, covenants and blessings ascribed to Israel in the Bible have been taken away from the Jews and given to the Church, which has superseded them. However, the Jews are subject to the curses found in the Bible, as a result of their rejection of Christ.

A few minutes later, after the bitter out of doors cold had forced him from his recollections into the beginning of what Father John had earlier said was to be his "Day of Decision," Drew once again delighted in both the physical warmth of Father John's study and the genuine human warmth of his friend and spiritual mentor.

"Tell me my son," Father John began, after he had poured his still shivering young visitor a cup of coffee and they had each settled into their respective chairs.   "What has the Lord laid upon your heart? Do you have any remaining questions before you join Mike and the rest of us in the glorious saved Body of Christ?"

Drew quickly reviewed the mental list he had assembled before this final and decisive meeting. "Father John, while, as you know, I've never been a practicing Jew," he began, "for the first time in my life you've shown me that I'm called to worship Yahweh, the Lord God of Israel----It seems to me that He and He alone is the creator of the Universe, the God of us all." He paused for a moment to better collect his thoughts. "Father," he continued, "To me, Yahweh is the God of the Torah, what you and the Church call the 'Old Testament'---and, it is the Torah that tells us that Yahweh alone will eternally be the one singular God of the Jews, a people whom He has chosen in an unbreakable covenant."

Despite, his efforts to the contrary, Drew found it difficult to control the emotion that was beginning to arise in his voice as he concluded: "Nowhere can I find any biblical evidence that the New Testament has superceded the Old or that the Church has somehow replaced the Jews and Israel!"

Father John noticeably slumped forward in his chair as he struggled to conceal his great disappointment. "The Apostle Paul," he began, "tells us in his letter to the Galatians that if we, through the Church, are saved by Christ through the power of the Holy Spirit, then we are the seed of Abraham and heirs according to the promise."

It was evident that the teacher had taught his earnestly seeking disciple well as Drew quickly responded, "It seems to me that your Jesus never intended to change the Torah of the Jews. He clearly told us in His Sermon on the Mount:

Do not think that I have come to abolish the Law or the Prophets; I have not come to abolish them but to fulfill them. I tell you the truth, until heaven and earth disappear, not the smallest letter, not the least stroke of a pen, will by any means disappear from the Law until everything is accomplished.[18]

"Surely," Drew exclaimed, "If the Torah remains unchanged, so must God's special relationship with the Jews as His chosen people also remain unchanged."

Seeing Drew's resoluteness on this point, Father John abruptly changed the subject to the ultimate, most fundamental doctrinal point of his teaching : "Drew, do I hear you—you who were born a Jew, acknowledging the authority of Jesus Christ in the New Testament? Have I truly succeeded in showing you that he is the Son of God, the promised Messiah, the head of His Body the Church through which and only through which salvation can be found?"

Father John paused for a moment, but continued before Drew could form a response. "Drew, my son," he earnestly pleaded, "Have you found your blessed salvation in the Church?"

Drew knew in his heart precisely how he was to respond. He had read and carefully studied the central teachings of both testaments of the Bible over the past several weeks and had spent many hours in prayer to a God whom he had only just begun to know but could only then barely fathom.

"Father John," he began, his tone and manner clearly showing his counselor the depth of his admiration and affection. "You have done so very much to help me along my way toward truth. Through what you have shown me I have come to know my God, the God of the Jews---to even begin to acknowledge to myself that I am a Jew! You have caused me to pray and to study, to seek and even in my own way to find---I thank you from the bottom of my heart for this."

He lowered his voice as he continued. "Father John, I am so sorry to disappoint you, but I see my salvation to be found only in Yahweh, the one God of Israel. I do not know or understand this Jesus Christ of yours who seems to me you have buried in the complexities of your Church." Drew felt the tears begin to well up in his eyes as he concluded: "Father John, I am truly sorry, but I can not, in all truth, accept the authority of either Jesus Christ or your Church."

With that, Drew stood, extended his hand to Father John, and turned to leave the study.

"Keep praying and keep seeking," Father John exclaimed in a trembling voice as Drew stepped through the portal of the study. "You need to find and come to know Jesus Christ---it is here in the Church and only here where He is to be found!"

"I will look for Him in other places," Drew whispered for his own benefit, as he stepped out once again into the waiting frigid world and began his long trek back to his campus dormitory. He was deep in prayerful thought as he proceeded and unaware that it had suddenly grown much colder and had once again begun to snow.

Chapter Eight

Capernaum, on the western shore of the Sea of Galilee
Spring, A.D. 27

Matthias' heart raced almost out of control as he caught site of Dory entering the walled city of Capernaum where he had taken up temporary residence in order to remain as close as he could to the Master and His unfolding, miracle filled ministry.

For the first time since he had begun his intense and ongoing discipling of Dory and her family several weeks ago, Dory had been permitted to come to him by herself, a clear sign of the trust and respect her father, Ariston, had afforded him as his relationship with this lovely Greco-Roman family from Hippos in the Decapolis had grown ever more close.

Matthias, who had been reared from his infancy to young manhood in the highly restrictive, monastic and celibate confines of Qumran, knew almost nothing of the emotional and physical relationships that his God had ordained between men and women. However, as he hurried to greet this extraordinarily beautiful, blue-eyed creature who smiled broadly and excitedly waved to him in their mutually compelling, recognition, Matthias marveled at the new and wonderful set of emotions he was only just now beginning to understand as his Creator's gift--- this all encompassing, incredibly wonderful manifestation of human love.

"How was your crossing?" he inquired as he took her hands in his own and their eyes met in an unspoken acknowledgement of their mutual attraction.

"Wonderful!" she replied, as she excitedly recalled her recent journey by boat. "Andrew and James had been waiting for me for just a few minutes when I arrived at Hadar. They had already filled their boat to near overflowing from their all night fishing."

"You don't smell a bit fishy!" Matthias teased as he playfully sniffed at her dark glistening waist length hair and then her body from a respectable distance. "Apparently, you, my dear brothers and the fish as well had a smooth crossing?"

"Indeed we did!" she replied happily. "The wind was just right and we were able to come the full distance in just over one hour."

"That certainly is to be greatly favored over the several mile hike around the north end of the Lake," he observed.

She squeezed his hands that she still held in her own as she changed the subject. "I am so pleased to be with you again, Matthias---. I know there must be much from the blessed Torah that you plan to share with me today, and I am so anxious to learn."

"Come, Dory," he replied, as he led her toward the city gate. "We will spend most of the day in a very special place---a place where the Master himself goes to escape the crowds. It's a holy place, simply because of His frequent presence there."

Suddenly Matthias' heart sank in despair as he noticed the small basket Dory carried and he rushed to the conclusion that she had prepared food for them which, he, as an Essene could not eat. He struggled, but miserably failed to suppress his emotions as he grappled for some escape from this difficult situation.

"Let me carry your basket," Matthias began, as they began their just over one mile trek from along the shore-side trail that would take them from Capernaum to the holy place of which he spoke, an otherwise quiet unimposing cave near the base of Mount Ermos.

Dory understood completely, and couldn't help smiling broadly in reaction to Matthias' obvious distress. "Don't be silly," she replied. "It's only a simple midday meal I had prepared for us this morning by a Jewish family at Kursi—it weighs very little."

They walked along, uplifted by the tender joy of their new, and still not directly vocalized young love. When they had traversed about half the distance to the base of Mount Ermos, Matthias gently, even tentatively took her free hand into his own, and she held it tightly, in what they both took to be an unspoken acknowledgement of the continuation of a very special relationship that had already inexorably bound them together.

"This is the place!" Matthias announced as they paused, and he pointed up towards the mountain from the place along the shore where the trail ended.

The entrance to Ermos Cave was almost completely obscured from view from where they stood by a single fig tree whose natural dark green camouflage was augmented by a dense carpet of tall, black-eyed, golden daises, covering the entire hillside. The lovely flowers were shifting to and fro as were the waves of the Lake below whose random movement was orchestrated by a gentle yet determined late morning breeze.

"There is awesome power in this place." Dory whispered as they entered the cave and sat side by side on a rough hewn wooden bench that had been placed there by some unknown benefactor.

Matthias did not immediately reply, remaining silent as they sat together, reverently taking in the incredibly beautiful scene before them. The Lake reflecting the sun, still low in the East at mid-morning, appeared to them as a heavenly jeweler's magnificent creation comprised of a seemingly infinite array of sparkling diamonds set in the deep sapphire blue water of the harp shaped lake.

The Golan Heights framing the scene they beheld to the East seemed to be an almost surrealistic border painted from a heavenly pallet of infinitely varied pastels by the very hand of God.

Matthias verbalized the awe of the moment they were both experiencing. "This is what our God was talking about when He told us through the prophet Ezekiel: *On that day I swore to them that I would bring them out of Egypt into a land I had searched out for them, a land flowing with milk and honey, the most beautiful of all lands.*[19]

"He is indeed the author of all beautiful things," Dory replied. Since I began seeking to learn more about Him, He has made everything in my life very beautiful.

"And you, my dear Dory," he ventured boldly. "You are among the most beautiful of His creation."

She blushed, and did not respond directly to his adoring observation. Instead, she reached for the basket that sat next to her on the bench. "Shall we eat before we study?" she suggested.

"By all means," he replied, his appetite accentuated by the excitement of the morning.

He took the generous loaf of bread that Dory had already removed from the basket. Looking toward the Lake, he bowed reverently as he held forth the loaf, broke it and chanted:

Barukh atah Adonai Elohenu melekh ha-olam, ha motze lekhem meen ha-aretz, Amen (Blessed art Thou, O Lord our God, King of the universe, who brings forth bread from the earth.)

With that, he tore off two generous pieces, one for each of them, and they quietly ate them together.

When they were finished eating, he took the freshly filled wineskin Dory had also brought along, and he held it forth, toward the lake, chanting:

Barukh atah Adonai Elohenu melekh ha-olam, boray p'ree ha-gehfen, Amen.

(Blessed art Thou, O Lord our God, King of the universe, who creates the fruit of the vine.) ·

With that, he opened the flask, drank deeply from it and passed it to Dory who did the same.

After their meal and a time of silent mediation, Matthias turned to the matter at hand. "In our earlier discussions with your family," he began, "we focused on the basic teachings of the Torah, because the Torah is the foundation of all Jewish understanding."

"Yes," Dory interjected, reflecting her quick mind and easy retention, "and we reviewed many of the things given by God through the Major

Prophets---especially those foretelling the forthcoming Messiah."

"You have been a bright and a good student," he praised without exaggeration.

She again blushed deeply. "It may only seem that way," she responded with sincere humility. "If it seems I have done well, it is only because of the skill and dedication of my teacher, and because I have read and reread the sacred scriptures you have so generously provided. The fact is," she declared earnestly, "I have come to love them all and they have already become a part of who I am."

Matthias continued his unabashed admiration and praise. "I must say that you have also come a long way towards understanding the intricacies of our Jewish tradition. After all, it is our traditions that have held my people together as a unified nation through all the many adversities we have been forced to endure."

"I know that I was born a Gentile, but it seems as if the very heart that beats within me has somehow become Jewish," she ventured.

"What you are experiencing is not in any way a physical change," he replied, knowingly, pausing for a moment to emphasize his next point. "It is rather your realization that *Yahweh* is the one true God, the God of His entire creation. The change you are feeling is spiritual, not physical. You were born a Gentile and for evermore you will remain a Gentile—just as I was born a Jew will forevermore will remain a Jew. The point is," he again paused for a moment, realizing the great importance of his next summarizing remark—"The point is," he repeated: "You have already begun to get a glimpse of who and what *He* is!"

"Only a glimpse---?" she replied in a way that revealed what she took to be his critical assessment of her spiritual growth.

"None of us will ever *fully* know Him until we meet Him face to face in glory," Matthias responded warmly. "The important thing is that we all continue to grow in our understanding," he went on, happily, as he realized he had been given a way to introduce what had been chosen for him to teach this day. "The Pharisees," he continued, "have been teaching wrongly that Yahweh is one indivisible God when in fact, historical main-line orthodox

Jews have understood since the days of Abraham that Yahweh is manifested in three persons or emanations!"

"How can that be," Dory inquired, seeking greater understanding, "when the Sh'ma[20] itself speaks of God being "*One*?"

He responded immediately, with conviction: "The Hebrew word used here for "One" is echad---a word that is used many times elsewhere throughout the Tenach . It means a unity that allows for a plurality---for example, it is written that a man and a woman will become *one* flesh.

"I think I understand," she replied hesitantly, "but if Yahweh is to be understood as three persons, then who are the other two?"

"Ahhh," he smiled at the perfect introduction: "According to Jewish tradition going all the way back to the time of Abraham, and according to very clear inferences in the Tenach, and even more pointedly, according to the central messianic theme that is written repeatedly in our sacred sectarian scrolls, Yahweh has long been understood to be manifested as three persons: the 'Father,' who emanates from the left pillar of what is known as the three pillar 'Tree of Life'; the 'Mother' who is also known as the 'Spirit of God,' who emanates from the right pillar and the 'Son' who resides as the center pillar.

"Then," Dory repeated to make sure she had understood: "You are saying that all three—the Father, the Son and the Spirit of God are all a part of the same, one true God, Yahweh?"

"That is quite correct," he smiled, inwardly rejoicing at her understanding.

"Help me, Matthias," she went on, somewhat hesitantly—"I understand the nature of the Father from what you have shown me as it is written in the Tenach, and I have a sense of whom or what might be His Spirit— but who, please tell me, precisely, who is the Son?"

He once again took her hands in his own, tears of joy filling his eyes, as he lovingly explained the profound central truth of his own understanding: "The Son of God, Dory---He is none other than Yeshua, the Master who even today walks among us performing miracles and teaching us from whence He came, His purpose and His plan to come again at the end of days."

"Tell me more of this," she sighed deeply at the wonder of what she had just begun to grasp.

"Our sacred scrolls provide the best summary," Matthias continued with the fervor of his own deep conviction. "They show repeatedly that the Messiah will be of the lineage of King David[21], that He will make two appearances—the first of which we have the great privilege to witness today as we see Him walking among us, and then, he will appear again at the End of Days.[22]

Most importantly, He has come to be the perfect atonement[23] for all the sins of the world in some way that I do not yet clearly understand—in a way that is not yet, but I am certain soon will be revealed for our full understanding."

"Yes!" she cried out her new understanding from the depths of her now divinely drawn soul, as she excitedly embraced her teacher. "*Yes! I believe!*"

***

That evening, just as the sun was beginning to set on the most profoundly important day of her young earthly existence, Dory was baptized by Matthias in the cool waters of the Sea of Galilee.

Later, they stood together arm in arm, silently taking in the wonder of the glorious scene set out before them, created it would seem, just for them, by the very hand of God. The setting sun refracted the last remnant of its intense red orange light in a shower of multi-colored diamond like sparkling gems emanating from a huge waterspout that cascaded into the Lake from the base of Mount Ermos.

"I love you, Dory," Matthias whispered barely audibly above the sound of the rushing water. "In my spirit I know that we are to be together in the service of the Master all the days of our lives."

She responded first with a tender kiss as she embraced this wonderful Jewish man she had come to adore even more than her own life. "I know this too, my darling," she replied as their eyes became fixed in a prolonged mutual soul penetrating embrace. "But there is much we must overcome before we can become man and wife." There was an admixture of sadness placated by her new yet already deep faith as she continued. "I already know in my heart that I am called to convert to your Essene Jewish faith. I am now praying and waiting upon the Lord to show us the way."

Chapter Nine

Rochester, New York, December, 1955

Mike Ryan, flashing his trade mark broad Irish grin, made a vain attempt to resurrect his roommate from the depths of the emotional doldrums into which he had recently become immersed. "Come on Drew!" he exclaimed. "Don't let this Church thing get you down! This was only round one! Your battle to find the truth has only just begun!"

"I know you don't blame me personally for anything," Drew responded dejectedly, "but I also know that you and Father John are both very disappointed in the way I've blown off your whole Catholic thing. You know, I really love you both and I didn't intend to hurt you---."

"Like I said, Drew, *forget it* for now! If you keeping seeking God, you can be sure that He will eventually reveal Himself in a time, way and place of His own choosing—not mine, not Father John's and certainly not your own!" With that Mike jumped off his bed from where he'd been holding forth and playfully attacked his roommate, embracing him in a crushing bear hug as he exclaimed, "Let's get serious, 'Mr. Vice President!' I think you've got bigger fish to fry for the moment. When is your father supposed to show up?"

"Just in time to take me out to dinner," Drew replied, not attempting to hide his growing dread at the prospect of an evening of unsolicited fatherly interrogation and counsel. "How would you like to join us?"

"Not on your life, Buddy," Mike replied resolutely. He donned his heavy winter parka and headed out the door. "You're on your own with this one! As for me, I choose to partake of the consistently lousy fair offered by our cafeteria rather than to share in the feast of nicely roasted young Jew your father is about to dish up after soundly raking you over the coals."

As Drew shed his sweat suit and selected more appropriate slacks and shirt for the evening ahead, he carefully reviewed the events that were about to bring his father to his dormitory door for the first time in the three and one half years since he'd begun his undergraduate education.

He smiled as he mentally shuffled the deck of possibilities for the umpteenth time and once again came up with the only logical conclusion: "It's got to be this religious thing again—some how I've managed to threaten the old man's security!"

Once he had accepted the validity of this now probable conclusion, Drew quickly began to put the flesh of recent events upon the skeleton of truth he had just deduced. He sighed deeply as he whispered for his own consumption: "You'd think he'd be proud to have me chosen by my new fraternity brothers as the vice president of the just established Mu Rho Chapter of Sigma Alpha Mu. What difference does it make that the 'Sammies', like Kappa Nu, are almost entirely Jewish?" Before he could frame his next silent thought, his anticipated visitor knocked loudly, announcing what to his son was the great challenge of his presence.

"Hey there big guy!" Mark exclaimed loudly, while gently placing his left arm around his son's neck. Simultaneously, he firmly shook his right hand, as if to provide just the right balance between fatherly love and proper man to man interface. "It would seem that congratulations are in order!" he exclaimed with genuine excitement.

Drew was more than just a little amazed, even flabbergasted by his father's presumed understanding and acceptance. However his erroneous assessment that his father was thus expressing approval of his own recent activities was immediately shattered.

Mark raised his arms above his head, clapping his hands together in the imitation of some mock pagan ritual as he danced full circle in front of his by now greatly confused son as he excitedly announced: "Take a good look Andrew Scott Sterling! The one who dances before you just happens to be the newly promoted National Carbon Company's Executive Vice President, Sales and Marketing---!"

Drew was doubly delighted by his father's most welcome good news; first because he was genuinely proud of Mark's amazing rise within his company and all the benefits that it represented, but also, more poignantly to the moment, he was equally grateful that this good news had apparently superceded any presumed criticism his father might have come to express about his own recent activities and commitments. "Dad, Drew exclaimed with genuine pleasure as he gave his father a bear hug, "I'm so very, very, proud of you and what you've accomplished!"

"Let's go find the best steak in Rochester!" Mark invited, "to say nothing of at least one bottle of the finest champagne money can buy!"

***

Some two hours later, as father and son were well into their second bottle of Dom Perignon and were just now finishing the last of their promised elegant and extravagant steaks at Gordon's Steak & Crab House, Mark turned their conversation to what Drew had earlier suspected was the subject of his visit. "What's this business of you being involved in starting up a new fraternity?" he tossed out the opening gambit.

"Sigma Alpha Mu," isn't a *new* fraternity by any means, Drew responded, trying to keep his tone inoffensive. "It's one of the biggest and oldest fraternities in the country—it's our chapter at the University of Rochester that's new!"

"But why now, mid way through your senior year?" Mark struggled, trying to keep his tone unchallenging. "I'm just more than a bit surprised that after all this time you've spent as a militant 'independent' you have suddenly decided to become a fraternity man?—And, may I add, why a new chapter and not one of the already well established houses on campus?"

Drew had been expecting this line of inquiry and he had already framed his response: "The Mu Rho Chapter will be the Sammies' experiment at ecumenical outreach," he replied instructively. "About a quarter of my new brothers are goys and to tell you the truth, I think they made me vice president because they think *I'm* a goy!—I've been keeping the family secret well, Dad!" he concluded, not quite able to conceal the hint of bitterness in his final remark.

"I guess my real problem here is simply one of not understanding! If I may ask, why, after you've always come across as some sort of anti-Semite, Semite— Why all of a sudden have you become a 'Mr. Big Shot' in a very Jewish, strongly pro-Israel, sometimes even militant national fraternity? I'm only wondering *why*, Drew—that's all??"

Mark had struck a highly sensitive chord in his son who now noticeably struggled to explain what was anything but clear to even himself. "Dad," Drew began, his voice and demeanor now subdued, even apologetic, "I don't know *why* but during these past several months, my closet friends, through no conscious choice of my own, have been Jewish---I find myself more and more gravitating to my, that is *our* people---It's sort of a love-hate relationship that I really don't understand myself---??"

"Has all of this anything to do with *religion*?" Mark probed more deeply.

"Not really," Drew replied. "You may not know this Dad, but I really made a great effort to find God starting way back in the days Grandma Amelia was trying to talk me into being Bar Mitzvah-ed. She just might have succeeded if *you* hadn't been so strongly opposed!"

"It was a practical necessity!" Mark responded, his own tone now somewhat apologetic.

"I know Dad, and I understand. I've always respected the need to protect your position."

Mark refused to let his son off the hook "I'm still not clear on where you stand religiously, Son," he came back to his earlier question. "Have you suddenly become a practicing Jew?"

"Not by any means, Dad—there is no need for you to be concerned on that account, but I have come to *know* the Lord God of Israel, that's all."

Mark, somewhat taken aback by his son's sudden intensity replied glibly in a feigned Yiddish accent: "Nuu, so next time you have a conversation with

him please give him my best personal regards! Knowing God *personally?*"
he continued sarcastically. "You are beginning to sound more 'born again'
Christian than anything Jewish I know about?"

"As a matter of fact, Dad," Drew replied, wondering if it was the last
of the expensive champagne he had just guzzled down that made him feel
so close to his usually very distant father---"As a matter of fact, Dad, " he
repeated for emphasis, "I have been searching for something more of God
than Judaism seems to offer— In fact, I've been looking into the Church for
what I have been seeking."

"Sweet Jesus!" Mark exclaimed, venting both his own great genuine
surprise and exasperation.

Drew, smiled at the perfect opening—"That's it exactly, Dad---Sweet
Jesus! I have been looking for *Him*."

Chapter Ten

Capernaum on the Western Shore of the Sea of Galilee, Summer, A.D. 27

It was, typically, stifling hot on this late July Friday afternoon. Even so, most of the nearly two thousand residents of the walled city were necessarily braving the furnace-like heat and very high humidity to scurry about from shop to shop properly provisioning themselves for the Sabbath that would, inexorably, arrive in a very few hours, providing wonderful holy rest from their daily labors and blessed relief from the torturing Summer sun.

Matthias and Kefa, (who would come to be known by the later English speaking Church as "Peter") had become close, even intimate friends during the past several months they had been walking together as brothers in Yeshua. Now they rejoiced together as they found a relatively cool place to await the Sabbath in the shade of a stand of acacia trees one hundred meters or so beyond the Capernaum city gate.

These two, Kefa, already an apostle, and Matthias, one of the inner circle closest to the Master, had been drawn together in a brotherly bonding that went well beyond their mutual adoration and total commitment to the Master. They relished spending time like this together: rejoicing in the ways and teachings of the Master, sharing their deepest thoughts and concerns, and, praying together as they felt led.

The two of them were so drawn together, perhaps because they were, in almost every way, markedly different. Matthias was strikingly handsome and well groomed. In stark contrast, Kefa was a rugged, course looking fisherman whose leather-like, permanently sun bronzed skin was punctuated by unsightly pock mark mementos of a nearly fatal childhood disease.

While they were strikingly different physically, perhaps they were even more dissimilar in their interaction with the people and situations they encountered.

Matthias interpersonal dealings were characteristically smooth and always considered.

Again in stark contrast, Kefa, although he was overflowing with love and concern, was impetuous to a fault. While he was always well intentioned, Kefa often lashed out without thinking, therefore relying on his dear friend Matthias and others to "sweep up the broken glass" he too often left in the wake of his sometimes even disastrous interfaces.

While the two of them were so very different in appearance, style and approach they held much more important things in common. First, their love for the Master had come to dominate every aspect of their lives and thinking. Out of this mutual and total commitment arose an out pouring of divinely instilled love that flowed from the depths of their beings and was strikingly evident to all whom they encountered. Even more was the deep and abiding brotherly love they shared with one another.

"Look at that poor tortured Roman," Matthias broke what had been a considerable time of silent mediation to comment on the approaching officer in full armor laden uniform. "He must be on the verge of collapse!"

"I will never understand the ways of the *goyim*!" Kefa quipped. "Nor is it in any way my desire to do so!"

"Why would this Roman come to *us*?" Matthias questioned in a whisper, while unable to conceal his immediate alarm, as the approaching officer, whom they could now see was a centurion, quickened his already hurried pace and headed directly toward the shaded place where the two of them were sitting.

They stood as the centurion drew close, introducing himself in faltering but adequate Aramaic. "Shalom, I am the Centurion, Marius, and I have come seeking help from the one called Yeshua. Do you know any of those close to this man who reportedly works many miracles?"

"Are you not a worshipper of the sun?" Kefa snapped rhetorically, pointing almost accusingly at the branded cross that formed an obvious and ugly scar on Marius' forehead. "Why would *you* seek help from the Son of the Living God, the Lord God of Israel?"

"Yes!" Marius replied unapologetically, "I am a follower of Mithra, god of the Sun, and this," he touched the ugly scar of his branded cross with the forefinger of his right hand. "This is the cross of Mithra that I willingly accepted as a sign of my allegiance to him and to my mighty emperor when I was first commissioned an officer in the Roman army." He paused for a moment, his tone becoming softer, humble, even pleading as he once again returned to gut wrenching purpose of his hurried seeking of their Master. "It is for Publius, my beloved servant that I come. He is desperately ill and about to die---I was so much hoping you would go to your Master and seek his help on our behalf??"

Matthias, immediately intervened, preempting what might otherwise have been Kefa's less than ecumenical response. "Yes, Marius, I will immediately bring your situation to the attention of Yeshua."

"Yes, *we* shall," Kefa agreed, not wanting to seem unnecessarily obstinate.

A short time later, the two of them found Yeshua relaxing, awaiting the Sabbath, in Kefa's house near the shore of the lake. Matthias spoke out respectfully, relaying the Centurion's request: "I believe that this man, Marius, deserves to have you do this, because he loves our nation. He even helped build our synagogue here in Capernaum."

So Yeshua went alone, on the way to Marius' house where Publius lay dying. He was not far from the Centurion's house when two young junior officers in Marius' command approached the three of them and addressed Yeshua on behalf of Marius'.

One of them spoke out: "Yeshua, our Centurion told us to convey this to You— "Lord, don't trouble yourself, for I do not deserve to have you come under my roof. That is why I did not even consider myself worthy to come to you. But say the word, and my servant will be healed. For I myself am a man under authority, with soldiers under me. I tell this one, 'Go,' and he goes; and that one, 'Come,' and he comes. I say to my servant, 'Do this,' and he does it."

When Yeshua heard this, he was amazed at him, and--- he said, "I tell you, I have not found such great faith even in Israel." Then the three young officers who had been sent returned to the house and found that Publius had been miraculously healed.[24]

***

Later that evening, just before the sun finally retreated to the other side of Mount Ermos, Matthias and Kefa were washing their hands together before they went to join the others for the bountiful erev (evening) Shabbat meal that had taken Kefa's wife and her mother all that day to prepare.

Matthias felt strongly led to share a great burden of his heart with this, his dearest friend and closest brother: "It was a wonderful thing to see the Master heal Publius," he began. "And he—being a *goy*!"

"The Master will do what the Master will do!" Kefa responded with just a hint of disapproval shadowing his complete agreement and understanding.

"Perhaps the Master is showing us we are to more closely embrace our non-Jewish brothers and sisters who have come to believe on Him?" Matthias offered suggestively.

"I think *not*!" Kefa snapped. "It was only a short time ago that He commanded the twelve of us: 'Do not go among the Gentiles or enter any town of the Samaritans. Go rather to the lost sheep of Israel. As you go, preach this message: 'The kingdom of heaven is near.' Heal the sick, raise the dead, and cleanse those who have leprosy, drive out demons. Freely you have received, freely give.' [25] My dear brother Matthias, could He have been any clearer? Yeshua is the *Jewish* Messiah! He has come to redeem us *Jews*!"

Matthias wouldn't let go. He sounded desperate as he continued with obvious passion. "Perhaps in healing Publius, a *goy*, Yeshua was showing us He has come to redeem *all* men---not just us Jews? Perhaps, my dear Kefa, it is only a question of timing! The Father in Heaven knows what a mess we Jews are in---! Just maybe Yeshua realizes that you twelve and the rest of us who are closest to Him will have all we can do to deal with our own people! Just maybe---think about it, Kefa---just maybe He has another agenda for the *Goyim*---another way?"

Suddenly, Kefa fully understood his brother's great passion. His heart sank sympathetically as he realized Matthias' great hurt, as they now approached the erev Shabbat table around which were already seated his dear wife, her mother and several other invited guests. All of them were already rejoicing together in their intimate fellowship with Yeshua who was seated in the place of honor at the head.

Kefa remembered in a flash of recollection how Matthias had hinted to him earlier in the week that his beloved Dory, the lovely *goy* from Hippos with whom he had become so helplessly infatuated, had never participated in a Shabbat meal and that she would be thrilled to do so. Kefa remembered how he had so insensitively and abruptly dismissed, even without a spoken reply, the very notion that Dory, a non-Jew, might eat at the same table with Jews---much less do so on erev Shabbat and at *His* table!

"Yes." Kefa replied in a barely audible whisper. "Perhaps the Master will provide another way for the *goyim*."

Now, as Matthias took his own treasured place at Kefa's table, having thus been poignantly and painfully reminded of the great religious, cultural and traditional obstacles that lay in the path of his intended life-long journey with his beloved Dory; unobtrusively and silently, he wiped away what he desperately hoped were his unnoticed tears with the swipe of a hand.

Chapter Eleven

Rochester, New York, June, 1956

Mark and Leila glowed with parental pride as they beheld the child of their youth walking across the stage at the River Campus of the University of Rochester to receive his Bachelor of Arts degree.

However, no words could even have begun to convey the depth and the breadth of the unmitigated joy that emanated from the absolutely radiant bull-dog shaped face of Grandma Amelia. She wouldn't, for any reason under the sun, have missed this momentous, unprecedented family achievement for which she inwardly claimed, rightfully or not, a sense of personal responsibility.

"I'm telling you, *Leila*!" she exclaimed, quite deliberately ignoring the presence of her son-in-law as the name "Andrew Scott Sterling" was announced over the booming public address system and, perfectly timed, Drew shook hands with the Dean of Men and then received his diploma. "Such a boy is this, *my* Drew! Nuu, maybe, who knows," she continued excitedly. "Who knows what will come next for this wonderful boy! Maybe, my grandson the doctor? Or, it wouldn't be so bad---My grandson the lawyer---?"

"Mamma! Stop already!" Leila interrupted. "For the next four years it is going to be your 'grandson the Lieutenant.' *Then* he can start living his life."

"I don't understand such craziness!" Grandma Amelia tortuously exclaimed. "Why would my darling Drew sign up for such a thing?"

Leila did her best to explain. "It was either join the Reserve Officer Training Corps or run the risk of being drafted---. Don't forget, many kids were pulled out of college and sent to Korea during Drew's first two years. Never mind, he was already committed to complete this training when the war ended, just before his junior year."

"Oyyy!!" Grandma Amelia wailed in protest. "Being a soldier is not a good thing for a nice Jewish boy!!"

"Not a *soldier*, Mamma!" Leila corrected with perhaps a hint of tactfully suppressed newly acquired inter-service pride. "Your grandson is about to be commissioned a second lieutenant in the United States Air Force!"

"Soldier, Sailor, Air Force, Schmair force!!" Grandma Amelia continued her now even more deeply Yiddish accented protest. "I'm telling you--- none of this is good for a nice Jewish boy!!"

Mark, who, predictably, had finally reached his breaking point provoked by his mother-in-law could no longer resist. "Why not?" He asked unemotionally.

"*Vhy not*!!" Amelia was outraged. "*Vhy not*!!" she repeated. "Have you ever heard of a *Jewish* general??"

"A few!" Mark relished in the implied victory of his impending response. "For starters, how about David, Joshua, Gideon and Moshe Dayan??"

***

Drew felt a profound sense of relief as he gripped his leather encased diploma and made his way to the gathering of his fellow graduates. They were assembled on the other side of the large stage. His heart surged at the prospect of what was yet to come---. Unobtrusively,he slipped his right hand under his heavy academic robe and into the pocket of his Air Force summer dress silver-tan "Class A" uniform. He reassured himself that the very special silver dollar that had resided on his dormitory desk these past four years was still in its newest proper place.

Although he had never dared to vocalize his growing heart's desire for a military career to *anyone* in his family, much less his grandmother, he had known for several years that this would be the course he would most likely pursue. He thrilled as the moment drew near later that morning, when, after he had removed his academic garb, he would reveal the uniform that would announce to the world that the first chapter of his emerging life's dream had now become a reality.

There were about two hundred family members and friends gathered to witness the commissioning ceremony in front of Harkness Hall, the red brick facility that housed both the Air Force and Navy ROTC programs.

Drew and his thirty classmates held high their right hands and, in unison, repeated what to him was an especially sacred and long anticipated oath of office:

"I Andrew Scott Sterling, having been appointed a Second Lieutenant in the United States Air Force, do solemnly swear that I will support and defend the Constitution of the United States, against all enemies, foreign and domestic; that I will bear true faith and allegiance to the same; that I take this obligation freely, without any mental reservation or purpose of evasion; and that I will well and faithfully discharge the duties of the office upon which I am about to enter, so help me God.."

In keeping with his class standing as an honor military graduate, Drew was the third newly commissioned officer candidate to be called forward by Colonel Harry Sullivan, Professor of Air Science and Tactics who crisply announced: "Second Lieutenant Andrew Scott Sterling."

"Oyyy!" Grandma Amelia whispered just loud enough to be heard by Mark and Leila who stood on her either side as if to lock her in place.

"*Shut up!*" Mark leaning toward her in the interests of privacy, commanded in a loud whisper launched directly into her now nearby ear.

Unaware of this combative family exchange, Drew moved smartly to a position directly in front of Colonel Sullivan, to whom he rendered a well practiced sharp hand salute.

Colonel Sullivan returned Drew's salute, then handed him his certificate of commissioning and a set of gold plated bars, the insignia of his new office. "Congratulations, Lieutenant Sterling," the Colonel who was well aware of Drew's intentions, offered with sincere warmth, "I wish you great success and God's speed in the career you have chosen." With that, they shook hands and once again exchanged salutes.

Mark and Leila, who before the ceremony commenced had been briefed on the traditional role they were to play, waited for their son in a designated place, just in front of the audience. Drew handed a gold bar to each of his parents who, as he proudly beamed, pinned the insignia in their proper respective places on his shoulder epaulets.

Over the many years of active duty that lay before him Drew would often fondly remember his father's most unexpected well wishes as he pinned his designated gold bar in place. "Never forget, son--- I am very proud of you and I love you very much!"

Having hugged his mother and firmly exchanged an expected manly handshake with his father, Drew turned to consummate what had long been only a dream. He turned and walked smartly toward the group of three ROTC detachment Non-Commissioned Officers who awaited the procession of new Lieutenants.

They took turns at garnering the traditional fruit of such occasions and it was Technical Sergeant Floyd Ebner, who had often encouraged and guided Drew during the past four years of his training who stepped forward and honored Drew with the first official recognition of his office. "Congratulations, Lieutenant Sterling" he exclaimed with sincere warmth as he rendered the newly commissioned officer a snappy hand salute.

Drew, failed in trying to suppress the great emotion of the moment as he returned the salute in the same manner it had been rendered, and then in the process of shaking hands with Sergeant Ebner included his long held silver dollar as a traditional token gift. With that, Drew turned away and began his walk into the beginnings of what was to be a long and wonderful life's adventure.

Chapter Twelve

Kursi in the Region of the Gerasenes, Autumn A.D. 27

Matthias heart raced in a surge of recognition as he saw Dory standing at the front of the sizable crowd gathered on the shore. These non-Jewish residents of the Eastern shore had come to greet the long anticipated arrival of the large, single mast, heavily passenger-laden, wooden fishing boat that was about to come ashore on the sandy beach of the natural harbor at Hadar.

It was a rare occasion indeed for *any* Jewish visitors to come from the western side of the Lake to what Jews then universally considered to be a potentially hostile, pagan region.

However, this particular visit was not entirely unanticipated by Dory and her family since it had been increasingly rumored throughout their thriving Decapolis City of Hippos, a short distance uphill from Hadar, where they resided with some two thousand other non-Jews, that Yeshua would one day soon journey to their area.

While the anticipated thrill of the Master ministering to her and her people here on their home turf was more than enough to mightily quicken her spirit, Dory had yet another deeply compelling personal agenda that caused her to rush toward Hadar when the boat, that potentially carried the Master, was sighted and loudly announced by a lookout posted on the lake-side of the city wall.

Dory's inner turmoil had been almost more than she could bear since she had last been with Matthias, several weeks ago in Capernaum, when she had been summarily excluded by Kefa from attending the Shabbat dinner in his home. According to Kefa's understanding, only Jews were considered clean and thus worthy to participate.

It troubled Dory greatly that Matthias, whom she had already grown to love and adore, even beyond her own understanding, had made no apparent effort to contact her during the ensuing several weeks. Now, as she saw the boat approaching and rejoiced that he would soon once again be in her presence, she desperately prayed that she might be able to show him the depth of her own unconditional love— that, together, they might find a way to overcome the cultural barrier that now threatened to separate them forever.

Then, suddenly, she saw him. He stood not far behind the Master on the deck of the approaching fishing boat. He waved to her in a way that somehow communicated his own returned deep love and devotion. It was in the next instant, when their eyes met that she knew with all of her being— this was the one who had been divinely ordained to stand by her side as her life's partner. Never mind the obstacles created by men! Nothing would obviate their wonderful, now mutually understood shared destiny.

The two of them walked along, hand in hand near the rear of the growing assemblage that followed Yeshua north, along the lake-side trail that led to nearby Kursi in the region of the Gerasenes. "I had hoped that the Master would come to Hippos," she spoke softly for Matthias' hearing only.

"The Master will do what the Master will do," Matthias repeated what was now a common expression of loving trust and acceptance among Yeshua's sometimes perplexed inner circle. "I feel certain He will one day honor your city with His presence," Matthias comforted. "You can be sure that He has a very special purpose for going this way instead." The truth of Matthias prophetic understanding soon became very evident.

Yeshua, followed in trail by the others, wound their way through the city of Kursi. As they did so, they were joined by a number of curious local residents. The now growing assemblage, led by the Master, made its way up the rather steep slope that led to several caves on the side of the mountain that had long served as tombs for the city.

"Dear God!" Dory exclaimed, disbelieving what her eyes struggled to convey to her shocked mind as she and the others now stood before a large centrally located tomb up on the side of the mountain. "I *know* this poor man—he is from our City!" She began to weep openly at the deeply tragic sight of the woefully decrepit creature who had once been among her closet childhood friends.

Matthias did his best to comfort her, holding her close as they beheld the one she called Athanasios. He was held by chains and shackles which he had pulled apart. Unable to be restrained, he roared about the entrance to the cave, foaming at the mouth, making sounds like a mad animal gone totally out of control. "How could a man fall into such a horrible state?" Matthias asked rhetorically, not really expecting a reply."

He was therefore startled when Dory began to explain: "We went our separate ways about two years ago when Athanasios became a priest of Helios, the sun god who is worshiped to this very day in Hippos. One day, more than a year ago, Athanasios just wandered off from our city without any explanation and he hadn't been heard from since, not until this very day."

A young man, a local resident of Kursi who was among those that had joined the assemblage led by Yeshua to the tomb, overheard Dory's perplexity concerning her childhood friend and he elaborated upon Athanasios' situation. "This poor man has lived in our tombs for several months," he explained. "No one has been able to bind him any more, not even with a chain! For he has often been chained hand and foot, but he has always managed to tear the chains apart and break the irons on his feet! No one has been strong enough to subdue him. Night and day among the tombs and in the hills he has cried out and cut himself with stones!"

Then, in an instant of divinely ordained clarity and recognition, Athanasios *saw* Yeshua who had been standing nearby. Now, completely unrestrained, Athanasios, ran to Yeshua and fell on his knees in front of him. He shouted at the top of his voice, "What do you want with me, Yeshua, Son of the Most High God? Swear to God that you won't torture me!" For Yeshua had just said to him, "Come out of this man, you evil spirit!"

Then Yeshua asked the demons who had possessed Athanasios, "What is your name?"

"My name is Legion," one of the demons replied, "for we are many." And he begged Yeshua again and again not to send them out of the area.

A large herd of pigs was feeding on the nearby hillside. The demons begged Yeshua. "Send us among the pigs; allow us to go into them." Yeshua gave them permission, and the evil spirits came out and went into the pigs. The herd was about two thousand in number. They were being raised to be sold as living sacrifices to the pagan god Dionysus: God of Sex, Wine and Intoxication who was then widely worshiped throughout the Decapolis cities. The herd of pigs, now filled with demons immediately rushed down the steep bank into the lake and was drowned.[26]

Those local residents who had been tending the pigs ran off and reported what had happened at the cave in the city of Kursi and in the countryside, and the people came out to see for themselves what had happened.

When they came to Yeshua, they saw that Athanasios who had been possessed by the legion of demons, was now sitting there, fully dressed and completely in his right mind; and they were sorely afraid.

Those who had seen Athanasios' miraculous healing excitedly told the people what had happened to him, he who had long suffered as a demon-possessed man. And, they told as well about how the demon possessed pigs had then gone in to the sea and drowned. Then, shocked and disbelieving, the people began to plead with Yeshua to leave their region.

It was then that Athanasios, begged to go with him. However Yeshua, who had other plans for this miraculously healed new disciple, did not let him come along with them, but instead He commanded him: "Go home to your family and tell them how much the Lord has done for you, and how he has had mercy on you."

With that, Yeshua turned and began to walk back towards Hadar and the awaiting fishing boat that would return him and those whom had accompanied him to Capernaum.

"Stay with us for a time!" Dory pleaded with Matthias, who now stood unmoving.

Tears of unbounded joy and love cascaded freely from Matthias' eyes, generated by both the miraculous healing they all had just beheld and the great all consuming love he felt for this woman who again stood by his side. Holding her close, he replied: "Of course I will, Darling. Nothing but the command of Yeshua will ever again take me away from your presence!"

With that, the three of them, Matthias, Dory and Athanasios, as Yeshua had commanded, began what was to become the central focus of their life-long ministry both separately and together: sharing the Good News of Yeshua with all, mostly Greco-Roman non-Jewish people, who had ears to hear; first in nearby Hippos,[27] and then later in the other nine Decapolis cities and elsewhere throughout this entire vast region that would one day evolve into what would be known, collectively, as the Eastern Churches.

From the beginning of their ministry later that very day in Hippos, when they first told of what Yeshua had done for Athanasios, all who heard were amazed.[28]

Chapter Thirteen

McChord Air Force Base, Washington, January 1958

First Lieutenant Andrew Scott Sterling sat quietly by himself in the back pew of the half-full Air Force Base Chapel. He had deliberately chosen the sparsely attended nine o'clock "early service" over the always packed house each Sunday at eleven. He wanted to avoid what to him would be the inevitable flood of well intended *pro forma* greetings from those who would feel called to welcome him, a curious, earnestly seeking, newcomer.

This was the third such early morning Sunday service Drew had regularly attended since he had recently been reassigned to this sprawling military complex near Tacoma, from the tiny, incredibly remote deeply frozen bastion of his first permanent duty location, Tatalina Air Force Station, Alaska, a Distant Early Warning Line site near the Artic Circle.

It had been, Drew now reflected, a crushing disappointment for him to "wash out" of pilot training near the end of the primary course. The gut wrenching words of the decision of the Flight Elimination Board meted out by the major who was its chairman would be indelibly written upon his heart: "Lieutenant Sterling, the Board has carefully considered your request for an additional eight hours of flight training to better prepare you for air to air combat maneuvers but quiet frankly, the needs of the service are that we are currently training fighter pilots. Thus, while we have confidence that you might eventually become a qualified multi-engine pilot, our opinion is that if you were to continue this current single-engine training that you might eventually kill yourself and perhaps others." He then warmed before he pronounced the final sentence: "Drew, you simply to not have the physical coordination and other aptitudes required of a fighter pilot. It is therefore the decision of this board that you are, effective this date, eliminated from further pilot training."

Had he been able to do so at that terrible moment, Drew now sadly recalled, he would have resigned his commission on the spot, thus giving up any expectation of an Air force career. In later years, however, it became clear to him what he could not have begun to understand at that time of intense disappointment: the God whom he did not yet personally know had another plan for his life.

It so happened that Drew *did* have exactly the right skills required of an Air Defense Intercept Director and he graduated at the top of his class from the rigorous air defense radar control training at Tyndall Air Force Base, Florida. This very new Air Force career field was being urgently implemented at the peak of the "Cold War" when the gravely threatening Soviet Union had amassed an enormous manned bomber fleet capable of obliterating the United States with nuclear weapons. Thus, the United States in cooperation with Canada had urgently created the North American Air Defense Command, the primary eyes of which were a string of early warning radar sites known as the "DEW Line" spanning the far reaches of the perpetually frozen North.

Little did Drew understand that this year of isolation in the far North was to be the forced sabbatical of his youth. At first it seemed to be only a time of relentless, often intensely challenging twelve hour shifts punctuated by shift end drinking sessions at the small officers' bar where his senses could be dulled sufficiently to permit a few hours of sleep before the next grueling twelve hours of staring at a radar scope.

It was however, during the mid-winter twilight and between the blinding snow blizzards that an Air Force Protestant Chaplain who was "riding the circuit" of the remote sites in the North managed to find his way to Tatalina Air Force Station's perilous snow-packed, orange dye marked runway. And it was he, Chaplain Captain Sheldon Thurman who planted the seeds of what was to spring forth and grow into a life long and abiding friendship with the young, still secretively, Jewish lieutenant—a friendship that began with a gift to Drew of sufficient interest to cause him to set aside the huge stack of *Playboy* and *Penthouse* magazines that were his daily fare in exchange for a bible that became the subject of his intense and growingly excited exploration. Sheldon's monthly visits to Tatalina had quickly become a highlight for Drew when the two of them spent long hours together discussing matters of theology during which Sheldon diligently defended his faith in the face of Drew's incessant curiously seeking challenge.

***

The compelling strains of the prelude to the first hymn snapped Drew back to the moment as he hurriedly opened his Armed Forces Hymnal to Hymn 333, "In Heavenly Love Abiding," and joined his voice with the others:

> In heavenly love abiding, no change my heart shall fear,
> And safe is such confiding, for nothing changes here.
> The storm may roar without me, my heart may low be laid;
> But God is round about me, and can I be dismayed?
>
> Wherever He may guide me, no want shall turn me back;
> My shepherd is beside me, and nothing can I lack.
> His wisdom ever waketh, His sight is never dim;
> He knows the way He taketh, and I will walk with Him.
>
> Green pastures are before me, which yet I have not seen;
> Bright skies will soon be o're me, where darkest clouds have been.
> My hope I cannot measure, the path to life is free;
> My Savior has my treasure, and He will walk with me.[29]

As Drew sang the "amen" and closed his hymnal, the words of this venerable old hymn took him back to Tatalina and his singular Artic winter outing. Few others had been bold or foolish enough to venture out into the deep snow drifts that literally engulfed the site's several buildings where access to the outside could only be gained through tunnels that demanded frequent clearing.

Never mind the high winds and the chill factor of sixty below zero that awaited him--- this was ptarmigan hunting season. Drew had heard that the elusive white game birds were reputed to be thickly present around the site. Perhaps it was his love of game bird hunting generated during his youth in Portland. Or, perhaps it was the "cabin fever" that now demanded his however brief respite from the prison-like confines of the site. Or, perhaps it was the delightful possibility of some small relief from the canned food based fair that made up the site's boringly limited menu.

It was probably a combination of these factors that generated Drew's passionate desire to check out the site's singular twelve gauge shot gun and venture forth into the frozen wilds just beyond his holed up confines.

As he struggled into his heavy parka, thus completing the tedious and meticulous donning of his multi layered artic survival clothing, it did not dawn on him that he was about to break the first rule of artic survival: "Always let others know where you are going and when you are expected to return." Without further regard for his safety, Drew pushed open the final door to the frigid outdoors, securely fastened his snow shoes, and with shot gun in hand ventured forth into the deep snow that had, by the incessant wind, been arrayed in a wave like series of huge drifts around the site. So deep were the drifts that the snow completely covered many of the very tall Alaskan Spruce trees that grew thickly around the now frozen facility.

Unmindful of any potential danger, when he was only one hundred yards or so beyond the site he flushed his first small covey of ptarmigan. Excitedly he hurried after the covey that had landed some fifty yards in front of him and were now scattered singly in the snow. He had only taken a few steps when his right snowshoe caught in the very tip of a completely covered spruce tree. Then, he now remembered in a kaleidoscopic recall, he tripped and somersaulted through the frigid air, landing head first in the snow. Instantly, he sank into the frozen drift to the full length of his body, held from further sinking only by his snow shoes that secured him, in this bizarre inverted position, totally alone, unable to move, and with no means of escape from what now occurred to him in a flash of dreadful recognition what surely was to be his slow but inevitable death by freezing.

Where was this God of the Jews his grandmother had persistently suggested that he embrace? Where was this son of Miriam who was head and guardian of Father John Lassiter's Roman Catholic Church? Where was this Jesus he had read about and pondered in the Bible given to him by his dear friend and mentor Sheldon Thurman?

Now, in the midst of his growing terror, as he struggled unsuccessfully to move his snow bound arms so that he might attempt to pull himself to the surface, he heard for the first time, a still quite voice whisper in his inner being. "---Call upon me in the day of trouble; I will deliver you, and you will honor me."[30]

At first, he ignored the voice, assuming it was a figment of his imagination and he continued in vain to move his snow-bound arms. Finally, exhausted and beginning to feel an insidious numbness working its way through the multi-layers of his artic survival clothing, and, as he paused for a time to better evaluate his situation he heard the same still quiet voice saying---" Call upon me and come and pray to me, and I will listen to you."

Now, for the first time in his young life he earnestly prayed to the God whom he had previously sought but had never truly known. In the very moment before he slipped into unconsciousness he cried out from the depths of his frozen tomb: Oh Lord God of Israel save me that I might live!"

He had no way of knowing how long he had remained on this path to his inevitable frozen end before he was awakened by a sharp an incessant pulling of both his feet from the surface. He now rejoiced that someone had miraculously come across his snow shoes on the surface and was pulling him into a renewed opportunity for life.

It had again begun to snow and Drew did not immediately recognize his artic survival clad rescuer as he now stood before him in the near blinding downfall. Before he could speak his benefactor intervened: "You'd better get back to the site, Lieutenant."

Drew quickly admitted, "I've lost my way," he responded pleadingly. "I don't know which way to go."

"Follow me!" his rescuer responded, turning with assurance into the storm.

Drew hurried in trail, and within a short time the two of them stood together at the entrance to the site's main tunnel. "I can't thank you enough, my friend." Drew exclaimed with relief. "I owe you my life."

"Never mind, Lieutenant," his rescuer replied, "You'd better take off those snow shoes and get inside where it is warm!"

Drew quickly complied, kneeling down to unfasten his awkward, yet life saving footwear. When he had done so, he stood up and invited, "Hey, let me buy you a drink!" He was deeply shocked when he turned to receive what he assumed would be an affirmative reply. He found, to his complete amazement, that he stood alone, utterly alone, at the entrance to the tunnel.

***

In the depth of his recollections, Drew had completely missed the weekly announcements and the congregational prayer. Now, he was snapped back to the moment, just as the Chaplain entered the pulpit to deliver his morning message. Tears began to flow freely down Drew's cheeks as he once again saw the sweet familiar face of his dear friend Sheldon who, like himself, had recently been reassigned to McChord. Little did he then know that the message Sheldon had prepared was meant especially for him:[31]

My purpose this morning is to demonstrate the absolute Jewish-ness of Jesus Christ, Yeshua as He is called in Hebrew, both as He was prophesized, and as He appeared during His First Century incarnation in Israel.

Yeshua was born a Jew:

He was and is a real, historical person, born in the Land of Israel, during the Roman occupation, in approximately the year 3 BCE. Abraham was the first Hebrew. He is called Abram the Hebrew. Yeshua is descended from "Abram the Hebrew." Abraham is the father of the Jews. Isaac was his son and Jacob was his grandson .

Jacob's name was changed by God to "Israel" and he had twelve sons from whom came the Twelve Tribes of Israel. One of those twelve sons was Judah, from whom we get the word "Jew." Although Judah was only one of the twelve, by 700 BCE the word Yehudee (Jew) came to mean any person descended from Abraham, Isaac, and Jacob.

The Messiah must be descended from the tribe of Judah as was King David, and he must be descended from King David himself. This is why the Messiah is called Son of David. Yeshua is from the Tribe of Judah. His earthly father was descended from David and His mother was as well. In Revelations 5:5 we read that Yeshua is called both "the lion of the tribe of Judah" and "the root of David."

Yeshua lived as a Jew:

He was circumcised on the eighth day.

He bore a common Jewish name, Yeshua, meaning "he [God] saves."

After his birth, Yeshua was presented to the Lord in the Jerusalem temple.

A sacrifice was offered for him - a pair of doves and two young pigeons - which indicated that his family was not wealthy. Thus, Yeshua was raised according to the Torah.

Yeshua undoubtedly received a Jewish education: at 5 years of age he would be ready for the study of the Torah, at 20 for pursuing a vocation, at 30 for entering his full calling. Yeshua entered his ministry at about age 30. By the age of 12 Yeshua was growing in understanding as he was found in the temple precincts "both listening and asking questions." On the outside Yeshua looked like a Jew. Certainly, being faithful to the

Torah, he wore the tsîtsith. In English these are obvious by the translations 'hem' or 'fringe of his garment' which later the crowds would be keen to touch in order to be healed.

Every year, Yeshua's family went up to Jerusalem to celebrate Passover, a tradition which Yeshua continued. Yeshua also kept the feast of Tabernacles (Sukkoth, 'booths'). "As was his custom" he also attended synagogue every Sabbath, even during his traveling ministry. In tithing, fasting and almsgiving Yeshua was totally Jewish.

Yeshua's disciples were Jews and they called Him "Rabbi". They sought Him because they believed the Torah and the Prophets. Yeshua self-identified as a Jew and as "King of the Jews." From His birth to His last Passover Seder Yeshua lived as a Jew.

Pilate, head of the Roman occupation, also recognized Jewish jurisdiction over Yeshua. Yeshua unequivocally identified Himself as the Messiah and as we have seen above, the Messiah must be Jewish.

Yeshua said He was the "King of the Jews" and, the "King of the Jews" must Himself be Jewish. The Jewish crowd also called Him "King of the Jews."

Yeshua died as a Jew:

Yeshua was delivered into the custody of the Jewish authorities. He would not have been placed under Jewish jurisdiction if He were not Jewish. Later, Yeshua was brought before the Sanhedrin where He was charged with an offense against Jewish Law.

Yosef of Arimethea, who was Jewish, laid Yeshua in his own new tomb. Therefore, Yeshua was buried in a Jewish cemetery and was buried according to Jewish custom of the time.

Yeshua was resurrected as a Jew:

Yeshua the risen Jew told his Jewish disciples to go out and teach all the Gentiles.

After eating, talking and walking with His disciples, Yeshua, "lifted up His hands and blessed them" with the Aaronic benediction as it is given in Synagogues and in Churches even to our day.

Yeshua spoke to Paul on the road to Damascus in Aramaic (Hebrew). Paul was fluent in Greek and possibly many other languages, but Yeshua spoke to him in the language of the Jews.

Paul did not become a believer until well after Yeshua's death and resurrection, yet an important part of his message is that Yeshua is a descendant of the Jewish king David.

Many years after His resurrection, Yeshua testified that He was the root and offspring of King David and in a time yet future, two of His titles will be Lion of the tribe of Judah, and Root of David.

In Conclusion:

My dear brothers and sisters in Yeshua, it is very clear from the Bible and from history that He who is called Yeshua was at once the Jewish Messiah, the Son of God and God Himself incarnate. Yes, Yeshua whose very name means salvation, our salvation--- He was born as a Jew, He lived as a Jew, He died as a Jew, and He was resurrected as a Jew. Yeshua is alive and Jewish now, and forevermore will be the same.

With that, Sheldon put down his notes and looked lovingly out over the congregation. While he was speaking to them all, in his heart, he knew that he was speaking directly to his friend Drew, whom he was thrilled to see sitting, enthralled, in the back pew.

"If any one here this morning who has not yet confessed their faith in Jesus Christ, Yeshua, as their Lord and Savior, and they feel called by Him through the power of the Holy spirit to do so now, let them come forward.

And so it was on that Sunday morning at McChord Air Force Base, Washington that Andrew Scott Sterling began his long and full walk with Yeshua, who like himself had been born a Jew.

Chapter Fourteen

Capernaum, December, A.D. 27

Matthias marveled at the indescribably glorious double rainbow that began at some unknown origin beyond Mount Arbel in the west and terminated out of sight, beyond the mountains of Bashan in the east. As had become his daily practice, before sunrise he had strolled to the lakeshore to pray. On this particular occasion, he had done so just after the heavy morning rain had ceased and the rising sun had provided a heavenly pallet for the Lord God of Israel to paint His remarkable double bow across the already pastel tinted canvas sky of the Galilee. Matthias now keenly felt the tender, all consuming embrace— the personal presence of his heavenly father as he stood there, enraptured. He raised his hands in praise and chanted: "Blessed are you O king of the universe who has brought forth this glorious day in which I seek to serve you fully, in accordance with your will."

"Blessed be your day, my brother!" Kefa's uniquely gruff, yet somehow at once clear and tender voice suddenly called Matthias back to this earthly moment. "I thought I'd find you here!

"And may your day also be richly blessed, my brother!" Matthias responded, his heart filled with love for this wonderful man of God. "Perhaps we can pray together for a time. It would seem that our heavenly father has painted a lovely double bow in the heavens that cries out for our recognition."

"Look again!" Kefa pointed to the sky above Bashan where just moments ago the special bow in the heavens had brilliantly shown forth. "His sign for us has announced its message and has already begun to fade."

Matthias turned at once, just in time to watch the last of the rainbow vanish before his eyes. "Praise be to God for giving us this day!" he exclaimed from the depths of his totally awakened being.

"The Master has called His twelve disciples together for breakfast at my house followed by a special teaching. I believe that you and a few of the others are to be there as well," Kefa announced his purpose in having thus sought out Matthias.

"As usual, my dear brother," Matthias replied, "I continue to be greatly blessed and honored by your kindness in inviting me to be present for these special moments near the Master."

"It is not I who calls you, Matthias; it is rather the spirit of God speaking through me," Kefa replied reverently.

***

Matthias was indeed awe struck by the unspeakable honor he felt at being present with the others as they finished the last of their morning meal. His heart filled with an intense, consuming love as his eyes for a wonderful moment met those of Yeshua who was seated at the head of the table surrounded by His twelve chosen disciples: Shimon, who was called Kefa, and Andrew his brother; Ya'akov the son of Zebedee, and Yochanan his brother; Philip and Bartholomew; Thomas Didymus and Mattatyahu the tax collector; Ya'akov the son of Alphaeus, and Lebbaeus, whose surname was Thaddaeus; Shimon the Zealous, and finally Judah Iscariot.

When they had finished eating, after He had concluded the meal with a prayer of thanksgiving, Yeshua turned to the purpose for which he had called them together. Addressing the twelve, He spoke to them directly of their special calling. Then He gave them divinely granted power over unclean spirits, to cast them out, and to heal all kinds of sickness and all kinds of disease. When He had finished doing this He commanded them saying: "Do not go into the way of the Gentiles, and do not enter a city of the Samaritans. But go rather to the lost sheep of the house of Israel. And as you go, preach, saying: 'The kingdom of heaven is at hand.' Heal the sick, cleanse the lepers, raise the dead, and cast out demons. Freely you have received, freely give. Provide neither gold nor silver nor copper in your money belts, nor bag for your journey, nor two tunics, nor sandals, nor staffs; for a worker is worthy of his food.

"Now whatever city or town you enter, inquire who in it is worthy, and stay there till you go out. And when you go into a household, greet it. If the household is worthy, let your peace come upon it. But if it is not worthy, let your peace return to you. And whoever will not receive you nor hear your words, when you depart from that house or city, shake off the dust from your feet. Assuredly, I say to you, it will be more tolerable for the land of Sodom and Gomorrah in the Day of Judgment than for that city!"[32]

***

Much later, as the sun was slowly setting on this most remarkable day, Kefa once again found Matthias at the lakeshore, this time upon his knees in deep, contemplative prayer. He approached, his dear brother and quietly knelt down beside him, joining him in this special time of communication with their greatly beloved Abba, the Creator of the Universe.

When, as all traces of the day had finally faded away through the ever changing glorious hues of the sunset that perfectly reflected the mountains of Bashan from the still, mirror surface of the lake, the two of them arose from their prayer and stood together under the already deep blue, star laden canopy of the new evening.

"Why is it that you look so troubled, my brother?" Kefa inquired with great concern as he beheld Matthias' deep sadness of the moment, given away by his still undried tears as they were illuminated by the moonlight.

"It is nothing," Matthias replied, trying, but utterly failing to conceal his own deep turmoil.

"Of course it is *something*, Matthias," Kefa enjoined; "something you should share with me so that we may together put your spirit at peace."

At that moment Matthias' resolve to maintain the privacy of his deep inner turmoil vanished and he began to pour out his heart to this, his closet brother in Yeshua.

"Kefa, my brother," he began, "Like you and the others, I was thrilled with all of my heart, a few days ago when the Master, in this very place, miraculously fed more than five thousand from our region—the way He healed many of them and it seems the entire crowd came to Him in faith. It was wonderful---."

Kefa interrupted, perplexed: "If it was so wonderful which indeed it was, how could this possibly trouble you?"

"Kefa," Matthias replied solemnly: "As far as I could see, all of those whom the Master fed and healed were Jews from this region—*none* were from the other side of the Lake or from any other region!"

"I can't see why this should trouble you," Kefa replied, still not understanding. "It seems to me that the Master ministered to those who had followed Him that day and they all, or at least most of them, just happened to be Jews---?"

"I suppose that may be so, Kefa," Matthias replied, "but taken with His command to you twelve disciples after breakfast this morning, I have grown to fear He has come only for us Jews and not for any others."

"Ahhh, my brother," Kefa sighed in his understanding: "You are concerned about your beloved Dory and her family??"

"Indeed!" Matthias replied, his voice choking with emotion, "I am *deeply* concerned about the salvation of *all* those Gentiles who are not descended from the twelve tribes of Israel---those from the Decapolis and those from all of the other nations."

Kefa came close to Matthias and embraced him. "Do not be troubled, my brother," he comforted him. "You can be certain that the Master has a plan to save *all* of His creation. None will be excluded—after all, look at what He has already done for Dory and Athanasios."

"But what of the others in Hippos and beyond?" Matthias enjoined. "If you twelve disciples are to go only to the Jews then who will bring the truth to the others?

"Trust Him, Matthias!" Kefa spoke assuringly. "Soon He will show us all His way for the Gentiles. But, for now we must understand that our own people, the Jews are greatly confused and horrendously led far away from the truth by the Sadducees and Pharisees."

"I'm certain," Kefa continued with resolve: "It was this great need of our own people that brought forth His command to us this morning. Be comforted, my brother. Yes, we are to go *first* to the Jews, but this in no way excludes what I know in my heart: His intention is to bring salvation to *all* of His creation!"

Chapter Fifteen

Eglin Air Force Base Florida, April 1959

"Welcome to Eglin, Lieutenant Sterling," Colonel Myron Lovell greeted Drew warmly as he extended his hand. "Congratulations on your selection as the best controller in the West, and best wishes for your success over the next six weeks as you work with your two outstanding counterparts from the Central and Eastern Regions."

"Thank you, Sir," Drew replied, trying to suppress the great pride he felt at having been chosen for this special duty from among several hundred other radar controllers, as he returned in kind the firm hand shake of the Chief of Defense Systems Development. "Helping develop the tactics package for the latest interceptor in the inventory will be an exciting challenge, to say the least."

"You'll be working with the best talent in the Air Force to perfect the F-101B Voodoo," the Colonel continued. "The six air crews who have been assigned to this project, like you, were hand picked by their own regional chains of command, as were all of the troops in the maintenance and administrative support teams."

"I'm really looking forward to working with all of you, Sir!" Drew replied excitedly.

The Colonel smiled warmly as he continued. "Good, Drew, so let's get down to business. For starters, I have set up an initial meeting for you three controllers at thirteen hundred hours, at the radar site we have dedicated exclusively to this project. I've made a staff car and driver available to run you gentleman around the base during the next six weeks."

"Very well, Sir," Drew responded as he stood, sensing that this initial meeting had come to an end. "Thank you so much for your hospitality."

"Speaking of hospitality, given that this is Friday, the staff and I would like to invite you and the rest of the team to a "happy hour" welcoming get together at the Club that should get underway around seventeen hundred."

"I look forward to meeting you all there this evening, Sir," Drew exclaimed as he saluted smartly, turned and exited the office.

***

Drew was clad in a fresh short sleeve shirt summer uniform that was in vogue year-long at Eglin when he arrived at the Officers' Club some thirty minutes before the scheduled gathering of his fellow F-101B project participants. Having to this point spent almost all of his three and a half year career at small, remote radar sites, he was at first somewhat intimidated by the huge crowd of "Happy Hour" celebrants that had gathered for some traditional end of week camaraderie and relaxation. Now, as he wound his way towards the crowded bar through numerous small cliques of mostly young officers clad variously in everything from dress blue uniforms to flight suits, his sense of detachment began to fade. As he watched them, with drinks in hand, engaged in a potpourri of animated conversation, the sum of which made up the very heart business of this huge testing and development complex, the strangeness of his surroundings was quickly replaced with a real and growing sense of belongingness.

"What will it be, lieutenant?" the young off duty airman bartender queried when Drew managed to shoulder his way near enough to the crowded bar to get his attention.

"An extra dry martini on the rocks, please," Drew responded gratefully.

Moments later, drink in hand, Drew worked his way back through the crowd until he noticed a still empty chair at a table already occupied by several flight suit clad aircrew who were engaged in lively and excited conversation. "Mind if I join you gentlemen?" he inquired.

"By all means!" the captain who was apparently the senior member of the group responded. "Always room for'one more! I'm Hank Tyler, in from Travis for the 'One Oh Wonder Bee' tactics development program. These guys are the rest of the aircrew, in from all over the place for the project."

"You've *got* to be kidding me!" Drew responded excitedly at the fortuitous coincidence of their meeting. "I'm Drew Sterling, from McChord. I'm one of your three ground controllers.

"Seems to me there's time for me to buy you gentlemen another round before the official party begins!" Drew stood, already anticipating their affirmative response after he had shaken hands with the rest of his just discovered new colleagues. "Let me see if I can grab one of the waiters who are floating around this place and drag him back here to take your orders."

It took Drew some time to finally spot a waiter near the opposite side of the crowded room. At the moment he seemed to be greatly enjoying an animated conversation with four young Air Force nurses while, presumably, he unhurriedly took their order. "Excuse me!" Drew interrupted, addressing the waiter, "but when you finish here I've got a table full of thirsty aviators who need your services!" As he spoke, Drew really looked for the first time at the four lady officers who were seated at the table. While, he quickly ascertained, they were all attractive, the one seated nearest to him immediately captivated his attention. Her shoulder length blond hair framed her strikingly beautiful face, the central feature of which was her huge, dancingly expressive blue green eyes. For an awkward moment that seemed much longer than its reality, Drew stood transfixed as he now exchanged what seemed like a prolonged frozen fascinated eye contact with this lovely young woman. Finally, breaking the moment, "I'm Drew Sterling," he managed to introduce himself. "We are TDY from all over the States for the F-101B project."

"Sounds exciting!" the object of Drew's attention replied warmly in a way that conveyed to him her mutual interest. "I'm Carla McKenzie. We're all here on permanent assignment at the base hospital. Welcome to Eglin,

Drew."

After Carla had warmly introduced him to her three fellow second lieutenant nurse tablemates, Drew felt emboldened to continue what had for him already become a quest. "We'll be here for the next six weeks," he began. "Will you ladies be in the Club again any time soon?"

"With my schedule," Carla replied, "probably not until this time next Friday."

The circumstances were such that it would have been awkward for Drew to have boldly asked for her phone number on the spot, so he resolved to seek her out in some way yet to be determined, certainly before another week had passed. "Okay, ladies," he presumably addressed the four while he was actually speaking directly to Carla, "Until then, if not sooner."

"Yes, Drew," she replied warmly. "That will be nice."

***

Drew awoke on Saturday morning with a substantial hangover from the repeated rounds of martinis he had consumed until he and his new colleagues were the last to leave the Club when it closed at midnight and these elite "One Oh Wonder Bee" team mates had by then solidly cemented their special relationship. Now, as he tentatively opened his eyes just before noon, as had been his last thought just after he had stumbled into bed, his first thoughts were of the lovely Nurse Second Lieutenant Carla McKenzie. Although he made a conscious effort to put her out of his mind until his head cleared and he could better evaluate the new flood of emotions their brief meeting had generated, Carla McKenzie remained the focus of his attention from this first moment of his awakening and throughout what remained of the day.

Vainly, he had hoped to find her eating lunch at the club, and then later he had hoped to meet here "by chance" that evening at dinner when he had deliberately waited for more than three hours in the entrance lounge. But, Carla, to his great disappointment, was no where to be seen.

Thus, now resolutely determined, Drew easily got Carla's phone number from the base locator and, just before nine that evening, he took a deep breath, dialed and waited expectantly to hear her voice.

"Lieutenant Ralston," the unexpected voice answered.

Drew did a quick double take. "Good evening, this is Drew Sterling. I'm trying to reach Carla McKenzie—apparently I have a wrong number."

"Not at all Drew!" she replied. "This is Maggie Ralston, Carla's roommate. We met last night, but as I recall you were not paying much attention to anyone but Carla."

"I'm sorry it was that noticeable, Maggie—Is Carla there?"

"I'm afraid not, Drew, she's working swings and won't be home until nearly twelve. I'll tell her you called."

"Thanks so much," he replied, trying to mask his disappointment. "Please tell her I'll try to reach her again soon."

***

Since that wonderful Sunday he had come forward to declare his faith Drew had never missed attending the early service at McChord Chapel. Thus, it was both instinctive and exciting for him that he do the same each Sunday during his six week assignment to Eglin. While the West Gate Chapel was several blocks from the Club where he had eaten an early breakfast, Drew enjoyed walking briskly there on this lovely Spring morning.

As he now turned towards the entrance of this place of worship his spirit quickened in a way he did not then immediately understand. Then, as he stepped inside the sanctuary and began to look for an open seat toward the back, where a scattered few other worshipers were already seated, his eyes confirmed the inner most longing of his heart. He turned into the pew and moved to her side. "Good morning, Carla," he greeted this object of his now pounding heart with a special blend of tenderness and excitement: "May I join you?"

"Of course Drew," she replied with equal poorly masked emotion. "Nothing could please me more."

Chapter Sixteen

Tel Hadar, On the East Shore of the Sea of Galilee
March A.D. 28

Matthias sighed with joyful relief as he sank down for a brief respite upon the soft carpet of meadow-green grass. This was a glorious place generously decorated with a carpet of multi-colored spring wild flowers that totally covered a small hill near the eastern shore of the Lake---a place called Tel Hadar.

"The Master has amazing endurance," he commented to his beloved Dory who had just settled down beside him. "Just look at the crowd that has followed Him...there must be at least four thousand! Some have come all the way with us from Sidon!"[33]

"But why wouldn't they follow Him?" Dory replied. "He has performed amazing miracles all along the way. Many who saw these things have come along to gather with us in this place."

Matthias choked with emotion as he added: "Dory, the truly amazing thing is *who* these people are. There may be a few Jews like me scattered among this multitude, but far and away these are *your* people, *Gentiles*! The Master has shown us something wonderful today! He has come for *all* of His creation—first for the Jews, but also for *all* other people! He has come for *everyone* who would simply believe, then follow Him!"

"Why are you two sitting on the grass when there is so much work to be done for the Master?" Athanasios exclaimed loudly, making himself heard over the excited din of the crowd after he had, in the confusion of the crowd, approached his two dearest friends unnoticed.

"What are you talking about, Brother?" Matthias teased with delight as he came to his feet and embraced the new arrival. "Don't forget that *we* are the ones who accompanied the Master all the way to and from Sidon while you were at Hippos."

"Taking life easy?" Athanasios retorted with mock offense, "By no means my dear brother and sister. You will be amazed at the number of the Master's new followers who have already come together to worship at Hippos—and this is only the beginning! Now tell me," he continued in a more serious vain, "how was your long journey with the Master?"

"Awesome! Simply awesome!" Dory exclaimed, jumping into the conversation. "Soon after we started home from Sidon the Master drove demons out of a young Canaanite woman; simply because of her mother's great faith, and that was only the beginning!"

"Yes!!" Matthias added excitedly. "From that point on wherever the Master went, many came to Him, the lame, blind, mute, maimed, and many others; and they were laid them down at His feet, and He healed them.[34] So many from this great multitude gathered here today have already marveled when they saw the mute speaking, the maimed made whole, the lame walking, and the blind seeing; and they have given the glory to the Lord God of Israel."

"Just look at Him now!" Athanasios pointed excitedly to Yeshua who had made his way to the top of the nearby knoll where He now stood with three of His disciples, Kefa, James and Yochanan. "It seems that He never tires of performing miracles!"

Unknown to Athanasios and the others who could not hear Yeshua's conversation with these three, it was indeed so that yet another great miracle was in the making.

Yeshua spoke with concern to the three disciples who stood with Him: "I have compassion on this multitude, because they have now continued with Me three days and have nothing to eat. And I do not want to send them away hungry, lest they faint on the way."

Kefa answered for the three: "Where could we get enough bread in this wilderness to feed such a great multitude?"

Yeshua then asked, "How many loaves do you have?"

"Only seven, and a few little fish," Kefa replied.

With that, Yeshua spoke in a loud voice to the multitude that had instantly grown silent and attentive. "Sit down on this beautiful carpet of grass." He commanded them." Let us give thanks to my Father in heaven, for it is time for us to eat."

Then, Yeshua took the seven loaves and the fish and gave thanks, broke them and gave them to His disciples; and the disciples in turn distributed these to the seated multitude. So they all ate and were filled, and when they were finished eating they took up seven large baskets full of the fragments that were left over. Now those who ate were four thousand men, besides women and children.[35]

Later, as Yeshua and these three of His disciples made their way towards the fishing boat that waited for them there on the shore, Kefa spotted Matthias and the other two in the crowd and hurried toward them. Reaching into a large satchel that he carried with him he hurriedly removed a small Torah scroll. "This is the blessed Torah that you have requested I bring to you for your teaching of the Gentiles at Hippos," he said, transferring this precious gift to Matthias. "May your endeavors for the Lord be abundantly blessed and bear much fruit, my dear brother."

Matthias gratefully took the scroll from Kefa, embraced him and then spoke: "Thank you my dear brother for your great faithfulness. Please pray for me that my voice may be heard and understood among these people."

"I shall so pray, my brother—but now I must go," Kefa declared as he quickly embraced Matthias then hurried to join the others who were already getting into the boat that would carry them to the region of Magdala on the other side of the lake.

After Yeshua and the three disciples had set sail, the multitude remained seated on the grass in awed silence, able to speak only in whispers for a time about the awesome miraculous feeding they has just witnessed along with the many other amazing miracles Yeshua had so recently done among them.

Finally, in mid afternoon, those who had come to this remote Galilee harbor reluctantly began to depart upon their long treks back to their respective homes, scattered throughout the countryside as far away as the sixty-five kilometers that separated this place from Sidon.

The two hundred or so who had come from relatively nearby Hippos now faced a one hour sharply uphill trek to the mountain top city. They now stood, silently awaiting some further direction from Athanasios, the once demon possessed madman who had been miraculously healed by Yeshua, then who quickly had emerged as their clearly acknowledged, and already greatly loved and respected leader.

"I am so pleased that you will now begin teaching us the wonderful truths of the Torah," Athanasios, said as he fondly touched the scroll that Matthias still held in his hands. I am so excited and hungry to learn more about our beloved Yeshua—how, as you have told me, He is prophesied in one way or another on almost every page of these five sacred books."

Matthias gave his eager student a gentle, understanding hug, and then lovingly replied: "We read elsewhere in the complete holy source of your excitement, 'Blessed are they whose ways are blameless, who walk according to the law of the LORD. Blessed are they who keep his statutes and seek him with all their heart.'" Then, with strong conviction he continued. "While the Torah was first given to us Jews, it was by no means intended to be embraced by us exclusively. There is much you will learn that applies to *all* God's creation, such as were written by the hand of God upon the Tables of the Law of Moses. But also, there *are* other instructions that apply *only* to us Jews, like, for example, the particulars of worshiping in the Temple."

"It seems that there is so very much for us to learn," Athanasios sighed at the depth of his own lack of understanding.

"Never mind, my dear brother," Matthias replied reassuringly, "this is no time to despair; we have not yet even begun!"

"Then, let's be on our way!" Athanasios invited. "The way is long and the climb is steep!" He then turned toward the mountain with its large plateau that towered before them about half way up the Heights of Bashan and, with Matthias and Dory close at hand and two hundred or so others close behind; they began the trek up the rugged mountain trail that led to their city.

***

"You people must be half mountain goat!" Matthias cried out as he struggled to catch his heavily labored breath after they had managed to traverse about half the distance to the mountain top city.

Athanasios and Dory, who were well acclimated by their frequent ascents chuckled understandingly. "Hang in there, my brother," Athanasios replied. "There is a natural spring just a bit further up the trail where we will stop for a time of rest and refreshment."

A short time later, after they had arrived at the promised haven and Matthias had drunk heavily from the spring and recovered from his labored breathing, he stood, looking west toward the lake far below and the incredibly beautiful vista that stretched out before him. The steep intensely green slope between them and the water was richly decorated with a seemingly unending carpet of tall butter gold daises with black centers that moved like waves on the sea. They were tossed to and fro by the sometimes brisk direction changing breeze that also provided some cooling comfort for those who struggled up the difficult trail with the blazing afternoon sun at their backs, testing their endurance. As he took in the indescribable beauty of the scene before him, his joy became complete when Dory came close beside him and lovingly placed an arm around his waist.

"Now you can see why we have a special love for this place," she exclaimed.

"Indeed I can," he quickly agreed.

"How long will you be staying with us," she asked somewhat hesitantly.

"I'm sure you know that my family will be very pleased to have you as our guest for as long as you may desire."

"I wouldn't want to take advantage of your hospitality," he replied. "Besides, I'm not at all certain I would be able to keep my mind entirely on the Torah with you so close at hand. Never mind," he continued, "this time

I will be staying with Athanasios and his family who were also kind enough to invite me."

"Okay," she replied, silently agreeing with his discernment of their need for physical separation. "But, you didn't answer me…How long will you be staying in Hippos?"

"I've been giving this a lot of prayerful thought," he replied, "and if you all agree, I will spend the first week of each month in your lovely city for the next year. My plan is to begin on the first day of the week and then to teach every day from sunrise to sunset. Then, after we spend Shabbat together, I will return to Capernaum."

She hugged him excitedly, and then kissed him on the cheek. "Your plan sounds perfectly wonderful!" she exclaimed. "I can hardly wait for it to begin."

Matthias awoke just before sunrise the next morning. He dressed quickly, and then, after a quick breakfast of chopped raw vegetables, olives and flat bread, Athanasios took him on a very quick introductory walking tour of the city.

"There are more than two thousand people living in this place," his host announced proudly, and we have taken many things beyond our language from the Greek culture that was the basis for the Great Alexander's founding of Hippos and the other nine cities of the Decapolis."

"Your language skills truly amaze me," Matthias replied. "It seems that almost everyone here is at least bi-lingual and apparently many are also quite conversant in Hebrew."

"Greek, of course, is the common language of our entire region," Athanasios explained, "but Aramaic is the common language of your people with whom we have many contacts. Then, those of us who most often intermingle with you Jews usually come to grasp Hebrew as a matter of course."

When they had traversed the large, sprawling residential area, they came to the city center where what was called the Forum was already teaming with early morning commercial activity. This more than one square city block area, paved with rectangular pieces of basalt rock, was filled with several rows of well stocked shops offering a great variety produce and what to Matthias was a very surprisingly large assortment of other attractive items.

When they reached the far side of the Forum, they continued walking northwest for another few minutes until they stood before a large, well constructed single story building constructed from large hand carved basalt blocks. "This building is what we call the Northwest Public Room," Athanasios explained. "It is here where we have been meeting and where you will teach us."

***

Matthias was deeply moved by the two hundred or so excited, attentive faces that greeted him when he stepped inside the large room. He was especially pleased to see that the front row was mostly occupied by Dory, her parents and what he later learned was her entire extended family.

Without further formality he moved to the stone podium at the front of the room where he placed then reverently opened the small Torah scroll he had received from Kefa.

"Let us begin at the beginning," he said as he started to read: "In the beginning God created the heavens and the earth."

Chapter Seventeen
Eglin Air Force Base, May, 1959

Drew walked briskly towards Carla's Bachelor Officer's quarters, his heart surging with anticipation as he excitedly looked forward to once again being with this lovely young woman who had become the object of his constant attention over the past five weeks. Since they had met at the Club during his first evening at Eglin, despite their separate very busy schedules, not a day had passed that had not found them together. Long evening walks, hand in hand, along the silver sanded shore; picnics on the beach; sea food dinners at the officers' Beach Club, mid-week and Sunday services at the Chapel— but so much more than just these expected activities of an emerging deep relationship. With every moment of every day that found them together, as each of them individually understood, but had not yet verbally shared with the other, they had already become inexorably bound together.

Drew pulled himself back from his thoughts as he reached Carla's apartment and filled with joyful anticipation, knocked on the door.

In the next moment, she was in his arms. They kissed passionately until, bowing to the unspoken but mutually understood physical limits of their relationship, they, however reluctantly, once again stood ever so close yet still apart.

"So, what's on the agenda for my day off?" Carla smiled broadly seeking to learn how Drew had planned the rest of their day.

He replied excitedly: "I've gotten a green light from Colonel Lovell, and since you've got a secret clearance, I've worked something really special for this evening. "I'll be controlling a flight of two "Voodoos" and an F-89J target right after dinner and you've been cleared to watch the proceedings."

"How exciting!" Carla exclaimed. "I've been so hoping to see how you guys work. You know, I don't mean to complain, but working in the OB GYN ward isn't exactly why I enlisted in the Air Force."

Drew smiled knowingly at her so far unfulfilled quest for military excitement. "I'm afraid this will only be just one more routine intercept mission to add to our data base. We've got the entire Gulf Training Airspace reserved so we can run a variety of approaches."

"Ohh Drew!" She exclaimed. "All of this may be routine for you but it's terribly exciting for me!"

***

The sun had just started to set over the Gulf of Mexico when Drew, with Carla dressed in her pin striped uniform at his side, met the three aircrews, each comprised of a pilot and a radar observer (known fondly as the "back seater") at the flight line for a pre-mission briefing. Carla had already become well known and accepted by these elite aviators by her frequent presence with Drew at their regular evening get- togethers at the Club.

"Looks like you've added some real class to your act, Sterling!" Captain Hank Tyler, the lead pilot, began. "Welcome aboard, Carla. I hope you find the mission interesting."

"That's got to be the understatement of the day!" she replied excitedly. "Thanks so much for including me!"

"Why not?" Hank quipped. "After all, you've become one of us guys!"

"Not hardly!" Drew exclaimed in feigned objection. "She's got more class than all of us put together---."

"She's got a lot more than that," Hank spoke with genuine admiration. "But, enough of that for now; let's get on with the business at hand."

***

The full moon had already begun to generously illuminate the twin white bubble domes of the radar control facility that was set in a closely guarded, chain linked fenced, remote section of the sprawling base.

"Good evening Lieutenant Sterling!" the Air Police sergeant who was posted at the site entry gate greeted formally as he snapped to attention and saluted the two approaching officers. "And good evening to you Ma'am," the sergeant greeted Carla. "I assume you must be Lieutenant McKenzie, but kindly show me your ID for confirmation, Ma'am."

"My goodness, Drew! How can you see where you're going?" Carla asked worriedly, as she clung to his arm in her momentary blindness as they entered the large, barely illuminated operations room.

"Not to worry!" Drew replied, as he guided her to the nearest of several large planned position indicators, more commonly known as "scopes" that made up the top semi circular level of three such scope packed levels. "Your eyes will adjust quickly."

"You're right!" she replied, b'inking her eyes for confirmation. "Wow! This place is impressive!"

"You can sit right here, next to me, where my intercept technician would usually sit," Drew invited his already fascinated guest. He now settled into the armed reclining office type chair directly in front of the scope and began to make fine adjustments to the greenish glowing display of radar returns painted by the "trace" of the air surveillance radar's antenna as it rotated six times per minute through its 360 degree circular coverage.

"I hope you don't expect *me* to do anything?" Carla asked with sincere concern."

"Not tonight," Drew laughed, hoping to set her at ease. "Everything is being recorded and we will reduce the data we need in the lab tomorrow. Just sit back and enjoy the proceedings—. Whoops!" he explained, pointing with the tip of a black grease pencil to the first of three clear radar returns that had appeared near the now offset apex of his display. "Put on your head set, Carla, that would be the target. He should be calling in very soon.

"Sea breeze control, this is Joshua zero one, ten miles, outbound, heading zero one zero, climbing through one thousand, squawking three," the pilot of the target aircraft (call sign Joshua 01) called in his initial position report.

"Joshua Zero One, Sea Breeze Control, Roger." Drew responded with snappy precision. "Squawk two," indicating that the pilot should set his IFF transponder to mode two for identification.

"Zero One, squawking two." The pilot replied as Drew pointed with his grease pencil to the now double line that appeared directly above what had previously been a single line, just above the radar "blip" that represented the aircraft.

"Zero One, Sea Breeze, Squawk three." Drew directed, as he explained to Carla. "This is just one more check for safety---the IFF trace should return to a one line display on this next sweep. "Ahh, and so it did," he observed.

"Zero One, Sea Breeze, radar contact, turn left heading one eight zero, climb to angels three zero, set speed at point seven mach when level."

Turning once again to Carla, Drew explained. "Now watch the blip turn to the left and roll out on a southerly heading.—Now here come the two fighters," he continued, not attempting to hide his own growing excitement as he pointed to two almost overlapping radar blips with associated single IFF markers that had just appeared not far from the main Eglin runway.

Carla watched and listened with fascination as Drew quickly identified the two "Voodoos" and then gave them their initial mission instructions:

"Jolly Zero Three flight, vector one four zero, climb to angels two nine, set speed point eight mach when level.

"Jolly Zero Three, Roger," Hank Tyler acknowledged Drew's direction. "Zero Three Alpha," the pilot of the "Voodoo" in close trail formation with his lead issued his own acknowledgment."

Having a moment to further explain the upcoming activity to Carla as the three aircraft climbed into their initial positions, Drew, using a clear plastic straight edge, drew a horizontal, East-West black grease pencil line across the center of his display.

"This track is where we will run the target back and forth across about one hundred miles of our airspace," Drew explained. Then, I will set up the interceptors on a variety of vectors running from quartering frontal to quartering stern approaches. We should be able to run about ten passes before we head them all for home.”

“Okay!” Carla replied. “It's a bit confusing but I think I get the general idea.”

“It will get much clearer after I run a couple of passes,' he assured her before he turned back to the business at hand, observing that the target aircraft had almost reached the grease pencil line that marked the center of the control area. “Joshua Zero One, port[36] zero nine zero, say angels (altitude in thousands of feet).”

“Sea Breeze, Zero One, Roger, turning port to zero nine zero, level angels three zero.”

Turning again to Carla, Drew explained. “Okay, now we have the target on track and at altitude heading due east and almost at altitude, and here come the interceptors, just where they belong, about fifty miles out and in good position for a set up.”

“Jolly Three flight, Starboard, two seven zero,” Drew directed. “You will have one target passing right to left, tracking, zero nine zero, ground speed six hundred, one thousand feet high.”

Drew again quickly briefed Carla. “The interceptors are now displaced about thirty miles from the target, heading due west and closing quickly. The trick now is to turn the interceptors to their attack heading of one eight zero at just the right moment.”

“When you are dealing with such high speeds, how can you possibly know that exact moment?” Carla asked, mystified.

Drew held up a plastic tool he had grease pencil marked with the technical vectors of his planned attack geometry. “This ‘Handy Dandy’ is helpful, but after you have done this a few thousand times it becomes instinctive—and here we go!”

“Jolly Three flight, in trail, Port One Eight Zero, when steady, your target will be forty degrees right at twenty five miles.”

“Sea Breeze, Zero Three, No Joy,” Hank reported having no radar contact as he turned into the target.

"Alpha, No Joy." Hank's wingman echoed.

Zero three steady on One Eight Zero, No Joy." Hank reported

"Zero Three, target now 38 degrees right at twenty miles." Drew advised.

"Zero Three has a radar contact, 38 right, 19," Hank advised, his breathing noticeably accelerated in the excitement of the moment.

"Zero Three, contact is your target," Drew confirmed.

"Zero Three, Judy," Hank's "back seater" reported that his airborne fire control system had now locked on to the target and that he had taken over responsibility for completing the intercept.

"Zero Three Alpha has a Judy," Hank's wingman reported.

"Roger Judy for Three and Alpha,' Standing By." Drew replied with noticeable satisfaction.

"All we do now is watch while the good guys shoot down the bad guy," Drew updated Carla who had been observing the attack with keen attention."

"See Breeze, Zero Three," Hank reported a few moments lbater, "Splash one F-89J."

"Roger, Splash." Drew acknowledged the successful completion of Hank's pass.

"Zero Three Alpha, Splash,' the wingman echoed Hank's success.

***

"Gee, this is fun!" Carla observed after Drew had guided the two "Wonder Bees" through five successful subsequent intercepts, each with a different attack angle.

"It is indeed!" Drew replied. This stuff never ceases to thrill me. But, everything you've seen tonight has been very routine." Little did he realize that the routine he spoke of was about to be suddenly shattered.

"Sea Breeze, Jolly Zero Three, I want to change the script a bit and perform a full power high speed run to check out some on going avionics issues before we head home. Please give Joshua and Alpha a steer home and keep me within the airspace while I put this beauty to the firewall."

"Roger, Zero Three." Drew acknowledged the lead pilot's discretionary changing of the mission while in flight, as he next complied by vectoring the other two aircraft back to Eglin and then turning them over to the Eglin Tower frequency for their final approach.

Having thus relinquished control of the other two aircraft, Drew now turned his full attention to Hank Tyler who was about to commence his, full power supersonic run headed east from the extreme western edge of the airspace. "Watch these blips get further and further apart," Drew explained to Carla as Hank pushed his throttles full forward, lighting the "Wonder Bee's" twin afterburners.

"Passing nine hundred," Hank called out his speed for recording both in his aircraft and in the ground control facility. "Nine fifty—nine seventy five"— he continued, the rapidity of his breathing seeming to keep pace with the now near record high velocity of his aircraft. "One thousand—One thousand twenty!" he continued.

Then suddenly, as if it were a clap of thunder, a loud blast pierced through the radio frequency, then gave way to sudden, utter silence.

Drew knew that some catastrophic event had occurred but at that moment he had no way of knowing the precise nature of the emergency that was unraveling before him. "Zero Three, Sea Breeze!" he repeated several times in vain as he attempted to reestablish radio contact.

"My God! What's wrong?" Carla asked anxiously, not expecting a reply as she saw that Drew totally absorbed in the situation, seeking some appropriate course of action.

"Okay," Drew responded, speaking more to himself than to Carla. "He's still flying, his speed is way down and he has apparently lost all radio contact.

"There it is!" he suddenly exclaimed, pointing to the four IFF bars that had just appeared above the radar blip, signifying that the pilot had declared an emergency.

Drew acted instinctively. "Zero One, understand you have declared an emergency. If you read me, squawk standby."

The next sweep of the radar showed that Hank had understood and momentarily turned off his IFF transponder.

"Resume your emergency squawk," Drew directed. "If you need navigational assistance, squawk two."

"Two IFF bars appeared during the next antenna sweep.

"Turn left heading 330. When steady, home plate will be twelve o'clock one hundred and twenty miles."

Drew watched as the blip representing Hank's stricken aircraft turned right through 330 degrees and continued turning to settle 50 degrees off the heading he had directed back to Eglin.

"Zero Three, you have overshot the turn by fifty degrees, begin a slow turn to the left."

Drew watched as Hank immediately complied. "Roll out now," he directed sensing the precisely correct moment. "You are steady on 330, home plate dead ahead at one fifteen.

Suddenly a barely discernable semblance of Hank's wind blown voice could be heard. "Sea Breeze, Zero Three, We popped the canopy. My back seater ejected and I lost my headset. Just got it back on, but I can't see anything! I'm flying by the seat of my pants."

Drew had already alerted Air Sea Rescue by phone to an impending emergency immediately after he had lost contact with Hank so he was ready to proceed. "Roger, we have already scrambled 'Dumbo'," He advised the stricken pilot as he quickly turned the just airborne SA-16 "Albatross" rescue aircraft towards the position where the incident had begun.

Now it was time for the most difficult of all questions. "What are your intentions, Zero Three?" Drew inquired of Hank with professional calm.

"Can you steer me back to the end of the runway with the same kind of timed turns we just did?" Hank inquired.

"Roger, we can give it a shot," Drew replied, "but it isn't in the book."

"Forget the book!" Hank replied. "Let's go for it. If need be I can eject when I get closer to home."

"Roger," Drew replied. Begin a slow turn to the right. We need about fifteen degrees--- You are right on the money, Zero Three," Drew then reported seconds later as Hank rolled steady.

For the next twenty minutes Drew conveyed heading and altitude adjustments to the stricken pilot who now managed to find himself in a position over Eglin in much better condition than he had been when the emergency had begun.

"Sea Breeze, Jolly Zero Three," Hank sighed with noticeable relief, "my vision has returned sufficiently for me to see the instruments and make the semblance of a safe landing. I'm switching to the Eglin Tower frequency at this time."

"Very well, Zero Three. Good day."

Drew, bathed in sweat, took off his headset and exclaimed. "Come on, Carla. Let's go meet this guy on the flight line."

The two of them arrived at the project parking area near Base Operations on the flight line, just as Hank safely landed his wounded Voodoo with its canopy noticeably absent, and began to taxi toward them.

"That was the most amazing thing I've ever seen," Carla commented, her breath still heavy with the intensity of their recent experience. "You were obviously wonderful, Drew, but all the way through this thing I knew that God had his hand on both you and Hank, to say nothing of the poor guy who got dunked in the drink."

"I know," Drew replied. "I was quietly praying through the entire incident. For that matter, I always pray before during and after each time I control aircraft."

She put her arm around his waste and continued. "Drew, I was praying too, all through this thing."

***

Later that night, after the entire project team including the rescued and unhurt "back seater" had closed the Club following a short but vigorous celebration, Drew and Carla began what had already become a traditional walk along the moonlit, silver sand beach.

They had walked along, holding hands for several minutes, each deeply lost in their own profound thoughts generated by the day's remarkable happenings. Finally, it was Drew who broke the silence. "You know, Carla," he began, "I truly love the Air Force and the kind of work I do but lately I have begun to sense that God has something else, something more important for me to do with my life."

Carla, somewhat disbelieving what she was hearing responded with surprise, "Drew, you are obviously one of the top people in your profession! Surely, you aren't thinking of getting out of the Air Force?"

"Heavens no!" he replied unhesitatingly, "I couldn't bear doing that--- but it just seems like I'm being called to do something else."

"Do you have any idea what that might be?"

"This may sound totally crazy to you—it kind of does to me—but I believe I am being called into the ministry."

She was overcome with a potpourri of emotions: her initial shocked surprise instantly overcome by a spontaneous outpouring of strong agreement, joy and love. "Ohh Drew!" she exclaimed, giving him a tight full body hug, then pulling back with her arms remaining possessively around his waste. "I couldn't be more thrilled and nothing could be more right. How about Chaplain Lieutenant Andrew Scott Sterling? It has a nice ring, doesn't it?"

"It's not quite as simple as that," he cautioned, trying to bring some sense of reality to her pronouncement. "First of all, I'll have to work some sort of a leave of absence for three years to attend seminary. Then, I'll have to be ordained, and then, here's the hard part: I'll have to be accepted by the Air Force Chaplaincy."

"Drew," she comforted, as she now once again held him close: "Listen to what the Lord says:

So I say to you: Ask and it will be given to you; seek and you will find;

knock and the door will be opened to you. For everyone who asks receives; he who seeks finds; and to him who knocks, the door will be opened.[37]

Drew's response was spontaneous and flowed from the depths of his soul. "Carla, I can't begin to imagine living such a life in His service without you by my side—I know we have only known one another for a very short time, but, Darling, I know that I love you with all of my heart—Carla, will you marry me?"

Her tears of indescribable joy were illuminated by the full moon reflecting from the breakers as they crashed along the shore, rushing towards the two of them, only to halt just before they touched them where they stood, just beyond their reach; only to relentlessly try again with unceasing repeated successive attempts to finally reach their goal. "Of course, I will, Darling!" she replied.

.

Chapter Eighteen

A Limestone Cave near Ein Karem
July, A.D. 28

Matthias and Dory paused for a moment to catch their breath and to take in the magnificent vista of the ancient village of Ein Karem with its lush, densely forested surrounding hills and valleys that lay just a few kilometers west of Jerusalem.

"We are nearly there," Matthias announced encouragingly, more to himself than to what he often teased was his "mountain goat" companion. "It will be so good to see Yochanan and I know he'll be both surprised and pleased by our unannounced visit."

"He certainly has chosen a remote place to continue his immersion ministry. It's a wonder that anyone is able to find him here," Dory spoke wonderingly.

"I'm certain the Lord is leading those here whom He has chosen. I pray He will continue to protect Yochanan from his many enemies who are led by Satan to end this wonderful ministry," Matthias replied.

"Here we are!" Matthias announced excitedly, as they rounded the final curve in the uphill path and found themselves just a few meters from the opening of a large limestone cave. "And we are not alone," he observed as a middle aged couple and their teen aged son suddenly emerged from the man-sized rectangular carved cave entrance. "Shalom!" Matthias greeted the family whose faces were aglow with the easily recognizable joy of an awesome spiritual encounter that had just transformed their lives.

"Shalom, indeed!" the head of the family replied. "Have you also come to be immersed by the Baptizer?"

"We have already been so cleansed," Matthias replied. "We have come to see the Baptizer for other reasons. He is my brother."

"Then you have indeed been greatly blessed!" this up to now perfect stranger replied as he moved forward and embraced Matthias. "The Lord God of Israel is doing mighty things through your greatly anointed brother."

Immediately after the family had bid Matthias and Dory a fond farewell and begun their trek down the path, Yochanan appeared at the mouth of the cave, as if to greet the next party seeking his special immersion for repentance. As anticipated by Matthias, he was both surprised and delighted to behold his precious brother and his lovely companion.

"Greetings, dear ones!" Yochanan nearly shouted in his enthusiasm as he rushed to Matthias and embraced him in a crushing bear hug, then, in a marked contrast, fondly turned to Dory and kissed her on both cheeks. "What a great joy it is to see you both! What brings you calling on me even in this remote hideout?"

"Quite frankly, dear brother, our beloved father, Eliezar, told me that you were in grave danger and he sent me to personally see about your safety. You must be aware that King Herod Antipas has been making all sorts of threats against you."

"You must tell our father not to be concerned. I have been about the Master's business and I know that our heavenly father holds me in the palm of His Almighty hand. Besides, Antipas doesn't have a clue where I've taken up residence—he and his minions know nothing of this lonesome cave."

"Not too terribly lonesome, it would seem," Matthias replied questioningly. "It is quite obvious that the word is out among the people and they are coming to this place to be immersed"

"Indeed they are!" Yochanan replied with great satisfaction. "On some days there are more than one hundred who find their way here."

"That is my point exactly," Matthias replied with unconcealed exasperation. "If *they* can find their way to you, then so can Antipas!"

"What would you have me do; give up my ministry?" Yochanan pleaded.

"This brings me to the message that comes from our father's heart." Matthias began to convey the real purpose for his visit. "I don't have to tell you that he is very close to our heavenly Father and the words he speaks are those of wisdom. Yochanan," he continued forthrightly, "our father desires that you immediately return   to Qumran and stay their in the protection of the community until all of these political threats against you have blown over."

Yochanan paused for several moments of contemplation before he replied. "Matthias, we both know that our father is a great and holy man who has our best interests at heart, but, please understand, I answer to a higher authority and I am persuaded to remain here and to continue about His business."

***

Some days later, as had become his custom, Matthias had arisen before dawn and made his way the short distance to the Capernaum lakeshore while the stars were still illuminating the heavens and the full moon was painting the barely rippled surface of the lake with a magnificent array of sparkling diamond like reflections.

He prayed from the depths of his soul crying out: "Blessed are you O King of the Universe who laid out the heavens and established the earth and whose power is reflected in the heavens above and whose glory is manifest throughout the whole earth. You are my God, there is none else."

"My Father is hearing and rejoicing at your praise." Yeshua spoke softly as He tenderly placed an arm around the still kneeling Matthias' shoulders. "And, my son, I greatly rejoice at the depths of your love and faithfulness towards me."

Matthias was awed and nearly overcome by this unprecedented intimacy with the Master. His voice was barely audible as he, through the depths of his emotion, managed to reply simply: "My Lord and my God."

"My son," the Master began to reveal the purpose of this pre-dawn encounter. "I want to speak to you about your brother, Yochanan. I know that you have not yet received word that he was arrested by Antipas and taken to prison, and that he sent two of his disciples to me to inquire: 'Are You the Coming One, or do we look for another?' I sent this message back to him: 'Go and tell Yochanan the things which you hear and see: The blind see and the lame walk; the lepers are cleansed and the deaf hear; the dead are raised up and the poor have the gospel preached to them. And blessed is he who is not offended because of Me.' Matthias, I have been teaching the multitudes concerning your brother, Yochanan: 'What did you go out into the wilderness to see? A reed shaken by the wind? But what did you go out to see? A man clothed in soft garments? Indeed, those who wear soft clothing are in kings' houses. But what did you go out to see? A prophet? Yes, I say to you, and more than a prophet. For this is he of whom it is written: 'Behold, I send My messenger before Your face, who will prepare Your way before You.'"

"Assuredly, I say to you," the Master continued, "among those born of women there has not risen one greater than Yochanan the Baptizer; but he who is least in the kingdom of heaven is greater than he. And from the days of Yochanan the Baptizer until now the kingdom of heaven suffers violence, and the violent take it by force. For all the prophets and the law prophesied until Yochanan. And if you are willing to receive it, he is Elijah who is to come."[38]

"Master," Matthias humbly replied in a barely audible whisper, "I am so greatly blessed and honored to have been raised to manhood in the same household and by the same father as this my brother whom I so greatly love."

"Arise, my son." Yeshua spoke with an outpouring of indescribable love as He gently helped Matthias to his feet. "We each have a destiny appointed by my Father. All men, myself included, must taste physical death before we rise again to live eternally in the presence of my Father." Yeshua held him close as he came to the central purpose of this early morning encounter. "Matthias, my son, according to my Father's will, your brother Yochanan's earthly walk has ended. He is already rejoicing with my Father in paradise.

You must now go to your earthly father and comfort him with these things I
have told you."

Chapter Nineteen

Lakewood General Hospital, Lakewood, Washington
October, 1960

Drew took no comfort from the stress filled faces of the three other expectant fathers who remained seated, as he paced back and forth in the waiting room of OB-GYN ward of Lakewood General Hospital, near Tacoma, Washington. Just an hour ago, despite her strong protestations that she was in false labor, he had rushed Carla to the hospital. "Never mind, my darling nurse," he whispered for his own benefit. "The doctor vindicated my concern—you were already crowning when we arrived and I am about to become a father!"

The impact of this impending reality generated a rush of concerns in the mind of this trying not to be nervous imminently expectant father. Although he had completed his first year of training at nearby Faith Seminary with a perfect 4.0 grade point average, the Master of Divinity degree he sought as his entrée to the Air Force Chaplaincy was still two years away and now his beloved Carla would no longer be able to work as she had done up to just a few days prior to this momentous evening.

Now, as he struggled to push these negative considerations from his mind, he prayed intensely for the Lord's comfort, guidance and provision and even more for Carla and their unborn child.

"Hey Drew!" Chaplain Major Sheldon Thurman burst into the expectant father's waiting room. "What's happening?"

"Glad you could make it, Shel," Drew replied with relief as he hugged his dear friend and mentor. "The fact is," he replied excitedly, "you're about to become a God Father and, among other things, I'm wondering how I'm going to support my family and stay in seminary for another two years?"

Sheldon was almost overcome by the joy of what he was about to convey. "You know, we can count on our wonderful God to be right on time for those who love and choose to serve Him!" And, just in case you ever wondered, you can count on me too. You and Carla have so much become the family I never had---."

"Of course I know and trust in His provision," Drew interrupted, "and I certainly trust in your loving concern—the way you constantly bless us." He paused, trying to suppress the outburst that was to follow. "I *know* He will guide us through this situation, and I *know* that you will be standing by our side—but---."

"I may fail you from time to time, my brother. After all, I'm only human. But you can always count on our wonderful God!" Sheldon again seized control of the conversation returning to his announcement. "It seems that the Chaplains' Board was very impressed with the results of your first year at Faith—Hear me—I said *very* impressed!"

"And just what does that mean?" Drew replied suddenly filled with great interest.

"For starters," Sheldon continued, "just in case no one else has told you, the Air Force Reserve captains' list will be officially announced tomorrow, but I got a look at it today. Congratulations, *Captain* Sterling!"

"Wow!" Drew exclaimed excitedly. "The extra pay will add a lot to my two weekend drills each month!"

"It gets much better than that, Drew," Sheldon continued. "I must confess that I've been doing some very strong lobbying in high places on your behalf—and, here's the deal! It seems, given your record and your performance so far in seminary, effective immediately; you have been recalled to active duty and transferred to the Chaplain's corps with full pay and allowances. Your duty assignment for the next two years will be to finish your training!"

Overcome with the sheer joy of what he was hearing, Drew collapsed into a nearby chair, unable to speak.

"There's more!" Sheldon went on. "Pending the award of your Master of Divinity and ordination, you will be granted a Regular Air Force commission in the grade of captain and immediately embark upon your career as an Air Force Chaplain."

The other three expectant fathers in the small room could not have avoided hearing Sheldon's exciting news and they now robustly joined in what had become a spontaneous celebration. "It looks like I should be handing out *two* cigars instead of one!" Drew exclaimed.

"I'd say an entire box would be even more appropriate!" Sheldon joshed, relishing in the happiness which had largely resulted from his own intense personal efforts.

After this spontaneous celebration, Sheldon and Drew resumed their more private conversation while seated side by side, somewhat removed from the others. "You know, Drew," Sheldon became more serious. "While it is in no way required, I would like to see you spend as much time as you can with our chaplain staff at McChord. This will give you a leg up on how we operate and it will also provide you with some precious time in the pulpit—sort of a practicum while you continue your studies at Faith."

"How can I begin to thank you for all this Sheldon?" Drew replied just beginning to take in the magnitude of all he had heard. "Of course I will spend time with you at McChord! What a great honor and opportunity for me to learn!"

"Here's how you can thank me, Drew," Sheldon replied while wiping away the beginning tears of joy that were now evident upon his cheeks. "I know in my spirit that our Lord has great and wonderful things planned for you *Chaplain* Sterling! I now challenge you to be everything you can be for Him!"

Before Drew could frame a response, Doctor Graham Garrison, the duty OB-GYN physician popped into the waiting room. "Lieutenant Sterling?" he inquired of those who anxiously waited.

Drew jumped to his feet, suddenly once again returning to the central focus of his presence in this place. "Yes, Doctor!" he replied with nervous anticipation. "I'm Lieutenant Sterling!"

"Then come along with me. I would like to introduce you to your perfect and healthy new daughter who is waiting for you in her mother's arms."

The incomprehensible joy Drew felt when he first saw his newborn daughter was only equaled by the all consuming mother's love radiating from the depths of Carla's soul that somehow illuminated the entire room and everyone who might have the great blessing of entering into their presence.

Drew, moving quickly to their side, made no effort to suppress his tears of utter joy. "She's so beautiful, Darling— how could she be anything else with you as her mother—those eyes, look at her eyes, they're enormous!— Sweetheart, are *you* okay?

"I couldn't be better, but I'm a bit weary," she replied.

"Then I'd better be going and let you get some well deserved rest."

"Not until we decide on this angel's name!" Carla insisted. "I know we've had this conversation before, but now it's time to make a final decision."

He smiled, knowing that she was only seeking confirmation of what she had already decided. "Okay, I know that you want to do everything possible to win the love of my family, especially Grandma Amelia's who has been something less than enthusiastic about you not being Jewish."

"You've got it, Drew!" she replied resolutely. "Let's do the old girl the honor of naming our first born after her dearly departed sister, and, if you don't mind, let's go with Ann as her middle name since this has become a tradition of sorts in my family."

Drew now, with typical new father hesitancy, gently picked up his daughter for the first time and held her close. "Welcome to the world Dory Ann Sterling," he spoke to her joyfully. "You are now the latest Dory in a long standing Grossman family tradition."

Chapter Twenty
The Jordan Valley, near Scythopolis (Bet She'an)
March, A.D. 30

Kefa, who had been close to Yeshua at the front of the procession during their long morning's walk south along the Jordan River towards Jerusalem, made it a point to seek out his dear friend Matthias during the midday rest and meal time. The two of them gratefully settled together onto the thick carpet of lush green grass generously decorated with blood red poppies that spread out in every direction from where they sat, as far as the limits of their perception could behold.

"It's so good to see you, my brother," Matthias greeted Kefa with a kiss upon each of his cheeks. "It has been some time since we've had an opportunity to be together."

"I'm so sorry, Matthias," Kefa explained apologetically, "but I've been by the Master's side almost continuously during these past several weeks. So much has happened—so very many amazing, awesome things! I hardly know where I should begin in sharing these wonders with you!"

"Do share what you are able," Matthias replied, anxious to hear these wondrous testimonies of the Master's latest ministry.

"Let me begin with the Master's recent trip to the north where we first sojourned at a most unseemly place called Panias, the very center of pagan worship—a virtual hotbed of evil. This is the place where the Jordan River begins by arising from deep within the earth, then rushing forth from a huge cave with a large overhanging cliff."

"Matthias," Kefa continued excitedly, "The twelve of us stood in front of a pool of water at the base of this cave and the Master taught us concerning the great Body of believers who would follow him now, through all the coming generations, and until the end of days. Matthias, I saw Him take up a small pebble from the bottom of the pool where it had been worn smooth by centuries of the water's polishing. Then, speaking directly to me, referring to the stone in His hand and speaking in Greek, the Master used my name which in that language is *Petros*, meaning small stone.

With this *Petros* in His precious hand, He pointed to the huge cliff above the evil cave and He said '*Petros*, you are *Petra*, meaning a large rock wall' and then, pointing back to Himself He taught us: upon this rock, speaking of Himself, I found the Body of my followers now and forevermore."[39]

"How very interesting," Matthias replied thoughtfully. "It would seem the Master was making it very clear that He alone, never any other, would eternally be both the foundation and the head of His Body of believers."

"Indeed," Kefa replied. "And there is so much more."

"Please, my brother, share these with me," Matthias waited expectantly.

"From this place called Panias," Kefa continued, "the Master led Ya'akov, his brother Yochanan and me on a rigorous six day walk to the very top of Mount Hermon. We had no idea why He was taking us to this high place, still covered with a thick layer of snow, and still very cold, but of course we trusted Him and we knew He had some very important purpose in all this."

"You must have been very cold and weary?" Matthias questioned.

"Amazingly not," Kefa replied. "It seems that the three of us were kept in some way wrought by the Master, perfectly comfortable and renewed with great energy to make this long hard climb."

"What happened there?" Matthias asked excitedly.

"Matthias, this was the most remarkable thing I have ever witnessed. There before our eyes, the Master was transfigured. His face shone like the sun, and His clothes became as white as the light. And then, Moses and Elijah appeared before us, and they were talking with Him. Then I asked the Master if He wished for us to make here three tabernacles: one for Him, one for Moses, and one for Elijah." Then, while I was still speaking, a bright cloud overshadowed us; and suddenly a voice came out of the cloud, saying, 'This is My beloved Son, in whom I am well pleased. Hear Him!' And when the three of us heard it, we fell on our faces and were greatly afraid. But Yeshua came and touched us and said, 'Arise, and do not be afraid.' When we had lifted up our eyes, we saw no one there but Yeshua." .

Matthias could hardly speak, so overcome was he with the magnitude of what Kefa had just revealed. Then, he noticed that his beloved friend had begun to weep and was deeply saddened. "Why do you sorrow, my brother, over such glad tidings?"

"There is more, Matthias," Kefa replied after he had regained his composure sufficiently to continue. "I know that I should not have shared this with you, but somehow, since you are practically one of us, I felt that the Master would have allowed this one exception."

"Whatever are you talking about, Kefa?" Matthias begged for clarification.

"Matthias, when we came down from the mountain, the Master commanded us saying, 'Tell the vision to no one until the Son of Man is risen from the dead.'

Don't you see, my brother, the Master was conveying to us that He was soon to die and He would rise from the dead."[40]

"Perhaps you misunderstood, Kefa. He may not have been speaking of His death being imminent, but rather at some time in the far, unknown future?"

"Oh no, Matthias, He has made it clear. He is soon to be with His Father in heaven. Ever since that time on the mountain top He has been showing us disciples that He must go to Jerusalem, and there suffer many things from the elders and chief priests and scribes, and be killed, and be raised the third day. In fact, when I challenged Him saying, 'Far be it from You, Lord; this shall not happen to You!' He rebuked me saying 'Get behind Me, Satan! You are an offense to Me, for you are not mindful of the things of God, but the things of men.'[41] It is thus that I weep"

"Be comforted, my brother," Matthias replied with great emotion. "You must know that the Master loves you deeply. Surely, He was only using you in this way to make a point."

"Perhaps," Kefa replied tentatively embracing Matthias' comforting suggestion. "In fact, immediately after He rebuked me, he told the twelve of us, 'If anyone desires to come after Me, let him deny himself, and take up his cross, and follow Me. For whoever desires to save his life will lose it, but whoever loses his life for My sake will find it. For what profit is it to a man if he gains the whole world, and loses his own soul? Or what will a man give in exchange for his soul? For the Son of Man will come in the glory of His Father with His angels, and then He will reward each according to his works.'"[42]

"Ohhh!" Matthias exclaimed, noticing that Yeshua had just risen from where He had been sitting on the grass, signaling that the noontime rest was now finished and it was time for them to continue their journey to Jerusalem. "The Master would have us be on our way! Thank you so much my brother for sharing these amazing things with me."

"There is so very much more, Matthias, that I have not yet shared—but, I will continue this testimony sometime soon. Now I must once again walk at the Master's side."

***

Yeshua and the others drew near Jerusalem late the next morning, having spent the night near Jericho. Now as they came to Bethpage, at the Mount of Olives, Yeshua sent two of His disciples, saying to them, "Go into the village opposite you, and immediately you will find a donkey tied, and a colt with her. Loose them and bring them to Me. And if anyone says anything to you, you shall say, 'The Lord has need of them,' and immediately he will send them."

All this was done that it might be fulfilled which was spoken by the prophet, saying: "Tell the daughter of Zion, 'Behold, your King is coming to you, lowly, and sitting on a donkey, a colt, the foal of a donkey.'"[43]

"So the disciples went and did as Yeshua commanded them. They brought the donkey and the colt, laid their clothes on them, and set Him on them. And a very great number of people spread their clothes on the road; others cut down branches from the trees and spread them on the road. Then these many people who went before and those who followed cried out, saying: 'Hosanna to the Son of David!

Blessed is He who comes in the name of the Lord! Hosanna in the highest!'

"And when He had come into Jerusalem, all the city was moved, saying, 'Who is this?' So the multitudes said, 'This is Yeshua, the prophet from Nazareth of Galilee.'" [44]

Chapter Twenty One

Tacoma, Washington
June, 1962

"What's bothering you, sweetheart?" Drew asked with intuitive sensitivity born of their three precious years of marriage. "How can you look so glum on a day such as this?"

"I'm *not* glum!" Carla replied with a transparency he had come to recognize and easily penetrate. "The fact is, Bekah was a bit restless all night and I didn't get a whole lot of sleep."

Drew who had been shaving in their attached bathroom finished the task, rinsed his face and went to his obviously troubled wife who remained in their bed that, along with the baby's crib, left little space for much else in the doll house size bedroom of their tiny rental house. He sat down next to her on the bed and they kissed tenderly. "Okay, Carla, fess up—what's bothering you on one of the biggest days in my life?"

"I'm sorry, darling," she replied. "It's just the reality of having to face your parents and your grandmother all at once. It isn't that I have any illusions that they accept me or even like me...."

Drew replied tenderly, "I know, darling, how difficult this must be for you, but it's a good thing all of them insisted on being here for my graduation and ordination. Surely this bodes well for their growing acceptance of you and our girls."

"It's just that they have been so terribly negative towards me in the past—my goodness Drew, how can you ever forget my first visit with your grandmother when she sized me up from head to toe then took you aside for her own supposedly private interrogation?"

Drew laughed, unable to contain himself at the memory she had provoked. "Sweetheart," he replied, trying to explain. "What she said was a very Jewish thing---."

Carla cut him off, remembering Grandma Amelia's biting words, deliberately spoken loud enough for her to hear, which she now repeated mockingly in her own version of Grandma's Yiddish accent: 'I only have one question, Drew— *Vhy*? Nuu, you couldn't find a nice *Jewish* girl'??"

"I'm telling you, Carla, the old girl will melt when she comes face to face with her two great granddaughters. She's already more than delighted that we named our first 'Dory' after her dearly departed sister, and how will she be anything but thrilled when she meets her and little Rebekah for the first time?"

"I suppose you're right, Drew," she replied with a hint of released tension. "I'm only glad there isn't room in the car for me and the girls and that you will meet them at SeaTac and take them all directly to the motel. That will cut down my exposure to them considerably."

"You know, Carla," Drew spoke out unable to conceal the sense of his own hurt, "my relationship with your family hasn't been what one could call ideal?"

"Drew, *they* have accepted *you*!" she retorted defensively.

"*Sure* they have!" he snapped sarcastically. "That gaggle of red necks you call kin folk haven't exactly lovingly embraced your *Jewish* husband, born again or otherwise."

Now it was Carla's turn to be defensive. "Drew, darling, you've got one terrible chip on your shoulder. Of course my family sees you as *different*. Why wouldn't they—they've never even seen a Jew close up before, much less have one marry their beloved vestal virgin daughter. Drew, give them a break—in their own way, they do accept you and love you very much!"

"Okay, enough already!" he replied, wanting to turn their conversation back to the moment. "Things really aren't as terrible or as threatening as you make them out. There will only be the faculty's dinner for the graduating class and their guests this evening, followed by the graduation, then, of course there will be all day tomorrow before they leave in the evening."

"Ohh Drew," she pleaded. "Whatever are we going to do with them all day tomorrow?"

"Well, I've been praying about that and I believe that the Lord has shown me we are to take them to the Rose Gardens at Point Defiance State Park. If the good weather holds, there is no place in the world more beautiful this time of year and all three of them are flower lovers."

***

They sat in the plush lobby of the Silver Cloud motel built entirely on an enormous pier that jutted out into Commencement Bay. Carla held Bekah in her arms as she struggled to control the pent up energy of two year old Dory who was anything but content to sit quietly awaiting the great moment she would meet her great grandmother for the first time. "Dory," she commanded her first born as she scurried toward the hallway leading to the first floor guest rooms. "Come back here immediately---!"

Before Dory could react to her mother's demand, Drew and the others appeared in her view and, without the slightest hesitation, she hurried on towards them with renewed determination. Then, in a moment that could have been nothing but Divine intervention, instead of rushing into Drew's outstretched arms, she unhesitatingly rushed instead into the outstretched arms of her great grandmother who scooped her up with an inexplicable outpouring of instantaneous mutual love and bonding.

"Oyyy!!" Grandma Amelia exclaimed, unable to hold back the tears of joy that flooded from large eyes dominating her bull dog like face. "You are so beautiful Dory Ann Sterling—Nuu, and so vhy not? You look just like me vhen I was a little girl!"

***

It was late morning after Drew's graduation and ordination. The five of them paused for a moment of rest to revel in the astounding beauty of the Fort Defiance rose gardens where they had wandered together, individually and collectively enraptured by the sheer glorious beauty of the place. They stood together on a pathway at the beginning of an archway of large pink, delightfully fragrant roses in full bloom, framed on both sides by long rows of exquisite, varying shades of blue and purple hydrangeas that pointed the way to the seemingly unceasing beauty of the continuing gardens just ahead.

"I'm telling you, such a place I have never seen," Grandma Amelia pronounced her approval while holding Dory's hand but speaking to no one in particular.

"*Ha Shem*[45] painted all of this with His mighty hand!"

Mark put his arm around his traditional adversary's shoulder as he replied.

"You know Mom, this is one of those rare occasions where I absolutely agree with you." Then, pointing east towards Commencement Bay and snow covered Mount Rainier that dominated the scene on this picture postcard perfect day, he continued. "Yes, who can deny that there is a God in heaven who created all of this?"

Carla who had been carrying Bekah in her arms all this time invited. "Come on everyone, there is much more to see. There are several hundred more roses at their peak in the gardens just ahead."

Grandma Amelia sighed as she sat down on a long wooden bench just under the rose archway. "Carla, darling, to tell you the truth I'm not getting any younger and you must be exhausted from schlepping our angel. Vhy don't I just take her from you and sit here in this beautiful place while the rest of you go ahead? I would like to see more, but I've already seen enough to give me wonderful memories for the rest of my life."

"I've even got a better idea," Drew interjected. "Why don't Dory and I sit here with you, Grandma? It will give us a wonderful opportunity to have a nice visit."

"Vaht a lovely idea, Drew, darling," Grandma Amelia replied, obviously very pleased at his suggestion.

Grandma Amelia broke the silence after the rest of them had moved ahead along the pathway and she, Drew and Dory sat alone under the rose arbor.

"Drew, darling, this has been such a good time by me. Last night at the dinner, the president and the dean treated me like I was some kind of royalty. I'm telling you, I've never met such warm loving people!"

"They are very special people, Grandma, but so are you. I doubt whether they have ever encountered anyone quite like you before, if you know what I mean."

"Okay, already, I know exactly vaht you mean, and I know that you mean it lovingly." She paused for a moment before continuing. "Drew, darling, I was so proud of you at your graduation. Imagine, my grandson, the captain with a master's degree with straight "A's" yet, and at the top of his class."

"Thank you, Grandma," he replied with genuine humility. "It has been a very difficult three years for all of us, but I am so pleased with how much I've learned and about the exciting years that lay ahead."

"Okay, darling, she replied, making it obvious that she was about to surface what to her was a troubling matter. "Vaht are you Drew; God forbid, a Christian minister, a rabbi in Christian clothing, or vaht —maybe something else that I'm missing?"

Drew who had anticipated such a discussion responded tenderly and without hesitation. "Grandma, I'm a Jew! I will always be a Jew. Nothing can change that, nor would I want to change anything about whom I have always been and who I am."

"Drew, Darling," Grandma Amelia responded thoughtfully. "You seemed so confused when you were a young boy, growing up. I remember the time when you hated everything Jewish---maybe even you hated me, just a little, because I vanted so much to see you brought up Jewish. I'm only asking, Drew, Vaht changed?"

Drew wasn't surprised by the depth of her understanding. "The truth is, Grandma," he slowly formed his reply. "I did rebel against everything and everyone Jewish, especially against my father who I saw as a villain of sorts who had created what to me was a terrible situation. But through all of this, never for a minute did I stop loving any of my family---especially you Grandma. I suppose it was just a question of me growing up and finally getting to know God."

"Last night," Drew continued, "I was ordained as a minister of God's Word—His Word, as it is understood by you and all Jews, but even more as it is also understood by Christians. Jews and Christians all believe in the same God, the Lord God of Abraham, Isaac and Jacob, the Lord God of Israel."

"That's not the whole story Drew!" she relied challengingly. "Vaht about this Jesus thing? Aren't you all putting Him in the place of God—the one God who is indivisible and cannot take on human flesh?"

"Grandma," he replied with deep conviction, "All your life you have been answering your own question every time you said the Sh'ma: 'Hear O Israel the Lord your God the Lord is *One*.' The Hebrew word for 'one' used here is echad which means here, and elsewhere in the Tenach, a unity that allows a plurality."

"Nuuu, so stop being so intelligent and kindly tell me exactly vaht that means Mr. Master's Degree!"

He smiled at his success in having led her to this point. "Let me give you one of the many examples from the Torah," he began. "Remember the verse that speaks to marriage when a man and a woman will become *One* flesh. Just like in the Sh'ma, the Hebrew word for 'one' used here is echad." He paused for just a moment collecting his thoughts before he got to his main point. "Grandma, Jesus, who believing Jews know by His Hebrew name, Yeshua, is not something outside of God but rather at one with God the father and God the Holy Spirit. Christianity is not a separate or new religion; rather, it is the *fulfillment* of Judaism. Yeshua was and is the expected Jewish Messiah. Most Jews miss this, but Grandma, I know with all my heart that this is the truth."

"So okay, already," she replied softly and without apparent objection. "This is all too much for me to take in much less understand right now. So," she continued, "I have just one more question for you right now. "How am I to refer to you when I tell all my friends about you and vaht you have become? Again, are you a Christian minister? A rabbi? Or something else?"

Drew smiled broadly. "I'll tell you what, Grandma, how about 'my grandson the Christian Rabbi Air Force Chaplain Captain?'"

She smiled broadly in kind. "Nuuu, maybe it would be better for all concerned, if you know vaht I mean, if I just refer to you as "my grandson, the rabbi!"

***

That evening, at Carla's insistence, she, Grandma Amelia, and the two children went by taxi to nearby SeaTac Airport while Drew drove his parents there in their antique compact Chevrolet.

Grandma Amelia, who had clung to the very last moment of her wonderful visit, until it was time to board her flight to New York, scooped Drew, Carla and her two great granddaughters up in one all encompassing embrace. Through her joyful tears she pronounced. "Drew, darling, you have such a beautiful family—and to tell you the truth, the girls look a lot more like their mother than they do me! I love you all so very much!" With that, not in the slightest way showing her eighty years, she turned and walked smartly into the jet way.

Chapter Twenty Two

Jerusalem
April, 14 Nissan, A.D. 30

"What a breath taking view!" Matthias observed as he sat down with Kefa on a wooden bench overlooking the Temple Mount from their elevated vantage point on the Mount of Olives across the Kidron Valley. "How awesome it is that the King of the Universe dwells in the heart of this place!"

"Indeed, it is more than we can fully comprehend, but equally mind boggling is that our Master, Yeshua who dwells here *among us* this very day is the only begotten Son of the Almighty—our promised *Mashiach*!"

Matthias sighed. "It seems like the great prophecies of the Tenach and the sacred scrolls of our sect are unmistakably unfolding before our very eyes so quickly that we can't even begin to fully understand."

"Yes, my dear brother," Kefa replied. "We are greatly privileged to live in this place at such a momentous time as this. In fact, this Pesach that we will celebrate this evening will surely be long remembered by all future generations. I so wish it were possible for you to attend the Master's Seder in the upper room that has been prepared, but He has, for His own reasons restricted his guests to just us twelve."

"Don't trouble yourself, my brother," Matthias replied reassuringly. "Who am I to question such a thing? Please believe that I rejoice in simply being here in the city of Jerusalem with Him and you all at this amazing time."

"My brother," Kefa continued, "if you have no other plans, Judah, one of the Master's four brothers, will be hosting a family Seder at his home in the walled city this evening and he asked me to convey his very warm invitation for you to join with him and others of the Master's family who have come from Nazareth to celebrate this feast. Yeshua's earthly parents, Yosef and Miriam will be there, as will his other brothers, Ya'akov, and Simon, and at least two of His sisters and all of their families.[46] It should be a wonderful and most memorable occasion!"

"I would be so honored to attend, "Matthias replied humbly, "but I would by no means want to intrude on such a private occasion---."

"You would in no way be intruding!" Kefa insisted. "The fact is, we are all one great family with the Master as its head. I can assure you, you would be the one who brought honor to those who shared your presence."

"Then, by all means, I gratefully accept!" Matthias replied with excited anticipation. "I only regret that Dory can't be with me for this very special occasion."

***

The family gathering around Judah's table had been everything Matthias had anticipated and more. The meal of roast lamb following the traditional liturgical celebration of the Jews' miraculous escape from bondage in Egypt was indeed memorable, but as the after dinner conversation continued, he could sense that Ya'akov, the blood brother of Yeshua, was drifting away significantly from the rest of the family's acceptance of Yeshua's messianic claims.

"To tell you the truth," Ya'akov announced with some hostility, "I think our dear brother has lost his mind. He may have delusions of grandeur, but to wave them in the face of the entire city is nothing less than to invite disaster. I just don't understand how he can be taking every opportunity to all who will listen to proclaim that he is the *Mashiach*—the promised one—the Son of God!"

"Perhaps, my son," his mother Miriam interrupted," He is proclaiming these things because they are true!"

"I'm sorry, my dear mother," Ya'akov replied sardonically, "but I just don't accept these outrageous claims. If all of you loved this dear man as I do you wouldn't be sitting here doing nothing while he sealed his fate? Don't you realize that he surely will be severely punished for what he has already said and done?"

"What's so terrible about proclaiming the truth?" Judah replied.

"How can you all be so blind?" Ya'akov exclaimed. "On Monday he literally attacked the money changers in the Temple to say nothing of his bold messianic claims to those in authority.[47] Then there was Tuesday when He spent the day preaching about the city in parables that pointed to himself as being the chosen one—even suggesting that he was one with God himself!" He sighed before sarcastically concluding his outburst. "At least he had the good sense to take Wednesday off from this outrageous nonsense."

It was now Yosef, Yeshua's earthly father who spoke as the impromptu spokesman for the entire family who unanimously stood in opposition to Ya'akov's rejection of Yeshua's messianic claims. "Even as we all deeply consider these momentous events, even now, our blessed, Yeshua, is with his twelve disciples in an upper room on Mount Zion. I know that I know in my heart of hearts—tonight is the beginning of His earthly end. Yet we are not to be troubled because a great victory will soon manifest itself in our presence."

Matthias who had, up to now, remained a silent guest throughout the already long evening finally spoke, and all of them listened with rapt attention. "I have had the honor of walking close by your son and brother since the very day He was immersed by Yochanan the Baptizer. I witnessed many of His almost countess miracles: how He fed the multitudes, raised the dead, drove out demons, healed the sick, and walked upon the water—and oh, so much more. I have listened to His teachings and heard His claims. I have looked into His eyes and seen the depth of His soul." He paused for a moment, and then continued, addressing Ya'akov directly. "I can tell you my brother! This man Yeshua is indeed exactly who and what He claims to be. He is the *Mashiach*! The Son of God! And, once more He is one with God and the Holy Spirit just as it has long been written in our sacred scrolls."

Ya'akov responded with skeptical interest. "Just exactly what are you talking about. What is it about the scrolls that make you believe they are speaking about Yeshua?"

"For starters," Matthias replied, "there are many references that point to our expectation that the Messiah will come to atone for our sins. This very core Essene expectation of an atoning Messiah has been at the heart of Yeshua's teaching. For example, it is written in our scrolls:

"He will judge me in the justice of his truth, and in his plentiful goodness always atone for my sins; in his justice he will cleanse me from the uncleanness of the human being, and from the sin of the sons of man, so that I can extol God for his justice and the highest for his majesty." [48]

"While for now it must remain a matter of faith," Matthias continued, "I know with assurance that Yeshua is on the very brink of fulfilling this prophecy in a way none of us can yet understand. He will indeed atone for all of our sins! Believe me dear ones, soon we will see this wonder of wonders revealed in our presence and what we see will be both terrible and wonderful."

Matthias paused for a moment, noticing that all present hung on his every word. "Then also," he continued, "It is frequently written in our scrolls that the *Mashiach* will also be the very Son of God who is descended directly from the line of King David. For example, in one place we read:

"And *Yahweh* declares to you that he will build you a house. I will raise up your seed after you and establish the throne of his kingdom forever. I will be a father to him and he will be a son to me. This refers to the branch of David who will rise with the Interpreter of the law who will rise up in Zion in the last days---."[49]

He then turned and spoke directly to Yosef and Miriam who were seated at the head of the very large table. "And you, Miriam and Yosef, His physical mother and appointed father, I am told that you both are descended directly from King David?"

"You speak the truth, my son." Yosef responded for the two of them.

Matthias continued, "And finally, our scrolls speak repeatedly that the *Mashiach* will appear imminently and then again at the end of days, following several clear signs, many of which have already appeared before us. Surely, these all point to Yeshua who has already come and who will come again. For example a dream of one of our elders is recorded in the scrolls that speaks beautifully to both of these comings of the *Mashiach* who is referred to as a lamb—indeed an unblemished lamb:

"And they were startled and shaking in front of him. And they shouted to the lamb, which was its second, which was in their midst: We are unable to be in front of the Lord. Then the lamb who led them turned, and climbed for a second time to the top of that rock and came to the flock and found most of them blind and astray. When they saw him they began to get alarmed in front of him, trying to return to their pens. The lamb took other lambs with him and came to the flock. --- I continued seeing this dream until the lamb turned into a man, built a Tabernacle for the Lord of the flock and took all the flock to the Tabernacle. ---.'" [50]

When he had finished, there was a time of complete silence that was finally broken by Ya'akov. "I truly do thank you Matthias, and I would genuinely like to believe all that you have said about my brother, Yeshua, and arrive at the same conclusions you have reached. However, try as I may I simply can't embrace the idea that the very human brother with whom I tussled and shared a bed—this very dear and wonderful man who he grew up to be---. I'm so sorry, but I can't find it in my heart that he has somehow been the Messiah in waiting, the chosen one of God, much less one with God Himself!" As he concluded, his earlier hostility had left and he quietly began to weep.

Matthias rose from the place where he had been seated and went to comfort Ya'akov, placing an arm around his shoulders. "Fear not, my brother, surely the wonderful truth will soon be revealed to you."

***

Matthias was awakened, from a fitful sleep by the shrill and alarmed voice of Kefa as he stormed into Judah's house and shouted to awaken those who had remained after the post Seder discussions that had continued long into the night.

"Matthias!" he cried out in anguish. "Where are you?"

"I'm right here, my brother, Matthias replied as a deep foreboding, and inner turmoil brought him immediately to full wakefulness. "What's happened?"

Kefa, weeping openly, struggled to maintain his composure as he spoke.

By now the others who had remained in the house had gathered around and listened intently to Kefa's sad and alarmed report: "Judah! It was Judah Iscariot that snake who betrayed Him!" Kefa exclaimed angrily. "Even the Master Himself said it would have been better if he had never been born!"

"Calm down, Kefa," Matthias tried to relieve at least some of his brother's pent up anger and outrage. "Tell us— *what happened?*"

"Well you all know that the Master has been intimating recently that He would become the perfect sacrifice for us all! Well, my brothers, it seems the time for this is at hand."

"How do you know this?" Matthias replied anxiously.

"To begin with, during our Seder, Yeshua made it clear that He would be betrayed that very evening and it would be done so by Judah. I can tell you all," he continued, his voice trembling with emotion. "Later, the Master, who took me and the two sons of Zebedee with Him, went to Gethsemane to pray. As we slept while the Master prayed, Judah came with some soldiers." He paused, struggling to continue.

"Yes, go on!" Matthias tried to comfort him. "What happened?"

"I awoke and then saw with my own eyes and heard it with my own ears," Kefa continued his report. "Judah pointed to Yeshua, betraying Him, and the soldiers seized Him and took Him before Caiaphas: the High priest, and the elders who were assembled.

Then Caiaphas confronted the Master directly saying: "I charge you under oath by the living God: Tell us if you are the *Mashiach*, the Son of God." The Master replied to him and the elders: "Yes, it is as you say, but I say to all of you: In the future you will see the Son of Man sitting at the right hand of the Mighty One and coming on the clouds of heaven."[51]

"How did Caiaphas react to the Master's claim?" Matthias asked, already knowing the answer.

Kefa relied with profound sadness. "Caiaphas tore his clothes and said, 'He has spoken blasphemy! Why do we need any more witnesses? Look, now you have heard the blasphemy. What do you think?'" And, Kefa concluded, his voice now only a whisper, "they pronounced that 'He is worthy of death!'"

"But surely there will be a trial before the Sanhedrin where He will have an opportunity to defend Himself?" Matthias interjected.

"I fear not," Kefa replied. "Caiaphas has already sealed the Master's fate. Early this morning, all the chief priests and the elders of the people came to the decision to put Him to death. They bound him, led him away and handed him over to Pilate, the governor. He is in the governor's mansion, awaiting some sort of decision as I speak. This is why I have hurried here to tell all of you what has happened so that you might be able to come with me to the Master's side and pray."

An hour later, as they stood outside of the governor's mansion, Kefa, again openly weeping, took Matthias aside, away from the large crowd that had begun to gather. "Matthias, my brother," he agonized between his soul deep sobs. "I have sinned beyond belief and I must confess what I have done and seek forgiveness."

"Nothing, absolutely nothing you may have done can be beyond the Master's forgiveness." Matthias comforted his dear brother.

"Matthias, even before I did so the Master told me that I would."

"What, Kefa? What did you do?"

Kefa looked towards the heavens and cried out. "My Lord and my God forgive me in the name of your Son Yeshua—just like He said I would, before the sun rose, I denied Him three times."[52]

Chapter Twenty Three

McChord Air Force Base, Washington
June, 1967

Chaplain Captain Andrew Scott Sterling warmly greeted the last of the worshipers who had attended the packed eleven o'clock service as he waited with anticipation for what had become his weekly critique by Carla, and more importantly Sheldon Thurman who had been his mentor and immediate supervisor during his initial assignment to the McChord Chapel team.

"That was beautiful, darling," Carla offered with a hug and perfunctory kiss. "Your message on the centrality of the cross is among your very best."

"Spoken like an adoring wife!" Sheldon observed as he joined the two of them and shook Drew's hand warmly. "You know, Chaplain Sterling, you have truly become the star of our preaching team during the nearly four years you've been with us."

"You are far too kind, Boss," Drew replied with genuine humility. "But if I've succeeded it is only because I've had a wonderful teacher."

Sheldon turning very serious replied, "Drew, you are a natural with a brilliant future. I've known that from the very beginning and it's been my great honor and privilege to get you pointed in the right direction by teaching you what little I know."

"Enough of the mutual flattery, already, gentlemen," Carla intervened. "Sheldon, what say you join us at the club for brunch—our treat?"

***

"How were the girls?" Carla inquired as she paid Cindy, the Sterling's regular Sunday morning baby sitter, then warmly kissed, hugged and released their third daughter, three year old Rachel, who now rushed to join her father and sisters in the Sterling's living room.

"Perfect little angels as usual," Cindy replied. "It's so sweet to watch Chaplain Sterling with his girls," Cindy observed as she pointed towards the three of them, Dory, Bekah and Rachel who, in what had become a Sunday afternoon ritual, were now rushing to fill their father's lap as soon as he had settled into his delightfully comfortable reclining leather chair. "I just love my weekly routine of attending the early service, then hurrying here to take over your girls so you can attend the eleven o'clock. It's like I've become part of your wonderful family." "You have, Cindy!" Carla replied with a gentle kiss on the teenager's cheek. "We love you very much, too."

Then, suddenly, Carla turned more serious as she continued, "I think we all need to be prepared for our time at McChord to end, and soon."

"Have you heard something?" Cindy replied with alarm.

"No, not really," Carla replied, but you know there's a war going on and it's only getting worse—and, don't forget, we've been here almost four years."

***

Late that evening, after he had led his girls in their bedtime prayers, Drew joined Carla in their bedroom, tidying up before calling an end to this typically very busy Sunday. He found her fondly holding the "Class A" uniform jacket he had worn that day and, as usual, hastily hung over the back of a bedroom chair rather than in its proper place in their closet. "My, Darling," Drew pulled her back to the moment from her deep thought, "is something bothering you? You seem a bit pre-occupied?"

"Heavens no!" she protested. "I was just looking at your pretty impressive decorations my dear chaplain. Two Air Force commendation medals for outstanding achievement is quite an accomplishment for a captain with just seven years in the service."

"You had a hand in both of them," Drew observed modestly. "Although, I'm sure you will agree that it was our dear Lord who saved Hank Tyler from going into the drink that scary day in our earlier life at Eglin."

"Of course it was!" Carla protested. "But it was you who He put there to handle the situation, and you did brilliantly! Then, of course, there is the second award for your vacation bible school program that has now been adopted by the entire Defense Department. You are really something else, Chaplain Sterling," she concluded with obvious adoration—"I'm so very proud to be your wife!"

"Carla," he responded in kind, "God put us together for His purpose and He has only just begun to reveal what He has in mind for us. We simply have to do our best to listen for His voice and then to obediently follow Him!"

She knew this was the opening she had been hoping for and she proceeded without hesitation. "Darling, there is a lot more displayed on this uniform than your very impressive medals." She pointed to the silver cross that signified its wearer was a Christian chaplain. Then, struggling to find the right words she continued. "Drew, does this cross really say who *you* are—sure you graduated from a conservative Lutheran Seminary and you're an ordained minister of the gospel—but really Drew, are you a *Lutheran*, or for that matter are you really a Christian?"

Given that he had often flirted with this same battery of soul wrenching questions himself, only each time to promptly turn away from what to him seemed the perpetually unanswerable, he knew exactly where his beloved wife was coming from. "Would you rather I exchanged the cross for a Star of David?" he quipped, trying but failing to keep his response light. "Sure," he continued, "religiously I'm a Christian, and for want of any other denominational choice, by default I must be a Lutheran. After all, I represent both Christ and this particular denomination in the chaplaincy—so, does that answer your questions," he tried unsuccessfully to close the matter.

"Not entirely," she responded, not wanting to let go. "The fact is Drew, you always have been and always will be a Jew, and in my book that is something wonderful! My point is that you're a Jew who happens to believe that Jesus was and is the Messiah that most of your people are still looking for." She now hesitated for just a moment before she came to her central point. "Drew, darling—*I'm* a Gentile Christian! You're a *Jewish* believer and there's no way you are or ever will really be a Lutheran."

"Okay," he responded somewhat defensively. "Given that, according to you, I'm not really a Christian or, God forbid, a Lutheran, and that I'm therefore parading around in my chaplain's suit with the cross under false pretenses, then just what is it that you would have me do—resign my commission and study to become a rabbi, or what?"

She knew exactly how to stimulate then deal with such of her husband's emotion driven protestations. "I was hoping you would ask?" she replied putting her arms around his neck and pulling him close. "The fact is there's a mixed congregation of believing Jews and Gentiles who call themselves "Messianic Jews" that meets in Federal Way every Saturday morning. I've already spoken to their leader who seems very nice and he has urged us to give them a try." Ready for an extended argument she was absolutely taken aback when Drew replied simply and inexplicably:

"Nuu, so vhy not??"

***

Their conversation during the forty-five minute drive south to Federal Way the next Saturday morning was mostly perfunctory. Carla hesitated to put in jeopardy what to her was a major victory. And Drew was deeply lost in thought, struggling with a potpourri of mostly conflicting sets of emotion: anticipation and fear; longing and rejection; sadness and joy—

"Turn left here," Carla directed, calling him back to the moment. "According to the map, it should be right around the corner in the next block."

She spoke first as they shared their first glimpse of the large Four Square Gospel Church that rented its facilities to Congregation Beth Simcha each Saturday. "Look at that parking lot!" she exclaimed. "There must be over one hundred cars—it looks full!"

Both of them were greatly surprised by the apparently large size of the congregation, having assumed that there could only be a very few such "born again" Jews and the odd Gentile who might be inclined to meet together. Now, as Drew took the last available parking place in the very large lot, he looked at his watch and noted they were fifteen minutes early for the eleven o'clock service, and there were already several other cars behind them that would now have to park along the street, a bit farther away from the sanctuary.

Drew's sense of anticipation and excitement grew and his spirit quickened as they stepped out of the car and started to walk, arm in arm, towards the entrance of the quite plain, yet lovely Church. Filled with peace, he found himself yielding to a sense that something very important was about to happen—something life changing in its significance.

Then he saw it. His heart started to race, pounding in his chest. His spirit soared on wings of eagles! He was filled with a strange sense of wonder and overwhelming joy! There, planted in the lovely, lush green lawn in front of the Church, was a simple wrought-iron Star of David. His eyes darted back and forth from this symbol of his long- suppressed, ethnic heritage to the plain Christian cross that rose from the top of the sanctuary. He felt Carla gently pulling at his arm, leading him along to some certain and wonderful destiny that was soon to be fulfilled.

"Shabbat Shalom!" a delightful, Holy Spirit filled sister greeted them exuberantly as they stepped inside the Church. "My name's Rosie," she said, introducing herself. "Welcome to Beth Simcha!" she exclaimed, as she gave Drew a tremendously warm "bear hug" greeting. "Shabbat Shalom, Rosie!" Drew returned her words, using the Hebrew greeting for the first time, only suspecting what it meant. Then, he found himself saying sincerely, "We're Drew and Carla Sterling. It's *good* to be here!"

Carla was on his arm, close enough that he was wonderfully aware that they were indeed one flesh, a Gentile and a Jew, a "one new man" couple joined together for some important purpose that was far beyond his understanding of the moment.

And then, in a flash, the reality of his entire spiritual being came into a new, sharp focus. As he scanned the already crowded, nearly full, large sanctuary for some available seats, his eyes fell upon the simple wooden pulpit. It was covered with a blue-colored altar cloth, upon which was emblazoned a white Star of David. As he looked up from the star to a large Christian cross mounted on the wall behind the pulpit, the incredible significance—the wonderful reality of the moment fell upon him and he began to weep uncontrollably. For the first time in his life he understood precisely *who* and *what* he was, the person God had created him to be, and he rejoiced in this discovery! He was a *Jew* who by His grace had been saved by the shed blood of his Messiah, Jesus Christ, who, he was later to know more intimately as Yeshua. Never, he thought, would he stop praising Him for that wonderful moment and all that was to follow in this, his new walk as a self-acknowledged and self-appreciated Messianic Jew.

***

While it was extremely sweet and fulfilling, however, the Sterling family's wonderful every Saturday walk with Beth Simcha was to be quite short lived. In fact it was on the evening of the sixth such consecutive Saturday that Drew rushed to answer the phone when they returned home after the service. He seemed a bit perplexed when he rejoined Carla and the girls after his brief conversation.

"Who was that?" Carla asked with just a hint of discerned concern.

"It was Sheldon," Drew responded, trying to conceal his own disquietude. "He's invited us to join him at the Club for dinner—he said it was important—can you get Cindy to watch the kids on such short notice?"

***

Sheldon was waiting for them in the foyer of the Club. "Let's begin at the bar," he invited since what I have to share with you calls for a bottle of champagne!"

Drew quickly tried to imagine what occasion his supervisor and best friend could possibly have in mind that was, for him, worthy of such an uncharacteristic celebration. He drew a complete blank. "Yes, Sir!" he replied with a growing dual sense of anticipation and concern. "I assume you're buying?"

They chose a quiet table near the back of the nearly empty lounge and when Sheldon had ceremoniously filled their glasses he got to the purpose at hand. "Well you two, it seems that I have both good and bad news, and I want to begin with the good!" He reached into his pocket and withdrew something that for a moment remained concealed. Instead of handing his gift to Drew, he presented it to Carla announcing with great joy. "Well, Mrs. Sterling, the good news is that you will be pinning these golden oak leaves on Chaplain Major Andrew Scott Sterling's Class A uniform but the bad news is that he won't get to wear them until he is about half way through his next tour of duty. Drew, "he continued with a mixture of excitement and concern. "Both events happened on the same day. The major's list came out this morning and you made it two years below the zone—and, not to put a damper on this of course, personnel came through with your reassignment to Ton Son Nhut Air Base, South Viet Nam. You are to report in sixty days for a thirteen month assignment as deputy base chaplain."

"I have been expecting the assignment!" Drew exclaimed. "But, certainly not the promotion! My goodness, *two* years ahead of my contemporaries? I thought only you did that sort of thing, Chaplain Lieutenant Colonel Thurman."

"It pays to have friends in high places, Drew," Sheldon replied. "Certainly, my friends in the Pentagon had a hand in this, but God has you in mind for some very big things—of this you can be certain."

Chapter Twenty Four

Jerusalem
April, A.D. 30

Kefa, walking arm in arm with Matthias, seemingly to give one another some physical as well as spiritual support, was the first of those closest to the Master to arrive at the home of Judah in the early evening.

"Greetings in the name of Yeshua, our crucified Master!" Judah welcomed the two of them with deep sadness somehow blended with pervasive joy into an unseemly emotional admixture that now shown forth as a reflection from the steady streams of unceasing tears pouring from his deep set, dark brown eyes; the hallmarks of his countenance made weary by the indescribable events of the past nearly seventy two hours. "Where are the others of our brothers who would come?" he inquired somewhat fearfully, as if he alone understood the incredible significance of what had recently occurred in the city.

"Be assured, they are nearby and will be with us soon," Kefa replied tenderly, seeking to give comfort to Yeshua's grieving yet inexplicably rejoicing earthly sibling. "This is the third day we have gathered together here to sit Shiva—nowhere else would seem to be appropriate!"

Before Judah could comment further, as if on cue, there was a loud bustling sound of new arrivals emanating from the entry way. Then, without delay, this ecstatically excited group of Yeshua's chosen disciples (except for Judah Iscariot who was not among them) presented themselves to those already arrived in the adjacent hewn stone salon.

"Welcome my brothers!" Kefa spoke for the rest as he, Matthias and Judah, went from one to another of the new arrivals greeting each of them with a holy kiss.

Then, unable to further contain himself until their mutual greetings were concluded, Mattityahu, nearly overcome with joy proclaimed in a loud voice. "Yeshua is risen from the dead! He appeared to both Philip and me this afternoon when we were walking together near the tomb. I truly did not believe this testimony when I heard it spoken by Miriam from Magdala and the other Miriam this morning, but I certainly believe what I have seen with my own eyes and heard with my own ears!"

"What Mattityahu has spoken is God's truth!" Philip exclaimed his agreement. "I too saw the risen Master and heard His voice! Furthermore, He told us to tell all of you to go at once to the Galilee where He would appear to you as well!"[53]

"Outrageous!" pronounced the highly agitated voice of an up to now unnoticed new arrival, who had entered the salon from an adjacent sleeping room. "Impossible! Nonsense! Vicious lies!" screamed Ya'akov, the eldest of Yeshua's earthly siblings. "What you are saying is nonsense! Sheer nonsense! Yeshua was my blood brother! I ate with him, fought with him, played with him—how can all of you be so greatly misled? Yeshua was a *man*, just like you and just like me! By no means was he one with God!" He paused for a moment sighing deeply in his own profound disbelief and frustration before he concluded his outburst. "I can't remain here with you any longer Judah.

How can I give and get comfort from you and these other blind idiots who would dare call a flesh and bones man their risen God?" With that, Ya'akov left their presence, slamming the heavy wooden door behind him.[54]

The seemingly interminable silence following Ya'akov's dramatic departure was finally broken by Andrew, the brother of Kefa. "Perhaps we *have* been misled," he suggested tentatively. "After all, we have heard only the second hand testimony of two emotional women and two of our own brothers." Then, he turned to directly confront the two who had given their testimony who now, as if defensively, stood huddled close together.

"Mattityahu and Philip, are you absolutely certain you have spoken the truth?"

The two who had been challenged began to weep, humbled by the disbelief of their brothers. Mattityahu, who had collected himself, was just beginning to utter a response, when suddenly the room was filled with a bright, near blinding light and the walls shook as if in resonance with a chorus of many silver trumpets. Then, miraculously before Mattiyahu could begin to speak, Yeshua Himself stood among them and quietly announced His presence: "Peace be with you!" All who were present were amazed and stunned by what they had just seen and heard.

Then, after Yeshua had spoken, He unabashedly displayed His pierced hands and punctured side for all of them to examine so that none who were present could later deny the truth of what they had witnessed.

As they began to mentally process the enormous miracle of the resurrected Yeshua, who now stood before them, they were filled with indescribable joy.

Then, instantly, they all grew absolutely silent as Yeshua once again began to speak: "Peace be with you! As the Father has sent me, I am sending you." And with that He breathed on them and said, "Receive the Holy Spirit. If you forgive anyone his sins, they are forgiven; if you do not forgive them, they are not forgiven"[55]

Yeshua then vanished from their presence just as suddenly as he had appeared.

When He was no longer among them, thrilled beyond their ability to understand much of the incredible significance of what had happened that day, they prayed and shared together long into the night until finally, in the wee hours of the morning they had all, in their sheer exhaustion, finally fallen asleep on floor mats scattered throughout the stone walled dwelling.

However, their rest was to be short lived owing to the just after dawn reappearance of Ya'akov who entered his younger brother's house just as noisily as he had departed only a few hours earlier. "Wake up my brothers!" he shouted loudly as he went from room to room stirring each of them to wakefulness, not growing silent until they had all sleepily assembled in the salon.

"Forgive me, my brothers! You were so *right* and I was so *wrong*!" Ya'akov proclaimed as one who had just re-discovered an indescribable treasure that at first he had tragically overlooked. "*Please*, my brothers," he now pleaded. "Hear my confession and accept my apology!"

"What confession?" Kefa asked, rubbing the sleep from his weary eyes.

"As you know," Ya'akov began, speaking with awe and humility in a barely discernable whisper: "I was with you and my brother when we shared bread and wine together at the Pesach Seder in the upper room. Little did we realize then that this was to be His last supper with us. I can tell you this," he went on, beginning to weep as he spoke, "I did not believe what He said then and I did not believe it last night when I left you all in anger—I did not even begin to believe any of His claims, much less that the bread and wine we then shared by His hand were to become perpetual symbols of his divinity. My God and my Lord—I was in such grave error."

As Kefa embraced Ya'akov comfortingly he asked: "My dear brother, what happened to so abruptly change your understanding?"

Ya'akov tearfully poured out his reply: "You may recall that I told Yeshua at our last supper together that I would not eat bread again until I saw that He had risen from the dead. Well, last night after I had so rudely left all of you, I went to the Garden of Gethsemane to collect my thoughts and to pray. I did so for a time, but then I soon fell asleep for I don't know how long." He paused for a moment trying to overcome the emotion that had rendered his voice an almost indiscernible trembling whisper. "Then," he finally went on, "I was awakened with a gentle kiss on my cheek. I awoke, and it was Yeshua, my brother, our risen Lord and God who stood before me. He had with him a loaf of bread which He blessed and then broke. He gave me a piece, saying: "My brother, eat your bread, for the Son of Man is risen from among them that sleep."[56]

Later that morning, after they had prayed together, the eleven apostles, with one accord, elected Ya'akov, the brother of Yeshua as the first leader of their new movement which was soon to become known as "The Way," and/or "the Nazarenes."[57]

***

Forty days later, the eleven of them stood, in awestruck silence on the Mount of Olives, each of them totally overcome by the utterly amazing miracles they had individually and collectively witnessed since their beloved Master had risen from the dead, and by what had just now taken place before their very eyes. This same risen Yeshua who had ministered to each of them and appeared to more than five hundred other witnesses—this same risen Yeshua who had proclaimed who He was and why He had come as God incarnate to be sacrificed upon a cross for the salvation of all who would believe—this same risen Yeshua who had promised to come again to this very place and then reign as King from Mount Zion for one thousand years—

This same risen Yeshua had been taken up into heaven while they had watched this indescribably glorious event with their very own eyes until a cloud finally hid their risen Lord from their sight.[58] Each of those who were closest to Him remained transfixed on the hallowed ground where they stood, unable to move, unable to speak for what seemed to be an interminable cessation of time and space until at last, as they were looking intently up into the sky where He had gone, suddenly two men dressed in white stood beside them. "Men of Galilee," they said, "why do you stand here looking into the sky? This same Yeshua, who has been taken from you into heaven, will come back in the same way you have seen him go into heaven." [59]

***

The thick living carpet of red poppies covering the hills of Bashan were a poignant reminder to Matthias of the recently shed blood of His Master as he made his way up the last of the steep climb to Hippos. Tears of remembrance and a new and even deeper commitment than he had earlier known, provided him with a perfect emotional backdrop for what lay immediately ahead at the end of his current steep upward trek. So very much had transpired during these momentous three weeks since he had last seen Dory, who after Yeshua, was the one great love of his life. "How can I begin to share with her and these other precious ones the incredible things I have witnessed with my own eyes?" he silently challenged himself as he reached the beginnings of the city and increased his pace to a slow run as he saw just ahead the basalt stone dwelling where Dory lived with her family.

***

"Matthias, my darling," Dory could hardly contain herself as they walked arm in arm towards the setting sun and a private place at the edge or the city overlooking the Lake. "I know you have things to share with me that you've held back from the others."

"Indeed, I do," he replied as he took her into his arms and they tenderly embraced. Then, after they had sat down, side by side on a large basalt outcropping overlooking the Lake, he continued. "Our brothers from Kursi must have already shared with your community many of the amazing, incredibly glorious events of recent days?" he ventured tentatively.

"Oh yes, they have!" she replied excitedly. "But, you, Matthias: you were there and saw these things personally: the crucifixion, burial, resurrection and then even His glorious ascension into heaven. You must share every detail with us--- all that you can remember."

"Of course I will, darling." He answered with deep commitment. "It is my destiny to spend the rest of my life sharing these very God ordained occurrences that I have seen and heard." He paused for a moment to properly set the stage for what was his planned central purpose of their evening stroll. "But, before I begin this greater work, there are other more immediate things I'd like to share."

She made a vain effort to control her own excited anticipation as she replied: "And I long to hear *everything* my darling."

"There are two important matters," he continued, suddenly turning very serious and carefully choosing his words. "At first, these may seem unrelated but indeed they are very much intertwined." She was somewhat taken aback by his sudden serious tone as she now hung on his every word.

"Have you heard about the Nazarene Congregation of believers on Mount Zion that began under Ya'akov's leadership two weeks ago?" he asked.

"Oh yes, our brothers at Kursi are very excited about this and describe it as the 'Mother Congregation' of what will grow into the universal Body of all those who follow Yeshua."

He was greatly heartened by the depth of her understanding of the recent profound events and their implications. "Then, surely you must also have heard that Judah Iscariot, the one who betrayed the Master, suffered a terrible death, leaving only eleven where twelve had been ordained?"

"Yes," she replied, wiping away the beginnings of her tears. "I was so deeply saddened to hear of such a terrible betrayal."

"Then," he probed, "perhaps you have also heard that the eleven who remained believe that they were guided by the Holy Spirit of God to elect another to take Judah's place among them?"

"Nooo," she hesitated, beginning to suspect what he was about to reveal. "I have heard nothing of this."

Sensing no other way to share the momentous news with the woman he loved, he spoke simply and unaffectedly in little more than a humble whisper. "They elected *me*, Dory. Although I am in no way worthy, they chose me to walk among those who were closest to the Master."

She was thrilled to the depths of her soul by what she had just heard. She burst into tears of joy as she embraced this dear man of God whom she had come to love as she loved none other than Yeshua Himself. "None of us are worthy, Matthias! Only He is worthy! Ya'akov and the eleven have chosen well!"

After their initial rejoicing, he managed to continue. "And there is more!" he added. "Much more!" Before He ascended into heaven, Yeshua instructed us to make disciples of all people everywhere, making it clear that while He had come first to the Jews He had by all means also come to save the Gentiles."

"I had heard none of this either!" Dory replied excitedly. "But of course, He had already shown us of His great love when He healed us, fed us and included us in His earthly teachings."

"Well," Matthias went on, "Ya'akov and the eleven who chose me to join them, were mindful of my seemingly special calling and love for the non-Jews of the Decapolis and they appointed me with the primary mission of bringing the Gospel of Yeshua first to the entire region of the Decapolis, and then as far and as wide beyond as I may be led."

"I am so thrilled for you, my darling!" she replied from the depths of her love filled heart. "Our heavenly Father has chosen you to do very great and wonderful things for Him!"

"No Dory," he answered, again turning very serious in tone. "You haven't understood these things fully. It is not I alone, but rather the *two* of us who have been called—I am to be the first of perhaps many Jewish disciples to the Gentiles and, if you will do me the great honor, my darling, you will stand by my side as my wife!"

Chapter Twenty Five

Ramstein Air Base, Germany
December 22, 1978

Chaplain Colonel Andrew Scott Sterling tried without success not to speculate about the *real* purpose of Sheldon's sudden visit to Headquarters United States Air Force Europe, announced only one day before his imminent arrival on this very cold winter morning. Perhaps he is just feeling his oats and enjoying the international travel perks of his lofty new position as Deputy Chief of Chaplains, he speculated quietly as twin engine C-20B Gulfstream III executive jet came into sight taxiing toward the V.I.P. ramp adjacent to Ramstein Base Operations.

Drew fought back a tear of joyful pride over the meteoric rise of his beloved supervisor and dearest friend as he caught sight of the single silver star prominently displayed above the door signifying the rank of its senior passenger. The sleek craft came to an abrupt halt in front of him and the ground crew hurried to position a portable jetway so that Chaplain Brigadier General Sheldon Thurman could place his feet upon the snow covered European tarmac without undue delay.

"Welcome to Germany, *General* Thurman!" Drew saluted smartly as he greeted the newly appointed Deputy Chief of Chaplains.

Sheldon returned Drew's salute and then gave him an uncharacteristically unmilitary hug. "Where else would I journey on my first official field visit as Deputy Chief?" he replied. "Who could be more important for me to call upon than the USAFE Command Chaplain, even though he is the youngest bird colonel in the history of the chaplaincy?"

"I would have chosen Hawaii over Germany," Drew offered. "In case you hadn't noticed, General, it gets cold around here this time of year!"

Sheldon continued to lay the groundwork behind his visit after the two of them entered the waiting staff car and the driver began the short drive to the Sterling's on base family quarters. "The fact is, I have been anticipating this visit for several years, ever since the day you made the profound decision to become an Air force Chaplain. I knew then as I know now that the Lord has much planned for your life—I'm really looking forward to some serious late evening discussion with you and Carla."

Carla, with Bekah and Rachel by her side waiting their respective turns, greeted their dearly loved guest with warm welcoming hugs at the front door of their quarters.

"Where's Dory?" Sheldon inquired with just a hint of concern.

"Have you forgotten—our eldest child is a freshman at the University of Maryland, Munich?" Carla replied teasingly.

"Of course not!" Sheldon replied in kind. "I just assumed she'd be home for the holidays and I was so looking forward to seeing my eldest Goddaughter."

"Not until tomorrow evening, I'm sorry to say." Drew replied. "She'll be taking her last final today. But, you'll see her for dinner tomorrow evening."

"It's not to be," Sheldon spoke, reflecting his genuine disappointment. "I've got to get back to Washington before the holiday break and I'll be taking off first thing in the morning."

Drew did his best to shrug off the obviously planned brevity of Sheldon's unexpected visit along with its uncharacteristic suddenness. "Well, at least we'll have time for a nice evening together," he commented, now becoming anxious to discover Sheldon's real purpose for having made this long journey.

This natural amphitheater on Mount Ermos ("The Mount of the Beatitudes") provides perfect acoustics enabling a normal volume voice spoken at its apex to be heard clearly throughout its very large extended wide area.

Ermos Cave at the base of the Mount of Beatitudes. Traditionally, this is one of the places to where Yeshua fled to get away from the crowds that followed Him.

A view from Ermos Cave looking out over the Sea of Galilee.

The pathway at Kursi leading from the ruins of the 5th Century Byzantine Church on the site to the first century Messianic Jewish chapel, just below the cave where the miracle of the swine was performed by Yeshua.

A retaining wall just below the chapel at Kursi. Although badly worn, the distinctly Nazarene Jewish symbols of the fish, menorah and "shoot" are still visible, offering a strong inference that this site was marked by very early Jewish believers.

The monument at Tel Hadar erected by the Israeli Government in 1999 marking the site of the "second feeding" of some 4000 mostly pagan/gentiles (Mark 8:1-10)

The road leading to the State Park at Susitta/Hippos.

"Black-eyed Susans" decorating the slopes of Hippos Mountain.

ew from the Gate to Hippos, looking back toward the arking area far below.

View from the poppy decorated top of the central apse of the Northwest Church at Hippos. Tiberias can be seen in the background on the other side of the Lake.

pillar from the Hellenistic Temple adjacent to the orthwest Church at Hippos, with the very early, perhaps st century, famous Christian anagram translated from e Greek as "Jesus Christ, Son of God, Savior."

A remnant of the First Century floor of what was apparently a "public meeting place" is clearly visible in this view of the 2003 Northwest Church exploratory trench.

A mosaic floor inscription in the floor of the Northwest Church at Hippos that is translated: "Heliodora offered half of the nomisma for the costs of the mosaic" The Byzantine monetary system was based on the solidus (nomisma in Greek), a coin of pure gold weighing 4.5 grams that was introduced by Constantine I in 309.

What appears to be a very early baptismal for the immersion of adults Found in the central ruins of Bet She'an, one of the Decapolis cities. The cross marking the mikvah-like facility is apparently original and is not of a typical Byzantine design, suggesting that this **may** have been a pre-Pauline site.

The ruins of what is obviously a very early church apse located at Bet She'an, adjacent to the cross marked "Adult baptismal" An official of the State Park at the site disclaimed that there was anything "Christian". to be found outside of a Byzantine Church that is outside the grounds of the main park.

A telephoto view of Pella, taken from near the Israeli/Jordanian international border. Pella, the place of refuge where the Jews fled in 70 AD was located on top of this very large "Tel" in modern-day Jordan.

***

Late that evening, after Carla had sensitively left them alone, the two of them basked in the joy of their time together in front of the remaining glowing embers of the fireplace and Sheldon finally got around to the central purpose of his visit.

"Drew, I have quite a potpourri of news to share with you—matters that were better dealt with face to face, and that's why I'm here."

Drew listened with rapt attention as he continued. "First, the really sad news, that is not yet for public release. As you know, General Haggerty's term as Chief of Chaplains has almost another two years to go, but I'm sad to report that he has just recently been diagnosed with a rapidly growing malignant brain tumor and he will be medically retired as of January first. The fact is he isn't expected to live more than another few weeks."

"Dear Lord!" Drew exclaimed in genuine shock. "He is such a dear man of God!"

"Well then," Sheldon continued. "Wait until you've heard the rest." He paused for a few moments, looking for some self-effacing way to continue. "Drew, the Chief of Staff called me in yesterday morning to tell me I will be the new Chief of Chaplains. This will be effective upon Chaplain Haggerty's retirement. He also told me that I'm being recommended for promotion to Major General."

"Wow!" Drew exclaimed, both saddened and thrilled at this totally unexpected turn of events. "I'm so sorry about Chaplain Haggerty, but so pleased that you'll soon be Chief."

Sheldon suddenly turned very serious and focused. "Drew, let me get to the real point of my visit. Obviously, as the new Chief of Chaplains, I will need a Deputy." He paused for a moment to let his words lay a thoughtful foundation for what was to follow. "Of course, you must understand that there are several excellent potential candidates for this position, all of them quite senior to yourself."

Drew thought he sensed where Sheldon was going—trying to let him down easy so that he wouldn't be overly disappointed at his non-selection for this general officer position. "Sheldon," he replied thoughtfully, "I'm the most junior colonel in the chaplaincy and woefully inexperienced compared to the rest."

"You're right on the first point, but very wrong on the second." Sheldon protested. "You may be the most junior colonel, but you are also the most decorated chaplain in the Air Force. Have you already forgotten the Air Force Cross you picked up for heroism in Viet Nam? Besides that, you have already been a huge success here in Europe! Anyway, none of this really matters. What does matter is that you are my personal choice for the position— no one else comes close!"

Drew was stunned by Sheldon's announcement and it took him several moments before he could respond. "I couldn't be more thrilled or flattered," he finally replied, "but wouldn't I be a difficult if not an impossible sell to the Chief of Staff?"

"I'll tell you Drew," Sheldon responded with fatherly like pride. "You've made every one of your field grade promotions significantly ahead of your contemporaries and there certainly isn't any reason in the world why this should stop now!

Drew," he continued resolutely, "If that was all there were to this I wouldn't be here. I simply would have recommended you for promotion to the Chief of Staff face to face and then fought like crazy for his approval— which, by the way, I'm certain he would have eventually granted. There's more than that to this, Drew---."

"And what might that be?" Drew replied, deeply perplexed.

"Drew, we've been very close *brothers* for a long time. Remember me? I'm the one who led you into the Kingdom. I won't pull any punches here. There are some things I need to know about your walk with the Lord *before* I recommend you to be my deputy."

Drew tried to lighten up the very apparent and sudden tension emanating from his dearest friend now turned unexpected inquisitor. "Well," he joshed, "I don't smoke, but I do drink occasionally and I am the husband of just one wife. What else could possibly be troubling you?"

"Look around the room Drew!" he began almost accusingly, pointing sweepingly around the well appointed living room. "Are you not the USAFE Chief of Chaplains and is this not Christmas week? Do you happen to see anything missing from what would normally be expected in the home of the senior *Christian* chaplain in Europe?"

"Ahhh!" Drew replied, still trying to lighten the tension. "You must be making reference to the absence of a well decorated pagan fertility symbol known as a Christmas tree? We haven't had one in our home for the past two years. The fact is the Easter bunny doesn't do much for us either, but we do celebrate and rejoice in the advent and resurrection of our Lord with all of our hearts and souls. Does this trouble you?"

"It's not just the absence of a Christmas tree, Drew!" Sheldon replied, his frustration becoming more apparent. "This is only symptomatic of what I've come to see as a more troubling underlying situation. Drew, tell me! Just how serious is this Messianic Jewish thing of yours? Has something happened to your faith! Has anything changed about where you stand with the Lord and with the Church?"

Drew was genuinely shocked at the depth of his dear friend's misunderstanding. "Sheldon," he began, "I discovered the Jewish roots of my faith two years ago—I'm a Messianic Jew, an ethnic Jew who believes in Jesus who I think of by his Jewish name, Yeshua."

"What about the Church!" Sheldon replied with deep concern. "You were educated in a conservative Lutheran Seminary and ordained as a Lutheran. Have you given up on all this?"

"Of course not!" Drew replied with obvious deep conviction. "Discovering who and what I am has only deepened my faith in Yeshua, the Jewish Messiah. Sheldon, you must understand that the first church was almost entirely Jewish and had no special denominational label like 'Lutheran.' They were mostly just Jews who, like me, believed Yeshua was the Messiah and they updated their Jewish worship in the light of the Messiah having come."

"Beginning in the first century there has been a small number of ethnic Jews, like me, who have believed in Yeshua, but regrettably, most of them were taught by non-Jewish believers that they too had to become denominational Gentile-like Christians and sever their connections with their Jewish heritage. Much of this came to a head in 1866 when the Hebrew Christian Alliance was formed in England and then later when the International Hebrew Christian Alliance was formed in 1925. Even then, Jews who sought salvation in Yeshua, Jesus Christ, were still required to join denominational Christian Churches and to renounce their Jewish-ness."

"All of this is very interesting, Drew," Sheldon interrupted, "but you still haven't answered my question. Are you still a *Lutheran*?"

"Let me continue with my brief personal history lesson," Drew replied warmly and openly. "The fact is, I never was a Lutheran anymore than, obviously, I was ever a *Gentile* Christian."

"When I first became a believer that day at McChord Chapel by coming forward and confessing my faith in your presence," Drew continued with deep conviction, "admittedly I was confused about just who and what I was and what if anything new I had become. Praise God, for the past two years I have understood that I'm a Messianic Jew! Not a Gentile Christian! Not a Lutheran! I'm simply a Jew who, like you, my Gentile brother, has been saved by the shed blood of Yeshua my Lord and my God! Nothing more! Nothing less! But, let me explain how we believing Jews finally got beyond the teaching and understanding of the International Hebrew Alliance."

"Yes, please do," Sheldon replied, obviously deeply interested in what he was being shown for the first time.

"In the nineteen sixties," Drew continued, "there were many Jews among the 'flower-power' dropouts in the United States and quite miraculously many of these, my Jewish brothers, were caught up in a great move of the Holy Spirit that led them to Yeshua. Even now, as we speak there is a major movement continuing in the United States where Messianic Jewish Congregations are being formed as an appropriate place for Hebrew Christians to worship Yeshua while retaining their Jewish identity. In fact, there are already thirty-three such congregations and many other Jews are now embracing Yeshua and flocking to join the movement."

"It really seems a shame that this new movement hasn't already become a denomination of its own and as such a recognized part of the Church," Sheldon observed.

"Dear God!" Drew replied emphatically. "Aren't nearly three thousand denominations enough? Besides, Messianic Jews, just like the various Christian denominations, are all over the lot theologically. We have everything from wild eyed charismatics to hard shell fundamentalists! Brace yourself my dear brother, but the fact is 'Jesus of Nazareth' did not come to found a new religion, he came as God incarnate—the expected Messiah of the Jews."

"Sheldon," Drew continued earnestly, "Yeshua lived his entire life without ever violating *any* of the more than 600 commands of the Torah, yet creating a new religion itself would have been an enormous Torah violation. The original followers of Yeshua were not part of a new religion— they were a sect of Judaism. Not a single New Testament writer refers to himself as being a 'Christian,' yet Paul continually identifies himself as being a Jew, even a Pharisee."[60]

Sheldon remained in silent, rapt attention as Drew continued.

"Sheldon, I'm sure you must be aware that many of our denominational theologians, even a shocking number of our Christian seminaries, are teaching that while Judaism was originally the one true faith, it has now been replaced by a new faith called 'Christianity.' This theology is totally counter to the teachings of the 'New Testament' that clearly tell us there is one true faith which was given once and for all time.[61] This means that the theology claiming Christianity has replaced Judaism is absolutely false!"

Drew now concluded passionately: "Christianity is too young to be the one true faith that was once given! The one true faith that was once given therefore must be Judaism! Better stated, my dear brother, all Jews and all Christians need to understand that the Bible clearly teaches that Christianity is the *fulfillment* or *completion* of Judaism and not by any means its replacement!"

It was nearly two o'clock when these two mutually devoted brothers finally concluded their deep and penetrating discussion of the Church, its meaning, composition and theologies. "I'd love to talk all night," Sheldon observed, after yawning deeply but tomorrow is another day and I've got a ton of paper work to plough through on the flight back to Washington. But, before we call it a night I would like to pray some mighty blessings on the one whom I am certain will soon become the first Messianic Jewish Deputy Chief of Chaplains in the United States Air Force, one Chaplain Brigadier General Andrew Scott Sterling!"

Chapter Twenty Six

Hippos
May, A.D. 30

The horse drawn wooden cart bounced to and fro as it rounded the final turn of the steep trail leading up to the mountain top city of Hippos and came into the view of the official welcoming party headed by Matthias with Dory, his soon bride to be, standing at his side. So greatly revered was this newly arriving distinguished visitor, indeed the rabbi who would join the young couple in wedlock, that the two of them were surrounded by the other eleven disciples of Yeshua and virtually all of the already many believers who dwelled in this Decapolis City as well as many of their fellow believers from the nearby Jewish settlement at Kursi.

It fell upon Ariston, the father of the bride, to be the first to offer the Hippos community's greeting to Ya'akov, the blood brother of Yeshua, and the first leader of the Jerusalem Body of Believers, who had traveled to this distant Bashan Mountain top city from the synagogue he oversaw on Mount Zion.

"Shalom Ya'akov! Our warmest greetings in the name of Yeshua, our risen Lord! I am Ariston, an elder of this community." With that he greeted the distinguished visitor with a kiss on each cheek that was returned with a genuinely warm embrace.

"I am delighted to be here for such a wonderful occasion!" Ya'akov replied, loud enough for most of the close gathered greeters to hear. "I have never seen such a beautiful place as your flower carpeted mountain or felt such genuine warmth as I now receive from all of you who have been so kind to gather here at my journey's end."

"May I have the honor to introduce my family," Ariston offered, as he, now arm in arm with Ya'akov stepped toward the gathered assembly. "This is my beloved wife, Theodora—Ya'akov bowed slightly making no physical contact. "This is my son Euclid," Ariston continued as the two men exchanged customary man to man cheek kisses. "And this, my greatly honored guest, as you have already long known, is my daughter, Heliodora, who you have come all this way to join in marriage with the Apostle Matthias."

Ya'akov, paused for a brief moment, and then smiled in a way that signaled his unqualified acceptance of this unique "mixed" marriage.

"As always," Ya'akov greeted the bride, "you are quite beautiful my dear, but even more, I have long known that your spirit is sweet, and overflowing with the love of our Lord." He now turned to Matthias and embraced him warmly. "Indeed, you have chosen well, Mathias. Your ministry will bear much fruit with your lovely Dory at your side."

***

The Sea of Galilee glistening in the late afternoon sun providing an exquisite backdrop for the traditional Jewish wedding *chuppa* (canopy) that the local congregation had erected on an elevated wooden platform in front of their basalt block constructed meeting place on the western side of the mountain top city.

Athanasios, the former demon possessed chained man who was now becoming well recognized as an evangelist and congregational leader, had worked closely with Dory to plan this landmark wedding—the first ever between a believing Jew and believing Gentile who had converted to Judaism. It was their great challenge to strike an appropriate blend between these two greatly divergent traditions that would most fittingly honor Yeshua.

Ya'akov, the officiating rabbi, Ariston, the father of the bride, and Kefa, the groom's dearest friend, stood together, waiting under the *chuppa* as

Matthias now made his way forward to the accompaniment of appropriately joyful and sacred music played by harp and lyre, and mounted the wooded platform to take his place under the ceremonial covering.

The four of them were dressed in simple yet elegant white robes created especially for this joyous occasion by the women of the local congregation.

Next came the bride, accompanied by her mother, Theodora, who beamed with adoring pride. Dory looked exquisite in her finely woven pure white cotton wedding robe. Her long jet black hair was covered with an elaborate silk head dress and her heavily veiled face kept private the tears of great joy that flowed freely from her large, deep blue eyes.

Now, to signify that this was the man she intended to marry, Dory accompanied by Theodora circled about the groom and his party seven times after which she took her place under the canopy at Matthias' right side.

So overcome was Matthias with the enormity of this long awaited moment that he was unable to focus on the details of the many blessings as they were being intoned by Ya'akov. Somehow, all that followed "In the name of the Father and the Son and the Holy Spirit" were blended into a holy blur that seemed to bathe his body, soul and spirit until his entire being was filled with an indescribable overflowing of happiness.

On and on the words flowed like a golden holy river from the lips of this great man of God as in and out of one reality into the other Matthias drifted from the realm of earth to the realm of heaven. In the midst of it all he found himself drinking of the first cup of wine, and then the second and, at last, it was almost finished.

Now, regaining his senses and returning to the moment, Matthias gently lifted his bride's veil, and turned to Kefa, to recover from him a very special gift he had been holding for Dory that would officially complete their ceremonial bonding as husband and wife. It was a lovely, pure gold pendant with chain, the medallion about two inches in circumference with her name, *Heliodora*, etched on one side, and on the opposite side, designed by his dear Gentile brother Athan, a logo to symbolize their faith, an anagram rendered in Greek, the language of Hippos, set inside a line drawing of a fish,: Ιχθυσ ("fish"), an abbreviation of: Ιησουσ Χριστοσ Θηου Υιοσ Σωτηρ ("Jesus Christ, Son of God, Savior").

Gently and adoringly he placed the chain around his bride's neck and recited what was then the traditional vow: "Behold, you are sanctified to me with this pendant, according to the Law of Moses and of Israel." Then, with God and the others gathered about to bear witness, he joyfully embraced and tenderly kissed his greatly beloved new bride.

***

Although the bride and groom had made their "escape" via Ya'akov's horse drawn cart to spend their wedding night and short honeymoon in a secluded cottage on the shore of the Lake near Tel Hadar, the men and women who had remained in Hippos for the night, along with the city's most important visiting personages, had separated into two groups for long late night discussions on a variety of matters of mutual interest. The men had gravitated to the public building where the congregation met after sundown each Shabbat and the women were gathered in several smaller ad hoc groups scattered throughout the city.

It was Ya'akov who opened the door to what was to become an important theologically significant discussion. "I want to congratulate you Athan," he began. "This synagogue you have created here in the Decapolis is most impressive and the wedding was certainly in keeping with the Torah and Jewish tradition."

"Actually," Athan began to frame his reply inoffensively. "From the beginning, we have referred to our group as a 'church' a word in our language that means a building or an assembly of people gathered together to worship. Our prayerful expectation is that one day this church of ours will become the first of many such churches throughout the world that will constitute the one true universal Church of 'Iêsous Kristos', as we would call Him in Greek or the Congregation of Yeshua as you would prefer in Hebrew."

"I hear what you are saying, Athan," Ya'akov replied gently, "But, there is a danger in your interpretation. Yeshua most assuredly did not come to start a new religion. He indeed understood and many times proclaimed that He was and is the promised messiah of the Torah —Indeed, He is the *fulfillment* of Jewish messianic expectation, not its replacement."

"What Ya'akov speaks is pure wisdom founded on divine knowledge," Kefa interjected. "The sacred scrolls at Qumran speak repeatedly of a Jewish Messiah who was to appear imminently and then again at the end of days. His first appearance, the one we have all just been privileged to witness was, as God almighty incarnate, to atone for all the sins of the world by being the one perfect sacrifice. His second coming will be to gather all believers together with Him on Mount Zion where He will reign as King of the Jews for a thousand years."

"Kefa is quite correct," Ya'akov added. "My dear brother Athan, when you consider this aggregation of all born again Jews and all born again Gentiles—it is neither fitting nor proper to think of us collectively, now or in the future, as *either* a universal church *or* a universal synagogue! 'Church' and 'synagogue' are merely buildings or people within such buildings."

"May I also add," Kefa interjected, we twelve disciples have heard from our Lord's own lips and otherwise discerned in our spirits the essence of all of this: Just as each of us has one body with many members, and these members do not all have the same function, so in Yeshua we who are many form one body, and each member belongs to all the others.[62]

"Do not fear my dear brother," Kefa continued. "While Yeshua came first for the Jews, remember that His final instruction to His disciples and ultimately to all believers is that we should make disciples of *all the nations*, not just the Jews.[63]"

"My dear *Jewish* brothers," Athan retorted with more than a hint of sarcasm, "Matthias, in his teachings here in our city, has been most kind to show us in the Torah how our God chose the Jews from among all other people—certainly that must mean that He looks upon you Jews with more favor than He does us Gentiles, at least according to *your* interpretation. Perhaps," he added sardonically, "we should be striving to become Jews so that we can enjoy the same favor with God that you have inherited as a matter of your birth?"

It was Ya'akov who replied on behalf of the others. "Athan, please understand that God chose us ethnic Jews for two principle reasons— certainly not because we were in any way better or more worthy than any other people—quite to the contrary! God has a way of choosing the most unseemly for His special purposes. In any event, entirely for His own reasons and purposes, He chose the Jews as the people from whom to bring forth Yeshua, and at the same time and in the same breath, he promised them the land of Israel as an everlasting inheritance."

"There are no hidden purposes or agendas here," Ya'akov continued, there is nothing more, nothing less. Yeshua died for *all* His creation. There is no favoritism in eternal salvation. Eternal life is just as eternal and in every way just the same for Gentiles as it is for Jews. All believers, Jews and Gentiles alike sit at the same table; each of us is a special, entirely equal part of the Body of Yeshua with Yeshua Himself sitting at the head."

"If I may summarize what we have been saying," Kefa offered, "It is perfectly reasonable and proper for you to refer to this, your congregation and the building you occupy here at Hippos as a 'church.' And, it is equally reasonable and proper for Ya'akov's mother congregation and the Upper Room where they gather on Mount Zion to be called a 'synagogue.' What we all must remember, however, is that it serves no purpose and carries with it all manner of confusion and potential harm to refer to all believers as 'the Church' or in any other way except as 'The Body of Yeshua' in whatever worldly language or languages such words may eventually be translated."

After a few moments of silence, Athan introduced a new subject. "If I may, my brothers, it seems to me that there will be an unending number of interpretations of the Tenach and of the words Yeshua spoke to us during His earthly walk that will eventually be written down—words such as those our brother Mattatyahu here present is currently recording in what is to be called *The Gospel according to the Hebrews*. Indeed, there is surely so much more that will likely *never* be written down.

"But," Athan continued, "as this Body of Yeshua expands out into the world, who will remember such fundamental practices as the proper ways to baptize, administer the Lord's supper, or for that matter, even such foundational matters as how and when to pray? If the Body is to look to its Jewish Mother on Mount Zion, surely this Jewish mother must provide specific guidance on at least the basic matters of our mutual faith and its practice."

It was Ya'akov who replied. "I have every confidence that God has these concerns of which you speak under His very careful and close control. He certainly alludes to this matter in the Tenach where we read the words of Jeremiah who shared with us: 'The time is coming,' declares the Lord, 'when I will make a new covenant with the house of Israel and with the house of Judah---'This is the covenant I will make with the house of Israel after that time,' declares the Lord. 'I will put my commandments in their minds and write them on their hearts. I will be their God, and they will be my people.'[64]

"I am confident my brothers," Ya'akov continued, over time, new books will be added to the Holy Scriptures —yes, beginning with Mattatyahu's gospel, but there will be other gospels as well and many other writings that will record the very fabric of our faith and salvation in Yeshua. Indeed, this has already begun."

"May I also add," Ya'akov continued, "We in the Mother Synagogue, as some of you have called us, have also seen a great need to provide guidance to the emerging congregations who will make up the Body of Yeshua all over the world. In fact, we will soon get about the business of providing instruction on at least the central matters of which you spoke, Athan: baptism, the Lord's Supper, and prayer. In fact, our dear brother Matthias, along with being the apostle to you here in the Decapolis and beyond, will also inherit this special task of compiling what is to be entitled the 'Didache,' or 'the Teaching of the Twelve Apostles' which will be a compendium of such guidance to the extended Body."

Chapter Twenty Seven

Ramstein Air Base, Germany
New Year's Eve, 1979

Drew unabashedly beamed with joy and pride as he looked about the living room of the Sterling family quarters to behold his beloved wife and their three precious daughters who were bubbling with excitement about his forthcoming promotion and relocation to the Pentagon. He gave the bottle of fine French champagne he was opening a small but deliberately effective shake that produced just the attention getting loud pop he had hoped for as he vigorously removed its cork stopper.

"Mazel Tov!—Happy New Year one and all!" he exclaimed loudly enough to succeed in getting the full attention of these four most important people in his life. "This is indeed an auspicious and increasingly rare occasion—all of us together as a family in the same place at the same time!"

"Never mind the sermon, Chaplain Sterling!" Carla teased. "The fact is, your wife and your girls are very proud of you and what you have achieved and it has fallen upon me to propose a toast if you would be kind enough to fill our glasses.

Make that a half-glass for Rachel," she added."

"Ahhh, Mom!" Rachel protested!

"Never mind, little one! You are only *fifteen*!" Bekah nudged the baby of the family in what was an ongoing normal sibling interchange.

"Never mind indeed," Drew interjected as he got to Rachel's glass last and poured her just enough for a generous taste. "Like the lady said, this is indeed and auspicious occasion!"

"I humbly accept that my direction has been superceded," Carla joshed as she raised her glass and turned suddenly very serious. "I would like to propose a toast to my loving husband, the adoring father of our three precious daughters, and the next Air Force Deputy Chief of Chaplains. Ladies, I give you soon to be Chaplain Brigadier General Andrew Scott Sterling, United States Air Force!"

"I'll drink to that!" Drew responded happily, raising his glass.

"Here! Here!" his four ladies shouted in unison as they partook of the bubbly together.

"I don't mean to throw a damper on this celebration," Drew commented after they had put down their glasses, "but this whole thing is not quite yet a done deal! Chaplain Thurman has only *nominated* me, but the Chief of Staff still has to approve it and so, technically, does the Congress and the President."

"Oh Daddy!" Dory protested! "Isn't all that stuff just so much pro forma? Hadn't the Chief of Staff *already* given his approval before you were ever offered the job and isn't the rest of it just a rubber stamp sort of thing? Never mind, I'm going to submit my application to Georgetown next week!"

"You're probably right, sugar," Drew answered his eldest, "but the fact is I am both very junior in years and time in grade— this whole thing is so unique we should be prepared for almost anything!"

***

Well after midnight and the dawning of the New Year, Drew couldn't find the solace of sleep as he tossed to and fro in their non-government issue king sized bed.

"What's wrong, Darling?" Carla questioned intuitively. "Are you too excited about all this to sleep---?"

"No, he replied thoughtfully, "there's more to how I'm feeling beyond just excitement—I don't really understand it myself. By the way, what's on the schedule for tomorrow?"

"Nothing really," she replied, "except of course the staff reception in the Club early in the morning—what a hideous tradition for a bunch of hung over people who would rather be someplace else."

"Are the girls doing anything special with us?" he continued.

"You've got to be kidding!" she replied laughingly. "The three of them are booked solid with friends all day and Dory's got another date with that gorgeous provost marshal's son she met at school in Munich. He's an Army brat but I guess we can cope."

"It sounds like they may be getting serious?"

"Could be, but it's a bit too soon to worry about that."

"Sweetheart," he continued in a more serious tone. "Since it will be just the two of us tomorrow, I'd like to take you for a very long drive in the country—actually to a very special place—a uniquely awful place that I've been putting off visiting for these past two years."

What on earth are you talking about, Drew?" she replied guardedly.

"I'm talking about Dachau, Carla—the Nazi Concentration Camp at Dachau! I *need* to go there and I'd like it very much if you'd come with me. If we push it we can make it each way in about three hours."

***

It was just after twelve o'clock when the two of them found themselves utterly alone as they crunched along through the heavily falling snow leading from the large now empty parking lot to the open gate of the enormous, desolate former concentration camp.

"We certainly seem to have this place to ourselves," Carla offered trying to put a touch of lightness into what she sensed was the growing despair of this dear man whom she so loved—this wonderful *Jewish* man who walked by her side."

"What else would you expect on a miserable New Year's day," Drew replied somewhat sullenly. "Everyone with good sense is home by their fires drinking eggnogs or whatever these folks drink on days such as this. It's amazing this place is open today. It's like no one seems to care about what happened here!"

"Here's the gate," Carla stated the obvious as she struggled in her very limited German language to read the huge wrought iron letters that were the central feature of the cracked open main gate to the camp. "Arbeit Mach Frei" she read tentatively.

"It means 'Work Makes Free!'" Drew snapped. "This incredibly transparent lie was supposed to motivate the 238,000 or so Jews who were murdered and then incinerated here. Of course, these were just a drop in the bucket considering the more than six million or so other Jews who were murdered by the Nazis in more than thirty such camps scattered about Europe. Dachau just happens to be more or less in our neighborhood."

"I can't believe they left the gate unlocked," Carla observed. "It must have been a mistake. It doesn't look like there's another living soul in the place."

"No." Drew replied in a sullen near whisper. But there are hundreds of thousands of Jewish ghosts here to greet us."

***

Their self guided tour of the camp had continued for over two hours during which they seemed to be directed by some grisly, unseen tour guide from ages past who had remained behind to show them the way. And what a way it was—drifting among the long abandoned wooden barracks, and other facilities. On and on the two of them wandered, mostly in stunned silence as the many camp facilities where they found themselves seemed unchanged even after the passing of more than thirty years.

"Dear God!" Drew exclaimed, struggling to catch his breath as their seemingly ghost-guided tour had now led them to a building labeled above its entry as 'Baracke X.' They entered and immediately found themselves standing before a huge, fully open heavy metal door. Above the door, equipped with what appeared to be rubber sealing gaskets, was a painted label in German denoting its purpose: "Brausebad," which Drew immediately translated to the English as "Shower bath."

The two of them stood silently, even transfixed, for several minutes before this open door which seemed to beckon them to enter this "Brausebad," until, after a time, Drew finally spoke, as if to himself, "I'm trying to understand what this door means beyond its obvious former purpose. It beckons me with something very personal—some deep meaning that somehow escapes me."

Without any verbal reply, Carla took her husband's hand and gently led him through the thick open door into the huge gas chamber that lay just beyond. Silently, they inspected the seemingly out of place, immaculately clean, attractively tiled floor and overhead false shower heads that had previously well served their grim purpose as entry ports for the lethal Zyklon B gas pellets that had transformed this otherwise peaceful appearing room into a chamber of horrors.

"Come, my darling," she said, as she gently led him further into another even larger connected room, a crematorium that was, shockingly, equally as horrific in both appearance and function as its adjoining killing chamber. There before them lay four open ovens.

Even now, more than thirty years since their last terrible employment these hellish ovens remained noticeably soiled with human remains—more than just traces—clearly visible, seemingly swept aside ashes of individually unidentifiable, but collectively not forgotten Jews who had been murdered and then incinerated with precise German technical efficiency in this indescribably evil place.

They remained silent during their long walk back to their now snow covered car through the biting cold of the approaching Bavarian Winter evening. There was little they could say, no words either of them could find that would not appear somehow trite after what they had just witnessed.

Now as they approached their car, Drew stopped suddenly and reached out for the comfort of his beloved wife who rushed into his open arms. His sobs began silently, then grew quickly into a torrent of tears—tears that were a baptism of sorrows flowing from the depths of his grieving spirit—his spirit that deeply longed to reach out and some how sanctify each of these unnamed thousands—these murdered Jews whom he could not deny were his people—his very own precious people who now cried out to him accusingly from their scattered ash remains, demanding, on their behalf, that he embrace and accept who and what he was, a Jew like them, but unlike them a Jew who still lived and functioned— a Jew who by the grace of God understood and embraced the one true way of salvation and eternal life. Deep within his being he heard his Lord crying out to him in a clear voice "Feed my sheep!"[65] And, at that moment the seeds of a new understanding and a different calling had begun to come forth.

Finally, when Drew's tears had ceased, Carla broke their long silence. "Darling, we've been here for more than two years and you haven't taken even a single day of leave. It's high time we took a couple of weeks off and went somewhere—just the two of us!"

She was genuinely shocked at his immediate agreement. "Yes," he replied simply. "Let's go to Israel."

Chapter Twenty Eight

Jerusalem
Shavuot, June, A.D. 30

Kefa and Matthias walked along together, a few paces ahead of the other ten disciples and the one hundred and ten or so other believers in Yeshua. They were, for the moment, lost to one another and the world around them, their spirits immersed in the depths of a divine esoteric cloud that seemed to carry them along as they began to ascend the magnificent, two hundred foot wide, native marble staircase that led to the southern entrance of the Temple.

It was almost nine o'clock in the morning on Shavuot, the Feast of Weeks and, the place was crowded with thousands upon thousands of Jews from all over the known world who had come to Jerusalem for this grand celebration in accordance with the God's call for them to do so as it had been written in the Torah.

It was exactly seven weeks—fifty days since Pesach, and these large crowds of obedient worshipers had come to be renewed in the covenant with their God as well as to commemorate the giving of the Ten Commandments to Moses on Mount Sinai.[66]

They had also come to celebrate the abundant harvest season in their greatly blessed Israel.

However, except for this relatively small band of Jewish believers in Yeshua, none of these many Jewish worshipers had even an inkling of the great promise the Lord God of Israel was about to keep as it had been spoken by Yeshua just before He had ascended into heaven from the adjacent Mount of Olives some six weeks earlier.

For it was with joyful expectation that these first followers of Yeshua knew with perfect assurance that they would not be left alone after their Lord had ascended to sit at the right hand of His Father. Indeed, Yeshua had promised that the Father would send them a comforter, His own Holy Spirit, and it was He whom they awaited.[67]

What they did not know, however, as they reached the top of the staircase and entered the sacred precincts of the Temple, was that the day, even the hour, was at hand when the precious, indescribably wonderful promised gift would be given to them and, forevermore, to all whom subsequently would become members of the Body of Yeshua.

When they had covered about half the distance between the South Entry to the Temple Mount and the Temple itself, it happened. Suddenly, the sound of a mighty rushing wind came as if from heaven, and it filled the whole place. Divided tongues, as of fire, appeared to them and one of these tongues of fires fell upon each of them. At that very moment they were all filled with the Holy Spirit and they began to speak with other tongues, as the Holy Spirit empowered them to do so.

Because it was Shavuot, Jews from every nation were present in the Temple Court. When this very loud, unfathomable combined sound of those speaking in many different languages burst forth, it confused everyone who was present. Yet, somehow through it all, inexplicably, each member of this large multitude clearly heard complete strangers speaking in his or her own native tongue.

All of them were amazed and marveled at what they were hearing and they said to one another, "Look, are not all these who speak Galileans? And how is it that we hear, each in our own language in which we were born? Parthians and Medes and Elamites, those dwelling in Mesopotamia, Judea and Cappadocia, Pontus and Asia, Phrygia and Pamphylia, Egypt and the parts of Libya adjoining Cyrene, visitors from Rome, both Jews and proselytes, Cretans and Arabs -- we hear them speaking in our own tongues the wonderful works of God." So they asked one another in their amazement,

"Whatever could this mean?" Others who were present mocked what was happening and accused them of having been drunk from new wine.

By now, Kefa and Matthias with the other ten disciples close behind had made their way through the amazed and perplexed crowd to the stairs leading up to the entrance to the Temple. Kefa took a position about half-way up these stairs and began to bring forth and amplify that which had long ago been prophesied:[68]

"Men of Judea and all who dwell in Jerusalem," Kefa began to exhort, "let this be known to you, and heed my words. For what you see and hear now are not men intoxicated by wine, as you suppose, since it is only the third hour of the day. But this is what was spoken by the prophet Joel: 'And it shall come to pass in the last days, says God, That I will pour out of My Spirit on all flesh; your sons and your daughters shall prophesy, Your young men shall see visions, your old men shall dream dreams. And on My menservants and on My maidservants I will pour out My Spirit in those days; And they shall prophesy. I will show wonders in heaven above and signs in the earth beneath: Blood and fire and vapor of smoke. The sun shall be turned into darkness, and the moon into blood, before the coming of the great and awesome day of the Lord. And it shall come to pass that whoever calls on the name of the Lord shall be saved.'"

"Men of Israel," Kefa continued passionately, " hear these words: Yeshua of Nazareth, a Man attested by God to you by miracles, wonders, and signs which God did through Him in your midst, as you yourselves also know -- Him, being delivered by the determined purpose and foreknowledge of God, you have taken by lawless hands, have crucified, and put to death; whom God raised up, having loosed the pains of death, because it was not possible that He should be held by it. For David says concerning Him: 'I foresaw the Lord always before my face, for He is at my right hand, that I may not be shaken. Therefore my heart rejoiced, and my tongue was glad; moreover my flesh also will rest in hope. For you will not leave my soul in Hades, nor will you allow Your Holy One to see corruption. You have made known to me the ways of life; you will make me full of joy in your presence."

"Men and brethren, Kefa continued, "let me speak freely to you of the patriarch David, that he is both dead and buried, and his tomb is with us to this day. Therefore, being a prophet, and knowing that God had sworn with an oath to him that of the fruit of his body, according to the flesh, He would raise up Yeshua to sit on his throne, he, foreseeing this, spoke concerning the resurrection of Yeshua, that His soul was not left in Hades, nor did His flesh see corruption. This Yeshua God has raised up, of which we are all witnesses. Therefore being exalted to the right hand of God, and having received from the Father the promise of the Holy Spirit, He poured out this which you now see and hear. For David did not ascend into the heavens, but he says himself: 'The LORD said to my Lord,' sit at My right hand, Till I make Your enemies Your footstool.' Therefore let all the house of Israel know assuredly that God has made this Yeshua, whom you crucified, both Lord and Savior."

Now when they heard this, they were cut to the heart, and said to Kefa and the rest of the apostles, "Men and brethren, what shall we do?"

Then Kefa said to them, "Repent, and let every one of you be baptized in the name of Yeshua for the remission of sins; and you shall receive the gift of the Holy Spirit.   For the promise is to you and to your children, and to all who are afar off, as many as the Lord our God will call." [69]

With that, Kefa turned, and with Matthias now at his side and the other ten disciples close behind, they continued up the stairs. The two of them quickly reached the portico at the top where several priests were waiting to receive the sacrifices from a seemingly never ending stream of worshipers who would have them offered at the huge Brazen Altar just beyond the entrance.

Kefa and Matthias were so filled with the Holy Spirit that when they approached the ordained priests of the temple, who would never have permitted ordinary worshipers to pass beyond the portico and into the Holy Place, stood back in awe, shielding their eyes from the near blinding glow of the Spirit that emanated from these two uniquely chosen ones of God.

Thus, without the slightest interference from the priests who stood as guardians of this holy place, while the other ten disciples mingled with the crowd at the entrance, Kefa and Matthias slowly and reverently passed beyond the golden chains there and then through the Holy Place itself. The two of them were mesmerized as they proceeded towards the veil leading to the Holy of Holies. Reverently, and filled with awe, they made their way through this exquisitely appointed place overlaid with pure gold furnished with Menorot and Tables of Shewbred on both sides and by the Altar of Incense that stood just outside the veil.

Matthias, awestruck, spoke first in an almost inaudible whisper. "Look! The curtain that was torn from top to bottom at the moment of our Lord's death has been repaired," he observed.

"And necessarily so from the perspective of these dear ones who do not yet know Yeshua and why He came," Kefa responded. "For they, for the moment, still seek righteousness in this place through the blood sacrifice of animals. Then, they yearn for the next annual Day of Atonement when once again they may be cleansed from all their sin."

"Never mind that the curtain has been physically repaired." Kefa continued. "No earthly band of priests could ever repair the *spiritual* curtain that was torn here! Yeshua made a way for us all through the shedding of his own precious blood!"

"Amen," my brother, Matthias replied. "Now *all* believers in Yeshua can pass through the curtain *spiritually* from any place. All who have thus been saved by His precious blood have direct access to our Lord and our Creator without the benefit of any priestly intervention or other sacrifice. Yeshua made a way for you and for me and for all of His creation!"

"Amen and Amen!!" The two of them shouted joyfully in unison.[70]

Chapter Twenty Nine

Jerusalem
January 15, 1979

Drew, with Carla close by his side, stood in reverent awe just inside the entrance to the very large plaza in the very heart of the Old City of Jerusalem that encompassed the open part of what remained of the Western Wall of the Temple, known to the world as the Kotel. Beyond this last venerable monument to the survivability, durability and faithful persistence of the Jews and everything Jewish, the Romans had long ago seen fit to pulverize virtually every remaining vestige of what had once arguably been the most holy and beautiful place of worship on earth.

Even now, the huge plaza that could easily encompass two football fields was teaming with several hundred mostly Jewish pilgrims who had come to pray there, as well as a great variety of other tourists from all over the world who had come for a variety of reasons, but most simply to behold this very unique and compelling place.[71]

Drew felt a mighty, profound stirring in his spirit. "Dear God!" he spoke, his voice quivering with the emotion of a long lost child at the moment of his homecoming, "How could I have waited so long for this moment?"

Carla replied with long suppressed, deep understanding. "Because, my precious husband, God brought you to Himself in a Christian world—and He did so for a great and wonderful purpose! Darling, you're a Jew, a long lost blood descendant of Israel who at long last, right on time, according to God's holy schedule, has come home to your people."

Drew did not respond immediately. Instead, like an iron filing drawn to a huge magnet, with Carla remaining by his side, he began to move reverently towards the huge, ancient, stone block wall. Neither of them spoke, even when they reached the restricted entry place guarded by two traditionally clad orthodox rabbis who made certain that the men and women were channeled to their respective separated places at the Wall and that heads of all male visitors were properly covered, issuing black cardboard constructed kippahs to those who did not bring their own.

Carla took her husband's hands into her own and gave them a loving, joyful squeeze as she turned to make her way to the women's section. Never before in their many years together had she known such a depth of special trust, respect and love for this Jewish man who was her God given husband, as she adoringly watched him place the proffered covering upon his head and begin to take the last several steps to a place that had just opened for him between two other worshippers at the Wall.

He now stood, his arms raised in praise; his hands making their first physical contact with the ancient stone. Tears of his indescribably satisfying homecoming flowed unabashedly down his cheeks as instinctively he cried out in a middle eastern sounding language he did not know but with certain knowledge that the words he lifted up to the very throne of God were words of praise, adoration and thanksgiving to His heavenly father who had brought him to this marvelous moment of homecoming. This moment would, forevermore, be indelibly etched upon the innermost parts of his being.

***

Late the next afternoon, the two of them stood atop a large concrete slab that only nine years earlier had served as the protective cover of a Syrian gun emplacement that selectively shelled Jewish communities along the Eastern shore of the Sea of Galilee. In fact, prior to the 1967 "Six Day" War during which the Israeli Defense Force reclaimed this strategically commanding position along with the rest of the Golan Heights, an entire generation of

Jewish children in this particular region had been raised like moles, forced to hide out in bunkers to avoid the daily viciously hostile outpouring of this and other Syrian gun emplacements along the eastern ridge of this mountain chain, frequently referred to in the Tenach as "Bashan."

"What an incredibly glorious place!" Carla exclaimed as they beheld the breathtaking view before them of the entire harp shaped lake.

"And what a picture post card day this has been," Drew replied. "Look, you can even see the Jordan river," he added as he pointed south toward and the just now turning emerald green Jordan Valley with its tiny stream, more a creek than a river, that now reflected the late afternoon sun as it snaked persistently onward, watering the richest farmlands of two nations as it flowed on to deposit its remaining tiny trickle in the Dead Sea. "The fact is, my head is spinning with the breadth and the depth of all we have seen and done these past two weeks—Dear God, the sheer beauty of it all!" he added as he made a sweeping gesture that took in the entire lake.

"Our Lord wasn't exaggerating when he called this amazing inheritance of your people 'a land flowing with milk and honey, the most beautiful of all lands,'"[72] Carla added her agreement. "Drew," she exclaimed, with heart felt emotion, "I've fallen in love with this place—with everything we've seen from north to south and east to west. And we've only begun to scratch the surface."

Drew quickly added his agreement. "The entire country is no bigger than New Jersey and yet, it seems, we could spend the rest of out lives seeing new and wonderful things and still not see it all! Perhaps the biggest miracle of this place is that God Himself chose it for so many interrelated divine purposes—all of them leading to the ministry, crucifixion, resurrection and soon return of Yeshua.

"Look, there Carla!" Drew exclaimed with the excitement of discovery. "Look across from where we are standing!" He pointed towards Tiberias, an alabaster white city on the opposite shore that had already begun to appear as a magnificent landscape rendered in lovely pastels by the just beginning sunset. "Yeshua's ministry started right there, just a few kilometers north of Tiberias! Just think of it: He multiplied the loaves and fishes and fed five thousand right, there at Tabgha! He preached the Sermon on the Mount right there on top of Mount Ermos! He performed all sorts of miracles right there at Capernaum!" Then, he moved his pointing finger around to the far Northeast shore. "And right there!" he continued. "Right there at Kursi He drove the demons out of the chained man and into a herd of pigs that went into the Lake and drowned."

When Drew concluded his summary of the biblical highlights of the Lakeshore, Carla, who had been totally absorbed in his teaching, felt compelled to ask, as she pointed to what appeared to be the ruins of an ancient mountain-top community just to the north of where they stood. "Drew, what is that place about two miles or so to the north, about half way to the top of the heights?"

"It just so happens that one of my professors did touch on this place during one of my doctoral courses on church history. It is, as I recall, one of ten ancient cities known, collectively, as the Decapolis. They were founded at the command of Alexander the Great to introduce the Greek language and culture to the Middle East.

The one you are pointing to was originally called by its Greek name, Hippos, but in modern times it is known by its Hebrew name, Sussita. Both names are translated the same in English: as 'horse.' They obviously chose this name because the mountain is shaped quite like the head of a horse."

"I don't have a clue why," she replied with a hint of mystery, "but I feel a special attachment—like I am being drawn to go there and explore the ancient city on top of this horse shaped mountain!"

He sighed deeply as he struggled, but failed to regain control of his emotions that were now spinning out of control. "I'll tell you, Carla," he now spoke sadly. "I don't know where Israel has been all of my life. Now that I've found it I can barely stand the thought of going back to the 'real world.' There simply isn't time for us to visit Sussita before we leave, to say nothing of the rest of the country that calls to me like I've never before been called."

"This doesn't have to be the end of it, Darling," she comforted him. They now stood arm in arm looking out across the Lake at the quickly fading glorious sunset of the final day of their first visit to the Land. "We can return again, perhaps even often. No, this doesn't have to be the end of anything—I would rather think of it as a beginning."

"Yes." Drew replied simply, "Yes, a new beginning."

***

"These marvelous two weeks here in the Land of your inheritance have given us a lot to think and pray about," Carla commented late that evening as she put the last of her things in her suitcase and zippered it shut. "I'll have to tell you Drew, I could live in this place and I'm not even the Jew in the family!"

Drew, who had been deeply contemplative and mostly silent since they arrived back at their hotel, carefully framed his response. "Did you know that there are literally hundreds of references in the Old Testament that speak to God's call upon all Jews to return to Israel?"

"I've been thinking about a few of these," he continued, "like Isaiah eleven, eleven and Jeremiah thirty-one, eight. These are certainly clear enough. It would be hard to make a case that God wasn't calling His people to come home!"

"Those are great verses, but," he added, " listen to Ezekiel eleven, seventeen: *'Therefore say: 'This is what the Sovereign LORD says: I will gather you from the nations and bring you back from the countries where you have been scattered, and I will give you back the land of Israel again.'* Carla, Sweetheart, what do you think the Lord is saying to *us* right now—not to all Jews in general, but directly to *me* and to *you*?"

"Last time I checked," she replied immediately, "you, were the Jewish spiritual head of the family and I was your goyisha Ruth. Remember what Ruth said at a moment like this: *'Don't urge me to leave you or to turn back from you. Where you go I will go, and where you stay I will stay. Your people will be my people and your God my God. Where you die I will die, and there I will be buried. May the Lord deal with me, be it ever so severely, if anything but death separates you and me.'*[73] Drew, darling, this is your call and I am with you whatever the Lord may show you He has in mind for us!"

"There is certainly a practical side to all of this," he replied thoughtfully. "If we were to go to the wild extreme and retire right now as a colonel with over twenty two years service we would receive more than four thousand dollars a month. If I don't mess up and become the Chief of Chaplains in a couple of years we would receive almost twice that much in a few years when I retired as a major general. That's one huge difference; to say nothing of the fact that being Chief would be a dream of dreams come true!"

"Didn't I hear someplace during the past week that a relatively well off Israeli family lives comfortably on about *two* thousand dollars a month! Be honest with yourself, Drew; couldn't just the two of us survive nicely on more than *twice* this amount?"

"It isn't just the two of us who need to be considered," he replied thoughtfully. "Don't forget the girls! We've been shelling out big bucks on these three darlings for as long as I can remember and I'm not under the impression the flow is going to stop any time soon."

"Take another look, Darling," Carla offered with a hint of sadness. "The three of them will be up and gone from our nest before you think. Dory will be a senior next year; Bekah a sophomore and Rachel will be just finishing high school. But, even so the Lord has provided well for us and we've managed to save even more than we'll need for their undergraduate education. There will even be enough left over for three grandiose weddings if that's how things manage to work out.

Money isn't the issue, Drew. If we were to retire and move to Israel right now we wouldn't be rich by American standards but we certainly would be *comfortable* by any other reasonable standard and our girls would continue to be well provided for.

It seems to me that the real issue here is just how you and you alone see the relative importance of The Reverend Doctor Andrew Scott Sterling becoming Chief of Chaplains in a couple of years and retiring as a major general with big bucks and all other things thereto appertaining. You need to weigh this against answering the Lord's call, if indeed that is what you are truly hearing, and responding right now, without a six year or so delay."

"As usual, my darling," Drew replied, "of course you are quite correct. There is no getting away from the conclusion that this call belongs to me and here is where I am----."

Before he could finish what he was about to say, the phone rang loudly, demanding an immediate response. As he hurried to the bedside table where the instrument stood, he was filled with a sudden foreboding, the essence of which was, sadly, true to his intuitive perception.

"Oh, Drew!" Carla hurried to him and embraced him comfortingly when he had concluded the short international communication. "I could certainly tell from your side of the conversation that you were speaking to your father---."

"Yes, it was Dad," he replied, cutting her off. "Grandma Amelia has had a major heart attack. She's in the hospital in New York, and she has asked to see me if it's at all possible---."

Carla took over the situation immediately. She picked up the phone and when the hotel operator answered "How may I help you" a few moments later, Carla, unable to conceal the urgency in her voice, replied: "Please connect me with the El Al ticket agency."

Chapter Thirty

Mount Zion, Jerusalem
Succoth, October A.D. 30

"I'm so thrilled to be a follower of your religion, Matthias," Dory exclaimed excitedly as the two of them stood together in the outer court of the Temple taking in the festive events that were unfolding before their eyes. "It's hard to believe it's been almost a year since Ya'akov guided me to my conversion."

"Without your conversion, we couldn't have become husband and wife," Matthias responded. But, my darling, please understand. By your conversion you have simply become a follower of my religion, Judaism—you have not become a Jew! God chose to make you a Gentile, just like He chose to make me a Jew. Nothing or no one can change our ethnic natures. Nor, is there any reason why we should want to be changed in this way.

"Your salvation in Yeshua," he earnestly continued, "was accomplished in the same way as mine—by the blood He shed for us all. Believe me, there are no advantages to being an ethnic Jew in the kingdom of heaven and certainly there are none here on earth."

"I *do* understand, Matthias," she responded trying to mask her annoyance with having once again heard what to her had always been quite obvious. "I'm proud to be whom and what I am: born a Gentile, 'born again' by the shed blood of Yeshua, and committed to embrace the Torah and Jewish tradition. I'm thrilled to be your wife, married into the covenant, and planning to raise our children as Torah believing Jews who know and love Yeshua as their Messiah and Lord."

"Just look at that," Matthias replied, well satisfied with her understanding and changing the subject. "One year ago I stood in this very place close enough to our precious Lord to touch Him. I and the others who knew Him rejoiced with Him at the four golden *menorahs* with four golden bowls at the top of each, like those now standing in this same place. Then, like now, there were four ladders, each leading to a bowl; and, there were four strong young priests climbing up with pitchers each holding nine liters of oil to pour into the bowls. Finally, when the bowls are filled, the young men will light the wicks made from their own worn-out drawers and girdles."

Suddenly, there was a loud expression of shared awe as the many hundreds of celebrants literally exhaled in unison and gasped loudly to catch their breath. "How glorious!!" Dory finally managed to shout as she and Matthias took pro-offered lit torches from the young priests and joined the others who were now dancing around the lit menorahs while the Levites played harps, lyres, cymbals, trumpets and innumerable other musical instruments. "Surely," she exclaimed in her excitement, "there is not a courtyard in Jerusalem that is not lit up by the light of these incredible menorahs!"[74]

"Something very wonderful is missing from this year's celebration!" Matthias shouted trying to be heard over the near deafening sounds of the jubilant crowd. "Last year Yeshua, Himself stood in the glorious light of these menorot and told all, that is all who had ears to hear: 'I am the light of the world---.'"[75]

***

On the first morning after the feast, Matthias was the last of the twelve to arrive in the Upper Room on Mount Zion for the first of many such full day meetings to be chaired by Ya'akov who had been named their leader by none other than Yeshua, Himself.[76] The other disciples and their leader now smiled in knowing unison as the late arriver made his way toward the only empty chair at the table.

"Well, my dear brothers," Ya'akov began, teasingly. "Now that our honeymooner has arrived for his very first formal meeting as a part of our very exclusive Council of Jerusalem, perhaps we may begin. How is your lovely bride, my son?" he added with paternal warmth.

"She is quite well indeed, my brothers." Matthias blushed, embarrassed by the focus of the entire group upon himself. "The fact is, praise the Lord, Dory is pregnant with our first child. We are quite thrilled by this, and by all the many other blessings that have come to us from His mighty storehouse in heaven."

All present beat their fists on the large wooden table where they were seated in celebration of Matthias' glad tidings. "Praise the Lord indeed!" Kefa exclaimed in reply. "May this child who will be the first from among our inner circle wax strong and grow each day in the faith of the Lord."

Beginning on this note of celebration, Ya'akov turned to the very serious business at hand. "My brothers we have been appointed and anointed by the King of the Universe, the very Creator of everything to make disciples of all men in every nation." He paused for a moment before he continued. "Just think of it my brothers, there are twelve of you, myself, and perhaps several hundred other Jews who have come to know Him. And yes," he continued, anticipating Matthias' brewing comment; "there are certainly some considerable number of Gentiles, mostly on the Eastern shore of the Kinneret (Sea of Galilee) who already know Him. But, hear me well! All of us believers taken together are a far cry from the 300 or so million men, women and children who are scattered about the now known world."

"Thenwhat are we waiting for?" Kefa interjected impulsively, "Let's get on with the Lord's work!"

"Thank you Kefa!" Ya'akov retorted in a tone revealing his deep frustration. "The fact is we have been called to do enormously great and wonderful things for the Lord! We may have the heart to do them, but, my dear brothers, we haven't even begun to pray over or even discuss any of the most foundational matters!

"How, precisely are we to go about saving the hordes of the unsaved?"

Ya'akov continued with growing passion. "What words from the Torah are we to share with them? What from the Writings? What of the extra- things that have been written down in our sacred scrolls for almost three hundred years? What words of our Lord that may never be written down that we have heard with our own ears? What wisdom and truth from our own precious Jewish heritage are we to share with these non-Jews of other nations? And, as if all of this were not enough my dear brothers, would you kindly tell me what we are to teach these legions of the unsaved— how precisely they are to go about worshiping the Lord?"

Ya'akov paused for a moment, trying with little success to reign in his growing emotion "By the way, he continued, "we haven't even settled yet upon how, where and when we redeemed Jews are to worship? How then can we light the way for others in things we have not yet come to understand ourselves?"

Ya'akov's face flushed as his frustration became more apparent. He struggled inwardly to maintain the outward demeanor he believed appropriate for the leader of the Jewish, Yeshua worshipping "Mother Congregation." He, who was the flesh and blood sibling of Yeshua, had no way of knowing then that he, because of his great righteousness, would soon come to be called, "Ya'akov the Just."

"Can you tell me, anyone of you, how precisely are we to baptize and how and when are we to celebrate the Lord's last Supper with us as He so clearly told us we should do in memory of Him and His incredible self sacrifice for us all---?"

Ya'akov's unexpected, emotional outburst was met with a time of stunned silence as the twelve quietly processed the enormous truth and seemingly boundless challenges their leader had just shared.

Finally, Kefa, notoriously the least timid of them all, responded: "My brothers, how very much my own faith is deepened by the divine wisdom our blessed Lord for having appointed His own blood brother as our leader. How comforting to know with absolute assurance that the Holy Spirit who dwells within each of us is leading and guiding the great and wondrous things we are called to do."

"My brothers," Kefa continued, "Ya'akov speaks the truth, but he speaks of doctrinal, organizational and administrative matters, all of which we must somehow address, but I ask you to remember what Yeshua commanded us to do, just before He ascended into heaven. Do any of you have even the slightest recollection of His having instructed us to create a new religion in His name? Who among you can recall even a hint that we were to even slightly be diverted from the Holy task He laid upon us to: '--- go and make disciples of all nations, baptizing them in the name of the Father and of the Son and of the Holy Spirit, and teaching them to obey everything I have commanded you. And surely I am with you always, to the very end of the age?'"[77]

"You have made my point exactly!" Ya'akov retorted. "By all means, our first priority is to evangelize, but may I ask, Kefa, how are you personally going to obey Yeshua's command to 'teach them to obey *everything* I have commanded you'? Do any of you individually recall *everything* He said when He walked among us?"

"Much of what our Lord taught us was first prophesied in the Tenach!" Yochanan, who, like the others had so far remained silent during this foundationally important discourse between Ya'akov and Kefa, now dared to venture.

"There is also much written in our sacred scrolls kept in the library at Qumran," Matthias added."

Now Mattityahu, who had also remained silent up to this point, spoke with deep conviction. "My brothers, the Tenach and our Scrolls provide us with prophecy of what was to come and indeed did come in the flesh substance and divine ministry of our precious, Yeshua. I ask you to kindly recall the wisdom of Jeremiah who spoke the words of the Lord: 'The time is coming,' declares the Lord, 'when I will make a new covenant with the house of Israel and with the house of Judah.--- This is the covenant I will make with the house of Israel after that time,' declares the Lord.

'I will put my law in their minds and write it on their hearts. I will be their God, and they will be my people.'[78]

"My brothers," Mattityahu continued passionately, his eyes glowing in the power of the Holy Spirit, "the Tenach is the written record of the Old Covenant that our God made with our people, the Jews. It has now fallen upon us who have walked with Yeshua; seen the things He has done with our own eyes; heard with our own ears the things He taught while He was among us. Yes, it has fallen upon the twelve of us, as we are led by the Holy Spirit, to write down *everything* we can recall about the Master's walk and teachings while He was among us. Then, just as the Tenach is the divinely inspired written reflection of the Old Covenant God made with His people, what we are about to write down will be a sacred treasure for our own and for all future generations—a sacred reflection of Yeshua, written by the very hand of the Spirit working through us. It is to be a beacon of truth from the very throne of God lighting the way to eternal salvation through the shed blood of Yeshua for all of His creation, Jews and Gentiles alike."

Ya'akov's frustration now turned to joy. "Indeed, my brothers, our Lord has spoken through Mattityahu Levi. Those among you who are so led by the Spirit, must immediately begin to record the substance of this *Brit Hadashah* for it will surely be the completion— yes, the very fulfillment of the Tenach. "

Then Yochanan, inspired by the Holy Spirit spoke again. "The Lord has just shown me to begin my recollections with the substance of what Ya'akov has just spoken. 'In the beginning was the Word, and the Word was with God, and the Word was God. He was with God in the beginning.'"[79]

Mattityahu spoke next. "And I too will write down what I have seen and heard— first in Aramaic, the everyday language of our people, and then there will be copies of these writings in Hebrew for the more scholarly and for those in other places who have learned our more formal tongue."

"You can be certain," Matthias added excitedly, "This Gospel of the Hebrews" will be quickly translated into Greek for the peoples of the Decapolis and for the many other nations who speak this language."

"Indeed," Ya'akov added, "These sacred writings you will now begin to bring forth will one day be translated into the languages of *every* nation so that all people everywhere may read, hear and believe upon Yeshua, the salvational Word that became flesh and walked among us."

"Each of you twelve," Ya'akov continued, his eyes now aglow with the revelation he was about to share. "Yes each of you will be divinely guided as to precisely where and when you are to go into the world. Some will depart immediately. Others will remain with me here on Mount Zion for a time, perhaps even for many years.

"The Lord has shown me," Matthias interjected. "I am to work with you from time to time here at Mount Zion between my various travels into the Decapolis and perhaps beyond."

Then Philip, who had been silent up to this point added: "and I too have just been shown that I whose Hellenized family gave me a Greek name—I too am to reach out to the Gentiles in the Decapolis, working with Matthias who will lead me in this outreach to these ten cities and where else beyond the Spirit may lead. Like Matthias, in between my various travels, I am also called to work with you Ya'akov, to help you accomplish all of the organizational and administrative tasks of which you earlier spoke."

"My precious brothers," Ya'akov continued joyfully. "You twelve who have been chosen—you are the *continuing* spiritual seed of Abraham—the New Covenant seed scattered forth into an unsaved world by the very hand of God—Holy seed out of which will spring forth the wondrous redeemed assembly of Jews and Gentiles who together are and forevermore will be the eternally living Body of Yeshua."

Chapter Thirty One

Royal Hospital, The Bronx, New York
January 18, 1979

"I'm so happy you two are here, Leila exclaimed as she fought back tears and gave her adored son a motherly kiss and embrace. You look simply gorgeous in your uniform," she observed with unrestrained pride."

"We came right from the airport, Mom," he explained. "We caught military space available hops all the way from Tel Aviv and didn't want to take the time to check into our hotel."

"It's a good thing you did, son," Mark interjected. "Your grandmother has been waiting for you—she speaks of nothing else."

"Well then," Drew replied as he took Carla by the hand and turned toward Grandma Amelia's room that was just beyond the door where they had all met. "Let's stop standing here and pay the darling a visit."

"I love her too, Drew," Carla said as she gently pulled away, "but, you need to see her by yourself—I'll join you later."

Drew silently accepted his wife's sensitivity as he smiled and then entered the room where his beloved grandmother lay.

"Hi Sweetheart!" he greeted her in a way that reflected his deep love for her born out of their long and special relationship. "You've got to stop giving us all such angst! It's a long trip from Germany to New York!" he joshed, then turning very serious he continued—"How are you grandma?"

"I'm telling you, Drew, Darling, I'm not feeling so hot, if you know vhat I mean. It is so vonderful that you came all this vay to see me. Nuuu, so where is your lovely goyisha vife?? She didn't come mit you?"

"Of course she did." Drew replied. "She just thought it would be nice if we had a nice private visit before she joined us."

"Let me tell you, Darling, goy or no goy, that girl is something very special—Nuu, and vhat of your lovely daughters—they couldn't come and see their great grandmother in the hospital??"

Not waiting for a response, she continued. "So how is it by you Drew? Your father tells me you vill soon be a general mit one star and then maybe later even two stars? Nuu, *my* grandson the rabbi vill be the *macher* from all the chaplains in the Air Force—Oyy! Such *nachas*!—My darling Drew—I love you so much!"

He came close and tenderly kissed away the tears that had begun to flow down her cheeks. "I've always loved you, Grandma," he proclaimed from the depths of his heart—you have always been the Jewish anchor in my life." He paused for a moment to collect his thoughts, then continued. "The fact is, Grandma, Carla and I have fallen in love with the Land of Israel."

"Nuuu, so vhat is not to love??" she replied mustering enough strength to sit up a bit more.

"It goes beyond that, Grandma—We are seriously considering retiring right now and making *aliyah*."

"You'd altogether give up this Christian Rabbi business—you would forget about the chaplain *macher* job— Tell me, Darling, for *vhat*?— How would you make a living in Israel?"

"Money isn't an issue," he replied, "We could live nicely there for the rest of our lives on my Air Force pension. To tell you the truth, Grandma, I don't know exactly what I would do there, but I do know that the Lord God of Israel is calling me to do this and that He will show me what He has in mind according to *His* schedule, not mine."

"Drew, I think it would be vunderful if you moved to Israel—if you started to live your life like a Jew instead of like a Goy—if finally you became who you are, vun of *Us* and not vun of *Them*!"

"Grandma," he replied thoughtfully, "I've finally come to understand that there are no *Us* or *Them* in the family of God. Jews and 'Christians' all worship the very same God. Yahweh is His name and He told us to exalt Him by it[80]—never mind that the Orthodox are afraid to do so and use all kinds of substitutes like 'Jehovah', 'HaShem', 'G-d', 'L-rd' and others.

"Nuuu, so vhat about Jesus the Christian?" she replied somewhat defensively.

Drew carefully chose his words and replied from the depths of his own deep conviction. "In the first place, this Jesus you speak of was a Jew, just like I am, and the Hebrew name by which He was first known is Yeshua, which in Hebrew means salvation."

"Grandma," he continued, the real problem that separates Jews from Christians is a misunderstanding of whom this Yeshua was, is and always will be." He now took his small print carry around bible from his uniform jacket pocket and found his place as he continued. "Grandma, the great Jewish prophet Isaiah described this Yeshua to us in great detail several hundred years before he appeared first among the Jews in Jerusalem. Here is what he said about the coming messiah, long before he was born." He began to read with authority, love and conviction:

> *Who has believed our message and to whom has the arm of the LORD been revealed? He grew up before him like a tender shoot, and like a root out of dry ground. He had no beauty or majesty to attract us to him, nothing in his appearance that we should desire him. He was despised and rejected by men, a man of sorrows, and familiar with suffering. Like one from whom men hide their faces he was despised, and we esteemed him not. Surely he took up our infirmities and carried our sorrows, yet we considered him stricken by God, smitten by him, and afflicted. But he was pierced for our transgressions, he was crushed for our iniquities; the punishment that brought us peace was upon him , and by his wounds we are healed.*

We all, like sheep, have gone astray, each of us has turned to his own way; and the LORD has laid on him the iniquity of us all. He was oppressed and afflicted, yet he did not open his mouth; he was led like a lamb to the slaughter, and as a sheep before her shearers is silent, so he did not open his mouth. By oppression and judgment he was taken away. And who can speak of his descendants? For he was cut off from the land of the living; for the transgression of my people he was stricken. He was assigned a grave with the wicked, and with the rich in his death, though he had done no violence, nor was any deceit in his mouth.

Yet it was the Lord's will to crush him and cause him to suffer, and though the Lord makes his life a guilt offering, he will see his offspring and prolong his days, and the will of the LORD will prosper in his hand. After the suffering of his soul, he will see the light [of life] and be satisfied; by his knowledge my righteous servant will justify many, and he will bear their iniquities. Therefore I will give him a portion among the great, and he will divide the spoils with the strong, because he poured out his life unto death, and was numbered with the transgressors. For he bore the sin of many, and made intercession for the transgressors. [81]

"Drew," she commented when he had finished, "You shouldn't tell my Leila but the truth is this person you have just read about sounds exactly like who the T.V. evangelists talk about on Sunday morning?"

"You mean you actually have listened to them?" Drew replied questioningly?

"Oyyy!" she replied, "Ever since you decided to become one of 'Them' I was trying to figure out what craziness you were thinking—how you could do such a thing.

"Grandma," he replied as he tenderly held her hands. "Again, I'm telling you. There is no *Them*—there is only *Us*, all of us who were born to gain eternal life through what this Yeshua did for us."

"Tell me again, Darling—vhat did Yeshua do for me?"

Drew opened his bible to the Gospel of John and read selectively:

"Let Him answer in His own words, Grandma:"

> *Then Yeshua cried out, "When a man believes in me, he does not believe in me only, but in the one who sent me. When he looks at me, he sees the one who sent me. I have come into the world as a light, so that no one who believes in me should stay in darkness. "* [82]

> *"For God so loved the world that he gave his one and only Son, that whoever believes in him shall not perish but have eternal life. For God did not send his Son into the world to condemn the world, but to save the world through him. Whoever believes in him is not condemned, but whoever does not believe stands condemned already because he has not believed in the name of God's one and only Son. This is the verdict: Light has come into the world, but men loved darkness instead of light because their deeds were evil. "* [83]

> *Yeshua said to her, "I am the resurrection and the life. He who believes in me will live, even though he dies; and whoever lives and believes in me will never die. Do you believe this?"* [84]

"Grandma," Drew asked longingly when he had finished reading. "These are words Yeshua spoke to others who came to know him and believe on Him about two thousand years ago. But He also was speaking to me and to you. He asked this woman of long ago if she believed and now He is asking you the same."

Her entire continence took on a remarkable transformation from fearfulness to complete peace as she replied, simply, "Yes, Drew darling, *Yes*, I do believe."

Drew again took her hands into his own and said, "Now, let's seal your new eternal life in Him with a short prayer. Grandma, repeat after me---" and she did, line by line:

"Yeshua, I am a sinner and I long to be forgiven of my sins. Please Lord wipe me clean—make me white as snow! I believe that You are the Messiah, the Son of God, one with the Father and the Holy Spirit, who came into the world as a man and who shed Your precious life as a perfect sacrifice for me and for all the world. Now, Yeshua, I invite You to come into my very being and to become the Lord of my life. I thank You Yeshua for what You have already done for me and for the world. Amen."

When they had further rejoiced together for a time, Drew, saying nothing about what had happened, guided Carla and his parents to Grandma Ameila's side.

"She looks so very peaceful now!" Leila observed when she now again saw her mother. "I can't believe the change—It's remarkable!"

About a half hour later, with those she loved most at her side, Amelia Grossman Cittrenbaum, entered the gates of heaven with a smile of joy illuminating her entire being.

Quite late that night, when Drew thought the others had gone to bed, he was prayerfully reviewing the momentous events of recent weeks and days in the comfortably furnished family room of his parents Scarsdale home where he and Carla would be staying until after Grandma Amelia's yet to be arranged burial in the Grossman family plot in a Jewish Cemetery on Long Island. "There is so much to be done," he mulled anxiously. "The funeral arrangements, getting the girls and the rest of the family here, and yes, finding sufficient time alone with Carla to make a well considered final decision about their immediate future."

"I thought I would find you here, Darling," Leila brought him back to the moment as she announced herself and joined him on the large leather sofa in front of the still glowing fireplace embers.

"So you couldn't sleep either?" he questioned.

"Not so you'd notice," she replied. "But I'm glad I found you here alone on the day of your grandmother's passing." Leila had been carrying a simply wrapped gift box when she entered the room and she now held it forth to her son. "She gave this to me for you a few days before she entered the hospital. She told me to give it to you after she was gone—it was as if she had some sort of premonition. She said that this was a 'special inheritance' meant just for you and that you would understand."

Not having even a hint at what treasure it may have held, Drew removed the simple wrappings, opened the box and withdrew its contents. He stood so that he could examine the beautiful tallit at its full length as well as the white and black kippahs that were included with the prayer shawl. There was a simple note between the folds of the tallit which he opened and read first silently and then aloud:

My Darling Drew,

This tallit and kippahs were my husband's, your grandfather who you never knew. I know that you two would have loved one another very much, like I love you and you love me. I know that he would have wanted you to have them. So, wear them in good health and with pride in being the Jew that you are.

Your loving grandmother,

Amelia

Without further comment, Drew carefully kissed the center of the shawl and put it around his shoulders; then, he placed the black yarmulke on top of his just beginning to bald head.

"Both of them would have been very proud of you, Drew." Leila said, wiping away a tear. "Just like your father and I."

"I know, Mom," he replied—"I know."

***

Chaplain Colonel Andrew Scott Sterling took a deep, fortifying breath, then stepped into the newly occupied office of his dearest friend, mentor and most importantly at this moment, the one man whom he considered more than any other to be his pastor. "Congratulations Major General Thurman!" he came to attention and smartly saluted the new Chief of Chaplains. "I know that this is the fulfillment of a long held dream and I'm thrilled for you, Sir!"

"Never mind, Drew," Sheldon replied warmly. "I will only sit in this place for two years and then it will likely become the end of your own rainbow. In the meantime, sitting in the office next door as my deputy isn't two onerous an idea, I presume!"

Sheldon had given him a perfect opportunity to open the Pandora's box that was his real purpose for making this side trip to the Pentagon before he and Carla returned to Germany. "The fact is, this is the very thing I've come to talk with you about. Carla and I have made a decision that will likely come as quite a surprise—." He hesitated for a moment, looking for the right words.

"Yes?" Sheldon questioned, showing the first hint from the deeply serious tone of Drew's voice that he understood something had gone terribly awry. "Please go on."

Drew did his best to rise to the difficult task at hand. "I don't intend to give you a sermon, Boss," he began. "But, I do want to begin with one of several hundred references in the Old Testament that speak to the same thing. Isaiah told us:

> *In that day the Lord will reach out his hand a second time*
> *to reclaim the remnant that is left of his people from Assyria,*
> *from Lower Egypt, from Upper Egypt, from Cush, from Elam,*
> *from Babylonia, from Hamath and from the islands of the sea.*
> 85

"Sheldon, the great prophet was talking about what is happening *today*. These are the end times. Our Lord will soon make His return, but before He does, ethnic Jews who have been dispersed all over the world must heed the clear biblical call to come home, to make *aliyah* to Israel."

Sheldon waited for a few of what seemed like endless moments as he framed his reply. "Drew, are you telling me that you, Carla and the girls are planning on moving to Israel?"

"Not exactly," Drew replied. "The fact is the girls are all agreed they will finish their education in the States—just the two of us will permanently relocate, at least at first---"

Sheldon cut him off. "A whole bunch of questions come to mind, Drew, but I don't have any real problem with your plans to move to Israel, as long as you are talking about four to six years from now— after you retire."

"This is the part you aren't going to like, Boss." Drew went on. "I'm talking about *right now*. I'm putting in my request for retirement as soon as I leave your office. It will be effective in sixty days."

Chapter Thirty Two

Mount Zion, Jerusalem
October 15, A.D. 30

The four of them: Kefa, Phillip, Matthias and their leader, Ya'akov, paused for a moment from what had become a somewhat heated and emotional discussion as they struggled to find agreement on how they were to meet the very urgent and compelling needs of the moment. They were seated at the large wooden table dominating the center of the Upper Room where they had continued to meet and worship, even after Yeshua's ascension. This was a sacred place that was universally agreed among the explosively growing number of new believers in Yeshua to be the birthplace of their new and unique expression of Torah fulfilled Messianic Judaism.

Ya'akov, rising to his responsibility, finally broke their self imposed silence. "My brothers," he began with controlled emotion. "There are so many matters to be resolved. To do so will take us many months, perhaps even years. *Again* I ask you; how are we to baptize? How are we to pray? In what manner and how often are we to remember our Lord's last supper with us? How are we to organize and administer our rapidly growing Body of Jewish believers in Yeshua? Where are we to meet— In synagogues, in homes, or in both? Are we to deal with women who love the Lord in the same manner as we deal with our brothers? The list seems to go on and on---?"

Matthias replied, taking advantage of Ya'akov's pause for breath: "Ya'akov, my brother, you have not included another most urgent matter.

May I also add: What, exactly are we to require of non-Jews in order that they might enter into our fellowship? Are we to accept them as full and equal members of our Body or are there to be certain distinctions?"

Kefa, making no effort to control his barely suppressed outrage, jumped to his feet and nearly shouted his unsolicited response: "*Of course* there are to be distinctions! Matthias, if I may, your Dory became one of us through her conversion to Judaism. Now, as a Torah observant follower of Judaism who also has, by His grace, become a believer in Yeshua, she is in every spiritual way the very same as all other members of our Body who by nature were born of Jewish parents."

"I ask you my brothers!" Kefa continued with rising emotion. "How can any of you, even for a moment consider fellowshipping with those who are forever ceremonially unclean? How can you even imagine the horror of sitting down to eat with those who eat the flesh of swine?[86]

"We only need to look to the miracles performed by of our risen Master," Matthias responded calmly, trying to temper the predictable contemptuous outburst of his dearest friend. "We must never forget the wonder He performed at Tel Hadar when He miraculously fed four thousand with seven small barley loaves and a few small fish. Remember, while there were certainly some Jews present, including both you and me, Kefa, the majority of these people were as you say, 'unclean, eaters of the flesh of swine.' You seem to forget that I sat down and ate with these people, and so did you, but more importantly so did Yeshua."[87]

Matthias paused for a moment to further gain the rapt attention of his brothers. Then, he continued with obvious deep love and unshakable conviction: "My brothers, our beloved Yeshua challenged the legally enforced separation of people as it is understood by many of our non-believing brothers, by inviting the whole multitude, Jews and Gentiles alike, to sit down and eat with Him— to share food with Him.

Then, He blessed the food in a traditional Jewish manner and He gave it to those of us disciples who were present to distribute."

When Matthias had once again taken his seat, Ya'akov continued. "My brothers, Kefa and Matthias have very well illustrated the great breadth and depth of our work that lies ahead. Yes, we must clearly define and boldly teach our Gentile brothers and sisters precisely what they are to do, how they are to worship, what is required of them to be fully accepted in our midst. Believe me, brothers, this matter alone is something that will require much prayer and divine guidance. My sense is, however, that this is not among the issues that we must get to immediately."

The attention of twelve seated with him at the table were riveted to their greatly loved and respected leader as he continued. "My brothers, the Gospel of our blessed Yeshua is spreading like wildfire throughout Jerusalem and beyond. Thousands, perhaps even many thousands of mostly Jews have already made statements of faith in our blessed Lord. Now, in keeping with His last commandment to you before He ascended into heaven, these new brothers and sisters must be baptized. This then, shall be the very first consideration on our agenda. How, precisely, shall we go about sealing the salvation of this growing multitude of newly committed believers who would enter into our fellowship? Surely, Yeshua was speaking of water immersion when He spoke of baptism, but how should this be accomplished and should there be any other elements in this initiation of new believers into the very Kingdom of God?"

***

The four of them: Ya'akov, Kefa, Phillip and Matthias stood at the entrance to the grotto that was situated just behind the building that housed the Upper Room. They had worked diligently, in deep and constant prayer for several days seeking the Lord's will for how they were to proceed with initiating the growing multitude of new believers into their fellowship. Finally, after they had individually confirmed to one another that they had heard the very same divine guidance through the intercession of the Holy Spirit, they had finalized the three part ritual that was to be followed for this sacred purpose. Even now, they were in the process of giving final instructions to the group of twelve komerim (deacons) they had selected and ordained from the inner circle of one hundred and twenty to administer these rites of initiation. Ya'akov, who had personally provided most of the meticulous instruction on how they were to proceed, smiled in satisfaction that God's will was about to be accomplished in this remarkable precedent setting, first institution of this sacred, salvation sealing ceremony.

"I now charge you all, my brothers, in the name of our precious Lord, Yeshua to go forth into this place and seal the salvation of these new brethren as you welcome each of them into our full fellowship. Your work will be long and demanding for many thousands of these soon to be saints who await the indescribable blessings that will come to them through your devoted service as conduits for this, our Lord's joyful, welcoming touch. And so my brothers," Ya'akov concluded his remarks, "the first group of twelve who seek baptism will now be called. They will be followed by other groups of twelve in a never ending succession, twenty-four hours each day except for Shabbat, until all who seek such baptism shall have been served. At the beginning," Ya'akov now pointed to the three disciples who stood at his side. "One of these brothers will be with you in each of the three chambers to participate, pray and to make certain that all goes well. May the Lord God of Israel abundantly bless you all."

***

Matthias greeted the first group of twelve men who would be baptized at the top of the hand hewn stone stairs leading down into the grotto. They were a mixed group, varying in age from young to very old, and from their dress and general appearance, Matthias marveled at how the Lord had included amongst them representatives from apparently every societal strata of the greater Jerusalem community. While they appeared very different and easily distinguishable by age and their physical circumstances, Matthias also noted that they shared one very imposing thing in common—both individually and collectively they glowed with the presence of the Holy Spirit within them that had recently taken up residence with their own spirits in His temple that had in fact miraculously become each of their bodies.

"Come along, my brothers." Matthias greeted them tenderly, bathing them in his own great love that shined forth from him as a glorious mantle that touched all who now followed him down the stone stairs into the first chamber of the grotto.

The very small amount of natural, seemingly deep blue, dimly glowing light that filled this place was barely sufficient for them to find their way, even as they were assisted by Matthias and the three komerim who were assigned to conduct this first part of the three part initiation.

"My brothers," Matthias began, "Let us recite together the renunciation of our sinful ways." The twelve now repeated Matthias' words as he paused between each phrase for this purpose. "With all of my heart---With all of my soul---With all of my Spirit---I totally and completely renounce Satan and his legion of demons and all the evil works of their creation."

When this was finished, Matthias continued. "And now my brothers, I ask you to to divest yourselves of all your clothing. When you are thus totally unclothed you will be given a vile of sacred anointing oil with which with the assistance of the komerim, you are to anoint your entire bodies.

When each of the initiates had meticulously followed these instructions, Matthias continued. "My brothers, I now ask you to repeat, after me, your confession of faith." Again, pausing between phrases, Matthias led the twelve: "Heavenly Father, I confess with my mouth and believe with all of my heart that Yeshua is the promised Messiah, Your Son--- And that He reigns with you and the Holy Spirit as the Holy God of Israel---I believe that He came into the world to dwell among us as God incarnate--- To forgive our sins and to show us the way to our salvation and eternal life in the Kingdom of Heaven--- I believe that He willingly went to His cross and suffered death, shedding His precious blood there as a perfect blood sacrifice for us all---I believe that he died as a man, was buried and that He arose from the dead on the third day---I believe that he ascended into Heaven---I believe that He will return at the end of days to take up His throne on this very Mount Zion where He will reign in glory--- I repent of my sins and will worship you all the day's of my life--- Because your word is truth, I confess with my mouth that I am born again and cleansed by the Blood of Yeshua! In Yeshua's name. Amen."

"May God richly bless you all, my brothers," Matthias continued after a few moments. "Hear now the words that were recorded in our sacred scrolls at Qumran many years before Yeshua came and walked among us:

And he will atone for all the children of his generation,

and he will be sent to all the children of his people. His word is like the word of the heavens, and his teaching according to the will of God. His eternal sun will shine and his fire will burn in all the ends of the earth; above the darkness his sun will shine. Then, darkness will vanish from the earth, and gloom from the globe. They will utter many words against him, and utter every kind of disparagement against him. [88]

"And now, my brothers, hear the words that Yeshua spoke that many of us heard with our own ears: *'I am the light of the world. He who follows Me shall not walk in darkness, but have the light of life.'*"[89]

At the moment Matthias read these words spoken by Yeshua, the komerim lit a large array of olive oil fed lamps that were placed on all of the walls of this chamber of the grotto. The effect was: Magnificent! Startling! Electric! as the multi-source flashing light was reflected from the fully anointed bodies of the twelve initiates who now danced about the enchantingly illuminated chamber, shouting out their praises to God for the great things He had done.

When they had finished their rejoicing, Matthias with some difficulty, once again managed to return them to a state of order so that they might proceed to the second part of their initiation. Having done so, he led them into the next chamber along the way of the branch of the complex catacombs that formed the grotto.

"It is here, my brothers," he pointed to a large Jewish ceremonial mikvah at the center of the chamber, "that you will be fully immersed three times in the ancient purification rite of our people." With that he descended the seven short steps into the spring fed running water as he beckoned the first of the initiates to follow him.

Now, as the eldest of the group of twelve, who was selected to be first in deference to his years, stood directly in front of Matthias who was, symbolically, the adopted sibling of Yochanan the Baptizer, Matthias placed his hands on the man's head and applied just a hint of pressure, proclaiming

"I baptize you in the name of the Father." As he spoke, the man squatted down in place until he was totally immersed, a condition insured by the water that for a moment covered Matthias' hands that remained in their place on top of the man's head.

As soon as the man once again stood in front of Matthias they repeated the immersion in the same manner, this time Matthias proclaiming; "I baptize you in the name of the Son." Then, when this was concluded, a third immersion followed with Matthias proclaiming: "I baptize you in the name of the Holy Spirit."

When this was finished, the other eleven initiates followed in turn into the water where they were baptized by Matthias in the same manner as the first. Joyfully, as each came up out of the water, all present shouted out praises to God for the wonder of His salvation and great goodness that He had bestowed upon them.

Finally, when all twelve had been so immersed and order had once again been restored, Matthias led the group into the next connecting chamber where the third and final right of their initiation was to be conducted.

With the twelve once again gathered about him, Matthias began to pray in Aramaic, the day to day common language of them all. "Heavenly Father, I know call upon you to release within each of these my newly baptized brothers the full and mighty power of your Holy Spirit that dwells within each of them. I ask this in the name of your Son, Yeshua, so that these twelve might be fully empowered to manifest the gifts and the fruit of the Spirit, even, as it may be according to your will, to perform miracles in your name."

Then, Matthias, with his arms fully raised above his head, continued to pray, but now in a language that was known only to His God to whom it was offered. As he thus cried out, he went from one initiate to the next, reaching out towards them but not quite making physical contact. As he did so, each of them in turn, fully overcome by the palpable power of the Holy Spirit that filled the room, fell over backwards, miraculously landing unharmed upon the solid stone floor where they lay for a time fully entranced.

After a time, one by one, the twelve of them arose and began to cry out praises to God for what He had done in a new tongue known only to the Holy one of Israel to whom it was offered. When all twelve had thus arisen and begun to pray, the room was totally alive in the Spirit with all of whom bore witness to this amazing happening weeping for joy and crying out praises from the very depths of their beings.[90]

***

Early the next morning, Matthias accompanied Dory to the entrance of the sacred grotto where she, having been trained and ordained as one of the komerot (deaconesses) was to participate in the initiation of the first group of twelve woman. These totally committed women were to receive the very same three part ritual ceremony as had the men on the day before, and, when this had been accomplished, they were to take their places then and forevermore as fully equal and fully participating members of the Body of Yeshua. For this is how it had been decided by Ya'akov and the Twelve Disciples.

***

Late that same evening, Matthias called upon Ya'akov who was relaxing for a brief time in the Upper Room. "Forgive me for interrupting your rest, my brother," he greeted his leader, "but I am persuaded that I have been led by the Holy Spirit to create a wonderful new symbol that represents the purpose and substance of our ministry. I've sketched this symbol on parchment and, if you are willing, I would like to share it with you."

"Of course I am willing, Matthias!" Ya'akov exclaimed. "How could I not be willing to share in such a wondrous gift?"

Thus encouraged, Matthias placed the parchment on the table immediately in front of where Ya'akov sat and he began to explain the lovely three part symbol he had been guided to sketch.

"Please take note, my brother," Matthias began. "The top part is a simple menorah, a long established representation of the very essence of our beloved Torah based Judaism. Likewise, the bottom part is a simple line drawing of a small fish. The Holy Spirit reminded me that Yeshua multiplied such small fish on two separate occasions whereat He miraculously fed first a large group of mostly Jews and next another large group of mostly non-Jews. I was further thus reminded that there were twelve baskets left over from the feeding of the Jews, one for each tribe, and that there were seven baskets left over from the feeding of the non-Jews, one for each of seven nations. Further, it was revealed to me that the fish will one day in the future become the universally understood symbol representing Yeshua, Himself, and the huge Body of mostly non-Jewish believers who will eventually follow Him."

"Notice also," my dear brother," Matthias continued his explanation. "The middle part of the symbol is made up of the overlapping stand of the menorah and the tail of the fish to form a perfect six pointed star. This star represents Yeshua, the Messiah, who was prophesized in the Torah as one who would come out of Jacob---a Scepter rising out of Israel."[91] (Note: In modern times, this precious six pointed star has become a universally recognized symbol of the contemporary State of Israel and all Jews everywhere.)

"Could it be any more obvious, Ya'akov?" Matthias concluded. "This wonderful three part symbol speaks directly to the unity that is already evident in our Body between Jews and Gentiles who are coming into the faith. But, even more, it speaks specifically to *Unity*, not *Uniformity*. The menorah and the fish are in many material ways and otherwise very different, as are the Jewish and Gentile believers in Yeshua they represent. Even so, as these two substantively different groups come together symbolically to form the six pointed star, they are thus made *One* Body of Yeshua by the eternal salvation they share in His precious shed blood."

"Yes, Matthias!" Ya'akov exclaimed excitedly when Matthias had finished. "I can confirm in my spirit that this symbol is indeed a divine gift, a seal that speaks to our Heavenly Father's heart's desire that there be unity in the Body of Yeshua, now and for all generations to come. "We must distribute this symbol as widely as we are able and teach its great and wonderful meaning at every opportunity."

Chapter Thirty Three

Tiberias, Israel
March 1979

The two of them stood arm in arm on the large meerpesset (balcony) of their lovely fifth floor penthouse apartment overlooking the city, the Sea of Galilee and the Golan Heights.

"Is this what you had in mind, Darling?" Drew, filled with awe at the view before them, asked as he gently pulled Carla toward him and kissed her with a love that reflected the depth of his devotion and the enduring bond of their already long and wonderful life together that had now taken such an unexpected and remarkable new direction. "I can't believe there's any place in the world any lovelier than this."

"This new home we've found is certainly far more than anything I'd even imagined," she replied. "I've been praying for an apartment with a view of the Lake and just look at what He's provided! He's opened up His storehouse in heaven and poured out all of this! Thank you Lord! Praise you!" She cried out her praise and thanksgiving over the lovely scene before them.

"This apartment may be *one* thing!" Drew replied joyfully, "but just look at these, Carla! Just look at *these*!" he exclaimed in wonderment, removing their just issued *taudot zahoot* (national identity cards) from his shirt pocket. "Can you believe it? These are *ours*! As of this very day, *we* are *citizens* of the State of Israel? Is there no end to His provision?"

"All of this is almost too wonderful to take in!" she added. "And, just two more days and our container will be delivered from Port Haifa. It will be so good to finally have this apartment furnished with our own things instead of making do with a few borrowed odds and ends. I still don't understand why Israeli Customs wouldn't release our shipment before today?"

"God knew and we knew all of this would go well." Drew replied, "But, there really *was* a possibility in the eyes of the government that we just might not be accepted as citizens, in which case both our container and the two of us would have been summarily shipped back to the States and that would have been the end of our dream!"

"Well, my love," she replied excitedly. "The fact is, albeit small and noisy, we do have a refrigerator in the kitchen, and it does just happen to hold a bottle of the finest Israel sparkling wine nicely chilled for such an occasion as this!"

***

They sat in borrowed white plastic chairs on the meerpessit, the now empty "champagne" bottle between them, as they watched the huge full moon, a glowing red-orange ball, rising before them over the Golan Heights, reflecting its sparkling light from the rippled surface of the lake in a way that seemed to be a very special blessing for their eyes alone.

"You know, Darling," Drew reflected happily, "It isn't that we've just been sitting around doing nothing these past six weeks. Living here has so far been a bit sparse, but on balance this has been an incredible time for us to at least start getting acquainted with this Land of our inheritance."

She replied with feigned sarcasm. "Neither one of us has ever been in better physical condition from all our on foot sight seeing! Oh, Drew! Won't it be great to finally be allowed to buy our car?"

"Indeed it will!" he replied happily. "As a matter of fact, now that we are full fledged olim hadishim (new immigrants) there is no longer any reason to wait. We should have our new Subaru in just a few days!"

"Praise God!" she exclaimed. "What a blessing it is we had sufficient savings to pay cash for both this apartment and a car—to say nothing of your Air Force pension that is more than adequate to meet our needs here in the Land."

"Not to mention the mutual funds we've been feeding all these years for the girls' education!" he added. "What a blessing that we should have no concern at all about money and can devote all of our energies to whatever the Lord has in mind for us here in the Land."

"Do you have any idea at all what that might be?" she asked, happy to have an opening into a matter they had not yet more than superficially explored together.

He waited a few moments, trying to frame his thoughts. "A bit more than a glimpse, I'd say," he replied thoughtfully. She waited silently for him to continue.

"I believe there's a huge gulf of misunderstanding born of bad teaching that has been separating the Church from 'born again' Jews from the very beginning. Even now there's a "them and us" mentality that continues to fuel a whole new outpouring of anti-Semitism.

"Anyway, Darling," he paused for a moment before he got to the substance of his reply that would guide them through all the years of their new life in Israel. "While I'm not yet certain just what direction it may take, I do know that my ministry here in the Land has to do with helping to restore unity among *all* believers in the Body of Yeshua."

He then continued with the conviction to explain his growing understanding. "I already see that there are two sides to this calling. First, our 'born again' Jewish brothers and sisters must learn to understand that they, and whom they often disdainfully label as "Christians" share the very same salvation in the shed blood of Yeshua.

"They need to *respect* Gentile Christianity as the vehicle through which the faith in Yeshua called 'Christianity' by most of the world, managed to endure after the first two or three centuries. In short, believing Jews must gently and lovingly be shown that *Church* isn't a dirty word and that their fellow believers in the pews of Gentile Christian Churches are not to be avoided but rather embraced for whom they are--- their very real brothers and sisters in Yeshua.

"Oh *yes*, Drew!" Carla agreed. "But, what you are saying could take several lifetimes to accomplish!"

"Indeed!" he replied. "And I have only outlined *part* of the problem. "The rest has to do with opening up the hearts and eyes of our Gentile Christian brothers and sisters.

"We must show them that the roots of our shared faith in Yeshua are indeed Jewish. They must also come to understand that while we share identical salvation in His precious blood, we do indeed remain ethnically different.

"Paul certainly made it clear that there are enduring physical differences between slaves and masters, between male and female, and there are certainly enduring ethnic, cultural and traditional differences between Jews and Gentiles who have been saved by Yeshua.

"Perhaps, for Gentile believers," Drew continued, "the most important thing they must come to understand is that there is potentially very little to be gained and very much indeed to be lost through living out a misguided yearning to somehow become Jewish; even as identically Jewish as those who were born of ethnically Jewish parents!"

"Doesn't Scripture speak to this point?" Carla interjected.

"*Twice*, in Revelations!" Drew immediately replied. Yeshua Himself spoke out strongly against the first century generation of "Wannabees" when He said: "I know the slander of those who say they are Jews and are not, but are a synagogue of Satan."[92]

"It sounds to me like you already have a pretty good idea what the Lord has called you to do here," she commented reflectively.

"I know there will be more—much more!" he replied with the confidence of his growing understanding.

***

"It's gorgeous!" Carla squealed with delight a few days later, as she, at Drew's side made their first walk around inspection of their shiny new, pearl white, 1979 Legacy at the local Subaru dealership.

"And, the good news is," he added. "It's paid for!"

"I'm so looking forward to our first self provided trip around the Lake!" she exclaimed as she put the picnic basket they had brought from their apartment into the trunk."

"Let's go!" he said excitedly, as he took his place for the first time behind the wheel of their lovely new means of conveyance.

***

"Why are we stopping *here*?" Carla asked as Drew pulled off the road into a parking place just beyond the entrance to the Church at the foot of Mount Ermos known as "Peter's Primacy." "I thought we were going to go right to the other side of the Lake and explore Hippos?"

"We shall!" Drew replied warmly. "But first, indulge me for a few minutes as we satisfy one of *my* long suppressed desires. Come on!" he pleaded excitedly. "This will only take a few minutes."

She followed him up a primitive metal staircase and onto a trail that led a short distance up the face of Mount Ermos, where nearly two thousand years earlier Yeshua had blessed the world with His Sermon on the Mount.

"Here we are!" he announced as they soon reached the entrance of a cave that was almost completely obscured from view from where they stood by a single fig tree whose natural dark green camouflage was augmented by a dense carpet of tall, black-eyed, golden daises, covering the entire hillside. This lovely, God-woven carpet was shifting to and fro as were the waves of the Lake below whose random movement was orchestrated by the gentle, yet determined late morning breeze.

"This place is called Ermos Cave," Drew explained. "Come, let's go inside."

Carla hesitated for a moment, and then she boldly stepped into the dark, cool interior of the cave which was large enough for them to stand together, side by side.

As she did so she immediately swooned under a powerful spiritual presence and had to struggle to remain standing. "Dear God!" she proclaimed as she stumbled onto a crude wooden bench that had been placed there by persons unknown. "*He's* here! The Spirit of the Lord is in this place!"

Drew followed her into this very special, holy place and, like she, immediately found himself gasping for air, barely able to breathe as he staggered to sit beside his wife. "Indeed, the Holy Spirit is in this place, just as I had been led by Him to believe He would be."

"This is one of those places near Capernaum," he explained, "where our blessed Yeshua came to pray and escape the crowd." He reached into his back pack and removed a small package he had prepared without her knowledge the evening before. "I thought it would be a very special experience for us to take the Lord's Supper in this place as a symbolic beginning of our new life and ministry here in the Land."

"How very precious!" she replied, still overcome by the rich spiritual presence in this place.

After Drew had given a sweet prayer of thanksgiving, and the two of them had silently repented for all they had done, said and even thought that might have been offensive to the Lord, Drew took a matzo from his improvised mobile Communion set.

"This may also surprise you, Darling," he announced, trying not to be prideful. "But I've already learned a bit of Hebrew." He then took the matzo and blessed it chanting: *Baruch Ata Adoni Eloheinu Melech ha Olam ha Motzee Lecham Mean ha Eretz. Ah'men.* (Blessed are You O Lord our God, King of the Universe, who brings forth bread from the earth). He then broke two small pieces from the matzo and handed one to Carla, then offered: "Yeshua told us that this was His Body, given for us for the forgiveness of our sin. Let us eat this bread in remembrance of what He has done for us."

When they had finished, Drew took a small bottle of sweet red wine from his communion kit and poured it into a silver chalice that he had also included. He then held up the chalice before them, saying: "In a like manner at the end of the meal Yeshua took the cup and blessed it saying (he chanted):

Baruch Ata Adoni Eloheinu Melech ha Olam Boray Puree haGefen, Ah'men
(Blessed are you O Lord our God, King of the Universe, who creates the fruit
of the vine.) Then, Drew continued: "Yeshua went to His cross where He
shed His precious blood willingly as the perfect sacrifice for the forgiveness
of our sin. Behold life is in the blood and eternal life is in Yeshua." He took
a drink from the chalice and then handed it to Carla who did the same.

When they had finished they remained silent for a few minutes of quiet
contemplation and prayer. Finally, Drew broke their silence: "Could we
possibly be more blessed than this?" he asked rhetorically. "I can hardly
cope with the reality that we are citizens of the Land where our blessed Lord
spent His life on earth—that we are sitting in the very place where He sat and
that even now His presence with us is almost palpable."

"And," Carla exclaimed, "Yeshua couldn't have chosen a more beautiful
place to seclude Himself from the crowds. The view from this place is
absolutely breath taking! I've never seen a body of water sparkle like this.
Just look at Tiberias! Can you believe it is our new *home*? It seems to be
a fairy tale city framed by palm trees and adorned with the entire world's
diamonds."

"Don't forget the Golan rising up from the opposite shore!" Drew
continued in the same deeply appreciative vein. "They are exquisite and
ever changing in their appearance—painted from a veritable pallet of colors
by the very Hand of the God who created them."

***

Some time later, when they had finally recovered sufficiently from their
spiritual encounter in Ermos Cave, the two of them continued their drive that
would take them around the North end of the Lake and then along its Eastern
shore. It took them about twenty minutes to reach Kibbutz En Gev that
consisted mostly of a large, lovely community built right along the shore.

"Okay!" Drew announced with feigned authority. "According to the
map," he opinioned, putting down the Hebrew annotated guide. "This must
be the turn off leading up to Sussita National Park?" With that, he turned

their new Subaru left off the highway onto a very primitive graveled road.

"Don't those round red signs with the white line in the middle mean we are not to enter?" Carla asked sounding disappointed. "I've so looked forward to getting my feet onto this place---."

"Never mind!" Drew answered. "There are also signs written in Hebrew that obviously are there to explain the details of the no entry restriction."

"What do they say?" she asked.

"How would I know?" he answered. "Do I sound like someone who reads and speaks Hebrew?

With that they boldly began a long very steep tedious climb up the slope of the Golan creeping along and often maneuvering sharply to avoid the innumerable potentially axle breaking huge washouts along the way.

"It seems like we are in a slow boat making its way across a golden sea," Drew exclaimed, referring to the dense carpet of black eyed golden daisies that extended in many places to rise up even from the gravel surface of the road that had now become more of a trail.

"It doesn't look like there's been another car along this road in years," he continued, almost to himself." But his comment only further spooked Carla who had just begun to notice the skull and cross bone signs posted on both sides of their decrepit narrow pathway. "Drew, Darling," she asked fearfully. "Just what do those awful signs mean?"

"Not much really," he replied trying to make light of their perilous environment. "Only that there are active mine fields on either side of the road and we had best have our picnic in some other more suitable location."

"Hey!" Drew announced excitedly when they had progressed about half the distance up to the several kilometer wide rich farmland plateaus at the top of slope that separated Israel from Syria, its virulently hostile neighbor. "I think we've arrived." With that he pulled the car off to the right side of the road, into a very narrow parking area that had apparently long since fallen into total disuse.

"Let's check out the sign!" he invited, leaving the car and moving through the thick, multi-colored wildflower carpet toward what appeared to be a barely discernable Israel National Park Authority sign. As he reached the sign, he saw that it marked the beginning of a rugged, straight up trail that apparently led to the ancient city that had become Carla's inexplicably passionate quest to visit and explore.

Drew, who noted that the sign was written in three languages: Hebrew, Arabic and English, began to read aloud the version in their native tongue:

> The city of Hippos, also known well as Sussita, was founded on this hill overlooking the eastern shore of the Sea of Galilee during the Hellenistic period in the second century BCE. The first residents of the city were pagans who later converted to Christianity. At their side was a small Jewish community as well. Most of the ruins visible today date to the Roman and Byzantine periods (first century BCE-seventh century CE). They include a city gate, a main colonnaded street, a defense wall with fortified towers, a sophisticated water supply system, a main square (the Forum). A reservoir, a sanctuary, churches, a baptistery, and more. The city was apparently destroyed by an earthquake in 749 CE and was never resettled. During Israel's War of Independence in 1948, members of Kibbutz En Gev, located at the foot of the hill, took military control of Sussita. It served as a front-line military command post until the Six Day War in 1967.

"Oh! Drew!" Carla exclaimed. "I am so excited about seeing this place! Let's get started!"

"Maybe it would be a good idea if we ate first?" he suggested warmly, trying not to dampen her enthusiasm. "It looks to me like the schlep up the trail is one we won't soon forget and it would be best for us not to carry anything but our water and camera."

When they had finished their picnic of fried chicken and potato salad while sitting on an obviously ancient hand hewn stone bench at the foot of the trail, Drew took a deep breath of contentment and offered teasingly: "Are you sure you are up to this trek? I know we are in good shape from all the walking we've been doing these past several weeks, but this looks like it may be the proverbial straw?"

"Darling, I can't explain it, but it's like I've been waiting for this moment all of my life. Come on, Silly! Let's get going!"

With that they struggled up the boulder ridden, agonizingly steep trail, stopping along the way every few minutes to catch their breath and to take in the beautiful scene that continued on all sides to unfold beneath them as they progressed toward the ruins of the ancient city on the plateau at the end of the trail.

Finally, they reached the ruins of the stone hewn eastern gate, and they paused for a time to regain their normal breathing. Then, the two of them continued along the now level trail searching expectantly for some sign of archaeological evidence that this place indeed had once been an enormously important early Christian center.

"Wow!" Drew exclaimed in exited discovery as he pointed just off the left side of the trail to the extensive wild flower strewn ruins of what seemed to him to be a very large, obviously ancient Church. "This must be the fourth century Byzantine basilica I found mentioned in my recent research! It must have been magnificent in its day!"

They stood together looking out over the very large ruins strewn area silently taking in the clear evidence of the one time prominence of this very large place of worship with its three perfectly preserved semi-circular apses.

"Look at this, Carla!" Drew announced with excited discovery. "There is a baptismal right behind the ruins of the altar in the central apse." He moved closer to more carefully explore his find. "It is obviously deep enough for immersion but far to small to hold more than a small child. Ergo—these people baptized infants by immersion. As far as I know, only the Eastern Orthodox follow this practice today."

"How do you suppose they baptized adults?" Carla conjectured.

"My guess is that they likely stuck with the Jewish principal of immersion and most likely did this in some yet to be unearthed mikvah-like adult baptismal or," he conjectured, "perhaps even in the lake below."

The two of them spent the next hour or so taking in every visible detail of the excavated ruins of this apparently very large and elaborate basilica that had lain here, untouched, since its very limited archaeological exploration in 1952. Finally, Drew announced. "Well, that's about all there is to see here for now, but you can be sure that one of these days some other group will get around to digging up the rest of this place, and you can be sure also that this will be an enormous challenge. Hippos was a huge city and the early evidence shows there were at least two other churches, and all manner of other city dwellings and residences that are just begging to be investigated."

"Oh! Drew!" Carla now begged. "Do we have to leave already? I, I---I want to stay here awhile longer."

"Me too," he replied tenderly. I doubt that we'll see much if any other signs of the extensive ruins that lie just below the surface, but let's meander across the place and have a look at the view these folks once enjoyed from the Western side of their magnificent city."

A short time later, after they had arrived at the extreme Western edge of the steep precipice that marked the Western side of the plateau, they stood looking west toward the lake far below and the incredibly beautiful vista that stretched out before them. The steep intensely green slope between them and the water was richly decorated with a seemingly unending carpet of tall butter gold daises with black centers interspersed with a generous sprinkling of blood red poppies that moved like waves on the sea, tossed to and fro by the sometimes brisk direction changing breeze that also provided some cooling comfort. As they took in the indescribable beauty of the scene before them, they were filled with both joy and wonder. They stood there arm in arm, deeply in love with one another and with the Lord God of Israel who had seen fit to bring them to this place, a very special gem in the crown of their magnificent, divine inheritance.

"Now I can see why I've had such a deep longing, even a special love for this very special ancient city," Carla offered reverently.

He quickly agreed. "I have clear sense, even more, a sure understanding that we will return here many times! I *know* in my spirit that this ancient city and what happened here are central to why the Lord brought us home to the

Land of our inheritance!"

Chapter Thirty Four

December, A.D. 30
Hippos

Matthias pulled once again with at the fastening strings of his hood to make it just a bit tighter in a vain attempt to escape the biting gusts of wind that lashed at his inadequately clothed back as he and Dory neared Hippos at the end of their late winter, bitter cold, and torturous assent to the summit. "Thank God we're almost there!" he cried out, almost inaudibly over the screaming bursts of wind that now swirled about them depositing a quickly accumulating frozen white layer upon the rock strewn surface around them.

Dory laughed, loudly enough to be heard over the raging wind. "Stop complaining my precious Jewish husband!" she replied, teasingly, as she, three months pregnant with their first child, danced about in joyful appreciation of what to her were normative "winter wonderland" surroundings. "Look at it this way, Matthias— Our God has given us the snow today that will very soon melt and bring forth the glorious flowers! Then, soon after the glorious flowers," she continued with tears of joy, He will bring forth the flesh of our flesh as a sweet testimony of His love in us and for us!"

Matthias hurried his pace to catch up with his lovely wife. Having done so, he grabbed her about the waist and pulled her close in a loving embrace. They kissed as the falling snow enveloped them in their own white veil of privacy. "You know," he teased, as he pulled away for a moment to catch his breath. "I could have married a nice Jewish girl from Bethsaida—one with a rich father!"

"And I," she replied very seriously, "I could have married one of my childhood Gentile friends and never come to have known the joy of my salvation in Yeshua!" Tears had begun to flow from her beautiful, very large, deep blue eyes and he gently kissed them away. "Matthias, my darling husband, because of *you* my life has been forever changed---."

"Not because of me—my precious Dory— it is all because of *Him*! In my heart I know He brought us together, a Jew and a Gentile made one flesh, so that together we might do great and wonderful things for Him."

***

"Welcome to my home!" Athanasios greeted his two very dear friends later that evening, after they had settled in for their extended stay with Dory's family. "It's so good to see you my dear brother and sister! It's been too long! Come, sit closer to the fire; it will warm your bones!"

The two of them gladly accepted the invitation as they sat down, cuddling close, upon the antelope hide that covered the earthen floor in front of the now roaring fire that cut through the biting cold embrace that held the entire city in its unrelenting grip.

"We've missed you very much as well, Athan," Matthias replied. "There were many things that kept us in Jerusalem and much more remains to be done, but now we are free from all this for a time in order to continue our work among our dear brothers and sisters here in the Decapolis."

"You've come just in time for our first congregational celebration of Yeshua's birth!" Athan announced excitedly. "We will do so in just three days, on Sunday, the Winter Solstice." He continued his hurried revelation before Matthias could voice a reply. "Our entire group will gather in the Temple of Helios, you know, the magnificent old structure very close to our own humble meeting place. We will gather there just before the sun rises—I am so pleased you two will be here with us for this wonderful celebration!"

Matthias, trying not to be overly critical and measuring his words very carefully replied: "You may not yet know this, Athan, but those among us who were close to Yeshua's family when He was a child have made it known to us that our master was born in the fall of the year, during the feast of Succoth. Why have you chosen the winter solstice, the birthday of the Sun God Helios, to celebrate the coming of the one true God into the world?"[93]

Athan, in turn, carefully measured his somewhat defensive reply. "It seems to me the very fact that Yeshua *came* into the world is the thing to be celebrated—not specifically *when* He came into the world!" He continued, not waiting for a reply. "My people have celebrated the birth of their ancient god Helios every year at this time for as long as anyone can remember. It is a long standing sacred tradition that will draw virtually everyone in our community to worship in the same place at the same time. What a golden opportunity it will be for those of us who already know Yeshua to share His truth with all of the many who do not yet know Him! I am so pleased that you will be with us to preach the good news of Yeshua to them who are still unsaved among my people!"

Matthias did not yet respond directly, changing the subject for a time. "May I also ask you, my brother; why have you chosen to celebrate this wonderful occasion in the Temple of Helios the Sun God?"

"One day," Athan replied fervently, without hesitation. "One day when our congregation has grown to include most of the people of Hippos, we will erect a mighty temple (ecclesia, church) to Yeshua, a sacred and worthy place of worship—mighty and beautiful in its structure that will greatly overshadow the already magnificent temple of Helios. Then all who see these two temples standing side by side will know with assurance who is the mightiest of all the Gods! But, for now, we must settle for using the already existing structure. What else can we do? Our very small meeting place is not nearly large enough to accommodate all of the many who will attend this great celebration."

"To tell you the truth, Matthias," Athan continued with obvious envy. "You Jews still have a mighty and glorious temple standing in Jerusalem. Even those of you who know Yeshua go there to gather in the spacious courts of that beautiful place. I fail to see the difference in your temple and our temple to Helios."

Matthias, turning teacher instructed in reply: "There are several key differences, my brother. First, those many Jews who do not yet know Yeshua, worship His father, Yahweh, there—He who is the one true living God. It is to Him that they continue to sacrifice animals, not knowing that Yeshua has become the once and for all great blood sacrifice that has superceded all other sacrifices. No Jew, saved by the blood of Yeshua or not, worships Helios or any other false god in their temple. In fact, saved Jews never go inside the temple. They only gather in the spacious courtyards because it is a large, convenient and holy place for them to meet."

"I see a great potential danger in your use of this Temple of Helios," Matthias carefully continued. "Many generations of your people have worshipped a false god in this polluted place.

"Since it has fallen upon me to bring them the good news of Yeshua, I will emphasize the point in my teaching that it is not the *place* but rather the *person* whom they are called to worship. I will teach them to keep their eyes upon Yeshua and away from the person and temple of Helios, a false god among many false gods."

"Amen, my brother," Athan replied in agreement. "I want you to know that I have already given this matter considerable and prayerful thought. In fact, I have claimed the Temple of Helios for the worship of Yeshua—Come, let me show you what I have done."

A few minutes later, after the three of them had ventured out into the biting cold of the morning, they stood just outside the entry of the magnificent colonnaded Temple of Helios. "I grew up loving this place," Dory offered mostly for her own benefit. "While I know in my heart of hearts that Matthias speaks the truth, it is very difficult for me to find any evil in this beautiful place."

"Is it any wonder?" Matthias replied resolutely. "Satan himself masquerades as an angel of light. The serpent appears beautiful to many eyes that behold him, and so does this place that is so very pleasing to the eye—an evil temple at whose altar a Satanic god receives the blood sacrifice of pigs!"

"When there is a time for the entire community to meet in worship," he continued, "it would be far better for all who seek the one true God to gather outside of your humble public meeting place." Matthias paused for just a moment to emphasize what was to follow.

"My dear brother," he spoke with the fervor of his deep conviction. "It would be far more beneficial for your people who love Yeshua to continue meeting in small groups in their homes, breaking bread together there just after the sun sets at the end of Shabbat. I must confess that I have a great fear, even a clear discernment that one day the Body of believers will be so focused on building mighty edifices that they will almost completely lose sight of Yeshua, the one whom they seek to worship."

"You are correct, Matthias," Athan replied somewhat sheepishly, "but, come, let me show you where my heart is by something special I have done." With that he led Matthias with Dory at his side just inside the entry to the Temple of Helios. Then, taking them behind the first pillar on the right side of the magnificently colonnaded structure he pointed to the anagram logo of his own creation he had etched deeply, in Greek letters into the marble: Ιχθυσ ("fish") an abbreviation of: Ιησουσ Χριστοσ Θηου Υιοσ Σωτηρ ("Jesus Christ", Son of God, Savior").

"It is thus I have claimed this place for the worship of Yeshua!" he declared with immense pride. "This is the very same faith declaring symbol that adorns your Dory's wedding pendant!"

"Again, my brother," Matthias replied, now more tenderly. "Much caution must be exercised by us and by succeeding generations as the *ecclesia* (universal Church) grows from this very humble place where it began, into a mighty force that will eventually bring the light of Yeshua to the entire world."

"My point is this, and I ask you to hear me well!" Matthias raised his voice in dramatic conviction. "Those who truly love Yeshua must never allow their places and forms of worship to take on more significance than their own personal relationship with Him, the precious one whom they have come to worship! As the Holy Spirit leads, I will speak more of this on Sunday morning."

Chapter Thirty Five

Ben Gurion International Airport
August 1989

Drew smiled broadly when he saw him as he looked over the heads of the crowd gathered at the arrival area in Terminal One of Israel's only international airport. Now Carla, who was standing close by Drew's side, saw him too, and she waved excitedly to catch the attention of this very special arriving visitor whom they both loved with a long standing deep affection and admiration.

Then, in a flash of joyful recognition, Chaplain Major General Sheldon Thurman, USAF (retired) caught the eye of his two enthusiastic greeters and waved back with his own returned shared joy to once again begin what had become an unscheduled but more or less regular annual visit with them since they made *aliyah*, to Israel, the Land of their inheritance, more than ten years before.

***

"It's incredible how this country is growing—despite everything!" Sheldon commented in wonderment as Drew skillfully navigated their now somewhat aged Subaru through the heavy, wildly undisciplined late morning traffic on the northbound lanes of the Ayalon expressway as it cut a determined swath through the center of Tel Aviv. "I never cease to be amazed at the ever changing sky line of this city! It would seem that God is preparing a place for His returning people!"

"The Spirit of God is palpable all over our little country!" Drew replied with unabashed excitement. "It is ever amazing to me how He has empowered His small remnant of just over five million Jews to accomplish such great things."

I'm thrilled for you both!" Sheldon responded with deep emotion. "Your aliyah to Israel has been a profound example of how He directs our lives! And, your obedience to His call has been an enormous witness to me and many others."

"We're thrilled to be here at such a momentous time in history— God is moving all around us, preparing the way for the ultimate return of His Son to Mount Zion!" Drew continued. "But, so much needs to be done before that happens!"

"Like for example!" Carla interjected. "The Golden domed abomination on the Temple Mount needs to be removed along with the rest of the Islamic presence in that place."

"Carla is so right!" Drew picked up on the theme she had introduced. "Satan is doing everything in his power to delay and disrupt God's plan of redemption that began in the Garden of Eden and will only end when Yeshua comes again! He certainly won't return to a place that has been so woefully desecrated!"

"Quite frankly, you two," Sheldon continued with obvious concern, "I'm deeply troubled over what's happening here right now and I'm especially concerned for your personal safety." His anger became increasingly obvious as he continued. "I can't believe how the world, *including* the United States, not only sits by but seemingly encourages the outrageous and baseless claim of a band of terrorist Arabs, who call themselves 'Palestinians', to the Land God gave the Jews as an everlasting inheritance. You're so right, Drew! It's just plain and simply *Satanic*!"

"I simply don't understand!" Drew replied with frustration. "These so called *Palestinians* have absolutely no history as a people. They were illegitimately spawned by the devil himself in 1964 as an invention of the

Terrorist Organization called the 'Palestinian Liberation Organization' whose charter it was and remains to kill every Jew and to destroy the State of Israel!"

"They seem to be doing a pretty good job on the killing part," Sheldon replied. "Dear God," by my reckoning they've already slaughtered 128 of your dear and innocent people since 1978, to say nothing of the 16 (including one American) that they killed in a vicious attack on a civilian bus just last month. "Forgive me, dear ones," his voice growing softer. "But, I'm concerned---deeply concerned about your safety!"

"None of this makes any sense," Drew replied, "until you put current events into a proper biblical context. No thinking Jew or Christian can legitimately find any interpretation of the Abrahamic Covenant[94] other than the Lord God of Israel's clear and everlasting gifting of the Land of Israel to His ethnically Jewish people. After all, in the very same breath that He made this eternal land grant to His people, He also promised to bring forth the Messiah (Yeshua) through these same chosen ones."

"Even so," Drew continued, "these so called 'Palestinians' are, among other things, insisting that Yeshua was a Palestinian and the Land is *theirs*! However baseless and otherwise outrageous these claims may be, the rest of the world headed by the United Nations with the shameful agreement of the United States is saying amen to the entire ridiculous non-biblical affair."

"It seems that if you keep repeating the same set of outrageous lies long enough, even you begin to believe them yourself," Sheldon interjected.

"Look at it this way," Drew went on. "Think of Israel as a box of matches placed in the center of a football field. The tiny box represents the five million or so Jews inhabiting a land mass about the size of New Jersey surrounded by more than 331 million mostly Muslim Arab enemies in a huge land mass consisting of seventeen contiguous, virulently hostile neighboring countries with one consistent central avowed purpose: the death of every Jew and the destruction of Israel."

"So, here's the deal being forced upon Israel by seemingly the entire world!" Drew summarized sardonically. "All we have to do is to give these folks one half of the match box, mind you, expecting nothing but empty promises in return, and at last there will be peace."

"And if you believe that," Sheldon replied emotionally, "I've got this bridge for sale in Brooklyn at a very good price---."

"The problem is, Shel," Drew continued. "The whole western world has swallowed this satanic bait, hook, line, and sinker and only our blessed God can set things right. The good news is you can be certain that He will---the Tenach, for example is crammed full of examples of His protection of His people Israel."

"Like for instance, Nehemiah nine-twenty," Carla interjected, quoting: 'For forty years you sustained them in the desert; they lacked nothing, their clothes did not wear out nor did their feet become swollen.'"

"Right on dear," Drew commented appreciatively. "Then, we read in the Gospel of John from Yeshua's final prayer for the protection of His Body of believers who were, at the time, mostly Jews:"

Holy Father, protect them by the power of your name-the name you gave me-so that they may be one as we are one. While I was with them, I protected them and kept them safe by that name you gave me. None has been lost except the one doomed to destruction so that Scripture would be fulfilled.

I am coming to you now, but I say these things while I am still in the world, so that they may have the full measure of my joy within them. I have given them your word and the world has hated them, for they are not of the world any more than I am of the world. My prayer is not that you take them out of the world but that you protect them from the evil one. They are not of the world, even as I am not of it. Sanctify them by the truth; your word is truth. As you sent me into the world, I have sent them into the world. For them I sanctify myself, that they too may be truly sanctified. My prayer is not for them alone. I pray also for those who will believe in me through their message, that all of them may be one, Father, just as you are in me and I am in you. May they also be in us so that the world may believe that you have sent me. I have given them the glory that you gave me, that they may be one as we are one: I in them and you in me. May they be brought to complete unity to let the world know that you sent me and have loved them even as you have loved me. [95]

***

They had already talked at length for several hours after dinner. Carla yawned and pleaded: "If you don't mind, it's way past my bedtime and I know you two want to have some one-on-one 'man talk.'" With that she stood and gave the two of them perfunctory good night kisses on the cheek as she began her retreat from the living room.

"You have been greatly blessed with a totally wonderful wife," Sheldon commented after Carla had left their presence.

"Indeed I have, my friend," Drew replied, suddenly emboldened by this moment of intimacy to ask a long suppressed question. "Shel, I've always wondered, but never asked. It's always been perplexing to me that you never married? Was this by some conscious choice or just the way things worked out in your life?"

"The fact is," Sheldon replied thoughtfully, "I never really went out looking for a wife. It just seems like the right mate never came into my life. In that sense, I look at myself as some sort of modern day Paul. In any event I'm perfectly satisfied the way things have worked out for me."

Drew replied with deep and genuine affection. "Perhaps, like Paul, God saw fit to keep your attention focused entirely upon Him and your ministry. I must say He has done much great work through your faith and obedience. I know for certain that without you, I might well still be walking among the legions of the lost souls of this world."

"Never!" Sheldon responded forcefully. "I just happened to be at the right place at the right time when God decided to move in your life. Drew, I have always known you were a man of great destiny! What God has in mind of you will not be deterred or even delayed by any man. I just happened to have the privilege of being on hand to observe His hand touching your life."

"Which, if I may, brings me to another matter that has been somewhat nagging to me," Sheldon continued. "Drew, what's going on with your spiritual life since you've been in Israel? From what I can tell from your infrequent mention, I surmise you and Carla have been unable to make any deep commitment to any one group here in the Land. What's going on?"

"I'm really glad you brought this up, Shel," Drew replied with visible appreciation. "I've been struggling with the situation here since the day we arrived ten years ago. But, before I tell you specifically where I'm at congregationally at the moment, please bear with me while I give you a better frame of reference concerning the contemporary Body here in the Land."

"I'm all ears!" Sheldon replied with great interest.

"It may be a bit of an exaggeration," Drew began, "but some credible scholars hold that there *were* some one million Jewish believers in Yeshua in Israel at the end of the first century. Even if there were just *half* this number, which is probably much closer to the reality, please consider, by most reckoning, there are no more than five thousand believing Jews in the Land today! Just think of it Shel---there are fewer than one tenth of one percent the number of Jewish believers in Israel today than there were some two thousand years ago! This is the shocking and dismal truth!"

"Dear God!" Sheldon replied, genuinely startled by what he had heard. "Please continue."

"Okay!" Drew went on. "It would be sad enough if even all five thousand or so Jewish believers of today were like minded theologically— but let me tell you, if you think that runaway denominationalism is a problem in the American Church please consider the Body here in Israel."

Drew paused for a moment to collect his thoughts, then continued, the sadness in his voice nearly palpable: "Our five thousand believers are fragmented into some 69 different groups scattered throughout the Land."

"There is less than a handful of what can be considered typical congregations by any Western standard. The largest have between two and three hundred regular attendees and are located in Jerusalem, Rishon Letzion, Haifa, and here in Tiberias. These larger groups are, typically, a near even mix of Jewish and ex-patriot Gentile Christians."

"The rest of the groups are quite small by American standards," Drew continued. "Statistically, the 'average' Israeli congregation has 47 members (29 Jews and 18 Gentiles)."

"Theologically and in worship practice less than half, 33 of the 69 congregations, fit into the typical American model/definition of 'Messianic Jewish.' Eight of these 33 adhere more closely to synagogue worship style and practice (*Torah* service, Jewish rooted liturgy, etc.). The other 25 who identify themselves as "Messianic Jewish" generally limit their association with Israel and things Jewish to celebrating the Jewish holidays and by using the Hebrew language (or by providing a Hebrew translation)."

While Sheldon listened in rapt attention, Drew continued with his overview of the Israeli Messianic Jewish Body: "Twenty of the remaining 36 congregations do not identify themselves as 'Messianic,' and they, and the other sixteen are rooted theologically and in practice in traditional main line Protestant denominations.")."[96]

"With respect to worship practice," Drew continued, "about half of the congregations describe themselves as 'charismatic'. The others either call themselves 'non-charismatic' or make no mention of this distinction."

"This is all rather disconcerting!" Sheldon interjected. "I had no idea that your Body here was in such disarray."

"I've saved the worst for last!" Drew replied with continued deep sadness. "Remember, Shel, there are only some five thousand or so ethnic Jews in Israel who identify themselves as being saved by the shed blood of Yeshua—this is something like one tenth of one percent of the Jews here in the Land. Okay, now consider this. About half of these self-proclaimed 'believers' militantly deny the Divinity of Yeshua! To them He may be the promised Messiah, or even the Son of God, but in no way is He to be considered as a part of any triune Godhead which they also deny!"

"My God! Drew, that's hard to believe!" Sheldon replied, genuinely shocked. "Where do you get your data?"

"Right from the lips of the so called rabbi of a large congregation that holds to this apostasy. He sat right across the table and boldly declared to me and to others that he, his congregation, and about half of the other ethnic Jewish believers in the Land held to this same shocking position."

"Shel!" Drew now continued with visible outrage. "Not only do these poor misguided souls hold to this one way ticket to hell. They are teaching it forcefully to all who will listen!"

"How can any responsible leadership allow such a theological tragedy to occur, much less to continue?" Sheldon asked out of deep concern for what he had just heard.

"You've found the key!" Drew relied. "There is virtually no viable Messianic Jewish national leadership in Israel!

"As I see it," Drew continued. "One core problem we have is the woefully inadequate preparation of our congregational leadership. Among our eighty, or so, so called 'congregational leaders', less than a third are seminary or Bible College graduates. The rest are entirely homespun and, in my view, woefully ill prepared to assume a pulpit."

"Despite all of this, Drew," Sheldon replied. "Even in these dismal circumstances you and Carla *need* a place to worship. Even the best of us will simply dry up and die spiritually without some sort of communal worship. What are you two doing about this?"

"The fact is, Shel," Drew responded without hesitation. "Over these past few years we've diligently tried several different congregations, each one of them for a time and each one of them so seriously deficient in one way or another that we simply could not be adequately fed there. I can't tell you how much we've prayed and how we've sought to find an on fire Messianic Congregation something like the one we left in the States, but none we've explored are in any way cut out of the same spiritual clothe as the one we left to come here--- to this Land of our inheritance."

"So," Drew continued, "for the past year or so we've been leading an intercessory prayer group in our home each Wednesday morning. We've had up to sixteen likeminded brothers and sisters attend, some from as far away as Haifa, and the group seems to be thriving in the Spirit and we are well pleased.

"Okay, the Reverend Doctor Andrew Scott Sterling, Messianic Jew,"

Sheldon asked with a hint of genuine accusation. "This small home group of yours may be meeting the needs of a few, but what of the huge national spiritual deficit? Why haven't *you* risen up in the face of this Israeli Body-wide fiasco? Surely, with Divine help, you have the training, experience and capability to raise this mess up to at least some more acceptable level of theological and organizational sensibility? After all, you *were* about to become the Deputy Chief of Air Force Chaplains when you chose instead to cast your lot among your deeply needy believing Jewish brothers and sisters? Isn't it just possible you are missing the call of the God who brought you home to Israel?"

"I don't think so, Shel." Drew replied thoughtfully. "I've spent a lot of time praying about this and I know I'm not called into pastoral leadership here in the Land. The fact is that the chaplaincy prepared me to manage a huge organization, not to pastor a congregation or a group of congregations. Just in case you never noticed, any given Air Force Chapel congregation changes faces each Sunday as folks continuously move on through the system. Shel, the *real* issue here is that I've never heard clearly from God that I'm to jump into this fray and lead it on to victory!"

"Then, just what *have* you heard from Him, my brother?" Sheldon probed. "*Why* did He call you here out of an incredibly successful career— away from the land of your birth, your children, away from all that you have previously known?"

"I'll tell you what, Shel," Drew replied with satisfaction. "The hour is very late, and I believe that the Lord has brought us to this point in our conversation for a very definite purpose. Come with me after breakfast and I'll show you what I'm only just now beginning to understand about my purpose for being here in the Land."

Chapter Thirty Six

Hippos
December, AD 30

Matthias struggled to suppress the deep emotion that rendered him nearly unable to speak as he looked out over the one hundred or so congregants crowded before him in the simple, unheated, basalt block building that served Hippos as a multi-purpose public meeting place. How very far, he conjectured, had the evangelism of this Decapolis community already progressed, but how very much more it still needed to grow; to reach out with the gospel of Yeshua to the other nearly four thousand unsaved local residents and also far and wide to the many entirely pagan communities scattered throughout this huge region that was called by many 'the Corner of Arabia.'

This was the fertile hill country beyond the Jordan river, eastward; an enormous area running all the way from Damascus in the north to Philadelphia in the south. It was a huge, richly fertile garden watered by the rivers Yarmuk and Jabbok bringing the gift of life to consistently bountiful grain fields scattered between the countless hills where flocks of sheep and goats and herds of cattle roamed from the foot of Mount Hermon in the north to the innumerable ridges of Moab in the far south.

"Dear God!" Matthias proclaimed in a whispered prayer born in the deep recesses of his soul. "How deeply—how completely, I cherish and adore this beautiful place and the people of your creation who dwell here; this place where you have called me to speak of your mighty works— to proclaim the blessed Gospel of your Son, Yeshua. Bless me now, O Lord as I speak of the Living Water that flows from your precious heart to these dear ones who are assembled here--- in the name of the Father and the Son and the Holy Spirit. Amen."

"My precious brothers and sisters in Yeshua," he began to speak with tenderness and compassion born out of deep love. "When I stood on the Mount of Olives with many of my Galilean brothers and beheld with my own eyes the glory of our Lord Yeshua ascending into heaven to take His place at the right hand of His Father; I and the others heard Him speak a final instruction with His precious human voice: *Therefore go and make disciples of all nations, baptizing them in the name of the Father and of the Son and of the Holy Spirit, and teaching them to obey everything I have commanded you.*[97] Oh, how I praise Him and thank Him with all my heart that it has fallen upon me to follow this great commission here in your lovely city of Hippos and far beyond, throughout this vast region called the Decapolis."

"I urge you now, dear ones, to pay very close attention to the words of this final instruction Yeshua gave us at the moment of His ascension into heaven. He told us to make *disciples* of all nations! He *did not* tell us to make all men *Jews*!

"There is a great distinction here," Matthias continued passionately: "One who was not physically born as a Jew can in any way become such a Jew in the flesh. A Jew is a person who is physically, not in any way *spiritually* descended from one of the twelve sons of our patriarch, Ya'akov, called Israel. Hear me well my non-Jewish brothers and sisters! Nothing, absolutely nothing can change the physical reality of what I have just spoken.

"Indeed," Matthias continued with growing passion, "let me also quickly say that it matters not at all, not one iota, that I am a Jew in the flesh and that certainly most of you are not! Yeshua came into the world and shed His precious blood as a once and for all sacrifice: for Jew and Gentile alike. Hear me well my 'born again' brothers and sisters: there is absolutely no distinction; no advantage or disadvantage between the salvation in Yeshua of any Jew and any non-Jew."

"On that great and glorious final day when all believers in Yeshua are called to sit at His feet in heaven, 'born again' Jews and 'born again' Gentiles—all who have been saved by His shed blood, will rise *together* and worship Him *together*, not one in front of the other, or one behind the other. Rather, we shall sing His praises and behold His Glory while we, in perfect unity, side by side, as we bow down together before Him.

"You may reasonably ask, my brothers and sisters: why am I telling you this great truth *now*, by way of introduction? Let me answer by sharing with you the next inescapable truth: Yeshua himself was, is and always will be a Jew! You may then ask: if both Jew and Gentile are equally saved by His shed blood, why does it matter at all that our Lord happened to be born a Jew? Let me tell you, dear ones the words I heard Yeshua speak with my own ears: He spoke for the benefit of us all: *He who says I abide in Him ought himself also to walk just as I walked.* [98] Hear His words well, dear ones! Yeshua is commanding all believers, Jew and non-Jew alike, to *imitate Him*, as closely as we are able, in every aspect of our lives!

"Again, I ask you to hear me well!" Matthias continued emphatically, "Yeshua was a fully Torah obedient Jew.   Thus, according to the commandment of His own lips we too, 'born again' Jews and non-Jews alike— all of us should strive to do the very same!

"According to my reckoning," he continued instructively, "there are 613 commandments in the Torah. These 613 individual precepts and commandments have in turn, traditionally been separated into three kinds: moral, civil and ceremonial.

"The moral commands are those which have permanent moral value, and are therefore absolutely binding upon us all without further discussion.

"Civil commands deal with the regulation of the life of the nation of Israel. Their applicability to other nations is arguable and remains open to considerable discussion.

"Ceremonial commands, on one hand, deal with specifically Jewish ritual requirements, such as sacrificial procedures which can be applied only in the one and only Jewish Temple. Temple sacrifice, of course is no longer required by those of us Jews who accept the truth that Yeshua became the final blood sacrifice for us all.

"These ceremonial commands, however, also include dietary instructions detailing such things as which foods can and cannot be consumed, as well as the seven holy Jewish Feasts.

"Viewed from a more practical perspective, and taking into account that Temple sacrifice has been superceded by the sacrifice of Yeshua: from the 613 commandments and precepts, there are today a total of 271 that can reasonably be obeyed by believers without restriction."

Matthias paused for a moment, looking out over his audience of mostly Gentile new believers who were so recently pagans as they seemingly clung to his every word. Deep within him he understood the great importance of what he was about to share, and he once again cried out silently from the depths of his soul for the leading of the Holy Spirit. Having found solace in doing this, he went on with his teaching.

"I must confess to you," he continued. "Our leader, Ya'akov, and those close to him who are guiding the Body of Yeshua from the first Messianic Synagogue on Mount Zion are still fervently seeking God's will for what, specifically, from these 271 potentially appropriate and 'doable' commandments of the Torah are applicable to you, our non-Jewish brothers and sisters. We have been in deep prayer, seeking guidance in this and we and you can be sure that such will be provided in God's good timing."

"While there is considerable disagreement among us," he cautiously continued, "there is even more upon which we agree. It is one aspect of this agreement that I feel called to share with you today and with all other non-Jews who might one day hear these words.

"It is certain," he now continued forthrightly, "Ya'akov and the rest of us in leadership agree—Jews and non-Jews alike, all who believe upon Yeshua, are also held accountable to embrace and meticulously follow all of the moral commandments as they were given to Moses on Mount Sinai."

"Dear ones," Matthias now spoke with deep emotion— "Principal among these moral commandments are ten of such great importance that they were written upon stone tablets by the very finger of God. Among these ten is the clear precept: 'You shall have no other gods before me.'"[99]

"Hear the words of this commandment well my brothers and sisters.

You dear ones here in Hippos and beyond, those who will one day hear and embrace the Gospel of Yeshua in the nations—the Creator of the Universe, *Yahweh* is His Holy name—He is commanding that you will have **NO** other gods!"

Matthias now paused confidently as he approached the core substance of his message. "As you all know," he continued with authority, "today is the winter solstice, the very day upon which non-Jews all over the world have traditionally celebrated the birth of Helios, the sun god. Let me say that I am well aware that you new believers in Yeshua have personally renounced Helios and come to understand that your salvation is in Yeshua, the only Son of the Living God Yahweh, the Lord God of Israel.

"Even so, I am also aware that your gathering here today was planned to celebrate the coming of Yeshua into the world—a convenient adaptation of a most *holy* event directly linked to a most *unholy* pagan tradition.

"Furthermore, I am told you were intending to have this celebration in the beautiful and elaborate Temple of Helios that stands right along side this very humble and simple building of stone where we now meet.

"Dear ones!" he continued passionately. "It is a great blasphemy for any one who proclaims the saving blood of Yeshua, to blend the worship of Yahweh, the one true God, and His only son, Yeshua with pagan practice and tradition.

"Brothers and sisters in Yeshua, you here in this small gathering at Hippos, you are indeed the very first group of non-Jews who have formed the very first non-Jewish place of worship. What you do here and now will forever influence the great and universal *ecclesia* that will arise from your humble beginnings."

Now, almost shouting, Matthias loudly proclaimed: "May the one true God forbid that the universal *ecclesia* of the future be populated with those who would substitute pagan traditions for the blessed truth of Torah. May there never arise even one great future place of worship decorated with sun bursts and other pagan idolatry in lingering veneration to the false god, Helios."

"Indeed, may all who proclaim their salvation in Yeshua learn and then teach those non-Jews who will follow you into the one true faith, that the life of Yeshua is intimately linked to the major Jewish festivals that are set forth by God in the Torah."

"Dear ones, I beseech you to hear me well. We have heard and believe that Yeshua was born on the last day of Succoth. Thus, He was conceived by the Holy Spirit during the festival of Lights, Chanukah. Further, we can also say with assurance that He arose from the grave on the third day following His burial during the Feast of Pesach and that the great comforter promised by Yeshua came during the Feast of Shavuot. Most assuredly, we can declare in absolute truth: Yeshua was **not** born on the Winter Solstice! I thus beg you in His name: Do **not** worship or proclaim the blasphemy that Yeshua came into the world as a man on this pagan rooted birthday of Helios lest you and those non-Jews who will follow you in future generations fall into the terrible trap of polluting the precious fulfillment of Judaism which is our shared faith."

"Further, I beseech you! Tear down this Temple to Helios! It is a great abomination! Dear ones, I urge you to worship *here* as a total Body in this simple unadorned place where we now stand on the great feast days, and on other occasions of community wide interest.

"Brothers and Sisters," Matthias continued with passion. "Even more importantly, I urge you to continue breaking bread together in your homes. Gather there together in small numbers each week, just after each Shabbat ends to be nourished by your fellowship with Him and with one another. Then, as your numbers continue to grow, start new such home centered fellowships. There is no end to how many of these there may one day be here in Hippos until all of God's children who dwell here have at last been saved by His shed blood."

Now, Matthias raised his hands and intoned the traditional Aaronic Blessing upon this non-Jewish congregation: *The Lord bless you and keep you. The Lord make his face shine upon you and be gracious to you. The Lord lift up His countenance upon you and give you peace.*

As he concluded this blessing he struggled to ward off a frightening prophetic vision that sent a deep penetrating coldness throughout his entire being and caused him to tremble uncontrollably in the place where he stood. What he was thus given to see with absolute clarity was a very large cathedral set upon a hill. There was a huge courtyard in front of this enormous edifice with a very large pagan phallic shaped tower at its center. From this phallus there radiated the likenesses of sunbeams etched in the giant paved courtyard.

Now suddenly, in the theater of his mind, Matthias found himself standing inside the great domed structure looking upward at its huge domed ceiling that was decorated with a giant sunburst that sent the actual rays of the sun throughout the entire enormous unholy gathering place.

As Matthias now looked toward what was obviously an elaborately decorated altar at the front of the sanctuary, he beheld a hideously adorned man dressed in a long flowing white robe decorated with many signs of the sun. The man wore a large split head piece that looked like the open mouth of a giant fish, and he held a crooked black staff in his right hand the center piece of which was a grossly distorted figure of Yeshua hanging upon his cross.

"Dear God!" Matthias prayed in a whisper heard only by himself and the one to whom he prayed. "Please, Lord God of Israel—I beg you that what I have seen will not become the future of the non-Jewish Body of Yeshua to whom you have called me to teach His precious gospel."

Chapter Thirty Seven

Hippos
August, 1989

"You're certainly being mysterious about all this," Sheldon commented as Drew rounded the northern end of the Lake and began to drive south along the eastern shore. Although it was only nine o'clock in the morning, the intense heat and high humidity had already begun to make their tormenting presence known, even above the normally very efficient air conditioning system of Drew's Subaru Legacy.

"I'll have to admit you've got me more than a bit excited—I sense a powerful leading of the Holy Spirit—like He's about to show me something very important through your revelation."

"I'm glad you're spiritually tuned up for a very difficult uphill walk on this stifling August morning, but I'm certain you'll find the effort very worthwhile." Drew replied. "But first things first," he continued, as he turned right off the main road onto a barely passable narrow graveled road that led towards the nearby shore.

After they had driven only a short distance, he pulled his car to a halt in the scant shade of a convenient date palm not far from the water's edge. "Come," he invited his curious and excited passenger, as he exited from the driver's side and began to lead the way across the fifty or so meters between where they had parked and the water's edge.

"What have we here?" Sheldon asked with deep interest as he pointed to some apparently very ancient ruins that had only been superficially excavated, exposing just the tops of what were apparently several basalt block structures still mostly beneath the surface.

"This place is called Tel Hadar," Drew replied, "and these are the trial dig ruins of an ancient Canaanite City that dates to the 15th Century BC. But," he went on, "for our present frame of reference there is something much more relevant about this place."

"You'll remember the account of the second feeding of the multitude in Matthew fifteen," Drew continued, "where Yeshua took a few small fish and seven loaves of bread and multiplied them to feed some four thousand, many of whom He also healed and blessed at the same time.?"

"Yes," Sheldon replied, "But, I've never really explored this account much beyond the surface of what is written."

"You're certainly not alone in this," Drew continued. "The Church generally gives much more emphasis to the first feeding that took place on the other side of the Lake. Some even hold that this second feeding is really just another expression of the first and that they are the same."

"Of course there were two separate feedings, one on each shore!" Sheldon protested the mistaken inference that he might think otherwise.

"Absolutely!" Drew agreed. "And, my friend, there is much to be learned from this account that is not specifically written in Scripture. For example, let me ask you a simple question. First, all but a very few of those He fed in this place were pagans; that is, they were not ethnically descended from one or more of the twelve sons of Jacob. We know from presumably reliable scholarly sources that, except for a few very small communities of isolated Semitic groups, this entire side of the Lake and way beyond was inhabited by non-Jews during the early first century. Second, it's very reasonable, I would think, to assume that at least some, and more likely many of those who were fed and healed by Yeshua here also immediately came to believe upon Him whom they had seen work these miracles before their very eyes."

"I think I am beginning to get a hint of where you are going with this— please go on!" Sheldon pleaded with growing excitement.

"Okay, let me summarize my considerable research over the past couple of years." Drew replied professorially. "Please remember, Shel, Sha'ul, also known as Paul, the Apostle to the Gentiles, didn't take his first missionary journey until 46 and, like his other evangelistic ventures, this first outreach was to unsaved Gentiles located *out of this country*."

"So," Drew continued with growing excitement, as he continued to unveil his hypothesis. "If there were up to some 4,000 newly saved, formerly pagan, followers of Yeshua standing in this very place where we now stand, some twenty of so years before Paul began his ministry, their presence begs several key questions. For instance, how did they react to the incredible miracles they had just experienced? How did they respond to the Holy Spirit that now suddenly dwelled within them? Where did they go to worship? What form did their worship take? Who discipled them? These are only a few of the many questions that can't be ignored simply because they are not directly addressed in the Scriptures."

"Do I hear you suggesting that there may have been a pre-Pauline Gentile Christian Church?" Sheldon conjectured, picking up on Drew's leading.

"*Absolutely!*" Drew replied. "In my spirit, I'm certain of it! There absolutely must have been a formidable and wide spread Gentile Christian Body that arose here in the Decapolis and beyond, both during and after the twelve years between Sha'ul's encounter with Yeshua on the Damascus road and his first evangelistic journey to the nations in 46!"

"Drew!" Sheldon, visibly stunned by what he had just heard, responded. "What you're proposing here is a rather remarkable new understanding of early Church history. If indeed there were such a pre-Pauline Church it would carry with it all manner of implications!"

"There is more, much more!" Drew continued." "But, next, we have one more place to visit before I take you on the *schlep* of your life to the very place where I believe this first Gentile Christian Church was founded!"

"I wouldn't miss this for anything!" Sheldon replied excitedly. "Let's get going!"

***

A few minutes later, after they had left Tel Hadar and driven south a short distance, Drew turned left off the main highway, then immediately right into the asphalted parking lot of Kursi National Park. "Welcome to the place of the miracle of the swine," Drew announced as he, with Sheldon in close trail, led the way through the main gate into the park, then alongside an imposing, one hundred yards or so long eight foot high wall, reconstructed from ancient basalt blocks, that now bordered this well maintained national treasure on its eastern side.

"Wow!" Sheldon exclaimed as they reached the end of the wall and turned left to behold the impressive ruins of the fifth century Byzantine Basilica that dominated the landscape before them. "Is *this* the place you are thinking might be early Gentile Christian?" he asked.

"Oh no, Shel!" Drew replied. "What you see here are the rather well preserved ruins of an early Byzantine Basilica and pilgrims' center. The place I have in mind isn't here, but I believe there is a close and very compelling connection between the two. All of this will become much clearer as we move along."

"Man, you weren't kidding about the climb!" Sheldon's face was bright red and his breath came in labored gasps as they reached the top of the steep graveled path and now stood just in front of an ancient weather worn retaining wall, just a few steps away from the end of the path.

Drew laughed. "This little jaunt is nothing compared to what comes next, but I can assure you that you'll find what lies just ahead quiet remarkable."

"I couldn't be more interested!" Sheldon replied reassuringly. "Please, Drew, tell me what you know about *this* place."

"For starters," Drew began, "this is a first century chapel that was obviously erected by believing Jews, just below the cave where Yeshua drove the demons out of the chained man. Please note that the Byzantine basilica below us is some three hundred or more years more recent than this earlier structure."

"Pardon me for interrupting, *Doctor* Sterling," Sheldon interjected with a hint of skepticism, "but how do you know it was erected by believing Jews and how can you be so certain of its first century dating?"

"I was just about to get to these points," Drew continued. "First, please look very closely at the still barely discernable graffiti on the retaining wall right in front of us. Obviously, what remains after more than two thousand years of exposure to the elements is only a trace of what must have originally been a magnificent display."

Drew now began to point to the specific graffiti features: "First, note the equilateral members of what appears to be a Christian cross at the upper left of the wall. In all likelihood this is a *tau*, the last letter of the Hebrew alphabet that was in use at the time of Yeshua. The Byzantine cross was significantly different and more ornate. The prophet Ezekiel and the Dead Sea scrolls both make reference to the fact that long before the coming of Yeshua, Jews made the sign of the *tau* on their foreheads as a symbol that meant 'salvation.'[100] Later, this symbol was retained by the Nazarene Essenes who were the first Jewish believers in Yeshua."

"Sooo?" Sheldon responded. "Are you saying that the several other 'cross' symbols that are quite visible in the chapel itself are also *taus* and not just simply Christian crosses as they have been widely used throughout church history?"

"I wouldn't bet the farm on this one, Shel, but to me it seems quite obviously so. In the first place they all have equal length extensions, and, the cross of Yeshua has *never* been used as a symbol by believing Jews. Let me go on to make my point that this chapel was indeed established by very early Jewish believers."

"By all means," Sheldon replied. "This is fascinating!"

"Look next, if you will at the upside down fish in the center of the wall." Drew continued. "The fish is a symbol of Messiah Yeshua that was used by the very first Jewish believers on Mount Zion. It was later adopted by the emerging Gentile Christian Church along with the Greek anagram that translates 'Jesus Christ, Son of God, Savior.'

"Now, here comes another clincher," Drew continued, pointing to a symbol, just to the right of the fish, comprised of a vertical staff with 'V' cross hatches. "This, my dear General, can be nothing other than a menorah, the quintessential symbol of Judaism.

"But, that's not all," Drew went on pointing to the much longer symbol that dominated the lower right hand side of the wall. "This may look like an extended version of the menorah symbol," he continued, "but there are seven cross hatched 'Vs' which make it a good example of a frequently used early Nazarene graffiti symbol pointing to Isaiah 11:1 *A shoot will come up from the stump of Jesse; from his roots a Branch will bear fruit.* I've found these Nazarene Essene calling cards all over the Galilee in several old synagogues and in such amazing places as Caesarea Philippi in the far North. It's a sort of logo that they apparently left wherever they worshiped."

"It would seem you have done your home work well, my friend!" Sheldon replied. "It would be difficult to dispute the Jewish origination of this place as well as your first century dating. But how, precisely, does this fit in with your hypothesis that there was a pre-Pauline Church on this side of the Lake and beyond?"

"As you may know," Drew replied. "There is a growing understanding that the Gospel of Mark is actually a compilation of the first hand remembrances of the Apostle Peter, who as you know from Scripture, was also very involved in evangelizing non-Jews. So, let's get back to the miracle that took place here and read of the first hand account written down by Mark in chapter five of his gospel: Remember, as Yeshua was getting back in the boat to return to the western side of the Lake, the now entirely healed and saved formerly pagan chained man begged to go with him in the boat. However, Yeshua told him instead to: *Go home to your family and tell them how much the Lord has done for you, and how he has had mercy on you. So the man went away and began to tell in the Decapolis how much Yeshua had done for him. And all the people were amazed.*

"Okay, here is my central point regarding this place that was marked by Jewish believers with this chapel some time, probably soon after the miracle. Yeshua Himself commanded the chained man to evangelize pagans in what obviously must have at least included nearby Hippos, a city of the Decapolis that was thriving at this time. Not only did he do so, but I believe from growing evidence that he also began to spread the Gospel throughout the other widely dispersed Decapolis cities.

"Furthermore," he went on excitedly, "both the Gospels of Mark and

Matthew establish that the now healed chained man turned evangelist presumably preached the Gospel in Hippos at some time *prior* to Yeshua's Tel Hadar feeding of the 4,000. My point here is that some if not many of these very 4,000 had already heard about Yeshua from their fellow former pagan, now healed and saved chained man."[101]

"And so, what do you conclude from all this?" Sheldon asked rhetorically.

"Sheldon," Drew replied with deep conviction. "It seems to me virtually inarguable that most of these four thousand folks were from nearby Hippos and environs and after they had been fed and healed, they simply returned home to their mountain top city where it seems reasonable to assume they must have established the very first Gentile Christian Church— long before Paul's encounter with Yeshua on the road to Damascus. This, my friend, brings us to the last leg of our journey for the day."

***

It was already mid afternoon when Drew and Sheldon began their laborious ascent up the steep, primitive, rock strewn trail to the ancient Decapolis City of Hippos. There was not a hint of a breeze to offer even a suggestion of relief from the blazing summer sun produced temperature well in excess of one hundred degrees with an accompanying torturous humidity of well over sixty percent. Even so, with Drew leading the way, they struggled upwards, stopping every five minutes or so to catch their breath and to drink heartily from the already warm water in plastic soft drink bottles that they carried along in their back packs.

"I'll give you this Drew," Sheldon gasped between labored breaths. "This certainly *is* the *schlep* of my life! I only pray that we'll both survive the experience."

Drew laughed. "Trust me Shel, Carla and I have been up here many times since we discovered the place and we're both still kicking! It isn't much further to the summit."

"I've never seen such a totally lifeless and burned up place," Sheldon commented as they navigated the nearly impassible last one hundred yards of their upward trek. "I can't imagine why anyone, even in antiquity, would choose to call this place home."

"Israel is a place of great seasonal contrasts," Drew replied. "You should see it in the late winter and springtime when it and the rest of the Golan are covered with a magnificent lush carpet decorated with ever changing successive displays of indescribably beautiful wildflowers!"

"Next time, I'll remember to visit you, when it's so lovely and I might add cool."

"Never mind," Drew announced, as they rounded a final turn and suddenly found themselves standing upon level ground. "Here we are! Now, it's only a short distance to the 'cathedral' where I'll begin to give you a 'Sterling's eye view' of this incredibly important place."

"It's really quite remarkable!" Sheldon observed a few minutes later when the two of them stood on a slight rise overlooking the mostly excavated sixth century Byzantine 'cathedral' that lay before them. "How do you account for those glorious fallen marble columns, with all of them laying in such a perfectly tidy row, pointing in the same direction?"

"First of all," Drew replied, "this, along with its counterpart in Damascus, was a major, regional center of the Byzantine Church from some time during the fifth century until it was devastated by a catastrophic earthquake in 749 AD that simultaneously destroyed every building in this city and many others throughout the Galilee. The columns are thought to have formed one side of a large prayer hall presided over by a regional bishop who tended his extended flock from this place."

"I'm certainly no expert," Sheldon observed, "but it seems to me that this 'cathedral' as you call it, is very similar in design to the Byzantine church we visited at Kursi?"

"Indeed it is!" Drew replied. "The fact is, the Byzantine Churches scattered throughout the entire Decapolis were all very similar in design. I've had the privilege of visiting all of them over the last several years and I am persuaded they formed a closely integrated hierarchal network under the ecclesiastical cover of the bishop who presided over them from the place where we now stand."

"This is all most fascinating," Sheldon replied, "but let me get right to the point. What is there about this place and/or this city that supports your hypothesis that this was the site of a supposed pre-Pauline Christian Church?"

"I'm glad you asked," Drew joshed his friend. "The fact is, when the Israeli Antiquity Authority excavated this site in the early 1950s they reported that a large round basket carved of marble hung from the center of its main entrance, and mind you, these entirely secular scholars speculated at the time that this basket represented Yeshua's Miracle of the Loaves and Fishes."[102]

"Obviously, if they were correct," Drew continued, "this adds a great deal of anecdotal credibility to my suggestion that many if not all of the 4,000 who were fed and healed by Yeshua at the very foot of this mountain did indeed return *home* to this place and subsequently worshiped him here. But, of course, we must remember that this 'cathedral' is *sixth*, not *first* century."

"Of course!" Drew added, "While this basket seems to point to a possible tradition in this city that began with Yeshua's nearby multiplication of the loaves fishes, it could all be just a remarkable coincidence."

"Drew, what do *you* really think about the significance of all this?" Sheldon asked seeking a revelation of his dear friend's innermost understandings. "You sound to me like a man with a compelling God given mission?"

Drew responded in kind. "The fact is, Shel, I'm certain that the Lord has called me to this place for a very important and definite purpose. I know that I know that I know---Gentile Christianity, as we know it, began in this city, long before Paul began to evangelize in the West. I also am persuaded that in the beginning these first Gentile believers were discipled by the believing Jewish community at Kursi with whom they were in a remarkable unity, a unity that I am continuing to learn characterized the entire Galilee."

"I *hear* what you are saying Drew," Sheldon replied with great sincerity mixed with concern. "I *know* you like few others, and I trust what you have been shown by God about this place. I know that He has called you to a great and mighty purpose in all this. The problem is, my dear brother," he struggled for the right words, "how are you going to ever convince the Church that its view of its own history is so very wanting when all you have to offer is a remarkably logical hypothesis proven mostly by anecdotal evidence and assumption?"

"Come with me," Drew invited in response, as he began to lead the way through the debris strewn nearly one kilometer distance from the 'cathedral' to the western border of the city.

"The 'cathedral' is only one of at least *four* early Christian churches that have already been discovered in this city," Drew explained, as they progressed slowly through the torturous boulder strewn landscape. "The other three are only barely identifiable from the surface, and indeed, there may be other churches here as well. My point is," he continued with conviction: "One day, soon I hope, the excavations of this city, together with its several churches will continue. When this finally happens, I am confident the archeologists who take on this enormous project will uncover conclusive evidence that proves my pre-Pauline Church hypothesis. The incredible truth waits for them and the world somewhere beneath this rubble where we are now walking.

"How many people actually *lived* in this city?" Sheldon probed.

"According to my archeologist friends at the University of Haifa, their best guess, based on the size of the residential area, is that there were about 4,000 or so residents of this city at its height."

"It's hard to imagine such a heavy concentration of churches among so relatively few potential believers," Sheldon observed. "I can certainly see why you're so fascinated with this place."

***

"Here we are!" Drew stated the obvious as they stood together at the precipice of a steep cliff looking down upon Kibbutz En Gev immediately below them with the Lake beyond. The sun had now begun to paint the first signs of its imminent setting, and the water seemed painted by a pallet of extraordinary hues framing the city of Tiberias on the opposite shore.

"I can certainly see God's hand on your life, Drew," Sheldon spoke with deep warmth and holy conviction. "I know He has called you to a special and glorious purpose that is somehow focused here in this city. I sense in my Spirit that He has only just begun to reveal the truth about His early church, and that you will continue to grow in your understanding exactly according to His schedule and for His purpose."

"Amen." Drew replied reverently.

Chapter Thirty Eight

The Upper Room on Mount Zion
March, AD 36

The twelve sat silently at the large table in the upper room waiting for their beloved and greatly respected leader, Ya'akov, to break the utter silence that had prevailed since Matthias, the last of them to arrive, had taken his place several minutes earlier.

The utter pervasive grief that filled the room cut to the depth of their souls and there wasn't the slightest doubt among them why they had been called from their various ministries throughout Israel to gather once again as a body in this place where the communal worship of Yeshua had begun not long ago, during the Feast of Shavuot when the promised comforter had fallen upon them as had been promised by their blessed, risen Lord.

"There is much, much trouble for us here in the Land," Ya'akov finally began to speak haltingly. "It would have been bad enough for us to endure the persecution rising up against us from the ranks of the militant Pharisees, but it has gone well beyond just simple persecution. These are indeed treacherous men who are so terrified of the truth that they have declared war upon those who embrace Yeshua, the author of all truth and righteousness." He paused for a moment, struggling to suppress the great anger that festered deep within him—seeking to destroy his joy, the very fruit of his unshakable conviction.

"My brothers," he continued. "It would have been terrible enough if these evil men had been satisfied with trying to destroy our sacred body of believers here in Jerusalem by driving them all out of the city, simply because of their belief in Yeshua—but, as you all must know by now, even that was not enough."[103] He paused again to wipe away his tears before he continued.

"My brothers, a leader who seems to have come from the very depths of the abyss has risen up among those who have chosen to destroy us—Sha'ul of Tarsus is his name. He is spiritually sick, inflamed with misguided passion—the hateful passion of one who would personally drag our brothers and sisters from their homes and haul them off to prison! But," he continued with profound sadness. "Even *this* it seems, is not enough for Sha'ul of Tarsus. I have learned from several who were there as witnesses, that this Sha'ul of Tarsus gave his enthusiastic consent to the horrible execution of our dear brother Stephen."

"Has he no mercy at all?" Kefa questioned in disbelief.

"From what I've heard reliably reported," Ya'akov continued, "it would seem this man, Sha'ul, has not the slightest bit of either goodness or mercy. Even as our beloved brother Stephen looked up and declared 'Look! I see the heavens opened and the Son of Man standing at the right hand of God!' these Pharisees, Sha'ul among them, cried out with a loud voice, stopped their ears, ran to him with one accord; and they cast him out of the city and stoned him until he was dead.[104]"

"This outrageous man must be stopped!" Kefa shouted angrily as he came to his feet and pounded on the table with his fists! "I would gladly thrust a dagger through his heart! The Torah teaches us: a life for life, an eye for eye, a tooth for tooth, a hand for a hand, a foot for foot.[105]"

"Have you already forgotten Yeshua's teaching on this verse?" Yochanan gently admonished his outraged brother. He told us: 'You have heard that it was said, Love your neighbor and hate your enemy. But I tell you: Love your enemies and pray for those who persecute you, that you may be sons of your Father in heaven.'"[106]

"The fact is," Ya'akov once again regained control of the gathering, "this Pharisee called Sha'ul will do even more unimaginable damage to us unless we find a way to change his heart---."

"Or kill him?" Kefa interrupted.

"Let us follow the words of our Master and turn our other cheek!" Ya'akov admonished. "Please, my brothers, hear me out!"

"As you all know," Ya'akov continued, "our brother Matthias has already successfully planted thriving and growing congregations in three of the ten cities of the Decapolis. It so happens that the membership of two of these, the group at Hippos and Scythopolis, are predominantly former pagans with only very minimal Jewish participation. However, the members of the congregation at Damascus, by far the largest and fastest growing of the three, are mostly Jewish brothers and sisters who were already living in that thriving city."

"I can say with assurance," Matthias interjected, "that these new Jewish believers are reaching out in a mighty way to the very large pagan population of the city and many of them are entering into our faith every day—very much like what has been happening here in Jerusalem, only with mostly pagans rather than Jews entering into the Kingdom."

"Indeed!" replied Ya'akov, "And is it therefore any wonder that our enemy, Sha'ul has targeted this very congregation as his next candidate for destruction?"

"How can you know this?" Matthias asked protectively.

Ya'akov replied with conviction. "I've heard this report from reliable witnesses who heard Sha'ul speak in some detail of his despicable plan. My understanding is he is planning to journey to Damascus in the very near future for that very purpose."

"He must be stopped!" Matthias demanded protectively.

"Indeed he must!" Ya'akov agreed emphatically. "My brothers, I now charge Matthias to set out for Damascus immediately. Matthias," he now spoke directly and earnestly to the most recently appointed of the inner circle, "you must warn the congregation there of their imminent danger. You must also encourage them and help them do whatever else may be necessary to protect themselves from this murderous Pharisee!

"Let us all now lay hands on our brother Matthias and pray for his success," Ya'akov concluded, speaking to the others. "Then, Matthias, you must depart for Damascus without delay."

***

Sha'ul was filled with both determination and hate as he and his party of thugs approached the outskirts of Damascus that, illuminated by the rising sun, were just becoming visible on the horizon.

"Our timing is perfect!" he declared more to himself than to the others. "We'll catch these Yeshua lovers at their synagogue in morning prayer. They'll be completely off guard and we'll slaughter their leaders where they stand."

"What of the rest?" one of those accompanying Sha'ul inquired. "What will become of them?"

"Have you learned nothing?" Sha'ul chided. "We'll drag them all off to prison, where for all I care they can spend the rest of their days with their flesh rotting for the glory of their fanciful savior!"

Just then, at the very pinnacle of his hateful ranting, a bright light from heaven flashed all around him, and he heard a voice say to him, "Sha'ul, Sha'ul, why do you persecute me?"

"Who are you, Lord?" Sha'ul asked.

"I am Yeshua, whom you are persecuting," he replied. "Now get up and go into the city, and you will be told what you must do."

The thugs traveling with Sha'ul stood there speechless; they heard the sound but did not see anyone.

Sha'ul got up from the ground, but when he opened his eyes he could see nothing. So those who were with him led him by the hand into Damascus to a safe place, the house of Judah, who was another persecutor of the followers of the Way. For three days he remained there blind, and he neither ate nor drank anything.

It was during this extended time while Sha'ul remained totally blind and helpless in the house of Judah that Matthias remained hold up in the

Synagogue of the believers: Jews and Gentiles; men, women and children who had been born again in Yeshua. It was there that they remained in deep communal prayer and fasting, seeking protection from the expected onslaught from their self declared, vitriolic enemy from Jerusalem.

On the third day of this self imposed incarceration, one of their number, a disciple named Ananias, who had been absent from the synagogue, burst into their midst to excitedly report his just concluded miraculous experiences to the assemblage.

"The Lord called to me in a vision, he thus testified: 'Ananias!'"

"Yes, Lord" I answered.

"The Lord told me, 'Go to the house of Judah on Straight Street and ask for a man from Tarsus named Sha'ul, for he is praying. In a vision this man Sha'ul has seen a man named Ananias come and place his hands on him to restore his sight."

"Lord," I answered, 'I have heard many reports about this man and all the harm he has done to your saints in Jerusalem. And he has come here with authority from the chief priests to arrest all who call on your name.'

"But then the Lord told me," Ananias, continued "'Go! This man is my chosen instrument to carry my name before the Gentiles and their kings and before the people of Israel. I will show him how much he must suffer for my name.'"

"Well, my dear brothers and sisters." Ananias continued, "What more could I do? I went to the house and entered it and finding this blind Sha'ul praying there, I placed my hands on him and declared: 'Brother Sha'ul, the Lord, Yeshua, who appeared to you on the road as you were coming here, has sent me so that you may see again and be filled with the Holy Spirit.'"

"Let me tell you, it was truly miraculous!" Ananias continued excitedly. "Immediately after I prayed, something like scales fell from Sha'ul's eyes, and he could see again. He got up and declared his deep faith and allegiance to Yeshua, and then requested water baptism without delay."[107]

Early the next morning, with the entire local body of believers bearing witness, after Sha'ul had privately been completely anointed with oil, had repented, and made a statement of his faith in Yeshua, Matthias baptized him through three separate full body immersions: (in the name of the Father-- in the name of the Son and in the name of the Holy Spirit) in the cool running water of the synagogue's mikvah.

Next, Sha'ul received baptism with the Holy Spirit, after which he wandered among the rejoicing congregation crying out praises to his beloved Heavenly Father in an unknown tongue and overflowing with an unbridled ecstasy that transported him to the loftiest of spiritual heights.

After these wonderful festivities, Sha'ul spent several days in Damascus, taking food and regaining his strength. During this time he met regularly with Matthias, who by the grace of their now fully shared God, had quickly become both his close friend and mentor.

"What am I to do my brother?" Sha'ul vented his deep frustration to Matthias early during their meetings together. "Our beloved Yeshua commissioned me with His own sweet voice: 'I will rescue you from your own people and from the unsaved people in the nations. I am sending you to them to open their eyes and turn them from darkness to light, and from the power of Satan to God, so that they may receive forgiveness of sins and a place among those who are sanctified by faith in me.'"[108]

"My problem is this Matthias! I certainly can teach the unsaved of the world the truths of the Tenach, and I can and I *will* proclaim to all who will listen the wonderful good news of Yeshua who is the Messiah of us all. But how, I ask you, my brother—how am I to teach them the very doctrines of their new faith: what precisely they must do to gain salvation; the method and the meaning of baptism; where, and how often they are to assemble in His name; and so very much more? How am I to teach them any of this when I know so precious little of any of these things myself? May our dear God forgive me, Matthias!" he now wept openly, making no attempt to conceal his deep sense of guilt driven frustration.

Sha'ul continued after he had managed to momentarily regain his composure. "While you and the rest who were close to Yeshua have been establishing the very fiber of this wonderful new expression of Judaism called the 'Way' I and the Pharisees who have been at my command have gone from place to place persecuting your people, even to the point of death! It would seem that I am beyond forgiveness and certainly beyond any hope of taking so much of what I do not yet know to people in the nations who know nothing!"

Now weeping uncontrollably, Sha'ul fell upon his knees in front of Matthias, pleading, "help me my brother, if I am not already beyond help. Show me if you are able, the things I must do; the places I must go, in order to prepare myself to undertake such an awesome ministry for our Lord."

Matthias gently helped Sha'ul to his feet and they sat quietly together in silence for a few moments before Matthias began to speak with clear authority and confidence. "My brother," he began. "Until the very moment you met Yeshua on the road to Damascus, you were a Pharisee. Every fiber of your being was guided by your deep pharisaic conviction that God was an indivisible unity and thus the Messiah whom you awaited could by no means be Divine, the very Son of God. Further, your concept of redemption had everything to do with doing good works to earn your way to an eternal reward and nothing to do with the idea that salvation comes to us as an entirely unearned gift as a result of our faith in Him."

"My brother," Matthias continued passionately. "All the while you were embracing these misguided understandings—before your very eyes which were even then blinded, the Essenes, the third great sect of Judaism, were flourishing all around you. To me this is an incredible mystery—virtually all but a relative few of the Jewish believers in Yeshua who have become the initiating heart of our now shared faith in Him were first Essenes. Essenic doctrine and understandings have been actively practiced throughout our Land for some three hundred years. It is also well recorded that many of these same core doctrines were being practiced some five hundred years before the beginnings of the current millennium as the central understandings of mainline Judaism."

"My point is this!" Matthias continued as Sha'ul clung to his every word with rapt attention. "This new understanding of Yeshua you have embraced with all of its wonderful implications will one day change the entire world. These wonderful truths that have taken on flesh in our midst are by no means a new religion. Our new and wonderful Yeshua centered faith is simply a much richer and much more complete understanding of Judaism! The faith you now share with those who call themselves 'Nazarenes' and/or the 'Way' is quite simply the fulfillment of Essene prophecy as it has long foretold the coming of the Divine Messiah, Yeshua. Long before He appeared among us, these prophesies concerning His life, purpose, nature, sacrifice—how He is to be worshiped and so very much more about Him were written down in our sacred scrolls at Qumran. They remain there even today in our extensive library where they are unceasingly studied by our priests!"

"How could I and my people have been so blind?" Sha'ul lamented.

"Never mind, my brother, and you are now indeed my *brother* in Yeshua. Who can explain the ways of our God? Now, it is for you to call upon His name and to listen. He will show you precisely how you are to prepare for your great and wonderful ministry!"

"He already has shown me," Sha'ul confessed. "I am to go to Qumran and study there at the feet of the masters who inhabit that amazing storehouse of truth and knowledge."

"In my spirit I confirm these things." Matthias replied. "The Lord has shown me you will receive the necessary knowledge and understanding from your study at Qumran from which you will create the very core doctrines of our faith. These doctrines will continue on until the very end of this age as holy truth— a Scriptural illumination of the New Covenant spoken of by the Prophet Jeremiah."

"My brother, if you are willing," Matthias continued, "I will take you to Qumran to meet my father, Eliezar, the High Priest, who, I am certain will be most pleased to oversee your time of study."

"Indeed, this shall be done, and soon!" Sha'ul replied with deep commitment.

Chapter Thirty Nine

The Galilee

June 2000 – October 2004

Drew could hardly contain his excitement as he burst through the door of their lovely, Tiberias penthouse apartment and shouted joyfully to Carla who had been sitting quietly on a sofa in the living room, reading from her bible. "It's finally happened Carla! By the grace of God, my prayers have been answered!"

"*What's* finally happened, Drew?" she replied soothingly, trying to calm the runaway excitement of her nearly out of control husband. "Why don't you just sit down for a minute or two to catch your breath while I get you a cup of coffee? Then you can tell me all about your meeting in Haifa this morning." With that, she headed for the kitchen, not waiting for a reply.

A short time later, after he had taken his first taste from his freshly filled mug, he spoke, much more calmly than before: "Okay!" he began. "Are you ready for this?"

Carla laughed teasingly. "Darling, I've being married to you for more than forty four wonderful years—I'm ready for *anything*!"

"Okay!" Drew began. "I originally scheduled this meeting with one of the top archeologists in Israel with the idea of discussing my working hypothesis regarding a pre-Pauline Church. Well, guess what? While he wasn't exactly enamored with my hypothesis, he by no means dismissed it out of hand."

"But, that's not the *real* news!" Drew continued emotionally. "It seems that a renowned Haifa based team of archaeologists will lead a consortium of other teams from the United Sates and Poland during the next several years to excavate the entire city of Hippos!"

"Dear God!" Carla gasped. "That *is* extraordinary news! When will they begin?"

"Well, my dear, I learned that they've already conducted a preliminary survey of the city and the first dig will commence in just two weeks, on the first of July!"

"Is there any way that we can be directly involved in all this?" Carla asked with growing excitement.

"Interesting you should ask," he teased. "They are looking for volunteers to participate in the dig and I signed both of us up this morning!"

"Fantastic! Absolutely fantastic!" Carla exclaimed. "I really don't want to wait for two weeks to see this place again! It would be so wonderful for the two of us to just walk around, and pray over the ruins as they are now, before all the commotion begins."

"I was going to suggest this very thing," Drew replied happily as he heard the confirmation of what he had taken to be a leading of the Holy Spirit. "How about late this afternoon, when it cools down a bit?"

"If you call one hundred and five degrees or so cooling down, then I'm all for it! I can hardly wait!" she replied.

***

"Not too shabby for a young fellow like me, just turned sixty seven," Drew breathed heavily as the two of them paused under the meager shade of a live oak just beyond the summit.

"Have a drink, Darling!" Carla laughed as she offered him first claim to the two liter bottle of water she had packed up the mountain. "You'd better hydrate a bit before you really start hallucinating."

"I'm not hallucinating and you know it, Carla! Deep down in your spirit you surely must agree that a pre-Pauline Gentile Christian Church once stood in this mountain top city. I *know* in my spirit that the Church, as we know it today, sprang forth from this very place! I also *know* with certainty that the series of archeological digs about to begin here will radically change the very face, substance, and understanding of early Church history!"

"Drew, Darling," Carla replied soothingly. "I really do agree with your hypothesis, but this archaeological dig season will be only the first among many that will surely follow. The truth is we may not live long enough to witness the definitive hard evidence proof of what you are seeking."

They had resumed their walk along the flat terrain of the mountain top plateau where the thriving, regional Metropolis had stood so long ago, before it had been utterly destroyed by a devastating earthquake in 739 AD. Now, as they approached the near center of the city which was to be the focus of the first season's dig, Drew added thoughtfully: "I'll tell you what, Carla! You're quite right! It *may* indeed take several if not many more dig seasons to absolutely prove my contention, but I can tell you *right now*—one or the other of these two very old Byzantine Churches holds the key, and, if I were a betting man, I'd put my money on this particular ruin!" With that, he took Carla's hand and pulled her up a short but steep rise to the level of the top of the central of three apses from which, just in front of them, the clear outlines of the almost totally still buried church could be seen. There were several fallen marble columns lying about and the remains of several basalt block walls were clearly visible.

"Yes!" he continued confidently, "I have a very strong spiritual sense that this buried treasure, this rubble that the Haifa team has named the 'Northwest Church,' because of its relative location to the other places of interest in the city—I *know* this place will somehow reveal a much earlier, now totally unknown, gathering place where our precious Lord Yeshua was being worshiped by newly converted pagans even many years *before* He encountered Paul on the road to Damascus."

***

October 7, 2004

Simcha Torah[109]

The day after the close of the Fifth Dig Season

Sheldon Thurman stood by Drew's side as they together beheld the most recently unearthed ruins of the Northwest Church. "Drew, it thrills me greatly that you've found at least something of the proof you've been seeking all these years!" His breathing was still greatly labored after their long and difficult climb to the site. "I'm not at all sure I could continue making this annual ascent much longer. It would seem that my many years are beginning to show."

"Ah come on, Shel!" Carla, who followed along just behind the two of them, taunted their devoted mentor and dearest friend. "Both of you old geezers have many more mountains left to climb and all for the Glory of God!"

"The fact is, Shel," Drew revealed, "We've learned a great deal during these five dig seasons; enough I believe for us to make a very convincing case that a pre-Pauline Church most likely *did* exist in this place. The fact is, based upon what we've learned here, I'm going to begin work on a series of lectures and ultimately a book that will speak to all this."

"Why are you *waiting* on the book?" Sheldon interjected. "Why not get this all written down now? What you've already learned by no means should be kept from a long misled and hungry Church! The unbridled truth is something everyone who proclaims faith in Yeshua needs to thoroughly understand."

"The *truth* is, Shel," Drew replied with deep conviction, "While we've already learned much, there are at least several more dig seasons ahead and I'm deeply convinced there will be much more solid evidence forthcoming. Certainly, what we already have will convince many, but many others will argue, and rightfully so, that our conclusions arise from a variety of sources, too many of them anecdotal, making it impossible at this point to provide a solidly uncontestable conclusion. Shel," he concluded. "I want to wait for at least another two seasons before I put all of this on paper for public consumption."

"Fair enough! Reverend Doctor Sterling, and spoken like a true scholar! The world may have to wait, but *I don't*!" Shel spoke, only half teasing. "I trust that you are about to guide me step by step through the highlights of what you've already learned."

"Indeed!" my friend, nothing could give me more pleasure, he replied as the three of them now stood at the top of the center apse overlooking the now almost completely excavated 'Northwest Church.'

"And we've *earned* the right to talk about this place, let me tell you!" Carla interjected. "Between the two of us, we've *schlepped* several tons of rocks and other debris from here during these five years. We've not only come to *know* this place, but we've also grown to love it very much—every exciting square inch of it!"[110]

"Well," Drew began to speak professorially, "The first season was pretty much spent opening up the place, although, as you can see, we did manage to expose much of the gorgeous mosaic floors that are surprisingly well preserved."

"Was there any early encouragement to suggest some implied proof of your pre-Pauline church hypothesis?" Sheldon interjected.

"In all honesty, not even a hint to this point!" Drew replied. "Essentially, the team found very compelling evidence that this was a classic, circa fifth century Byzantine Church that had been constructed and appointed pretty much as expected for such a sanctuary during this period of Christian Church history. But, let me proceed to the second season, Drew continued. "That's when things began to get really interesting!"

"My husband is a master of understatement!" Carla interjected.

"Before I get into details of the church itself," Drew continued, as he pointed to a debris filled area, dominated by large fallen marble pillars, immediately to the left of the Church, "let me introduce you to its immediate neighbor, dubbed by the team as 'The Hellenistic Compound.' The pillars you are looking at were a central part of a very large pagan temple most likely erected in honor of Helios, the pagan sun god, who along with several other well known Greek and Roman pagan deities were widely and exclusively worshiped in this place and elsewhere on this mountain from the third century BC until the early first century AD. Thats when Yeshua inaugurated Gentile Christianity in a crowd of some four thousand people from this city whom He miraculously fed and healed, right at the bottom of this mountain at a place called Tel Hadar."

"Are you suggesting that these early Christian believers may have worshipped Yeshua in this *pagan* temple until the fifth century when they finally got around to building this Byzantine Church right next door?" Sheldon inquired skeptically?

"Not for a moment!" Drew replied with conviction. "Now let me show you how things began to get very interesting indeed. Even while the team was expanding the uncovered areas of the fifth century level laterally in every direction, they also, towards the end of the second season, had both the wisdom and the curiosity to begin to explore what might lie beneath. Towards this end they dug a series of shallow trial exploratory trenches at various places of interest throughout the exposed top level."

"What did they find??" Sheldon interrupted excitedly.

"In a word, they found enough to whet their appetites sufficiently to make this downward search a priority during the next season."

"But what *did* they find. Drew?" Sheldon demanded.

"Get this, Shel," Drew replied, savoring the moment. "They found clear evidence of three well defined lower level floors that could possibly be explained as lower levels of the existing fifth century structure, or floors from an earlier Christian sanctuary built on this same site, or the remains as an extension of the immediately adjacent pagan temple, or perhaps as some much earlier structure that may simply have been some sort of public meeting place. The fact is, at that point the team was still sorting through all of the very generous pottery and other artifact evidence to try and make some sense out of all this."

"The team must have really been chomping at the bit to explore these lower floors during the next season," Sheldon surmised."

"Things get a bit sticky on this point." Drew replied. "We must all remember that discovering possible chinks in early Christian Church history is not a first priority with this very appropriately scientifically and historically oriented team of mostly secular scholars. Needless to say, I did every thing but get down on my knees and beg for a redirection of their primary focus, but that focus always was and still is to reveal the city of Hippos the way it was when it was devastated by an earthquake in 749. Obviously, to best satisfy this underlying objective the team was and is rightfully oriented to digging and exposing laterally in all directions rather than by first looking for the earliest underlying evidence of civilization as it might appear just above bed rock and then working up."

"Are you telling me that they just stopped this downward exploration at the end of the second season?" Sheldon asked incredulously.

"Not at all!" Drew replied. "While the emphasis was now clearly lateral, downward exploration became only of secondary interest. Even so, at the end of the third season they dug a very provocative trial trench in the northwest part of the nave that led them to a much earlier floor—a clearly defined floor they surmised that could well have been connected with a much earlier, otherwise unpreserved structure."

"So," Sheldon replied, "Did the team follow through with this find in the fourth season or, as you said earlier, did they concentrate on expanding the top level fifth century church?"

"First off," Drew replied, "for the first time in my hearing the team developed a working hypothesis: the 'Northwest Church' was built upon the remains of both Hellenistic and Roman temples, most likely, as a symbolic gesture meant to signify the victory of Christianity over Paganism."

"Thus," Drew continued, "while deferring any further concentrated downward exploration, they attributed the clear evidence pointing to earlier structures that existed beneath the top level Church, to very early pagan temples. Thus, they discounted, for the time, the possibility that there could have been as well, or even instead, an earlier, perhaps even first century place of Christian worship."

"Let me quickly add," Drew spoke almost defensively, "I directly confronted the team with this conjecture of mine and they assured me that their conclusions to the contrary up to this point were anything but final and that the matter would definitely be further explored during the coming season and perhaps beyond."

"So, that was it for the fourth season?" Sheldon probed.

"The fact is," Drew replied with obvious respect, "the team made some remarkable progress during this season, more, from my point of view, than during all of the other earlier seasons combined."

"Like what?" Sheldon asked.

"For starters," Drew replied excitedly, "they dug yet another strata graphic trench, this one right in front of the main apse. This time, from my point of view, they hit the jackpot! In the words of the team chief for this part of the dig which I have committed to memory what they found are 'the remains of *pre-church* architecture: a channel and a floor that abut a wall which was later re-used by the builders of the church.' Furthermore, both a coin and pottery they found at this level have been dated to the early part of the first century! This is dynamite, Shel! They are claiming to have found the floor of an early first century pre-church structure the foundation of which was used, at least in part, to construct the present top level fifth century church. Shel, Carla and I *saw* this ancient floor with our own eyes! I photographed it before they covered it up until some indeterminate dig season of the future, perhaps never again to be further explored!"

"This certainly is exciting to say the least," Sheldon agreed to the find's overall importance. "But, by itself it by no means offers *absolute* proof that the structure they found was the pre-Pauline place of worship you have been looking for during the past five years! What it does offer, it seems to me, is some very compelling anecdotal evidence that points very much in the direction you seek to travel! Tell me, Drew, what else did the team find this season?"

"Actually, Drew replied, "Beyond the remarkable pre-church structure we've been discussing, the team concentrated mostly on exposing the southern aisle of the church. In the process, while they were cleaning the mosaic floor of the aisle, they found two fascinating Greek inscriptions incorporated into the beautifully preserved mosaic floor which covers the entire southern aisle. Come," Drew invited as he led the way, "I want to show you the one of these that speaks very clearly, directly and compellingly to Carla and me."

Drew now led them the few steps to the new position in the southern aisle. He pointed to a very clear Greek inscription worked into the mosaic, translating as he read the single line: *Heliodora offered half of the nomisma for the costs of the mosasic.*

"Heliodora," he continued, "was probably a deaconess or perhaps simply an otherwise significant benefactor. Constantine personally established the Byzantine monetary system which was based on the *nomisma*, a coin of pure gold weighing 4.5 grams."

"Most interesting," Sheldon commented.

"It's *a lot more* than simply interesting!" Carla added. "Shel, beyond Drew, I wouldn't share what I am about to tell you with anyone, not even our girls---."

Sheldon listened with rapt attention as she continued with great emotion.

"The fact is, from the very time I saw this place from afar, during our first visit to Israel some twenty five years ago, I've been drawn here in a very compelling and spiritual way I do not yet fully understand. You may think I'm some sort of a nut," she offered apologetically but---"

"But *nothing!*" Sheldon interrupted with deep conviction. "You are one of the most committed and spiritually attuned believers I've ever known, Carla! I *know* that the Lord must have something very special for you here---please go on."

"Well, the fact is, I married a Jew and I've always rejoiced in the amazing and wonderful new world Drew's heritage has opened up in my life. While I never really got to know her extremely well, like Drew, I had a very special and deep love for his grandmother Amelia, the mother of his mother."

"This may sound terribly silly, Shel," she continued, "But both Drew and Grandma Amelia shared with me *after* I had insisted that we name our first daughter 'Dory' that there has always been a 'Dory' in her family for the several generations we have been able to trace. The really odd thing about this I've learned is that our Dory's great, great, Grandmother was called 'Dory' which was a shortened version of her actual given name: 'Heliodora.'"

"Odder still," Drew added. 'Heliodora' is clearly a Greek name with no Jewish connection, at least not any we've been able to find."

"Okay!" Carla now stated with confident conviction. "Let me just go ahead and say it! Sheldon, somehow *I know* in my spirit that I'm directly connected to this very place and to this particular Heliodora, not because of my own direct heritage, but by virtue of my marriage to Drew!"

Sheldon waited for a few moments to allow what he'd heard to sink in. "Okay, you two," he now spoke with certainty. "I believe that the Lord has given me a word of knowledge that you are indeed connected to this place, Carla. It has everything to do with you, a Gentile, and Drew, a Jew, becoming, according to the promise of scripture, one flesh. I can tell you this," he continued with obvious conviction. "Sometime in the very distant past, another Jewish man and another Gentile woman who was named Heliodora shared a great love and a great destiny in this place."

"I totally agree with what you have heard from the Lord," Carla replied with equal conviction."

"And so do I, Shel." Drew agreed. "And, now it's my turn for shared revelation," he continued. "Shel, during these past five years of digging and moving this mountain we've come to understand something deeply moving and precious. What we've heard as the central message for the entire Church underlying all of this is the very same as the central message of the word of knowledge you just shared with us regarding the series of mixed Jewish and Gentile marriages that somehow seem to characterize this place. Both what we have come to understand, and your word of knowledge, speak to the same thing: *Unity*!

"We have come to understand that deep within the heart of this place rests a vital and God given message for the world today---a message of unity in His precious Body of Yeshua that you and another two billion of so Gentile believers have always known as the Church."

"Come, Shel," Drew gently led the way out of the "Northwest Church" proper and into the center of the adjacent Hellenistic Compound midst the fallen pillars of its Temple of Helios. "I have saved the very best for last. I have something very important to show you here but we must hurry, before the sun sets entirely over the western shore."

Drew now fell to one knee alongside of one of the several large, fallen marble pillars that dominated the area. "You'll have to bend down to see this, but believe me, it is worth the effort!"

Sheldon squatted down beside Drew and strained to see where he was pointing, to a barely visible Greek anagram etched into the solid stone. "Dear God!" he gasped in surprise. Is this what I think it is?"

"Indeed it is!" Drew confirmed it is a logo that has been used by the Gentile Christian Church since its inception: an anagram rendered in Greek, the language of Hippos: Ιχθυσ ("fish"), an abbreviation of: Ιησουσ Χριστοσ Θηου Υιοσ Σωτηρ ("Jesus Christ, Son of God, Savior").

"I challenged one of the senior archeologists on the team as to the presumed age of this inscription." Drew continued. "His opinion was that the inscription was not earlier than early first century and not later than early sixth. That really doesn't add anything more to my proof system other than yet more anecdotal evidence, but still, I find it most interesting if not compelling!"

"And now, my brother," Drew continued, "I have one more very important thing to show you that arises from what we have just seen, but I want to do this in the context of a sunset over the Sea of Galilee, and if we hurry, we will be in the right place at exactly the right time. Come, you two. Follow me to the Western edge of the city!"

***

"This is a truly spectacular ending to an unbelievably spectacular day!" Sheldon declared appreciatively as they looked out over the beautiful Sea of Galilee, majestically reflecting the exquisite overlapping tints of the sunset."

Drew, standing at Sheldon's side, affectionately placed an arm around his shoulder as he pointed first to Tiberias, nestled on the far shore, directly opposite from where they stood. "Follow along with me as I point out the very places where Yeshua ministered directly to His Jewish people during most of His three year ministry. Look, there is Mount Ermos from which He preached the Sermon on the Mount!"

"Yes, I see it!"

"And there are *Tabgha*, the place where He fed and healed five thousand mostly Jews."

"Amen." Sheldon acknowledged.

"And nearly in the same place," Drew pointed, "you can see what the church calls *Mensa Christi*, 'the Table of Christ' from which he told his disciples to throw their net on the other side and then, many days after His resurrection from the dead, he shared breakfast with them."

"I am seeing much for the first time, Drew!" Sheldon replied.

"And now, moving right along beyond The Bay of Parables, Gennesaret, and Magdala, we come to Capernaum, Yeshua's home away from home. Shel," Drew continued with great fervor. "The entire New Testament is crammed full of the wonderful things He said and the amazing things He did in these very places—things He said and did first for the Jews."

"Now, I implore you my brother, take a good look at the shape of the Lake. It is truly one of a kind—shaped like a harp, a symbol of peace love and unity!

"Shel, like the elders from the Book of Revelations who are singing praises to God without ceasing, I can practically hear a chorus of angels singing of Unity in the Body from their vantage points all around this precious Lake. Mind you, I'm not just speaking of the Western side and the sacred places there we've just pointed to, but follow me further and look a short distance beyond the northern end to the eastern shore and you'll find the wonderful place called Tel Hadar. Remember, this was the place where He conducted the second feeding; this time He miraculously fed some four thousand pagans, many of whom He also healed and many of whom I believe soon after became those who held forth in worship from this very city where we now stand. Perhaps, as I truly believe, they did so from a simple structure that now lies in mute evidence buried beneath the so called 'Northwest Church!'"

"Move along with me, further, Shel," Drew continued his pointing tour of the Eastern Shore. "Next you will find Kursi where He freed the chained man from demons and then drove them into a large herd of pigs. It seems very probable to me that these pigs were being raised to be used as blood sacrifices to Dionysus, the pagan God of sex and wine, right here in our local Temple of Helios.

"But, let's look on the bright side!" Drew continued. "I have no doubt that believing Jews who built the chapel at Kursi to mark the miracle also were commissioned by God to disciple His new Gentile converts right here in our beloved Hippos!"

"Pardon me for rambling on so much, Shel, but this brings me to the central truth we've learned from all this. There is a blessed Unity here! Just listen and you will hear the angels singing in testimony to the truth of what I am saying. Yeshua ministered to mostly Jews on one side of the Lake and to mostly Gentiles on the other. He ministered first to the Jews and then to the Gentiles. But, He never for a moment ministered with less salvational purpose to the Gentiles than He did to the Jews. I know that I know that I know—His heart was, is, and always will be that there not be two *differently* saved, unequally yoked bodies of believers, but rather two *physically different* but *spiritually identical* bodies who, joined in perfect and blessed Unity, will worship Him now and forever in genuine love as brothers. This was the very substance of His central message to us that he preached to all who would listen during the time He walked among us, and this is the central message of the scriptures that have come down to us through the ages!"

The three of them remained completely silent before their heavenly master when Drew had finished, as the last of the fading sunset reflected from the tears that now wet their three faces.

"I have one more thing to share from this place." Drew finally broke their silence as he took a piece of golden jewelry from his pocket and held it out to his dearest friend.

"What's this, Drew?" Sheldon asked curiously.

"It is a pendant made as an exact replica taken as a "strike" from the face of a recently rediscovered first century artifact on Mount Zion. It is called 'the Messianic Seal of the Jerusalem Church.'"

"There are actually eight such surviving artifacts that bear this ancient symbol," Drew continued." This symbol apparently was developed by very early Jewish believers from the Synagogue in the Upper room on Mount Zion. I know the people who hold the original artifacts and I trust them implicitly—I have held these pieces in my hands and I *know* that they are genuine. I also was present when another dear and trusted friend of mine who is an artist, sculptor and historian took the strikes while I watched. He then later made molds from the strikes and it was one of these molds that was used to produce this pendant."

"This looks terribly important, Drew," Sheldon exclaimed as he examined the three part symbol. "What is your interpretation of its meaning?"

"Please take note, Shel," Drew replied. "The top part of the symbol is a menorah, very much like the one we saw etched on the retaining wall of the first century chapel at Kursi."

"Likewise," Drew continued, "the bottom part is a simplistic fish. But, the really fascinating part of this design is the middle part that is made up of overlapping stand of the menorah and the tail of the fish to form a perfect Star of David. Could it be any more obvious, Shel?" Drew questioned. "One of the very first Jewish believers, perhaps even one of the twelve apostles, created this symbol to speak directly to the unity that literally thrived around this lake, and undoubtedly elsewhere during the early first century when both Jews and Gentiles were coming into the faith, even while Paul was still a belligerent Pharisee who thrived on tormenting Jews. Just *look* at it and listen to it speak of Unity: the Menorah is obviously a symbol of Judaism and all things Jewish. The fish is just as obviously a symbol of the Christian Church with Yeshua at its head. And, the two of them come together in the

Star of David which is clearly a symbol of our forever blessed Israel!"

"There are only three of these pendants in existence at the moment," Drew explained as he pulled an identical piece attached to a gold chain he had kept hidden from Sheldon until this moment. "Carla is wearing another, and this one is for you."

Chapter Forty

Hippos
January, AD 62

"Greetings in the name of Yeshua!" Matthias exclaimed as he gave a bear hug embrace to Sha'ul of Tarsus who stood at the open door of his humble basalt block home in the center of Hippos' crowded residential district. "You look extremely well, my brother," Matthias observed. "Come in, have some cool water from the depths of our cistern and sit down for a time to recover from your long journey."

"Even the climb to your beautiful mountain top city offered me no challenge," Sha'ul replied with no hint of pride. Perhaps you've heard something of my three very long journeys since the last time we met? I'm about to embark on a fourth, this time to far away Rome. Thus, my body, I'm certain like your own, has become accustomed to the physical rigors one must endure while sharing the Gospel of Yeshua with the unsaved!"

Sha'ul paused reflectively for a few moments before he continued: "From the Jews five times I received forty stripes minus one. I have been beaten with rods; I've been stoned; in journeys often, in perils of waters, in perils of robbers, in perils of my own countrymen, in perils of the Gentiles, in perils in the city, in perils in the wilderness, in perils in the sea, in perils among false brethren; in weariness and toil, in sleeplessness often, in hunger and thirst, in fasting often, in cold and nakedness -- besides the other things, what comes upon me daily: my deep concern for all the churches."[111]

"I certainly understand!" Matthias commiserated. "I know *exactly* what you mean. How wonderful is our God who fully prepares and enables us to do the things He has ordained."

"I am so pleased you've taken time from your busy travels to visit us for a few days," Matthias continued warmly. "We have so very much to share. What a joy it will be for Dory and me to bask in your sweet presence and great wisdom."

As if on cue, Dory came through the door carrying a large leather shopping bag overflowing with fresh produce she had just purchased from several different vendors in the nearby city market. "Greetings!" she warmly welcomed the guest whom she had never before met. "You must be Sha'ul! I've heard so much about your greatly blessed ministry from Matthias. We're so very pleased you've come to honor our home with your presence."

"The pleasure and the honor are mine!" Sha'ul replied graciously. "What is the news of your daughter 'Heliodora' whom I'm told you address as 'Little Dory?'"

"The years of our lives have passed like the light of a quickly fading lamp." Dory replied, amazed that this extremely challenged and involved man of God would know anything of their family. "It seems our 'Little Dory' and her husband, Alexandros, the son of Athanasios, have a Heliodora of their very own, along with three strong and beautiful sons!"

"You two will leave a remarkable legacy in their precious flesh," Sha'ul replied, "as well as a mighty legacy in the spirit born of your remarkable ministry here in the Decapolis and well beyond."

"Our ministry pales in its insignificance alongside yours, my greatly esteemed brother," Matthias interjected. "What great and wonderful things the Lord has done through you: By His grace, you have almost single-handedly established the Christian Church in the Western world, but so much more than this! You have, by the leading of the Holy Spirit, established and intricately defined the theology and doctrinal substance of the faith of those who now embrace Yeshua and who will embrace him in all future generations."

"The Body of Yeshua is like a lovely hand woven silk carpet," Sha'ul replied. "Viewed from its underside, one can see that all its threads run either horizontally or vertically and without exception every individual thread touches every other thread.

"Then turn the carpet to its topside and behold, before you is a lovely work of art.

"What I am getting to is this, Matthias," Sha'ul continued. "It was you, my brother, who introduced me—I who was ever so recently an evil, murdering Pharisee—to the wondrous truths long known and meticulously recorded by your people the Essenes. It was you who took me to Qumran and set me upon my long and devoted journey of studying in your wonderful library." He paused for a moment to suppress his rising emotion sufficiently to continue.

"Matthias, my dear brother, it was because our wonderful Lord saw fit that your thread and mine should cross and then become intimately and remarkably entwined for His divine purposes that I have been able, in my own humble way to serve Him, to understand that I and you are new creations; the old has gone, the new has come! We are indeed ambassadors for Yeshua who has given us the ministry of reconciliation.[112] He chose not to count our sins against us and then, by His grace, He is using us to carry His message of reconciliation to the world. Matthias," Sha'ul now spoke in a whisper born of his deep humility. "If our threads had never crossed, nothing I have been allowed to do in His service would have been possible."[113]

"Come, Sha'ul," Dory took their obviously weary guest's hand and gently helped him to his feet from the simple wicker chair where he had been sitting. "You must lie down and rest until the evening meal. I have no doubt that you and Matthias will talk very late into the night and you must prepare yourself for this wonderful sharing that surely lies ahead."

***

"Your darling wife was certainly right about the length of our delightful discussions," Sha'ul commented to Matthias as they sat across from one another on simple wooden benches in the late night coolness of the local congregation's simple basalt block meeting place. "It will soon be morning but I have not grown weary in the slightest."

"Nor have I, my brother," Matthias replied, fully alert. "The Lord has blessed us with this wonderful time together. We've already been sharing for several hours and it would seem we have only just begun."

"I'm so pleased how your ministry has progressed here in this city, and throughout the Decapolis," Sha'ul commented. "I have found such a consistent tendency among the nations where I have been blessed to plant congregations for them to build elaborate places of worship—ornate buildings, one bigger and more ostentatious than the next. Yet, I do not see this here in Hippos. You obviously meet each Shabbat in this simple public gathering place and even more importantly you seem to be following Ya'akov's Jerusalem model of small at least weekly gatherings of no more than twenty who break bread and worship our Lord together in private homes."[114]

Matthias fought to restrain the laughter that arose within him. "My dear brother, if you only knew!" he began." The truth is I had to intervene in a mighty way to dissuade these dear ones from gathering together in the elaborate Temple of Helios the sun god that stands directly adjacent to the humble public meeting place where we now sit. Then, when I was finally able to convince them that such a pagan shrine would not be an appropriate place to worship the Lord God of Israel, they immediately wanted to embark upon constructing a large and ornate "Christian" place of worship that would, at the very least, rival the Temple of Helios in both size and attractiveness. Believe me, Sha'ul," he continued, "It was no small thing for me to *finally* persuade this congregation that the Lord God of Israel looks upon each one of us as individual temples of the Holy Spirit, and when we worship Him collectively, it is our unified spiritual power that most pleases Him, not the size, or man made 'glory' of the place where we have gathered together for such congregational worship".[115]

"When the curtain of the Temple was torn from top to bottom at the moment of Yeshua's death on the cross," Sha'ul interjected with deep conviction, "the way was opened up for each of us to meet our Creator face to face in the Holy of Holies."[116]

"It is indeed a blasphemy of the Holy Spirit," he continued, "to suggest that some grandiose physical structure called a 'church' or a 'synagogue' or by any other name is required as the place from which a believer in Yeshua can properly communicate with the Heavenly Father."[117]

"Worse still!" Sha'ul became increasingly passionate as he spoke. "Yes worse still is the heretical notion that a hierarchal succession of ecclesiastical layers is either necessary or desirable with the mortal human leadership of each successive layer somehow spiritually 'accountable' to or irrevocably under the spiritual 'covering' or 'control' of the next upwards mortal layer."

"Certainly," Matthias interjected, "you made a clear statement of this 'Doctrine of Accountability' in your inspired letter to the Romans where you wrote, *all* believers, now and forever, will one day be called to give an account of their lives to Yeshua.[118]

"It would seem that we share many of the same misgivings about the emerging 'Church'," Sha'ul lamented. "I shudder at the thought that one day soon an army of mere men called 'priests' may rise up from the very mold of their pagan predecessors—an army of well intentioned but grossly misled men who will come to understand and widely proclaim to easily seduced ears that they and they alone are empowered to forgive sin, and to do so under the authority of yet another man— an ultimate high priest called 'Papa' who has been elected by still other mere mortals to sit upon some imagined throne of Yeshua here on earth. Yes, this mere man, this 'Papa' will sit upon a pagan rooted evil throne from which he will loudly proclaim his own infallibility as he attempts to take the very, holy place of the Creator of the Universe!"[119]

"And there is so much more, my brother," Matthias moved on to yet another matter that concerned him deeply. "So very many of these dear new believers have seemingly been led by the Holy Spirit to embrace our Torah based faith and then almost immediately been led astray by the enemy to set aside the very Torah upon which Yeshua Himself was first promised and then came forth."

"Indeed, it is as you speak, Matthias!" Sha'ul agreed emphatically. "Again and again I have attempted to teach that our faith is not a new religion but rather the continuation—the very fulfillment of Judaism. Again and again, I have proclaimed that the Torah is the good, true, very Word of God

--- the foundation from which the Holy Spirit has drawn them by grace into their faith.[120] But, sadly so often what I teach has been wrongly interpreted or worse still, fallen upon deaf ears."

"What I have seen," Matthias interjected, "are several new congregations that not only have come to discount what you rightfully assert to be our 'God breathed' scriptures but in their holy place they have substituted their former pagan practices and traditions!"

"I know!" Sha'ul replied with deep sadness. "And then, these poor misguided dear ones have gone to the next logical step in their gross misunderstanding to embrace the notion that their new, pagan based 'church' has replaced the original Torah based faith, along with Jewish traditions, all other things Jewish, indeed, even Israel itself. So many, like the Galatians, have already twisted my words and meaning on this central doctrinal understanding."[121]

"It seems to me," Matthias added, "that we must immediately focus our teaching upon correcting these heretical, even apostate understandings before the spiritual cancer they are spreading throughout the Body of Yeshua can no longer be excised."

"Sha'ul," Matthias continued with passion, "I'm told there are already more than one half million Jewish believers in Yeshua in Israel, and throughout the Diaspora. Praise God that you, other evangelists have also enjoyed remarkable success in bringing the Good News to the nations. Even now, there are many thousands of former pagan believers who are worshiping Yeshua, the Jewish Messiah, in a vast array of so called newly planted "Christian" churches. Inevitably," he hammered home a central calling of God upon his heart, "by the grace of God, the numbers of these Gentile believers will soon vastly exceed our own."

"Sha'ul, my brother," Matthias almost shouted: "We must never even for a moment let them forget the pure and wonderful Essenic, Jewish roots of their Christian faith—the rich spiritual soil of Mount Zion from which they sprang forth as a shoot from the stump of Jesse!"[122]

"Furthermore," Sha'ul interjected, "all believers in Yeshua— Jews and Gentiles alike must come to clearly understand the meaning of what I teach regarding the identical nature of the salvation afforded to them all, irrespective of ethnicity or any other consideration. All believers are saved by the shed blood of Yeshua and have thus become 'one, *spiritually* new man.' I'm deeply troubled that my teaching on this crucial point may be misunderstood by many who will rush to the very erroneous conclusion that Jews and Gentiles are made one in Yeshua in *all* respects, both spiritually and in the flesh."[123]

"I share your concern about this," Matthias replied. "Your meaning seemed clear enough to me as a Jew when you wrote that there would be no difference in gender, no slave or free and that all who believed were the 'Seed of Abraham' and thus transformed into a collective 'Spiritual Israel."[124]

"Perhaps I've failed to make my meaning clear." Sha'ul lamented. "Even our beloved brother Kefa has declared that my teachings are hard to understand and that the home synagogue on Mount Zion enjoys a wonderful peace when I'm abroad."[125]

"Sha'ul, the hour has grown well beyond simply late and the birds are beginning to welcome the sun rise with their sweet song. Let's go rest our weary bones for a time and then continue our wonderful sharing after we've enjoyed some restful slumber."

"And my brother," Sha'ul added: "As we close our eyes let us whisper and thus seek the precious words of our wonderful unifying Lord as a foundation for our dreams: *Do not think that I came to destroy the Torah or the Prophets. I did not come to destroy but to fulfill. For assuredly, I say to you, till heaven and earth pass away, one jot or one tittle will by no means pass from the Torah till all is fulfilled.* [126]

Chapter Forty One

Tiberias
November, 2004

"I'm certainly glad you decided not to make a big fuss about my birthday!" Drew exclaimed with a sense of feigned relief as he and Carla made their way to a central table in the over-the-water section of Decks, a posh gourmet restaurant on the Tiberias waterfront.

"Well you know it isn't everyday one's husband turns seventy, but after all, you are my spiritual head and if you wanted a quiet evening well---."

"You know," he observed, "it's really kind of weird. This place is practically empty! You'd expect it to be packed on a Friday evening--- even with many of the tourists scared off by the Intifada."

"Carla grinned from ear to ear as she faced her husband who was seated looking towards the water. "Well you never know, maybe some folks will show up later—after all, you've kept your birthday such a big secret who would know about it anyway?"

A moment later, right on cue, Sheldon, who had traveled from the States that very morning for this auspicious occasion, quietly approached from behind, and placed his arm around Drew's neck. "*I* would know about it, Drew! Happy, happy birthday!!"

Carla squealed with delight at the success of her well engineered surprise, as Drew, barely able to recover from the sweetness of Sheldon's presence, hugged them both from the depths of his appreciation.

A short time later, just after they had retaken their seats, Drew exclaimed excitedly: "Well, this certainly calls for a bottle of champagne--!"

"Actually, Darling," Carla interrupted with unconcealed delight, it calls for *several* bottles!" And again, right on cue, a loud chorus of loving voices from the sweet assemblage of dear ones who had gathered behind him cried out in perfectly orchestrated unison: "Happy Birthday Daddy!!"

Drew, taken by total surprise, wept with absolute joy as he hugged each of his darling daughters, their husbands, whom he greatly respected and adored, and then with overwhelming love, he emotionally greeted his six grandchildren: Dory's two boys and two girls, and Bekah's two girls.

"Sorry I couldn't contribute to the grandchildren collection, Daddy," Rachel whispered in her father's ear for just his hearing as she gave him yet another loving embrace.

"Never mind, Darling," he replied from the depths of his heart. "All three of my girls are *perfect,* just the way you are!"

After the baked Alaska desert that followed the predictably wonderful meal featuring lamb shoulder grilled over charcoal, Carla interrupted the ongoing cacophony of multiple, excited conversations to announce: "Ladies and gentlemen! If you will kindly look towards the sea, you will see the rapid approach of a tour boat that has been chartered in the honor of our birthday boy as well as for all of your benefit. I feel certain that the Reverend Doctor Andrew Scott Sterling will be delighted to give us a hands on around-the-lake lecturing tour of the biblical and associated archeological points and interest along the shoreline.

***

Very late that evening, after all but Drew, Carla, Sheldon and Dory had wearily retired to their rooms at the Sheraton Moriah, the four of them who remained sat together in the Sterling's living room, still glowing from the loving intimacy of this very special celebration. "I just can't tell you," Drew addressed no one in particular, "I can't begin to tell you how wonderful all of this has been—that my entire family traveled all this way, just to wish me a happy seventieth!"

"The fact is, Daddy," Dory seized the moment, turning suddenly very serious: "Our agenda extends a bit beyond just simply being here with you and Mom on this very special day. It seems that your daughters have individually and collectively reached a prayerful conclusion and I am to be the spokesperson appointed to share our thoughts with you two."

"And," Sheldon interjected supportively, "I am in full agreement with what you are about to hear and have been appointed by your girls to stand with them in this."

"For goodness sake!" Drew replied bewilderedly. "What ever are you two talking about?"

"Mom and Dad," Dory continued, "We think the time has come for you to come *home*! You aren't getting any younger. Your health is getting a bit shaky. You've lived a zillion miles away from those who most love you for over twenty-five years!"

Drew gently interrupted. "In the first place, Dory, we *are* home! We love this place more than any other we've ever known or imagined. We've lived in this same apartment for more than a third of our entire lives, and we will one day be buried side by side in a Christian cemetery that overlooks our beautiful and unique lake."

"As for our health," he continued thoughtfully, "I may have high blood pressure, high cholesterol and low everything else that should be high, and I may be wearing out the carpet between our bedroom and bathroom but at least I'm getting some exercise out of the experience. Dory, darling, we're both under the care of a wonderful array of physicians who stand at the leading edge of world-wide medicine. We couldn't find better care any place in the United States, even if we needed it."

"What about Mom's hips?" Dory continued pointedly. "Isn't it so that she may one day soon need to have complete replacements?"

"I've been seeing the head of orthopedics at Rambam Hospital in Haifa," Carla interjected. "He's among the very best specialists in the world. I couldn't do better!"

"Okay!" Sheldon continued with a new approach. "Listen to me

Drew! You've written several books focused on teaching the Jewish Roots of Christianity to the Church! You've been instrumental in introducing the Messianic Seal to the world! Perhaps, most importantly, you've begun a growing wave of home congregations here in Israel that is just now catching on and is already spreading like wild fire in the United States! And, perhaps most importantly, you've become widely known as an advocate of unity and reconciliation between believing Jews and believing Gentiles!

It seems to me that your work is essentially finished and it's time for you and Carla to at last be able to spend the rest of your golden years living in peace, close to your dear ones!"

Dory jumped back into the fray before her father could reply: "To be perfectly honest, Daddy, all of us are worried sick concerning your safety. It isn't like you two were sitting quietly in your apartment enjoying your retirement!"

"Daddy," Dory continued emotionally, "please don't get the idea that your writings and lectures that characterize Islam as modern day paganism; your outspoken and often quoted opposition to the Israeli government's ongoing obsession to give away large portions of the Land to their Arab enemies in direct violation to the clear teachings of Scripture have gone unnoticed! Daddy, don't you think that you are more and more becoming a probable target for extermination?"

Sheldon added: "Alas, Drew! Your safety is really the crux of this whole argument. The rest of what you've heard is really secondary."

Drew smiled contentedly as he replied. "Isaiah said it best:

I, the LORD, have called You in righteousness, and will hold Your hand;

I will keep You and give You as a covenant to the people,

As a light to the Gentiles, to open blind eyes, to bring out prisoners from the prison,

those who sit in darkness from the prison house.[127]

"Dear ones," Drew went on, "In my heart, I know there is much more for me to do and I'll continue working in His vineyard until I draw my final breath.

No one may listen to my lectures or read my books; nevertheless, this in no way diminishes my need to press on in my Lord's service."

Drew paused for a moment to collect his thoughts. "There are *only* some *five thousand* believing Jews in Israel scattered among more than one hundred highly divergent congregations. There were at least *five hundred thousand* like minded believing Jews at the end of the first century. Worse still, at least half of this comparative handful of believing Jews have been led by false teachers to embrace the apostasy that Yeshua is somehow not Divine, but rather instead, just an important prophet. I ask you, *who* is going to persuade them differently? Certainly it's not the rest of the Body here and abroad that knows the horrendous consequences of such an apostasy, but who haven't even begun to address the problem! Instead, they have chosen a terrible silence over correction in the interests of some sick sense that this will somehow promote unity."

"On the other fringe side of the Body, there are those many who are widely promulgating the incredibly unscriptural teaching currently raging throughout the church that all Gentile believers, or, variously, *all* Gentiles period, are actually blood descendants of the so called "Lost Ten Tribes" of Israel. Further that these so called "Israelites" all up to *six billion* of them, are called by God to take up their presumed inheritance of ten twelfths of the sacred land of Israel!"

"Who could believe such *unmitigated nonsense?*" Dory interjected.

"Most recently, some sixty million or so Hispanics have proclaimed they are descended from the Sephardic Jews of Spain and as such they, yes *all sixty million of them*, are called to populate the Negev! I'm telling you, this is a real movement, however fancifully it may seem, and no one in the church, to my knowledge has even raised a single voice in opposition!"

"Dear God!" Drew continued passionately. "There are some two thousand six hundred protestant denominations in the United States and more than half of these believe that the Church has replaced Israel. Thus, many of them don't even blink an eye when buses filled with Jews are regularly blown into oblivion by Arab suicide murderers throughout our precious God given, everlasting inheritance."

"Who is going to teach them differently?" Drew now stood and shouted from the depths of his frustration filled being. "Who is going to teach even the President of the United States the profound biblical error of calling for the establishment of a so called 'Palestinian State' on the sacred God given Land of Israel?"

"Sheldon, my dear brother! Dory, my greatly loved daughter!" he now confessed his own inadequacy "Of course I understand the unlikelihood that *anyone*, much less I or your mother can do very much if anything worthwhile to deal with any of these heart rendering issues. But I do know this: The Lord God of Israel called us both home to Israel where we have taken up our inheritance, and it is from this place that He would be most pleased for us to stay and continue to do battle with the forces of darkness that surround and threaten to consume us—even if such battle amounts to nothing more that a quixotic flaying of our arms at an unhearing, uncaring and totally unresponsive world.

"No," he now concluded sadly, in an almost inaudible whisper. "Certainly there is nothing I or any other mere mortal can say or do to correct the creeping neo-paganism that has insidiously transformed the traditional fundamental Judeo-Christian society we grew up in and so foolishly took for granted. How utterly hideous is this 'New Age' Aquarian monism that has spawned an almost universal supra liberal Church. A Church that, among many other of its horrendous positions, openly ordains a homosexual clergy, encourages full term abortion, and blatantly ignores God authored scriptural imperatives. Even worse, a Church that consciously distances itself from anything and everything whatsoever that might even hint of some distant connection between their thus newly defined "Christianity" and the traditional Judaism from which the original, God authored, *Torah* based faith of their fathers first arose, here in Israel and then in the world beyond."

Chapter Forty Two

Mount Zion
May, 68 AD

Matthias wearily lowered himself into the simple wooden chair that had long been understood to be his place at the table where Symeon, a first cousin of Yeshua, now sat in the place of honor at its head—the place from which 'Ya'akov the Just,' the blood brother of the Lord, had long led the original twelve disciples who were the founding Body of Jewish Believers from its very beginning, until, alas, he had been murdered by the "Wicked Priests"[128] in the Temple Court nearly six years earlier.

Try as he might, Matthias still deeply grieved over the tragic loss of this great man of God whom he had held in life, and continued to embrace in memory with the same respect and affection he had bestowed only upon two other men: Kefa, his, dearest friend and beloved brother in Yeshua, and Kefa's long standing antagonist, Sha'ul of Tarsus. Certainly, he conjectured, as he waited for this 'urgently' called meeting to begin, he truly did love and respect Symeon, but no one, he felt deeply, could by any means begin to compare in wisdom or spirituality to the now, already long departed Ya'akov.

Sadly, he concluded, it was only his deep devotion to both Kefa and Sha'ul, from which he was now able to draw the spiritual refreshment and strength he needed to rise above his already many years and continue to meet the ever increasing challenges of his widespread and demanding ministry.

How often, recently, he silently accused himself as he sat waiting for Symeon to begin, had he seriously entertained the idea of simply spending the rest of his days on earth resting peacefully in the arms of his beloved Dory, the undisputed greatest of all his earthly treasures. How sweet, he now thought it would be to quietly wait with her in their beloved Hippos for the expected coming of the Lord. If this were not yet to be, then joyfully and expectantly they would wait together for the day when they would at last enjoy a glorious reunion with their eternally precious and wonderful Yeshua when they bowed down before Him in heaven.

Matthias was snapped back to the moment as Symeon at last broke the silence and began to speak.

"My brothers, these times in which we live and witness to an often unhearing and uncaring world are at once deeply sad and very perilous. I ask you to bear with me as I recount the terrible events that have led to the situation we are facing here in this city today.

"As you know," he continued, "Just two years ago, Flavius Josephus, a young and inexperienced scholar who was a totally ill prepared general, attempted to lead the Jewish forces in the Galilee against a band of zealots. Unfortunately, the local politicians who had spent their lives building a power base there resented the intrusion of this haughty Judaen outsider, and Josephus thus found himself battling against his fellow Jews more than against the Romans. In the end, as you know, the Romans utterly defeated all Jewish forces in the Galilee. What you may not know is how very great the loss of life from all of this was. My brothers, I am very sad to announce that the final figures have now been reported and recorded. During this terrible fracas more than one hundred thousand Jews were killed or sold into slavery! And, it would seem, these horrors are only the beginning. Even now, these Jews who tasted the blood of their fellow Jews hunger for even more. Right here in Jerusalem they have already killed most everyone in some position of leadership who was not as radical as they. Thus, all the more moderate of our government leaders have been slaughtered by their fellow Jews, not a single one of them has even been touched by the Romans.

"Consider the irony of all this, my brothers," Symeon continued. "Even now, our real enemy, the Romans, is preparing a siege of the entire city. I know in my spirit that if we do not act quickly, this can only lead to a terrible collective disaster for us, the Jewish followers of Yeshua."

"Are you suggesting that we of the 'Way' stand together against the military might of Rome?" Kefa asked impulsively.

"If it was the will of God that we should so stand," Symeon gently replied, "then I have no doubt that He would deal with us in the same way He did with David and Gideon of old, but I am persuaded He has ordained another way for our people here in this city."

"And what may that be?" Kefa forthrightly inquired.

"It is here that I turn to you, my brothers, and more specifically to you, Matthias. The Lord has shown me clearly that all the Jewish believers here in the City are to flee en masse to some as yet undisclosed place of safety. He has also shown me that our brother Matthias has long been preparing this refuge for our people and he will at once know the very place of which I speak."

All eyes turned to Matthias, who now, with his hands raised in pronouncement, began to speak. "My brothers, you already know that my ministry over all these many years has been to teach the Gospel of Yeshua to the many pagan communities throughout the Decapolis and beyond. With God's leading and for His great glory, many congregations, or 'churches' as they are called by these people who are called 'Christians,' have arisen in every major community and in even many small villages from the shores of the Sea of Galilee to as far away as Damascus. Even, long before my beloved brother Sha'ul began his mighty evangelistic outreach to the West, hundreds of thousands of former pagans were already loudly proclaiming their wonderful and glorious true understanding that Yeshua, the Messiah, the Son of God, is Lord!

"My brothers," Matthias continued with obvious assurance. "From all of these formerly pagan communities, at this urgent season, our God has chosen only one as His place of refuge for our people. This place is Pella, a relatively small community that lies among rugged hills and sharp valleys about two miles east of the Jordan River and some seventeen miles south of the Sea of Galilee. Scythopolis (Bet She'an) another Decapolis City lies just across the river, about eight miles to the northwest.

"It is in this place," Matthias continued with firm conviction, "where our Jewish brothers and sisters in the Lord will be welcomed with open arms and in His great love. You can be certain that these now 'born again' former pagan residents of Pella clearly understand and rejoice in the Jewish roots of the wonderful faith and salvation we all share in Him."

"I have a clear confirmation in my Spirit that this is the place of His choosing," Symeon announced."

"Amen!" The eleven other disciples, who had not yet spoken to this matter, agreed in unison.

"So be it!" Symeon proclaimed, as he began to lay out the steps just ahead. "All of us in leadership must quickly and quietly alert our people in the city that they will begin their flight, three days from today, at sunrise.

"Matthias," Symeon continued, "will begin a hurried journey to Pella immediately after this meeting to alert these dear ones to the multitude of unexpected Jewish refugees who will very soon nearly inundate their quiet city. You can be sure that the Lord will show them precisely how they are to make ready."

"Kefa, you will lead this huge assemblage of our people on their flight to Pella. Matthias will meet you a short distance from the City gate to welcome you all to your new temporary home.

"You may be surprised at the next," Symeon continued, "but the Lord has also shown me that the other ten apostles and the inner circle are to remain on Mount Zion with me during the terrible upcoming siege. It is His will that an organized presence of Jewish believers always remain here in Zion."

Instead of ending the meeting at this point, Symeon kept his place silently for a time as he struggled to frame what he must next share. The twelve of them soon grew individually and collectively disquieted as they waited and wondered what might next follow. Finally, with great emotion and deep sorrow, Symeon began to speak.

"My brothers, if I had shared with you what now I must, before we settled upon the immediate work that must be accomplished for the survival of our people, we would have been overcome by a grief so great that surely we would have been stricken incapable of accomplishing His purpose."

"I know of no way to sweeten what I have to tell you, or to lighten the grief this terrible news will bring. I will only ask that we spend the rest of the day and night here in this sacred place fasting and in prayer.

"My brothers, I learned early this morning that our beloved brother Sha'ul of Tarsus was very recently arrested in Rome where he was then martyred: torn apart by wild animals in the arena before a cheering crowd in the presence and with the encouragement of the Emperor Nero."[129]

While all who were present were utterly shocked and bereaved by the news of Sha'ul's terrible end, it was Matthias who uncontrollably screamed out his grief and tore the cloth of his robe.

***

Matthias had mindlessly hurried along on his assigned journey to Pella, so overcome by grief that he was almost oblivious to his surroundings as he paused only for brief moments of rest and refreshment during the two day non-stop trek.

Now, on his way home, as he had proceeded only a short distance from Pella, Matthias marveled at how well his precious and ever faithful Lord had given him the strength to conceal the depths of his grief from the many dear and deeply warm brothers and sisters of Pella who had enthusiastically received the news he had brought to them of the oncoming mass of Jewish visitors as both welcome and good tidings.

He prayed earnestly as he retraced his steps toward Jerusalem. "Lord, I have sought to serve you with all of my heart and all of my strength since the day you first led me to your Son Yeshua, and now, I rejoice in this great work you have given me. I pray that you will protect your people as they come to this city of safety, and I pray also that you will forever hold my darling Heliodora and our extended family in the palm of your ever mighty protecting hand."

***

Yehuda Ben Amos was a Zealot, a member of a Jewish faction that traced itself back to the revolt of the Maccabees in the 2nd Century BC. The name "Zealots" would first be recorded by the then Jewish historian Josephus as a designation for the Jewish resistance fighters of the war of 66-73 AD.

This term "Zealot" applied to Yehuda Ben Amos and the others of their time who were like him because of their fervent, extreme veneration of the Torah and their deep hatred of all non-Jews and even more so of other Jews who lacked their own religious fervor.

Yehuda Ben Amos was such a Jew—a Jew who had inexplicably turned against his fellow Jews of less radical persuasion. He had recently tasted Jewish blood and, in his sick mind, thus embarked on a frenzy of blind murder of all these 'lesser Jews' who came into his notice.

It was in this frenzied lust to kill that Yehuda Ben Amos first heard the approaching mighty crowd of those who were obviously Jews, joyfully singing a psalm of David in unison:

> The LORD is my shepherd; I shall not want. He makes me to lie down in green pastures; He leads me beside the still waters. He restores my soul; He leads me in the paths of righteousness For His name's sake.
>
> Yea, though I walk through the valley of the shadow of death, I will fear no evil; For You are with me; Your rod and Your staff, they comfort me---. [130]

Yehuda Ben Amos, the Zealot, was filled with both joy and frustration as he quickly concealed himself behind some large boulders at the side of the road. He joyfully marveled at his good fortune in the happening upon such a large number of vulnerable, approaching targets for his wrath, but at the same time he was nearly overwhelmed by the frustration of his own obvious personal limitation to take on such an enormous crowd with a single spear. Certainly, he could kill one, or perhaps even two of these devils before the others counter attacked and killed him, their assailant.

It was thus, in the midst of his planning on how best to proceed that he saw yet another Jew, approaching from Pella, in the opposite direction, a Jew who now wiped the tears of an obvious deep grief from his cheeks s he walked along, oblivious to his surroundings, but apparently on his way to greet the now approaching, close by crowd coming from the direction of Jerusalem.

***

Matthias neither saw his assailant's approach from behind nor felt more than a brief moment of shocked pain as the spear entered his body and passed through his heart.

By the grace of God he was allowed to see two final visions as Yehuda Ben Amos quickly withdrew the spear from his now lifeless body and hurried away from the scene of his treachery.

First, Matthias saw with perfect clarity the face of his beloved Dory, her deep blue eyes just now forming tears of a sad but also promise filled farewell. Then, he saw the sweet face of his beloved Yeshua who held out His mighty arms in joyful welcome as He spoke: 'Well done, my good and faithful servant! You have been faithful with a few things; I will put you in charge of many things. Come and share in your master's happiness!'"[131]

Chapter Forty Three

Jerusalem

November, 2004

"I'm so pleased you've decided to stick around for a few days of sightseeing, Dory." Drew addressed his eldest child who was seated with her mother in the back seat of their venerable Subaru.

"There's so much I want to see here, Dad," she replied. "The boat tour around the shore was wonderful, but how could I leave Israel without visiting Jerusalem again and this place Hippos that seems to have become so centrally important to you and Mom?"

"It was sad saying farewell to the rest of our wonderful family at Ben Gurion this morning," Carla commented. "But it did give us a perfect opportunity to continue the short distance to Jerusalem."

"I must say," Sheldon observed from the passenger seat next to Drew, the new Yitzhak Rabin Cross Israel Highway from Afula to the airport is nothing less than world class---Israel has really done itself proud."

"As a matter of fact," Drew commented, "this new road cuts a good forty-five minutes off the old three hour trek between Tiberias and Jerusalem."

"To tell you the truth, I *much* preferred the old route down the Jordan Valley then up that lovely windy way through the Judean Wilderness," Carla interjected.

"Oh, Dad! Why didn't we go the way Mom is talking about? It sounds so beautiful!"

"It certainly is beautiful, my dear," Drew responded with a hint of irony. "It is especially so in the late winter and spring when the wild flowers are blooming. But," he continued sardonically, "unless you'd look favorably upon getting your life cut short by an AK-47 in the hands of a Palestinian terrorist, or the more likely prospect of simply being stoned by a bunch of little boys in training to become suicide bombers, *believe me*, I've chosen the best route for our purposes!"

"It's shocking that you Israelis are not able to travel safely within your own country!" Sheldon exclaimed.

"Never mind!" Drew replied. "Outrages like this have become a way of life in the Land that God gave us Jews as an everlasting inheritance. Why should we be concerned with the trivia of highway selection when our own secular government, cheered on by the rest of the world, is seemingly working overtime to find new ways to give this Land of our everlasting inheritance to our Arab enemies? Just think of it; if we manage to wait long enough there may soon be *no* highways left for us to worry about!"

***

Less than an hour later, the four of them stood on top of the Ramparts Walkway that surrounded the Old City of Jerusalem. "The views from the top of this ancient wall are simply awesome!" Dory exclaimed as she pointed just across the Kidron Valley from where they stood to the multi-layered Jewish cemetery that seemingly covered every available square inch of the Mount of Olives. "Why is the place so crowded and how did all those tombstones get shattered?"

"Rabbinical Judaism has some novel understandings invented by the Pharisees." Drew replied. "Even today these folks hold that there will be a resurrection of the dead at the end of days, but only from this one place in the world, immediately adjacent to the Temple Mount. Thus, those who are buried here get first dibs on being raised up while other righteous Jews who have been buried elsewhere will literally leave their graves and roll along under the earth and sea until they arrive at this very place from which they too will rise into heaven.

"By the way," he continued. "Before the Jordanians decided to become our 'peace partners' in more recent times, they saw fit to desecrate every Jewish grave they could lay their hands on---hence the shameful pile of rubble you see before your eyes.

"I can't for a moment imagine how Yeshua would return to such a completely desecrated place as this!" Sheldon shouted to make himself heard over the deafening, hideously amplified mid-day Muslim call to worship, an uninvited, intrusive, sickening blast that assaulted the individual and collective sensibilities of the vast Jewish majority of Jerusalemites from multiple thousands of electronic speakers thus paralyzing the entire city and environs five times each day.

"The prospect of Yeshua's sweeping aside the rubble to stand once again on the Mount of Olives from which He rose and then promised to return is painful enough," Drew replied. "But," he continued sadly, "also behold the Temple Mount where once the Holy of Holies stood—the earthly abode of the one true God! Behold the new pagan temples now crowding the place that have swept aside all things holy and in their place have created an evil fount of satanic glory to be unceasingly raised up to the unholy of unholies. No!" Drew concluded with profound sadness, "I can't even begin to imagine that Yeshua would stand in such a place. But, then again, there is a biblical precedent that may show differently."

"What would that be?" Sheldon asked incredulously.

"Don't forget that Yeshua Himself founded His Church at Banias, which at the time was the very center of the world's paganism. Then, incredibly, He let the place stand until 363 when He finally got around to utterly destroying the cave, idols, niches and several temples with a mighty earthquake that spread a wave of destruction throughout all of the North."

"Daddy," Dory interjected. "Are you saying that Yeshua might come back to this terrible place as it stands today, and then only later get around to making it pure?"

"I'm only saying that we should not limit God by imposing our own human understandings upon Him. We must never forget that it was He who created us—it wasn't the other way around."

"Drew, darling," Carla tenderly reminded her husband, "don't forget, you booked our tour of the Western Wall tunnel for one o'clock---only twenty minutes from now."

"You're quite right, my dear," he replied with thanks. "Carla and I have already shared this deeply meaningful experience several times and are always anxious to do so again, but this will be a first for the two of you and I wouldn't want you to miss it for anything! Come, follow me: the entry place is only a few minutes away."

Drew began a preview of their upcoming tunnel tour as they now descended from the ramparts and walked toward their destination in the Kotel (Western Wall) Plaza. "Many visitors in the last 2000 years," he explained, "have been wondering where the Temple stood and where the Holy of Holies would have been. The underground walk we are about to take spans the whole length of the Western Temple Wall from the time of King Herod.

"Many visitors ask why the 'Wailing Wall,' as it used to be called, is the most important wall of the Temple complex and why the Jews pray almost exclusively on this side?

"The answer is that the Holy of Holies was situated on the western side of the Temple plaza. After the destruction of the Temple and with it, the Holy of Holies we Jews have been praying in this sacred place for centuries, at the site where we knew that the Holy of Holies would have been closest. We will soon be standing just a few yards opposite of that very location, which is at the middle of tunneled section of the wall we will now explore."

The four of them huddled together a few steps behind the last of the otherwise guided public tourists who had just entered the well illuminated ancient passageway.

"This is the longest wall of the former Temple platform of Herod and stretches nearly 500 meters, Drew continued. Only 70 meters or so is visible today in the large plaza where Jews from all over the world come to pray.

The rest of the wall can only be seen here, underground.

"This tunnel, exposing the underground section of the wall, was opened in several stages after 1967, although some parts are even older. The last short part was opened during the Netanyahu government which as you may remember caused an enormous Arab upheaval.

"This ancient corridor we have just entered," Drew continued, turns eastwards to the wall. It was built in the early Arab period and served as a secret underground passage. Interestingly, the arches on the left supported a 12.5 meter broad bridge with an aqueduct in Herod's time which brought water from Solomon's Pools to the Temple."

About fifteen minutes later, during which Drew had continued to point out the biblical historical and archeological highlights along the way, they at last neared the center of the buried segment of the wall, and with it, the deeply sacred object of their quest.

A few meters further along they came upon a blocked passage in the wall. "This is the location of 'Warren's Gate,' named after its discoverer," Drew explained. "There were four gates leading into Herod's Temple. It was from here that the High Priest in the Temple would perform his rituals in the direction of Jerusalem and to the people who lived on the western hill."

Drew now paused as they approached a place on the wall with nothing more than a simple bench to indicate that it was the very special place he had been seeking. He waited until others in the larger group that preceded the four of them had moved on before he continued.

"During the early Muslim period (639-1099 A.D.)," he explained, Jews worshiped from this very place in a synagogue called 'the Cave.' It is in this very place that the Foundation Stone of the Temple has long been revered. According to ancient Jewish tradition, the stone stood at the 'navel of the world' from which life was created. And upon this stone, the Holy of Holies was placed, which, in the time of Solomon, contained the Ark of the Covenant.

"The historical works of Flavius Josephus and modern day scientific scanning methods have clearly confirmed the understanding of Scripture: This place where we now stand is indeed only a few steps removed from where once stood the Holy of Holies of the Temple, where Yahweh, the Creator of the Universe manifested Himself in Shekinah glory."

Drew looked at the faces of the three dear ones with whom he had been sharing and he knew that they indeed understood the significance of what he had been sharing. They, like him, even after the passing of more than twenty five centuries, were deeply overcome by an obvious lingering presence of the Holy Spirit, who even now, inexplicably, filled this place with some clearly discernable residual presence of His indescribable power and glory.

"If I could convey but one simple truth to a waiting and desperately hungry world," Drew tearfully cried out from the depths of his soul. "It would be, as it is recorded in the gospels of Matthew, Mark and Luke[132]: At the very moment of Yeshua's death upon the cross, there was an enormous earthquake! The lintel at the top of the curtained door leading into the Holy of Holies was torn from top to bottom making a way from that moment and forever more for every believer in Yeshua to freely enter into this Holiest of all places and there enjoy direct, unlimited access to the Creator of the Universe. No longer was any manner of priestly intervention required! No longer was there a need for the blood of sacrificed animals! It was at this indescribably sacred door that He did it all for us and for all who would follow Him in future generations. This, Dear Ones: This wonderfully Holy and Sacred place— *This is the door where it began!*"

***

"What an incredible experience, Daddy!" Dory exclaimed, still overcome by their recent proximity to the Holy of Holies even some fifteen minutes after the four of them had retraced their steps and were now once again standing in the open sunlight of the Kotel Plaza."

"Your father makes quite an impassioned tour guide," Carla commented.

"This is an experience I could repeat often," Sheldon added appreciatively."

"Well, Drew replied," if you all don't mind, I'd like to spend some private time at the wall. I so enjoy praying there in the spirit while my orthodox brothers are praying nearby in Hebrew thinking I'm a foreign visitor holding forth in some weird language."

"You don't mind if I join you?" Sheldon asked.

"Of course not," Drew replied. "I am certain you'll find this a very satisfying experience."

"And we ladies will be praying right alongside you in the women's section," Carla added.

"Wonderful!" Drew replied. "Let's all join up again right here when we're finished."

***

Ibrahim Abu Aita had spent most of his just ten years on earth in training to hate, denigrate and destroy all things Jewish, but also, as opportunity might present, to bring violence and even wanton death upon these detestable Jews, the enemy of his Palestinian people whom, he already had learned in some detail, had not only viciously stolen their sacred Palestinian land, but who, collectively, stood as a stumbling block that prevented the creation of an independent State of Palestine as it had been endorsed by all of the nations of the world, and more importantly, as it had long been promised to his chosen ones, by Allah, himself.

Ibrahim, who lived with his parents and eight siblings, in a crowded two room tenement in East Jerusalem, was thus born an Israeli citizen and therefore free to visit this sacred place as often as he might please. Thus, he came here often, and most recently even more than once each day where, as was his practice, along with several of his friends, to observe these detestable Jews who stood at the base of the wall immediately below, praying and flailing themselves against its ancient black stone.

Each day, as Ibrahim observed this carrying on below, he became increasingly incensed with blind hatred for these mostly black garbed beasts who appeared to him to be more demons than men.

Even now, the festering within him finally came to the moment that demanded a violent response, and with no preplanning, or pointed central purpose, he picked up a nearby large stone that weighed some ten pounds, and threw it randomly toward those detestable Jews who were praying below.

In a sudden flash of recognition, Drew saw Yeshua face to face, and even more, he heard an audible voice speak to him from heaven, a voice that seemed to come from a place immediately behind from where he now stood: "Well done, my good and trustworthy servant; you have been faithful over a few things, and I will now make you ruler over many things in heaven, but not just yet. I have much more for you to do. Come to me now and enter into the joy of your Lord!"

At the very next fraction of a moment when Drew turned and began to obediently step toward the beckoning voice, a sharp projection on the stone that had been cast from above by Ibrahim made contact with his flesh, cutting an almost surgically precise shallow swath down the entire back of his head and torso as its great force threw him forward, rendering him unconscious and bleeding profusely onto the hard pavement of the plaza.

***

"Daddy, are you sure you're really up to this?" Dory asked with great concern only five days after they had returned to Tiberias from Hadassah Medical Center in Jerusalem where Drew had received extensive emergency treatment.

"Of course I am, Sweetheart. It was only a few stitches and beyond being a bit stiff, I'm sure I can make it up the hill. I wouldn't miss showing you Hippos for anything. Today is our last chance since you and Sheldon will be heading home in the morning."

"You know, Drew," Carla offered protectively, we really don't need to have you along for this. I can take Sheldon and Dory up there and I certainly know my way around the place."

"Of course you could," he objected, "But just bear with me as I hobble along and the four of us will make it just fine!"

***

The climb to the summit had been long and difficult for Drew, but he never once had entertained the notion of turning back. He had shown these two dear ones the various archeological testimonies regarding his understanding that this was the location of the very first Gentile Christian Church, and as such, the very genesis of Gentile Christianity itself. Now he was content to lead them to one final place, the western edge of the city. Joyfully and together they took in the glorious scene as the sun was beginning to set over their precious Lake and their beloved Tiberias beyond.

Now, after they had relished together in what was nearly the last light of the day, they turned and began to make their way back through the still long untouched large residential section of the city that would be the future focus of yet to be scheduled seasons of archeological excavation.

"*Look at that!*" Dory exclaimed as she pointed to the left side of the path towards what were barely visible, unidentifiable ancient ruins. "I saw something *glowing* there just now!"

"Go and have a look!" Drew encouraged. "But be *careful*! Watch out for snakes! This is the time of the year and the time of the day one can encounter deadly vipers in such places."

Not to be dissuaded, Dory, with the others protectively following close behind, hurried toward the place of great interest she had only just moments before observed.

Suddenly, there it was, brought to the surface by almost countless successive seasons of rain, resurrected from its burial of many centuries. "*Look at this!*" Dory exclaimed excitedly. "It's a golden pendant and chain. It's in amazingly good condition and there's Greek written on both sides!"

She handed it to her father begging: "Tell me, Daddy! What does it say?"

Drew was genuinely astounded by what he held in his hand, as were the others when he translated the words from the ancient Greek into the English . of today. "You all know of the ancient anagram first used by the very early Christian church." He explained. "On one side of this beautiful piece," he continued, his voice quivering with excitement, we have rendered in Greek, the language of ancient Hippos, and set inside a line drawing of a fish,: Ιχθυσ μεανινγ 'fish', an abbreviation of: Ιησουσ Χριστοσ Θηου Υιοσ Σωτηρ meaning 'Jesus Christ, Son of God, Savior.'"

"On the other side," Drew continued in stark amazement, "we have the first name of a woman to whom this exquisite piece was obviously given, probably as a wedding pendant which was used in the Middle East long before the wedding ring came into vogue.

"What name is written there, Daddy!" Dory begged, almost out of control in the excitement of her precious find.

"The name written here is *Heliodora*," he replied, hardly believing his own words. "This must be *yours*, our own precious Dory," he tenderly added as he placed the lovely piece of ancient jewelry around his daughter's neck.

Afterword

I had the privilege of spending a good part of this past summer in the United States, teaching the Jewish Roots of Christianity at Faith Seminary, and enjoying some long overdue visits with our three precious daughters and their families.

The major downside of this extended absence from Israel was two-fold. First, I reluctantly had to defer my final polishing of this manuscript until I returned, and second, much to my great consternation, I was not on hand to participate in the most productive and exciting dig season ever at Hippos.

What awaited our happy homecoming was an exciting account of the recent dig season's highlights, saved for us by our dear friends Jacob and Anna Weinberg, as this summary had appeared in the *Jerusalem Post* on August 15th. The relevant part of this newspaper account follows:

Ancient riddle eludes archeologists
By JUDY SIEGEL-ITZKOVICH

University of Haifa archeologists digging in the ancient city of Hippos-Sussita have uncovered more than what they expected this season. One of their surprises was the discovery of a lintel from a structure built during the Byzantine era with Jewish symbols, which was originally thought to be a synagogue, but now believed to be a church.

The sixth season of the archeological excavation at Hippos-

Sussita overlooking Kibbutz Ein Gev on the eastern shore of the Kinneret, has produced several astonishments like the lintel, says Prof. Arthur Segal of the university's Zinman Institute of Archeology. The lintel was uncovered in a public building in the southwestern residential quarter of Sussita, which according to Ancient Jewish sources indicated that such a synagogue existed in this predominantly Greek city.

Segal later reached the conclusion that it was actually a church. He explained that the structure could have served first as a synagogue and later been turned into a church. In another explanation he suggested that the synagogue may have existed in close proximity to the church, and following the synagogue's destruction the lintel was reused in the church.

The sixth season has come to an end and Segal hopes that next summer the riddle will be solved.

This *Jerusalem Post* article was accompanied by a photograph of the lintel, of which I immediately tried to secure a good quality digital copy. However, for reasons yet unclear, the *Jerusalem Post* did not offer access to this photograph.

I thus contacted the team's leadership who I have come to know and greatly respect. They most kindly provided me with an excellent set of pictures that depicted both the lintel and the just excavated synagogue/church site where it was found. However, understandably, they requested that I not republish these pictures at this time until they have had more opportunity to study the implications of all this and to further explore the site.

While "a picture may be worth a thousand words," photographic evidence is not absolutely needed in the present context for me to share my own preliminary conclusions.

First, "lintel" is defined as "a horizontal structural member, such as a beam or stone, that spans an opening, as between the uprights of a door or window or between two columns or piers." Lintels decorated with various religious symbols were a standard feature incorporated into the entrance ways of, from what I can determine, virtually all ancient Jewish synagogues.

It is thus most interesting to take a look at four representative examples of other such decorated synagogue lintels that have survived the ravages of time:

Synagogue	Location	Principal Lintel Features	Meaning
Katzrine	Golan Heights	One large wreath	The use of garlands, wreaths and festoons dates back to ancient Greek times and it was adopted into the Christian religion as a symbol of the victory of the redemption. The laurel wreath is usually associated with someone who has attained distinction in the arts, literature, athletics or the military. The ivy wreath is symbolic of conviviality (gaiety or joviality). The wreath and festoon together symbolize memory. It is an Ancient symbol of victory.
Bar lam	Near the Lebanese border	A winged figure on each side surrounding a large wreath.	The winged figures may symbolize angelic guardianship. The wreath, as at Katzrine may symbolize "victory."
Capernaum	Near Tiberias	Clusters of grapes and a pot of manna.	Clusters of grapes are a symbol of the Jewish people. Manna symbolizes God's provision of the bread of life.
Gamla	Golan Heights	Palm trees	An ancient jewish symbol of the Tree of Life

Let us now turn to the quite remarkable and distinctly unique lintel that was recently uncovered at a new site in southwestern Hippos. First, as to its features, which are very unlike any other Synagogue or Church lintel I have seen during my research:

- A large bird, facing to its left, is depicted with a very long continuing beak that ultimately blends into and becomes the base of a festoon (wreath open at the top). At first glance, I took this bird to represent an eagle. On closer examination and investigation, it became quite clear to me that this figure was instead meant to symbolize a pelican.

- There is a cluster of grapes stemming from the extended pelican's beak that are placed just below the bird's feet.

- The base line of the festoon is surrounded by two infinity symbols (lemniscates) a mathematical symbol dating from 1655 that has its origins in a much older religious symbol with the same meaning.

$$\infty$$

- There is a closed circle placed in the open space at the top of the festoon. The circle is an ancient Christian symbol that represents eternity and the everlastingness of God Who has no beginning and no end.

Let me now say without reservation that I find this newly discovered lintel to be of *enormous* significance! However, let me emphasize that what follows are *entirely* my own, independent conclusions that may or may not be shared by others.

Having thus offered this disclaimer, I have concluded:

First, early in the first century, this new site, along with the apparent first century "public meeting place" found beneath the Northwest Church, might very possibly have been *a*, if not *the,* first (transitional) Messianic Synagogue(s) (populated mostly by gentile believers) or, stated differently, a precursor of the later, entirely Gentile Christian Byzantine Church.[133]

I base this conclusion in part on a number of scriptural, historical and archaeological evidence, both documented and anecdotal, as already discussed in the foregoing pages. Much more pointedly, however, I base this conclusion on my own, what seems to me to be an obvious, interpretation of the symbology that is clearly scribed on the recently discovered Lintel:

- The pelican is an ancient Christian symbol of Yeshua's atonement.[134] The pelican was believed to draw blood from its own breast to feed its young. As previously stated, this symbol much more clearly represents a pelican than it does an eagle, as others may suggest. Hence, I see this figure as a deliberately rendered very early first century representation of the atoning Messiah, Yeshua.

While there has been some later Jewish use of the pelican symbol, for example on grave headstones, this limited application seems to be imitative of what presumably originated as an entirely Christian symbol for the atonement of Yeshua. Some might argue that the several uses of the word "pelican" in the Old Covenant speak to some earlier Jewish application. However, I find only textual rather than graphically symbolic uses in each of these cases and consider them irrelevant to the present question.

If indeed the pelican is a "very early Christian symbol for the atonement of Yeshua," then this lintel at Hippos may likely be the origination of this tradition. Obviously, you can't get much earlier in the history of Gentile

Christianity than this presumed early "synagogue/church" at Hippos.

- Clusters of grapes are a well understood and widely used ancient Christian symbol representing the Lord's Supper. What more fitting symbol than this to demonstrate the partaking of this holy sacrament in this very early communal setting?

- The festoon is a well known universal religious symbol depicting victory, and more specifically, as a Christian symbol, victory over death.

- The two renderings of the lemniscates (infinity symbol) depicted as an extension of the pelican's beak, seem to me to clearly represent the eternal life granted to believers through the atoning death of Yeshua. The fact that there are *two* such renderings instead of one may represent the two appearances of Yeshua; one that had only recently already occurred and a second that was expected at the end of days.

- The circle at the top of the festoon, I believe, represents the Jewish rooted *eyn sof* (infinite) understanding of the Godhead.

In summary, Drew Sterling, a fictitious protagonist of the foregoing pages, would have been thrilled, as am I, by this most remarkable recent discovery at Hippos. While I am very confident that future dig seasons will continue to reveal much further convincing supporting evidence, this recent find most certainly adds immediate credence to the hypothesis that there was a pre-Pauline Church at Hippos and, by logical extension, there was such an early Gentile Christian presence throughout the entire widespread region of the Decapolis.

Of even more central importance is the ever increasingly believable conclusion that even decades before the Apostle Paul's conversion on the Damascus road, the very first ecclesia (churches) of Gentile Christianity sprang forth from the rich soil of Israel and not from Rome as it has, up to now, been traditionally understood.

As the title of this novel attests, I firmly believe that the curtain leading into the Holy of Holies of the Temple in Jerusalem was torn asunder at the moment of Yeshua's earthly death upon the cross, to open the way for *all* believers to have perpetual, uninhibited access to the Godhead. But also, please consider this. A lintel is a very critical structural component of a door. The genuinely amazing lintel recently found at Hippos may well indeed have been a critical component of the door to this inaugural sanctuary of Gentile Christian worship. Indeed, it may well have been *The Door Where it Began.*

RRF

Tiberias, Israel

August, 2005

(Endnotes)

[1] Isaiah 40:3-5

[2] For specific Dead Sea Scroll references and quotations, see Raymond R. Fischer, *Full Circle*, pp 58-79

[3] Ephesians 2:8

[4] Ezekiel 1:4

[5] John 1:26-27

[6] Revelation 5:13

[7] John 1:29-31

[8] a paraphrase of Isaiah 53:1-6

[9] 1Yochanan 4:7-8

[10] 4Q246 I 7-9, II 1-7

[11] Mattatyahu 3:13-15

[12] a paraphrase of Mattatyahu 3:11

[13] Ezekiel 1:26-28

[14] paraphrase of Matt 3:16-17

[15] Matt. 4:23-25

[16] Dead Sea Scrolls, "Book of Secrets" 4Q299-301, 4Q301 F.1

[17] Matt. 5:3-20

[18] Matt. 5:17-18

[19] Ezek 20:6

[20] Deut. 6:4

[21] CD VII 15-16, 18-19

[22] 4Q174, frag. 1-3, 10-12 4Q20 4 2-10

[23] 4Q174 1-3, 6-9 CD-A II 2-5

[24] Luke 7:1-10

[25] Matt 10:5-8

[26] The very plausible notion that the pigs of Kursi were intended as sacrifices to the pagan god Dionysus was suggested to me by my dear friend and author, Todd Bennett, and is used here with his blessing.

[27] Luke 8:39

[28] Mark 5:1-20

[29] Waring, Anna L. "In Heavenly Love Abiding" (1850) from *The Armed Forces Hymnal*, page 333.

[30] Psalm 50:15

[31] The "sermon" presented here is gratefully acknowledged as a paraphrase of an excellent article taken from www.jesusisajew.org

[32] Matt 10:1-15

[33] Sidon also known as Tyre, was an ancient city on the Mediterranean coast of what is modern day Lebanon

[34] Matt 15:21-31

[35] Matt 15:32-38

[36] During the opening decades of Air Defense operations, the USAF used the Naval terms "port" for left and "starboard" for right.

[37] Luke 11:9-10

[38] Matt 11:1-14

[39] Matt 16:18

[40] Matt 17:1-9

[41] Mark 16:23

[42] Matt 16:21-27

[43] Zech 9:9, Matt 21:5

[44] Matt 21:1-12

[45] HaShem in English is "The Name." It is used by observant Jews so as to avoid using the name of God thus risking taking His name in vain.

[46] Roman Catholics believe that Mary was a life-long virgin and that Jesus was the only child that she gave birth to; he was her first-born and last-born child. The Bible identifies four "brothers" of Jesus: James, Yosef, Judah and Simon. He also had at least two "sisters." (Matt 13:55). However, their exact number and names were never recorded. Some Catholics believe that Jesus' brothers and sisters were in fact half-siblings; they were children of Yosef by a previous marriage. Other Christians believe that the 6 siblings were really cousins or close friends.

[47] Matt 21:1-16

[48] 4Q264 1 1-3

[49] 4Q174 frag.1-3, lines 10-12

[50] 4Q20 4 2-10

[51] Matt 26:64 vf

[52] Matt Chapters 26 and 27

[53] There are somewhat different accounts of the immediate post resurrection appearance of *Yeshua* to the women and to the disciples. Mark 16:12 speaks to His appearance to two unnamed disciples. I have, with no other basis, taken author's license here to suggest that these might have been Mattatyahu and Thaddaeus.

[54] John 7:5

[55] John 20:19-23

[56] Taken from the Gospel according to the Hebrews as quoted by Origen and recorded by Jerome (*De viris inlustribus* 2)

[57] The book of Acts has multiple references wherein Ya'akov (James) is seen as the first leader of the first Jewish believers in *Yeshua* (see Acts 12:17, 15:13, 21:18). The

apocryphal Gospel of Thomas includes the following discourse between *Yeshua* and His disciples: (Saying 12) "The disciples said to *Yeshua*, 'We know that you are going to leave us. Who will be our leader?' *Yeshua* said to them, 'No matter where you are you are to go to James the Just, for whose sake heaven and earth came into being.'"

58 Acts 1:9

59 Acts 1:10-11

60 Acts 21:39, 22:3, 23:6

61 Eph 4:5, Jude 1:3

62 Romans 12:4-5

63 Matt 28:19-20

64 Jer 32:31,33

65 John 21:17

66 Exodus 34:22-26

67 John 14:26

68 Joel 2:28-32

69 Acts 2:14 -39 (paraphrase)

70 See Hebrews 6:19; 9:3 and 10:20

71 From December 1947 until the third day of the Six Day War, June 7th 1967, Jews were not able to approach the Kotel. After the Six day War the buildings placed against the Kotel were removed and the entire area in front of it was cleared, leveled and converted into a large paved open space. The area was partitioned off; one third is reserved for women and two thirds for men. The Kotel once more became a place of pilgrimage and prayer for Jews from all over the world. On the first day of Shavuot after the Six Day War, a quarter of a million Jews swarmed to the Wall, for the first time in 20 years.

72 Ezekiel 20:6

73 Ruth 1:16-17

74 Mishna, Sukkah 5:2-4

75 John 8:12

76 The Gospel of Thomas, logion 12

77 Mattatyahu 28:19-20

78 Jer. 31:31, 33

79 John 1:1-2

80 Psalm 34:3

81 Isaiah, Chapter 53

82 John 12:44-46

83 John 3:16-19

84 John 11:25-26

85 Isaiah 11:10-11

[86] Leviticus 7:19-21

[87] Mark 8:1-10

[88] Dead Sea Scrolls (4Q541 9, 1, 1-6)

[89] John 8:12

[90] I have done my best here to create here an accurate fictional setting of a very detailed claimed to be factual account of this Nazarene three part initiation ceremony recorded by two Roman Catholic historians who have reported on the earlier accounts of two "church fathers," St. Cyril and St.Egeria. For further details, see Fischer and Schmalz, *The Messianic Seal of the Jerusalem Church*, page 52-53, foot note 123.

[91] Num 24:17, 2Pet 1:19

[92] Revelations 2:9, 3:9

[93] There is much anecdotal historical and biblical evidence and a number of scholars that support the position that Yeshua was born during the Fall feast of Succoth. There are however other positions argued with various levels of believability. No credible scholarship, however, affirms December 25, the birthday of the sun god Mithra as the day of Yeshua's birth.

[94] Genesis 15:7-8, 17:2-14; Acts 3:25

[95] John 17:11-23

[96] Hansen and Skjott, *Facts & Myths about the Messianic Congregations in Israel*, Casperi Center, Jerusalem, 1999

[97] Matt. 28:19-20

[98] 1 John 2:6 (a paraphrase from third to first person)

[99] Ex 20:3, Deut 5:7

[100] Ezek 9:4, CD-B, XIX, 5-13, 15

[101] For the miracle of the chained man see Mark 5, Mattatyahu 8 and Luke 8. For the miracle of the second feeding see Mark 8 and Mattatyahu 15

[102] Concordia University, http://virtual dig.org, article "History of Hippos"

[103] Acts 8:1-3

[104] Acts 7:57-58

[105] Deut. 19:21

[106] Matt 5:43-45

[107] paraphrase of Acts 9:3-18

[108] Acts 26:17-18

[109] In synagogues that read from the actual Torah scroll a great ceremony is made of rewinding the scroll. It is considered an honor to be called up to help with this task. Also, the Torah scrolls are carried in a circle seven times around the sanctuary in a joyous parade called "hakafot". Children are given flags or small scrolls to follow in the procession. Candles are put in the ark in place of the scrolls, a reminder of God's law being our light:

Psalm 119:105

Your word is a lamp to my feet and a *light* for my path.

Also, as *Yeshua* reminded us when He was at the Temple on Sukkot:

John 8:12

When *Yeshua* spoke again to the people, he said, "I am the **light** of the world. Whoever follows me will never walk in darkness, but will have the *light* of life." We take delight in our celebration of the Torah as mentioned in Psalms:

Psalm 119:77

Let your compassion come to me that I may live, for *your law is my delight*.

Psalm 119:162

I *rejoice* in your promise like one who finds great spoil.

Psalm 119:174

I long for your salvation, O LORD, and your law is my *delight*.

Sweets are appropriate at this celebration to remind us:

Psalm 119:103_

How *sweet* are your words to my taste, sweeter than honey to my mouth!

As believers we can rejoice in the Living Word:_

John 1:14

The Word became flesh and made his dwelling among us. We have seen his glory, the glory of the One and Only, who came from the Father, full of grace and truth.

(Article taken from www.israelharvest.com)

[110] The following is an adopted, factual summary taken from the official Hippos/Sussita archeological reports from 2000-2004.

[111] 2 Cor 11:24-28

[112] 2 Cor 2:5

[113] 2 Cor. 5:16-21

[114] Acts 2:47

[115] 1 Cor 3:16

[116] Heb 10:19-23

[117] Acts 7:48-50

[118] Romans 14:12

[119] Ex 34:7, Mark 2:7

[120] Romans 7:16

[121] Galations 3:29

[122] Isa 11:1-2

[123] Eph 2:15

[124] Romans Chapter 9, Gal 3:28

[125] 2 Pet 3:16, Acts 9:31

[126] Matt 5:17-19

[127] Isa 42:6-7

[128] In the Dead Sea Scrolls, the Essenes frequently referred to the high priests, of what they considered to be the "polluted" Temple, as the "Wicked Priests."

[129] Neither history nor Scripture records the precise means of Paul's death which is traditionally held by most scholars to have been, variously, by beheading, crucifixion or by tearing apart by wild animals.

[130] Psalm 23:1-4

[131] Matt 25:21

[132] Matt 27:51, Mark 15:38, Luke 23:45

[133] Up to now, there have been three other circa 5th century Byzantine Churches uncovered in the City of Hippos. The current dig has yielded a fourth and there may well be others revealed in future dig seasons.

[134] The **Physiologus**, a second century work of a popular theological type, described animals both real and imaginary and gave each an allegorical interpretation. It told of the pelican drawing the blood from its own breast to feed its young. The physical reality which probably resulted in this legend is that the long beak of the pelican has a sack or pouch which serves as a container for the small fish that it feeds its young. In the process of feeding them, the bird presses the sack back against its neck in such a way that it seems to open its breast with its bill. The reddish tinge of its breast plumage and the redness of the tip of its beak prompted the legend that it actually drew blood from its own breast.

The **Physiologus**, and later Latin Bestiaries of the Middle Ages, found the action of the pelican, so interpreted, as a particularly appropriate symbol of the sacrifice of Christ the Redeemer shedding His blood, and thus the symbol of the pelican grew to have a wide usage in Christian literature and art. Thomas Aquinas did indeed use the figure of the pelican in his beautiful hymn appointed to be sung in Thanksgiving after Communion, the **Adoro Te Devote**:

"Pie Pellicane, Jesu Domine,
   Me immundum munda Tuo sanguine. (verse 3)
   O Loving Pelican, O Jesu Lord,
   Unclean am I but cleanse me in Thy blood."

(from an article: The Medieval Pelican," found at www.kwantlen.ca)

DISTRIBUTION & CONTACTS

To order more copies of this book or
Bob Fischer's other books and DVD teachings:

In North America:

Olim Publications of California
1725 Aston Place,
El Dorado Hills, CA 95762
Tel.(916) 939-1519
e-mail: stroebel@sbcglobal.net

(Or) Visit our Web Site:

www.olimpublications.com

To Contact the Author -

Raymond Robert Fischer:

Olim Publications
P.O. Box 2111
Tiberias, Israel
Phone 972 4 6720535
e-mail: olim@012.net.il